The Melody of the Soul

MUSIC OF HOPE SERIES

Book One

The Melody of the Soul by Liz Tolsma
Published by Gilead Publishing, Grand Rapids, Michigan
www.gileadpublishing.com

ISBN: 978-1-68370-040-1 (paper)
ISBN: 978-1-68370-041-8 (eBook)

Edited by Julee Schwarzburg
Cover directed by Larry Taylor
Cover designed by John Wolinka
Interior designed by Amy Shock

Printed in the United States of America

The Melody of the Soul

MUSIC OF HOPE SERIES
Book One

A WWII Women's Fiction Novel

LIZ TOLSMA

GILEAD PUBLISHING
PUBLISHING
Grand Rapids, Michigan

To the Dead

A grave among graves, who can tell it apart,
time has long swept away the dead faces.
Testimonies, so evil and terrible to the heart,
we took with us to these dark rotting places.

Only the night and the howl of the wind
will sit on the graves' corners,
only a patch of grass, a bitter weed
before May bears some flowers.

–Jaroslav Seifert

Whoever saves one life,
Saves the world entire.

–Talmud Yerushalmi,
Sanhedrin 4:12

To my mother,
Lenore Tolsma.

Your love has taught me what family is truly all about.
I so admire your dedication to those you hold dear. We don't
often honor your heritage, so I strove to do that in
this book. Anna is named after your grandmother,
Anna Kostachek Kovaly.
I love you!

Czech

Babička – grandmother
Beruško – a term of endearment. Literally: ladybug
Děkuji – thank you
Dršťková polévka – tripe soup
Houskový knedlík – dumplings made from bread and shaped like a loaf of bread before being sliced and cooked on top of a stew or goulash
Ježíšek – baby Jesus. Comes from the mountains on Christmas Eve to bring gifts to the children.
Koláček – a sweet yeast bread often topped with prunes and farmer's cheese or a poppy seed paste
Máma – mother
Ne – no
Pan – mister
Paní – missus
Ponorky – literally submarines, or those who hid and had to dive underground in case the house was searched.
Slečna – term of address for an unmarried woman
Táta – father

German

Danke – thank you
Fräulein – unmarried woman
Guten aben – good afternoon
Halten sie – stop
Hauptmann – Wehrmacht rank equivalent to captain

Hauptsturmführer – most common SS rank during WWII, equivalent to a captain

Ja – yes

Mutti – mother

Nein – no

Oberleutnant – Wehrmacht rank equivalent to 1st lieutenant

Schnell – quickly

Vater – father

*A*nna Zadoková held her mother's tiny body close. If only she could imprint the feel of her on her skin. She breathed in her scent, a combination of rose water and fried onions. Everything she loved best about her. A light mist dampened them both.

"Be a good girl, *beruško.*"

"No, *Máma, ne.*" She peered over *Máma*'s shoulder and stared at her father. "*Ne, Táta.* I'm going with you. My deportation notice might not have come with yours, but it will come at some point. The entire family must go together. We won't allow them to separate us."

"And what about your grandmother?" *Máma* smoothed Anna's hair from her damp brow. "It's a blessing from God that neither of you got your notices. For now, you're safe. You can take care of *Babička*, and we can go in peace, knowing she'll be looked after."

Anna bit her trembling lip to keep away the tears clogging her throat. "Please, let me go with you. Over the years, we prayed together, laughed together, cried together. This, too, we should do together." Her heart drummed against her ribs with the knowledge of what she faced, what her decision might cost her. She turned and surveyed her younger sisters, Jana and Lada, standing to the side, clutching the two bags allowed them by the Germans.

Prague's exhibition hall loomed behind them, the large wooden structure nothing more than a run-down shack. Other Jews filled the yard, eyes wide, faces drawn. Outside, flimsy wooden partitions separated dozens of toilets. If you had to relieve yourself, you had to do it in full view of everyone present. Anna couldn't say a word. Were the Nazis determined to degrade them?

Máma sighed, dark half-moons beneath her brown eyes. "*Ne, ne.* If you stay, at least I don't have to worry about you. Or my mother. That's one less burden for me to carry."

Táta stroked Anna's cheek. Deep lines etched his face, lines that hadn't been there before. He took off his hat and rubbed his bald head. "Don't do this to your mother and me. In the middle of the sorrow of leaving everyone and everything for an uncertain fate, we're comforted that you and *Babička* will be safe. Perhaps you will survive. The Americans have joined the fight. Not long now, and they'll be here."

"*Táta*, I can't survive without my family. I'll die of a broken heart. I, I ..." She swallowed lest she give up control.

"We can't lose all of our children. David also got his notice. He'll be on the train with us. Why you didn't get yours, only the Lord knows. But we believe He did it for a reason."

Anna pursed her lips and set her jaw. "What difference does it make if it comes today or tomorrow? The Nazis want to cleanse Prague of Jews. Even the Christian ones."

Táta flashed her a wry grin. "I have your grandmother to thank for your stubbornness."

"That stubbornness will serve me well in the camp." She locked her knees so her parents wouldn't see her tremble. Should she go home, or go with her family? Her stomach clenched. At least if she went with them, she would have them to help her.

Máma squeezed Anna's hand and stood as straight and regal as ever. "Anna, turn around and go to the house. Now."

Her sister Lada, only eleven years old, cried. "*Máma*, can't I go home, too? Why do we have to come here?"

Táta rubbed his youngest daughter's shoulder. "This is what God has planned for us. We'll submit to His will and pray for His protection." A muscle worked in his cheek.

Anna clung to him. "We should have gone to America with Uncle

Ivan when we had the chance. We would have been safe. Why did you listen to me? Why did we stay?"

"That wasn't God's plan for us. It's too much to explain now."

But she didn't understand. How could it be His plan for them to be parted this way?

A tall, scrawny young man approached them, his long, black coat flapping in the breeze. Anna gave Jakub Meles, David's friend and a member of the Jewish Council, a half smile.

"What are you doing here?" He finger-combed his unruly black curls.

Táta set down his battered case and patted Anna's hand. "We got our notices to report. We understand that David did, too. Have you seen him?"

"Why is Anna here?" He leaned in, and Anna only heard his words because she stood next to *Táta*. "You know the council draws up the deportation lists. David begged me, so I had her name and *Paní* Doubeková's stricken. He was afraid his grandmother wouldn't survive the camp, and he wanted Anna to stay and watch over her. I cannot save her if she shows up here. Send her home."

Táta's drawn face brightened. "God's provision." He gathered Anna to himself like he had hundreds of times when she was a child. "Do as I say. Leave us. Be safe. May the Lord go with you."

The tears, close to the surface all day, streamed down her cheeks in a torrent. "*Táta*. Oh, *Táta*."

He held her a moment more before pulling himself from her embrace. Moisture shimmered on his angular face. "This is the hardest thing I have ever done. I have loved you from the moment your mother told me you were on your way. Your tiny face captured my heart and hasn't let it go. My sweet, sweet Anna, my *beruško*, do this one last thing for me. Go home. Take care of your grandmother."

Her father kissed her cheek, turned her toward their flat on Salvátorská Street, and gave her a gentle push in that direction.

After she walked half a block, she turned back. Her family strolled hand-in-hand into the exhibition hall.

In the distance, a train whistled.

Chapter One

Prague, early fall 1943

*A*nna Zadoková clutched her violin to her chest. Her sheet music fluttered to the floor as she peered from behind the lace curtain to the street below.

"Well, child, don't just stand there. Tell me what you see."

Anna might laugh at her grandmother's impatience if a black Mercedes emblazoned with a swastika didn't sit parked in front of their apartment building. Instead, she sucked in her breath and turned toward her. "Nazis."

"Here?" *Babička* didn't open her half-closed eyes, but grabbed the carved arm of her chair tighter until her gnarled knuckles whitened.

"Yes, here. Of all places." Anna couldn't corral the wild beating of her heart. "But we won't be here for long." She turned her attention to the commotion on the road. "What are we going to do? *Máma* and *Táta* told me to keep you safe."

A young, lean officer stepped from the car, unfolding himself to his full height. My, he towered over the others. He blew out smoke from his cigarette. A shock of blond hair peeked out from under his hat, visible to her even at this distance. He couldn't be more than twenty-five. Handsome? Maybe under different circumstances.

But she couldn't forget what the Nazis had done to her family. She might never see *Máma* and *Táta* again because of them. *Ne*, his outward appearance may be pleasing, but darkness and ugliness pervaded his heart and soul.

Just like his countryman Reinhard Heydrich, the Butcher of Prague.

The man who deported and killed an untold number of Jews. Friends from the conservatory. Neighbors. Her only cousin.

The man barked at his driver and pointed in the direction of their flat. Anna grasped her bow hard. He was moving into this building? She forced herself to relax her fingers lest she snap the bow in two. There were no empty apartments.

Anna's knees turned to mush, and she leaned against the window sill to keep from crumpling to the ground. There might not be a vacant flat now, but there would be one in a matter of minutes. Would he arrest the young family below them, or Anna and *Babička*? Or both?

She turned from the window, unable to watch any more of the unfolding scene. "He . . ." Her voice squeaked, and she swallowed to clear it. "He is coming here. We have to be ready to leave. I'll pack a bag for you and bring your coat."

Babička bit her lip. "Thank you, child."

Anna's heart skipped in her chest, unable to find a steady rhythm. "*Babička* . . ." And then she dove into her grandmother's arms, trembling like a child in a thunderstorm.

"Hush, now, hush." *Babička*'s words flowed over her, gentle as a spring rain. "The Lord protected us before. He will again."

"I don't see how. I just don't see how. What about *Máma* and *Táta*?"

"They're safe in the palm of His hand."

If she could stop time and remain in *Babička*'s embrace forever, finding balm for the ache in her chest. But soon, the soldiers would burst through the door and arrest them. They had to prepare. She stood, taking a moment to steady her wobbling knees and straighten her pleated, navy blue skirt. Not that it mattered. Not that it mattered one bit.

She moved to the back bedroom she shared with *Babička* and pulled the well-worn tan suitcase from under the large feather bed. She stuffed the small case with all their warmest clothes and sweaters. From the bathroom, she grabbed *Babička*'s heart medicine and a bottle of vitamin tablets.

Where was *Babička*'s Bible? She would want it. Need it. It wasn't on the small, round bedside table. Perhaps in the kitchen where she had read it earlier this morning. But though Anna searched high and low and snatched the last of their *houskový knedlík*, bread dumplings, brought by a friend from their church, she didn't locate her grandmother's most treasured possession.

She returned to the bedroom and stood by her dresser, tracing the painted rose trailing down the Bohemian glass jug her parents gave her on her sixteenth birthday. Had that been only seven years ago? Of all the treasures begging to be stuffed in the suitcase, this was the one calling the loudest. But it might break during the journey. She left it alone.

Before her melancholy grew, she turned away and shut the door. The old parquet floors squeaked under her feet as she returned to the living room. Much to her relief, *Babička* sat in her chair, her Bible open in her lap.

They were Christians, yet the Nazis arrested and persecuted them for their ethnic heritage. For the blood which flowed in their veins, no choice of theirs. What had they ever done to the Germans to deserve this treatment?

"We're ready to go, *Babička*." Anna draped her grandmother's scratchy, gray wool coat over a chair and placed her grandfather's on top of it. A fall chill hung in the air, winter biting at its heels. Two coats would keep *Babička* warmer than one. Anna brought her own long, brown coat from the large walnut wardrobe, the yellow star sewn onto it proclaiming their identity to the world.

They sat beside each other on the rose-sprigged, Victorian-style sofa, the soft ticking of the Bavarian cuckoo clock on the wall the only sound in the room. Anna clasped her grandmother's cool, fragile hand. What would life have been like in America? They should have gone.

Babička bowed her head, closed her eyes, and moved her lips without uttering a sound.

Then, from downstairs, shouts and screams rang out.

Horst Engel studied the Baroque-style brown stone building adorned with ornate triangular pediments above each window and carved wreaths beneath each one. A large, engraved swag accented the arched main entrance. But even his attempts at an architectural analysis of his new home weren't enough to shut his ears to the screams of the small child ripped from his mother's arms.

Horst couldn't turn away.

The little boy's face reddened. Fat tears raced down his dimpled cheeks. The mother, a conspicuous yellow star on her coat, lunged for her son. His fellow officers rewarded her instinct with a gun butt to her head.

He averted his gaze at the sight of blood gushing from her temple. That wasn't necessary. None of this was. *Vater* said this assignment was better than fighting in a trench somewhere, but Horst had a difficult time understanding how that might be. Nevertheless, his father, an influential man in the Nazi party, had paid for this commission for his son.

This was not what his life was supposed to look like. Not any of it. And it wasn't because he was afraid to fight or even to die. For a right and just cause, he would give his life without hesitation. That's what a good officer did. But not like this. Scenes like this churned his stomach. Reminded him of his past. Brought on the nightmares.

He crossed his arms over his midsection and leaned against the black car, the metal warm on his cheek.

"Are you ill, sir?"

Horst startled at the voice of his young driver and snapped to attention. It would not do for him to be caught slouching. "*Nein*. Just fatigued."

"I'll tell them to hurry removing this Jewish family. It might take some time to clean their filth, though."

"Don't." Horst turned to the soldier whose name he couldn't remember at the moment. "Give them what time they need."

"Very good, sir. We want all to be in readiness for you."

The man misunderstood, but Horst didn't correct him.

A soldier, armed with a rifle, led the father from the home, his shoulders slumped, a muscle jumping in his cheek, his hands clenched. Horst gritted his teeth.

Something fluttered in an upstairs window. A lace curtain parted for a moment, a flash of time. The slightest glimpse of a young woman with dark brown hair and pale skin. Like an apparition, she vanished. Who was she?

He returned his attention to the family his soldiers led away. The guards shoved the father, a bright yellow star on his coat, inside the canvas-covered truck. He drew his wife and child to him, tears coursing down the woman's battered and bloodied face.

Horst swallowed hard.

The truck revved its engine and screeched away down the narrow street.

He couldn't take it anymore. Squaring his shoulders, he strode to the building and entered the first-floor flat.

For many years, *Vater* drummed into him how vile and filthy the Jews were. But not these. A large bow window brightened the cheerful living space, a bright red rug on the floor, a well-worn green sofa along one wall. Only his mother kept house this well, this clean. The lady of the home must have worked very hard.

He moved toward the couch. If he could put his feet up—

He tripped. A tin train engine sat on the floor in the middle of the room, one a child pulled with a string. He'd had one similar when he was young, fascinated by locomotives.

Horst picked it up and turned it around in his hands. Much of the black paint had peeled off. It had been loved. Treasured. Perhaps by more than one generation. He searched the flat for a bedroom and stashed the toy into the deep recesses of the wardrobe, behind several dresses.

The woman's flowery scent reached him and he slammed the door shut. His heart raced.

Boots sounded on the scarred wood floors. He once again donned his Nazi officer persona and went to meet his compatriots.

"Are the accommodations to your liking, sir?"

The boy's name eluded him. "*Ja, danke.* That will be all for now."

The house fell silent, and that was fine with him. His head pounded. Oh, to be home in his room with the smell of his mother's cooking and the scent of edelweiss filling the air.

He sat in the old, overstuffed chair in the corner of the living room and sank into its depths. If he closed his eyes, he could almost feel the warmth of *Mutti's* potato soup in his middle.

His stomach growled. What had they left him to eat in this place? He wandered to the kitchen. Neat and spotless, just like the other rooms. The cabinets, however, produced little for dinner. He discovered a tin of ersatz coffee and put the pot on the stove to brew.

As he waited for the water to boil, a strange sound floated around him. Beautiful. Haunting.

Mozart, if he was correct. He listened a moment more. Yes, *Violin Concerto Number Three.*

And played to perfection, the technique impeccable. His mother loved music and often dragged him to symphony concerts. When he was a teenager, it had been against his will. First he was soothed, then he learned, then he appreciated. Now, reached out to recapture those days.

He needed that beauty.

Anna allowed the last note of the concerto to float on the air and die away. She closed her eyes and held her breath for a moment, letting the quiet wash over her.

For that instant, and that instant only, she was free. The world was a good and happy place.

Yes, it was risky to play when the Nazis declared it illegal for Jews to have instruments. But she kept her violin's voice quiet. Right now, the music calmed her.

A knock on the door brought her crashing to earth like a flaming fighter plane. Her breath whooshed from her lungs.

These days, anyone might be on the other side. Did she get careless, lost in the music when she played? Did the Nazi downstairs hear her?

She glanced at *Babička*, sleeping in the chair, mouth wide open. Beside her sat the run-down brown suitcase, the leather handle worn, the fabric frayed at the edges. Would it even survive the trip to the camp?

Was this the time they waited for? Anticipated? Dreaded?

She wiped her hands on her deep blue skirt, sucked in a deep breath, and opened the door.

The officer from the street.

She locked her knees to keep them from failing her.

He strode into the flat, his eyes icy blue. In one sweep, he assessed the room. And them. He removed his peaked cap, an eagle on the crown, and tousled his dark-blond hair. He nodded at her. "*Hauptmann* Horst Engel. And you are?"

As she released the air from her lungs, she prayed the words would not squeak out of her throat. She never expected the Nazi deporting them to introduce himself. She answered in German, a language she and many Prague Jews were fluent in. "Anna Zadoková. And my grandmother, Jana Doubeková."

Babička stirred and opened her eyes, startling for a moment.

He nodded in *Babička*'s direction, then returned his attention to Anna. "You played that music?"

She stepped back, grasping at a wobbly side table for support. He'd heard. How could she have been that reckless? What should she say? Denying it would only bring on his ire. Acknowledging it would, at the least, add their names to the deportation notices.

After a few moments of silence, *Hauptmann* Engel cleared his throat. "Bring your violin and come with me."

She again glanced at the suitcases, packed, ready to go. And what about *Babička*? If only her voice worked. "Sir?" The word squeezed out between her tense vocal chords.

He turned toward her, his eyes the color of steel. "*Ja?*"

"My grandmother? And our suitcases?"

"The grandmother may come. The suitcases? You won't need those where you are going."

Chapter Two

*A*nna draped *Babička's* coat over her shoulders. The Nazi from downstairs may not allow them to take their valises to the camp, but she refused to let her grandmother freeze to death, no matter what the cost might be to herself. The cries of the family from the downstairs flat rang in her ears, though they were likely on a train by now, racing toward their awful destiny.

She grabbed her violin as he'd commanded and gave one last, long gaze at their suitcases. She itched to pull her grandmother's heart medicine and vitamin tablets from them. Perhaps they would help *Babička* survive. For a little time, if nothing else.

As they followed *Hauptmann* Engel into the hall, she peered back into the little apartment they'd called home for the past three years, ever since the Nazis confiscated their large, comfortable flat in the Christian section of town. That one had had four bedrooms, a modern kitchen, a large, formal dining room with a crystal chandelier, even a spacious music room with *Máma's* grand piano. The housekeeper had maintained it all in spotless fashion.

Then the Germans had forced her family into this tiny place on the edge of the Jewish Quarter—all except David, her older brother, who had moved into a flat with his intellectual friends, much to her parents' consternation.

Still, they'd made it a home, and it showed. The zig-zag parquet floors shone, the windows in the living room's bay gleamed, and the pillows on the well-worn flowered couch sat fluffed. The pungent tang of cabbage and vinegar hung in the air. The officers billeted here would think the family left for an outing and would return at the end of the day.

Anna tamped down the rising tide of tears. Over the past years, she had cried enough. At least she had her violin. In her head, even now, rang the notes of Mozart's concerto. It quieted her heart.

Babička held onto Anna and grasped the hand-smoothed banister, her steps slow and halting. She hadn't descended the stairs in months. These days, even Anna rarely did.

What would their friend, *Paní* Buraneková, say when she came on her usual Saturday to bring them food they could no longer buy for themselves? Would *Hauptmann* Engel lay in wait for her, ready to arrest her for assisting Jews? Anna forced herself to step forward. She shivered.

When they reached the first-floor landing, the soldier didn't usher them through the entryway. Instead, he opened the door to the Schniz's flat and motioned for them to enter.

Ne, it was his apartment now.

On trembling legs, she led *Babička* through the door and into a place laid out much the same as theirs. She removed her shoes, as did her grandmother. Before, when the Schniz's lived here, she had visited them, had sat on the parquet floor in the living room and played with the little boy.

She dug her fingernails into her palms. Maybe the pain from the action would cover the pain in her heart.

"Welcome." *Hauptmann* Engel opened the drapes on the bow window, inviting in the light and giving a view of the quiet, narrow street. He pointed to a spot in the bow. "Is this a good place for you to play? Do you have enough light? Didn't you bring any music?"

Anna controlled the smile that wanted to break out on her face at his fussing. "*Ja*, this is fine. I don't need any music. It is all in my head." Though she'd just had the music before her, the hours upon hours she practiced fused the notes into her brain. She would never forget. No matter what the Nazis did to her.

She sat *Babička* on the green couch, took her violin from its case, and stood beside the window. Her fingers trembled. Would she even be able to play a single note with him sitting beside her grandmother, staring at her? Placing her in the window for all of Prague to see that she broke the law?

"You may begin."

The music rose from deep inside her, swelling in her chest, commanding her fingers to draw the bow across the strings. It lifted her from this place and this time, to a spot where beauty lived. And then she closed her eyes and coaxed the notes from her instrument. The world disappeared as the melody rose and fell, intense, passionate, breath-robbing.

The final tone reverberated in the room. *Hauptmann* Engel's applause jolted her back to the present—to the small flat on the edge of the Jewish section of Prague where a Nazi officer congratulated her on a job well done.

"Bravo, bravo. Shall we have another piece?" He glanced at *Babička* for approval. And she nodded. What other choice did she have?

"Do you know Vittorio Monti's *Csárdás*? It's such a beautiful Italian folk piece. I heard it performed in Rome once."

"*Ja*, I know it." She played it almost every day. Again, she lingered in the raptures of the haunting music until his cheering yanked her away.

"Come, sit. I'll get you a glass of water."

He disappeared into the kitchen. With a click, he opened the cabinet and shut it again. The water ran. When he returned, he handed her the glass, the drink moistening her dry mouth.

"You play like a master. Where did you study?"

She swallowed hard. "The Prague Conservatory. It was forced to close before I finished."

"*Ja*, that is too bad. But you have a great deal of talent."

"*Danke*." She studied the Nazi, handsome in his olive uniform, an eagle over a star stitched just above the right pocket. His pale blue eyes glittered, like he took true pleasure in her recital. Never had a German been kind to them. What was going on?

He patted *Babička*'s gnarled hand. "You must be very proud of your granddaughter."

"I am. The Lord blessed her with a wonderful gift. With the others gone, she is my joy."

"And the rest of your family?"

Was he hunting for useful information? Lulling them into a sense of security while attempting to locate others to ship off to Terezín?

Then again, they didn't have to worry. There was no one left for the Nazis to turn in. "They were deported this past winter."

He leaned forward. "I'm sorry to hear that."

How could he be sorry? How many Jews had he himself arrested and sent to an uncertain future?

"My brother and both of my sisters were promising musicians."

"Ah, so your talent runs in the family. Did you play an instrument, too, Frau Doubeková?"

Babička's dim gray eyes took on a dreamy luster. "The piano. I lived for a while in Vienna and studied there."

"Did you know Gustav Mahler?"

"I met him once."

"I'm impressed."

Why would he be pleased *Babička* knew an Austrian Jewish composer?

"I played in many salons over the years, until I married my dear husband and the Lord gave us children. But always we had a piano in our home, and I spent many happy hours in front of the keyboard. My children and grandchildren grew up with music filling the house."

"Where are they all now?"

"My son emigrated to the United States. My daughter, son-in-law, two granddaughters, and a grandson got their deportation notices."

"I'm sure you miss them. But to grow up with music surrounding you ..." He nodded, and a slow smile spread across his face, a deep crease curving from the side of his nose to his chin. "I didn't always appreciate music. Over time, though, the rhythm of it filled me, and I grew to love it."

Anna closed her eyes to stop thinking of him as handsome. And kind. That last image of her parents and sisters walking into the exhibition hall flashed in front of her. That was what Nazis did to those they considered lower than them. That was the kind of man he was.

He slapped his knees and rose. "Thank you for the private concert. I would like you to come and play for me every day after dinner."

Again, she was stuck with no other option but to agree. There was no way she could get out of this without earning his wrath. Then one idea came along, and she held onto it. "My grandmother is very tired by that time of night, and I must help her get ready for bed."

Babička flashed her a scowl. She didn't like Anna's lie.

"It won't be late. You can bring her with you. I'm sure she would like to hear you play."

"She hears me all day long."

"Or I can come to your flat for the performance."

She bit the inside of her cheek until she tasted blood. A German officer in her apartment? *Ne*, she couldn't allow him to get that close. "I will come to you."

How much more would he demand of her? And how long before he tired of her music and sent them to Terezín?

"Halten sie."

Patricie Kadlecová froze in place at the German soldier's command, the strap of her grocery-filled shopping bag wrapped around her right hand. Behind her, a train whistle blew.

Was this the day? The day the Gestapo came for her and sent her to the very place she worked to keep her Jewish friends from?

It might well be.

Around her, the hustle and bustle of life in Prague continued. Families greeted friends and relatives coming to visit from other parts of the country. Sweethearts kissed each other good-bye as one or the other departed the city. Nazi soldiers patrolled the train station, their eagle eyes sharp, their German shepherds straining on their leashes to sniff out criminals.

Criminals like her, who went to the country for food she couldn't get in the city—an illegal act she committed once a week, when she took the train to a small town, then a cart to a farm to purchase food and milk.

The officer approached her, no weapon in his hand. She shivered and clenched her fists. He held out a ration card. A stolen one.

Did he know?

Could he tell?

"You dropped this." He waved it.

She snatched it and stuffed it into the bag of potatoes, onions, and bread, all covered with clothes to hide the contents from prying eyes. "*Děkuji*. I'm grateful." She had been careless. The cards were precious, necessary to sustain life. And obtained at a great price.

The German, who spoke excellent Czech, flashed her a dazzling smile. Light brown hair peeked from beneath his hat, pulled down, obscuring his eyes. His features were angular. Hard. "Let me walk you to your destination, *Fraulein* ..."

"Kadlecová." Her stomach flipped like the trapeze artist at the circus she'd attended as a child. Why would he make such an offer? "I wouldn't want to trouble you, Officer ..."

"*Hauptsturmführer* Stefan Jaeger. It is no trouble at all." He clasped her hand, his fingers clammy. He grabbed her bag from her. "Quite heavy."

She nodded, instead of speaking in a trembling voice.

"So much for a single woman to carry."

A statement, but it demanded an answer. "Books. I like to read." All the lying she'd done as a child came in handy now.

"But it is such a burden to you. Let me help. Which way to your home?"

She gritted her teeth. What now? Her house hid secrets no Nazi officer should discover. "This way." She pointed in a direction without any idea of where they would end up. She could bring him to Georg's. He wasn't home. But taking this soldier there was also a bad idea.

"My mother was from the Sudetenland and spoke Czech. I've been here since we annexed this area. Prague has enchanted me. It has such a cultural heart. Such a rich heritage."

One he was trying to destroy. Patricie nodded. "I agree."

"So, you have traveled?"

"Somewhat." Why did she converse with this man? In addition to being much too forward, he was the enemy.

"Where?"

Why wouldn't he leave her alone? "Austria. Germany. Switzerland."

"That's a good bit of wandering. Why those places?"

"I was a music student and toured with a small ensemble." Why was she telling him all this?

"Ah. What instrument do you play?"

"The oboe. At least, I used to." Because of a German decree, the conservatory stood shuttered and forlorn. The sting of it bit her chest. Her hands missed the smooth wood of her instrument, her lips longed for the tickle of the reed.

"But you were able to go places."

He hypnotized her. Her muscles relaxed, but she forced herself to remain on guard. He might have singled her out. Perhaps he already knew what she wanted to remain hidden. "I didn't appreciate it like I should have."

"I know what you mean. Now that I live here, I'm understanding more about the Czech way of life. About the people."

Not enough to know that the Czech didn't open up to strangers.

She led him in circles. She couldn't keep doing this. Soon, he would spot the Charles Bridge for the second time and figure out her deception. Like the cogs of a machine, her mind whirled. Then she slapped her forehead. "Oh, I meant to purchase eggs. I need them for dinner. Thank you for your kind offer, but I won't keep you."

She attempted to pull her bag from his grasp, but he covered her hand and clung to it. "Have dinner with me on Friday."

For the second time today, he stopped her in her tracks. "Excuse me?"

"Dinner. At Café Imperial. Give me your address, and I'll send a car for you."

"I'm not sure . . ."

"This is an offer you can't refuse."

She tried in vain to take a deep breath. He narrowed his perfect Aryan eyes and pursed his lips into a straight line.

"I should be honored to join you."

Should be honored. But instead, the hair on her arms bristled. What would happen to her if he discovered her secret?

Chapter Three

The windshield wipers on Stefan Jaeger's official car beat out a steady rhythm as he and Horst flew over the Czech countryside, the deluge obscuring much of the bucolic scene. Out there, farmland spread over the low hills. Gold and red tinged the edges of the leaves on the trees. Off in the distance, a train whistle blew.

Horst pressed his nose against the passenger-side window. Who was on that train? A family off on an autumn holiday? Jews headed the same place as him?

"I don't see what going to Theresienstadt has to do with architecture." Horst rubbed the door handle as he pushed back the urge to fling it open and jump out. He'd only have sixty kilometers to cover to get back to Prague.

Stefan tapped the steering wheel. "You'd be interested to know that this camp, a former fortress, was built in the shape of a six-pointed star. Prophetic, don't you think?"

"I suppose. But why this insistence that I go?"

"I know you like art and music, and there are a great many talented Jews there. They are planning a concert tonight that I thought you would enjoy attending. After I finish my work."

Many more words teetered on the edge of Horst's tongue, but he bit them back and instead leaned against the headrest and stared at the car's ceiling. Stefan was wrong. He would rather be anywhere than listening to Jewish prisoners perform for their masters' enjoyment like so many trained animals.

"It's not all bad for them there." Stefan tapped the brake as the car rounded a curve. "They have work to occupy them and are able to enjoy the arts. This outing for you is meant to be a diversion after all those hours in that dark office in Prague."

"I get out enough to inspect the buildings around the city, to make sure that we don't bomb any cultural treasures we want to preserve."

"Still, it's nice to get away from time to time. Now cheer up. We're here."

Thin, haggard, wizened people crammed the muddy streets of what had once been a sleepy garrison village. In their eyes, Horst spied nothing but hopelessness. Small children, dressed in little more than rags, shuffled between buildings. Soldiers surrounded a group of men with pickaxes returning from their work detail. The place stank of decay, disease, and death. Like rotting teeth.

An officer, all spit and polish, greeted them. "*Heil* Hitler."

Horst straightened his cramped legs and returned the salute, as did Stefan.

"I trust you had an uneventful trip."

"*Ja*, just fine. *Hauptsturmführer* Neubaum, this is my friend, Horst Engel, Minister of Architectural Preservation."

"Glad you could join us. Dinner is all set out. Nothing as fine as in the city, but hearty fare nonetheless." The captain led the way through the command headquarters to the dining room. "*Hauptsturmführer* Jaeger tells me you appreciate good music."

Horst nodded. "*Ja*, I do."

"Who is your favorite composer?"

"Wagner."

"Of course. The Führer's favorite. You are a wise and discerning man." Neubaum rubbed his golden mustache, an exact replica of their leader's. "You will be very impressed at the level of talent on display this evening. Theresienstadt is home to many of Prague's finest musicians."

Home. Anna. How long before she played her violin in this place? Before she became one of the vacant-eyed residents just hoping to survive?

Fine china and crystal, set on the long tabled, glittered in the chandelier's light. Neubaum indicated where he wanted Horst and Stefan to sit. Women prisoners marked with the yellow star on their maid's uniforms served wurst and spaetzle and potato pancakes. They stared at the food with their dark eyes and licked their lips. Horst forced his attention on his meal.

"How long have you been in Prague, *Hauptmann* Engel?"

"Only a short time. I was stationed in Vienna before that."

"And what do you think of your new post?"

"My family and I often took holidays here when I was a child, so I'm familiar with the city. I'm glad to see the beautiful old buildings weren't damaged during the invasion. It would be a pity if the world lost such amazing architecture."

Stefan lifted his beer stein. "If any harm comes to them, it won't be because of the Germans, I assure you. The Russians or English would be to blame."

"That won't happen. Czechoslovakia is part of the German Reich now." Neubaum bit a piece of veal from his fork.

The conversation turned to people Horst hadn't met yet. He should have stayed in the city where he could have listened to Anna's private concert. A time of balm for his soul.

When the meal ended, they made their way through the three inner courtyards of the Magdeburg barracks to the hall where the performances were held. Neubaum nodded in the direction of one of the overcrowded buildings. "Another transport left today. We'll empty this place yet."

"Where do they all go?"

Stefan and Neubaum stared at him as if he'd asked how to get a man to the moon. "Surely ..."

Neubaum chuckled. "To the east. Treblinka, Auschwitz. Part of the final solution. You haven't been behind a desk that long, have you?"

Horst laughed along, trying to make his chuckle as real as possible. "*Nein, nein.* I simply didn't know which camps this one fed. Those aren't important details in my office."

A new odor accosted him. Something like the time he burned his finger on the hot stove. His eyes watered, and he fought to keep his dinner in his stomach. He didn't ask what it was. No need to appear foolish again.

Probably for the best he didn't have the answer.

Bodies crammed the music hall. The voices of the prisoners rose and fell, some in German, some in Czech, some in other languages he didn't recognize. An open window provided small relief from the stench of the unwashed bodies packed inside. He restrained himself from digging into his pocket for his handkerchief. Instead, he reached for a cigarette.

They passed the Jews, packed shoulder to shoulder, and moved to the best seats, the ones reserved for the German officers. Four chairs occupied the raised the stage. Neubaum leaned over. "A string quartet tonight, starring Egon Ledeč. You have picked a good evening to be here."

At the top of the hour, four Jewish men entered and sat down. They tuned their instruments and adjusted the music on their stands. The curly headed man with the receding hairline nodded three times, and they launched into a piece by Mozart.

This wasn't an amateur group. The bows flowed over the strings as the music rose to the rafters. The silkiness of the sound enveloped Horst and carried him from this place and time to a world he could only describe as beautiful. The notes caressed him, soothed him, and filled him.

As the final measure sounded, the room held its breath for a moment before leaping into wild applause. The four musicians stood and bowed, their faces beaming and radiant, no longer hopeless. Horst rose to his feet and clapped with all his might. Not even in Berlin had he heard such a fine performance.

Stefan tugged on his coat and pulled him into his seat. "You are making a spectacle of yourself. A Nazi doesn't acknowledge Jews in such a manner."

Horst shrugged but held his hands still. "Why shouldn't we reward their accomplishment? They must have practiced for hours and hours."

"They are Jews." For Stefan, that may have been answer enough. For Horst, it was not.

After the applause died away and the room emptied, Neubaum

tapped Horst on the shoulder. "Since you were so enthusiastic about the show, let me introduce you to tonight's musicians." The captain led the way to the stage where the four Jews returned their instruments to their cases.

The group huddled together as Neubaum made the introductions. "This is Egon Ledeč, Viktor Kohn, Paul Kohn, and David Zadok."

Horst stared at the tall, gaunt young man with dark hair which stuck out in every direction. Against all conventions, he shook the Jew's hand. "Zadok, you say?"

The musician nodded.

Horst turned to his fellow officers. "Why don't you head back without me? I'll join you in a few minutes. I have some business with this Jew."

Stefan's gaze hardened, but he nodded. "Don't be long." His words were deep and slow. He and Neubaum left.

Horst turned to David. "You have a sister named Anna?"

The man's bottom jaw dropped open. He nodded. Light shone from his hazel eyes.

"I live in the flat below her and your grandmother."

David's knees buckled, and he sat in his chair with a thump. He grasped the edge of the seat. "How are they?"

Horst sat beside Anna's brother. "I just moved in and have only met them a few times, but they appear to be fine. How long has it been since you've seen them?"

"Eight or nine months."

"What about the rest of the family? Anna mentioned parents and two sisters."

A shadow crossed David's face. He swallowed several times. "They left on a transport east several weeks ago."

To an extermination camp.

He couldn't erase the image of Anna from his mind. Soft, sad eyes which filled with tears when the subject of her family came up. Or the image of his mother, risking his father's wrath if he found out, going to their Jewish neighbors the morning after Kristallnacht, helping them to sweep the glass which littered their jewelry shop.

She wouldn't want him to turn his back on this man and his sister. "What can I do to help?"

David held his violin bow and stared after the lean German as he walked down the concert hall's aisle and out the door into the cold and rainy night. Horst. He'd said his name was Horst.

Which was more stunning, the fact that the man knew both Anna and *Babička* or his offer of help? He was a stranger. David didn't know him in the least.

Viktor snapped his fingers in front of David's face, breaking his trance. "What was that about?"

David shook his head. "I don't know. The man is a Nazi officer who knows my sister and grandmother. Yet he spoke to me and offered to help us."

"Help us how? To get on the train east?" Viktor pointed in the direction of the tracks.

"To bring us food and medicine."

"And you believe him? Look around. You can't trust a single German. They are out to eliminate Jews from the face of the earth. Not a word of what he said was true."

David scoped out their surroundings. This one was packed with Jewish prisoners doing nothing more than existing, shoulder to shoulder. The rotten stench of filthy bodies mingled with the odor of sauerkraut and pervaded the very walls. And this was a palace compared to the room he shared with ten other men. They slept on rough mattresses along with lice and bedbugs.

"That man did this to us." Viktor shook his head. "He brought us here, and he's going to ship us out of here."

"He could be our savior."

"Our savior?" Viktor laughed a single, curt chuckle. "There is not going to be any savior. No one will rescue us from this place. Our only savior is our music. Our temporary relief from the hardship we call life."

David set his bow in his case and closed the lid. *Táta* and *Máma* taught him about a different Savior. They said if you believed in Him, He would grant you release. Some release it turned out to be. Last time he checked, he didn't see a Savior lifting anyone from this hole because they believed.

Nothing but a bunch of rubbish.

David sighed. "Music and sleep. The only times one can forget this place." And even sleep didn't provide the release he craved. He longed for. He only had his music to cling to.

He rose and picked up his instrument case. "Come on, Viktor. I'll race you to the room."

His short, balding friend grinned. "Like I'm in a hurry to be back there."

They left the building and trekked through the muddy courtyard, the muck oozing through David's cracked shoe sole. No moon shone to light their way, but at least the persistent shower stopped. "And what about Anna and *Babička*? He lives in the flat below them."

Viktor let out a low, long whistle. "That can't be a good situation."

"*Ne*, it can't. I'm very worried. That officer seems to have taken a liking to Anna. What will that mean for her? For both of them?"

Viktor hustled to keep up with David's long strides. "Remember, you can't trust him. This may be a trap."

"How?"

"He might be looking for them, waiting for you to spill the information he needs to nab them. Watch what you say."

"But he knew all about them."

Viktor shrugged. "That's the Germans' job. They know everything about us. There is nothing private when it comes to the Jews. Their persecution of us is relentless. Watch and be wary. Stay away from him. Don't let him near you. That's my advice."

"And it's good advice." But for his sake and for Anna's sake, he might not follow it.

Anna paced the tiny living room in the tiny apartment, stopping in front of *Babička*. "He wants me to play for him again. Play for him. Like I'm his personal musician, put on this earth for his pleasure and his alone. What do I do?"

"You do as he bids."

"Just like that. I create music for him." A knock broke off Anna's argument. "And there he is. I want you to come with me. I refuse to go to his flat alone."

Anna flung open the door, thinking she would see the Nazi officer. Her day got much better when she discovered *Paní* Buraneková on the other side with a bag full of groceries. "What a nice surprise. I wasn't expecting you until tomorrow."

The older woman, her thin gray hair in a knot on the top of her head, chuckled. "I can come back tomorrow, if you like."

Anna ushered her into the sunny flat. "Only if you bring us *koláček*." Prune and cheese-topped Danish. Her mouth watered.

Paní Buraneková led the way through the double doors into the narrow kitchen. "You always were a dreamer, Anna. That is what I love about you." Their friend from church pulled bread, paprika, and a small package of tripe from her sack. "A special surprise for you. Enough to make *dršťková polévka*."

Anna's stomach rumbled. How long had it been since she'd had tripe soup, her favorite dish?

"How is your grandmother today?"

"Come and see for yourself."

Babička sat in the bay in the living room, a book in her lap, her gaze fixed on the scene outside. "More going. Always more going."

Paní Buraneková went to her longtime friend and sat in the worn wing chair opposite her. "Don't worry. Let's praise God you haven't received your notice yet. He'll take care of you."

Babička turned to Anna, her gray eyes lacking their usual luster. "It's not for me that I fret. It's my Anna. I've lived a full life. She hasn't." She rubbed the back of her neck. "But the Lord's way is not our way."

"True enough." *Paní* Buraneková shook her head. "What is this world coming to?"

Another knock startled Anna from the scene. Her heart rate kicked up a couple of notches. There were penalties for helping Jews. Severe penalties. She nodded at *Paní* Buraneková. "Go to the kitchen."

The older woman furrowed her brow. "I'm visiting a friend. If that is wrong, then let them send me away."

Anna stared at her. How could she say such a thing?

"I mean it. I refuse to live my life in fear or to stop from doing what is right. Answer the door."

Anna hissed at her. "I can't let you take that risk. Please, at least go to the kitchen. I'm going to be leaving with him in a few moments."

Paní Buraneková relented and did Anna's bidding. Only then did she crack the door. "Hello."

Hauptmann Engel smiled through the small opening. "I came to hear you play for me again this evening. May I come in?"

Like he needed to ask. Dark laughter built in her chest, and she pressed her lips together to keep it contained. He could force his way in any time he pleased. She stepped back. He entered and removed his shoes, perhaps intending to stay.

Shadowy splotches formed half-moons under his pale blue eyes. The crease around his mouth was deeper, as if he'd aged in the past couple of days.

"What would you like to hear?"

"Something melancholy." He stared over Anna's left shoulder. "Good evening, Frau Doubeková."

It was a good thing *Paní* Buraneková remained in the kitchen, away from his prying eyes. "You were gone for a while."

"I was away on business. I'd like to talk to you about that, actually, if I may."

What did he have to say? That Jakub could no longer keep their names from the deportation lists? She sat on the tattered, flower-speckled couch.

He folded his frame onto the low seat and lit a cigarette. "I was at Theresienstadt."

Anna glanced at *Babička*. Her grandmother sat with her hands clasped. In resignation, possibly. "I know about it. In Czech, it is Terezín."

"I listened to a very fine string quartet while I was there."

Now he would tell her what a wonderful place it was, how the Germans would protect her there, and even allow her to play her music.

But that's not how it was. "You enjoyed it, *ne?*"

"Very much." His eyes softened. "Egon Ledeč was part of it."

The name struck a chord in Anna's heart. "My brother used to play with him. They practiced for hours upon hours." She swallowed hard.

"Your brother was one of the performers."

Anna grasped the armrest and clung to it. "David? He was there?" She had a difficult time breathing enough to get the words out.

Babička joined Anna on the couch. "Are you sure?"

Hauptmann Engel nodded.

Anna swiped a tear from her eye. "What about the rest of my family?"

Chapter Four

vening fell over Prague, and darkness descended. Blackout shades covered the windows and dark paper snuffed out street lamps and headlights. Patricie flew down the stairs, not wanting *Hauptsturmführer* Jaeger anywhere near her apartment. Inside, the crevices and crannies hid stolen ration cards and lists of Jews her arm of the resistance aided.

Hauptsturmführer Jaeger grinned when he saw her, but no warmth radiated from the smile. "You look lovely tonight."

His touch chilled her. She drew her coat tighter over her suit. "Thank you. May I say, you cut a dashing figure." And he did. His dark uniform complimented his fair coloring, the belt cinched around his small waist. At the sight of the red armband with the swastika, Patricie shuddered. How would she keep her nerves under control all evening?

He showed her to the car, every inch the perfect German gentleman. She slipped into the leather interior, the buttery suppleness of it caressing her skin. He slid into his seat and pulled away from her humble apartment building. "This is far from where I met you, is it not?"

"I enjoy the walk."

"With such a heavy sack?"

"I needed to buy eggs. The challenge is to get to a shop before they sell out. This way, I had plenty of places to try before I got home."

He stroked the seat beside her. "Come now, we all must live with the rationing. In the end, life for all of us will be much better."

She slid the tiniest bit toward the door. "Of course."

"You have lived here all of your life?"

"*Ja.*"

The small talk continued until they arrived at the restaurant. Warm, rich wood paneling set the ambiance. A phonograph played soft violin music in the background.

The maître d' greeted them with a snap of his heels and a Heil Hitler. "It is good to see you tonight, *Hauptsturmführer* Jaeger. Your table is waiting."

Hauptsturmführer Jaeger offered her his elbow as the man led them to the best location, in the far back corner of the sumptuous room. They passed square tables covered with crisp, white linens and set with the finest Dresden china, pink and yellow and purple flowers painted on it. Much more delicate than the bright, primary-colored Czech ceramics.

He pulled out her chair and waited for her to be seated before turning to the waiter. "*Danke*. We will have our wine now." He situated himself across from her.

"You must come here often. He knows you."

"Often enough, but never with a woman as beautiful as you."

"You flatter me." Patricie crossed her legs one way, then the other. "But I'm plain, and I know it. Look at me. Mousy brown hair. Green eyes set too far apart. Nose a bit too big."

"I only ever state the truth."

And all she did these days was lie.

The maître d' returned with their wine. She capped her glass. "None for me, *děkuji*. If I could please just have some water?"

Once the man poured *Hauptsturmführer* Jaeger's drink and left, the Nazi officer leaned across the table. "I know all about you."

She gulped. Where was that waiter with her water? "You do?"

"The child of a store manager and a typing pool employee. Two brothers. Graduated from school with mediocre grades, studied at the music conservatory, now is a store clerk. How did I do?"

Too well. Underneath the table, her legs shook. "Very good." She was forced to work in a clock shop because the Nazis stole her music from her. The part of her that lived and breathed. That came alive. Helping the Jews filled a small part of the void. "Where did you get all that information?"

"I have my ways. Nothing escapes my notice."

Of course it didn't. "I suppose, then, you are perfect for your position. But you have me at the disadvantage. I know nothing about you."

"There is not much to tell. My father passed away when I was young. I took care of my mother and younger sister, looked out for them, watched over them. I was commissioned and joined the SS when I completed my university studies. And now, I'm here."

With a great deal of effort, she gave him a small smile. "I'm glad you are."

"Tell me more about yourself. How is it you know every part of the city so well?"

The waiter brought her water, and she downed a gulp of it. "Even before the war, *Máma* and I visited the elderly and helped them in any way we could."

"A compassionate soul. But why help strangers? Didn't you want to look out for your own family?" He slicked back his light-brown hair.

"We all need someone's kindheartedness from time to time. They taught me, and teach me, many things. I learn from their wisdom. Everyone has their useful place in this world." She clamped her mouth shut. Where did those words come from? She'd said too much. That's why Czech children were taught from early on to hold their tongues around strangers.

Hauptsturmführer Jaeger laughed, a sound as cool as a mountain stream. "In their own ways, I suppose." He played with his spoon. "You don't have to be nervous around me."

She forced herself to sit back in her chair and unclasp her hands. "I'm not." Yet another lie. "I've never been to such a place like this before, though."

"None of your other boyfriends brought you here?"

"I've never had time for relationships with men."

"Always too busy helping others."

"Is that a bad thing?"

"I don't know. You tell me."

An icy jolt shot up her spine. "What do you want with me, *Hauptsturmführer* Jaeger?"

His smile revealed a row of even, white teeth. "Call me Stefan. No need to be so formal."

"We are a formal people." Patricie cringed. She would never call or even think of a stranger by his first name, least of all a Nazi officer.

"I like a beautiful woman who is a mystery. At the station the other day, I picked you out of all the others, with your heavy canvas bag. You say you help other people. What people do you help? And why do you help them?"

Patricie clasped her hands together even tighter and prayed that he would never discover her secret.

Anna sat on the edge of the sofa as dusk softened the light in the apartment. She searched *Hauptmann* Engel's face for the answer she wanted. The answer she dreaded. She squeezed *Babička*'s hand so hard, her grandmother let out a small squeal. "What about the rest of my family? You saw them at Terezín, *ne*?"

He rubbed his broad forehead. "I'm sorry." His husky voice was little more than a whisper. "David told me that they were taken away on a transport several weeks ago."

"Away? To where?" Her insides turned as cold as Prague in the winter.

"I haven't seen a camp for myself."

"What are they like?"

Hauptmann Engel crushed out his cigarette. "May I speak to you alone, Anna?"

Could she trust him? Perhaps. He had no reason to tell them about David. Foolish, maybe, but she went with him to the hall.

He leaned against the staircase's wrought-iron railing, shoes in his hand, then cleared his throat, his Adam's apple bobbing. "I didn't want to upset your grandmother."

"I need to know where my parents and sisters went."

"Despite what the Germans tell Prague's Jews, Theresienstadt is not a nice place. There are crowded conditions, disease, and starvation. If you are a musician, your life might be a little easier. You don't have to work as hard, and you might end up with better living conditions."

Hauptmann Engel evaded the question. Goosebumps raced up and down her arms. "What about the rest of my family? David and I were the only musicians. *Máma* hasn't played since David was born. Jana and Lada are still very young."

"I don't know where for sure, but from Theresienstadt, the Jews are taken to camps farther east. These camps are part of the final solution. The plan to rid the world of Jews."

Her knees buckled. *Hauptmann* Engel caught her before she hit the floor. In his embrace, a strange warmth flooded her. He led her to the top step and helped her to sit. "I'm sorry to shock you."

"There has been talk, but no one could prove it. Not a single person who went there has been back to tell about it. It's . . . it's hard to hear. So, they are . . . are, you know, then?" She couldn't say the word. Couldn't force it past her lips.

He sat beside her. "Those who are able to work are spared. Perhaps . . ."

"Two middle-aged people, one with a bad back, and two young girls. How much work are they able to do? I'm afraid there is no hope for them." His image swam in front of her eyes. She couldn't allow him to see her break down. "Please, will you excuse me from playing for tonight?"

"Of course. Do you need anything?"

She shook her head. Even if he could right her world again, she refused to accept help from the very kind of person who had likely murdered her beloved parents and sisters.

As Horst once again entered the transition camp at Theresienstadt, he attempted to shut out the sights and sounds that accosted him. The old people who tottered around the grounds on stick-like legs. The piles of corpses thrown like refuse on the side of the street, too many dying each day to be buried. The aroma of rotting flesh and the pungent stench of human excrement.

How could the world think the Germans protected the Jews here?

Only the music was beautiful.

He made sure to arrive in the late evening when the inmates scheduled a concert at their captors' command. And as he hoped, the barracks where the German guards lived were empty of almost all their residents. Though missing the performance was unfortunate, he needed to have it this way.

In the near-darkness, he slipped into the yellow-painted administration building. If they ever needed to flee this place in a hurry, the Germans had much to burn. They were nothing if not meticulous in their record-keeping.

All the better for him.

He held his breath as he crept up the stairs in case one of them should creak. The memory of the tears that had welled in Anna's eyes as she feared the worst for her family haunted him. Drove him. What if *Mutti* disappeared without a trace? He wouldn't be able to stand the not knowing. The awful wondering at her fate.

For Anna's sake, he had to find out.

Why he was willing to risk his life for a Jew, he didn't have an answer. She was beautiful, to be sure, with large eyes and dark hair that fell in soft waves around her heart-shaped face. More than that, she was sweet and vulnerable. Perhaps that was what had sent him on this crazy, heart-pounding search. Since that one awful night so many years ago, he couldn't endure that look of helplessness and pain in another creature's eyes.

He reached the top of the stairs and the records office. He turned the office's door handle. Locked. Just what he expected.

He reached into his pocket and pulled out a hairpin.

Good thing he had a female neighbor. As he'd left Anna's flat the other day, he'd picked up the pin on the landing, thinking to return it to her the next time they met.

His hands shook so much, the pin fell to the floor. Outside, on the street below, the voices of fellow soldiers who'd had a bit too much Czech beer tonight hung in the air. They sang the song all wrong, then laughed.

His stomach turned to a block of ice. The voices passed, then faded. He dared to relax and draw in a deep breath.

After retrieving the pin from the floor, Horst jiggled it in the lock. It took awhile, but at last it clicked, and the door opened. He pulled down the blackout shades and turned on the light.

The record keeper was neat and organized, and in short order, he located the file cabinet that held the records for each individual who passed in and out of these arched gates. He sorted through the folders until he got to the Z's.

Of course, quite a number of people named Zadok resided here. A popular surname in Prague's Jewish community. And he'd neglected getting the names of Anna's parents and sisters. The chore in front of him grew much more tedious.

After a few minutes of searching, he located David's file, which listed his parents and sisters who were also in the camp with him.

A floorboard in the hall creaked.

Horst stopped. He stood stock still, not breathing, not listening.

No more noises. He allowed the air to rush from his lungs.

Flipping through the files as fast as possible, he discovered the ones he wanted. He pulled them from the drawer, sat down, and set them on his lap. After a brief scan of each, he had the information he needed. That Anna and her grandmother needed.

Before he returned the files to their places, the door swung open.

An imposing SS officer filled the entryway. "What are you doing in here?"

Horst froze.

Chapter Five

$\mathcal{S}$oft light filtered into the chilly living room of Anna's apartment. Though *Babička* napped in the bedroom, Anna lifted her violin to her chin. *Babička* said the music lulled her to sleep. She never shushed Anna or told her not to play.

Today, she chose Paganini's *24 Caprices* as her music selection. She'd won an award for it long ago. Before the world went crazy. The challenging arpeggios, trills, and intervals kept her mind and fingers occupied, transporting her from this insanity. She poured her passion into it.

She played it through twice, hating for it to end, for reality to intrude once more. As she lifted her bow from the strings, there was movement in the doorway. Her very dear friend who grew up next door to her stood in the entrance. "Ester." Both tears and a smile threatened.

Ester Taborová gave her own sad smile before stepping into the room. "How long have you listened to me?"

"Since halfway through the first time." She pushed a long, dark strand of hair from her face.

Anna hugged her and motioned for her to sit on the sofa beside her. "And you didn't say anything?"

"You know I like to listen to you. I can't play such a challenging piece, so I watch you and pretend."

"And what brings you by?" Anna returned the violin to its blue-velvet-lined case.

"I wanted to see you. To find out how you are doing, especially with a Nazi living downstairs from you, or so I hear. It's bad enough to have the man in the neighborhood."

"Up to this point, it's not been too terrible. He's nice, as far as

Germans go. He hasn't been unkind to us. He hasn't taken my violin away or turned me in. In fact, he likes me to play for him." What possessed her to list Horst's positive attributes?

Ester's nut-brown eyes widened. "And you do?"

"What other choice do I have? When he commands, I obey. Maybe he'll keep us around longer if I perform for him. Between that and Jakub, perhaps *Babička* and I will have a chance to live. And he brought the most wonderful news."

"Is there such a thing as wonderful news these days?"

"Partly wonderful, anyway. He had to go to Terezín and, while he was there, he saw a concert." Anna restrained herself from jumping up and down on the rosy cushion. "David was one of the musicians."

A grin broke out on her friend's face. Ester had been sweet on David for years. "He's alive?"

"For now he is." A laugh gurgled in Anna's throat.

"And the rest of your family?"

Did Anna dare to tell Ester what *Hauptmann* Engel had shared with her? They would end up at Terezín sooner or later. In time, their number would be called to go to the camp in the east. Anna bit her lip. "I don't know."

They both sat silent for a few minutes. At last, Ester reached into her pocket. "I don't want to diminish your joy over David, but I have some bad news of my own."

Anna held the paper in her trembling hands. She didn't need to read it to know just what it said. "Your deportation notices."

Ester nodded. "I'll be joining your family in Terezín. Yours will come soon, I expect. Prague is almost empty of Jews. The Butcher of Prague may be gone, but he's still having his way with us. Before too long, Jakub will have to put you on the list, because there will be no one else."

Anna's body numbed. "You leave soon, *ne*?"

"The day after tomorrow. My mother is in a tizzy, my sister is crying over leaving her friends. And I'm scared. What if they do to us what the Butcher did to *Táta*?"

The ear-splitting ring of the gunshot that took *Pan* Tabor's life still reverberated in the street. Though they had scrubbed the wall Heydrich had lined him up against, the blood stain would forever mar the bricks.

She squeezed Ester's hand. "I will miss you. Do you remember hiding in your mother's wardrobe, amongst her fur coats, eating the *koláček* we swiped from the table?"

"The cook was so angry with us. We should never have done that. And what about the time we went swimming in the river without permission? I thought you were drowning, so I pulled you to the bank."

"And how we giggled over boys and planned our grand weddings, with huge vases of flowers and lace gowns." A lump in her chest weighed on her. "Oh, Ester, I'll pray for you." What more could she say?

"Thank you. That helps. What else can we do? We pack our two bags each and go to the exhibition hall at the appointed time."

Images of that day last winter flashed in front of Anna's eyes. Her family walking into the hall. And now, to lose this friend who'd brought her such joy in the many years they lived beside each other.

If only . . .

Her heart broke into a thousand little bits, like a piece of fine china smashed on the ground.

A shot of adrenaline rushed through Horst's body at the sight of the SS officer in the office doorway, leaving him mushy-elbowed and weak-kneed. He stood on wobbling legs and gave as lusty a Heil Hitler as he could manage. "Good evening, sir."

Thunder crossed the officer's oval face. His blue eyes flashed. "I asked you a question. What are you doing searching through those files?"

What was he doing here? His mind raced, searching for an answer. He must have been crazy to think he could get away with helping a Jew. "I needed to check on some files, sir."

"You are not answering my question. Let's start with another one. Who are you?"

He raised his head and summoned every bit of strength he possessed to sound confident. "*Hauptmann* Horst Engel, sir. I'm the

Minister of Architectural Preservation in Prague. There is one building I'm particularly interested in that was most recently owned by Jews. I need to speak to them about one change they made to the building, but I cannot locate them."

"Why would you care about a Jewish dog and what he did to a building? Burn it down."

"Sir, to destroy such beautiful architecture—"

"Who let you in here?"

"Someone passing by. He had to get back to duty, so he couldn't stay." Horst stuffed the folders into the drawer and slammed it shut. "I have the information I need." With another Heil Hitler, he strode out of the room, down the steps, and out the door.

Once outside, he leaned against the side of the building, the brick rough beneath his palms. He drew in shaky breath after shaky breath. He had to calm down. That had been close. Too close. The officer might yet write him up. He could face discipline. At least he hadn't shot Horst on the spot.

When his breathing returned to normal and a good amount of time passed after his encounter with the SS guard, Horst scurried to his car. He peered all around to be sure no one watched him. He slipped a few bread rolls into the pockets of his pants, along with a small wedge of cheese and a couple sausages. In the darkness, he prayed no one should notice the slight bulges.

From the records, he discovered David resided in the Magdeburg barracks. The same building where they first met after the concert. With perfect posture and sure strides, he made his way down the street. As curfew passed, no one moved about, but many sounds floated from the old stone buildings lining the road. Violin music. Children's laughter. The anguished cries of the dying.

The deeper he plunged into the ghetto, the more unbearable the smells. Cooking fires and falling leaves should perfume the air. Instead, the odors were indescribable. Gut twisting. Eye watering. Vomit inducing. He closed his mind to what caused them.

He located David's building with little trouble. His stomach rolled more than a ship on a stormy sea at what he discovered inside. Men packed the tiny rooms. Not a few of them lay on thin mattresses on the floor, sunken, hollow shells of their former selves. His eyes watered at the overpowering odor of human bodies and death.

All conversation stopped the minute the prisoners recognized Horst's uniform. Palpable fear permeated the walls and filled the space.

After a moment of adjusting to the interior's dim light, Horst spotted David. The man stiffened as he approached. "Why are you here?"

"I have something for you."

David motioned for Horst to join him in the hall. "What?"

Horst pulled a roll from his pocket. "It's not much."

"Don't give it to me in front of the others in the room. They'll kill me before I even sink in my teeth."

"I'm sorry. I didn't know you lived in such miserable conditions."

"What did you think? That we are on holiday here?" David wrung his hands. His voice rose in pitch. "This may be a transition camp, but your friends will be just as happy if we don't live to be transported elsewhere. It will save them the trouble of packing us into the train."

Horst stepped back. "They don't tell us underlings any more than they tell you."

"And you want me to believe that?"

"Believe what you want. I'm trying to help you." He withdrew the cheese and sausage and offered them to David.

David's hazel eyes darkened until they grew almost black. "This will only prolong my suffering one more day. You saw the conditions."

This conversation veered off the path. He expected gratitude. "If you would rather not have my help ..."

David grabbed the items. "There. Now, you have done your good deed for the day. You can feel good about yourself. Go home, put your feet up, and enjoy your evening. Next time, don't come unless you have enough to share with all the men. Or a way out of here." With that, the man with the wild hair turned on his heel, then spun back around.

"If you want to help me, take care of my grandmother and my sister. Don't let anything happen to them. Keep them from this despicable place." With that, he disappeared into the room.

Without paying attention to his surroundings, Horst stumbled to his car. Not until he was halfway back to Prague did the realization strike him that he never told David what he'd found out about his family.

Even before *Hauptmann* Engel disappeared, David consumed the roll and the sausage. He wanted to save it, to savor each little bite, but once he put the soft bread into his mouth, the bread baked only this morning by his calculations, he couldn't control himself. The morsel slid down his throat into his empty belly.

By the time he made it to the cheese, his stomach ached. He slipped the food into his pocket, the one without the hole. Maybe it would stay there and not rip the worn fabric.

After wiping his hand across his mouth to rid his lips of any telltale crumbs, he sauntered back into the room and to his mattress beside Isaac.

"Hey, Zadok, what did that Nazi want with you?" With such a boyish face, Isaac appeared much younger than his almost thirty years.

"Nothing. I've done nothing to earn this attention."

"Does he have it in for you?"

David coughed into his handkerchief and stuffed it into his pocket. He didn't have to look. It bore a red stain. "I don't know what he wants with me."

Simon sat up on his pallet. "You must be the teacher's pet."

"Shut up, Simon." Isaac leaned forward. "Nobody wants to be a pet to the Nazis."

"Not even if it saves his skin? I'd volunteer."

David didn't have the strength to fight this battle. "Let it go, Simon. Whatever that German wants with me has nothing to do with you."

"Are you hatching a daring escape plan?"

"I thought I told you to shut up." Isaac clenched his fists.

"Stop it. Both of you. We're the intellectuals, remember? We don't use violence. Only reason." For long hours, they had sat in Prague's cafés and coffee shops, debating reason and life and existence. To the Czech, it was almost a sport.

Simon crossed his arms. "And I have a hundred reasons why that Nazi singled you out."

David lay back. "None of them correct. Because I have no idea what he wants."

All at once, Simon appeared in front of David, leaning over him. "What are you hiding?"

Did he see the bulge? Sweat rolled down David's face. "Not a thing."

"You're not telling the truth." Simon reached into David's right pocket and came up empty.

But the other pocket held the cheese. He should have eaten it. Or fed it to the rats. With all his might, he pushed Simon off and stood. Now with the advantage, David hovered over Simon.

The man wasn't sick. He'd come in from Prague not too long ago and was in better shape than David. He pushed David and landed a fist on his cheek. Pain raced through his skull. His ears rang.

Adrenaline pumped into David's system. He summoned all his strength and socked Simon in the stomach.

Fists flew. Others joined the fight. After a time, David lost track of who hit who. One punch landed on the side of his head, another on his chin, yet a third in his midsection. He now understood what it meant to see stars.

Simon got a hold of David's neck and squeezed. He couldn't breathe. The world darkened. Simon was bent on killing him. David didn't have a choice. He held up his hands in defeat.

Simon let go. David fell against the wall and slumped to the floor. The metallic taste of blood filled his mouth. "You win. Are you happy? We've turned into the Germans. Barbarians, settling differences by fighting."

Simon spit. "You started this by not sharing what is in your pocket."

"Have it your way." David pulled out the hunk of cheese. "If it will make you happy, it's yours." He threw it into the middle of room.

Like moths to a light, the men clambered to the bit of food. The fight resumed, this time over Horst's offering. David sat against the wall, out of the fray.

For a moment, Simon stopped scrabbling. "From now on, you will share with the rest of us, or I will kill you with my bare hands."

David licked his lips. If he believed in God, he would pray that *Hauptmann* Engel would stay very far away from him.

Even though a light mist fell on the awakening city, Anna hurried down the stairs from her apartment. She drew her coat around her to keep out the chill.

Why did she stand in the predawn mist? Over the years, she'd said enough good-byes to friends and even her own family. Still, she wanted to see Ester one last time. Perhaps for the last time ever.

Would she ever be reunited with her parents or her siblings? Would they ever celebrate another name day together? Would they sit at the Christmas dinner table and feast on carp? Would she and David ever play music together again?

If it weren't for her parents' command to watch over *Babička*, Anna would tell Jakub to put her name on the deportation list and get it over with. What good was it to live if you had no friends or family to share your life with? Moisture dampened her face, in part from the drizzle, in part from her tears.

Five minutes later, Ester and her family emerged from the neighboring building. The four of them moved with hunched shoulders.

"Ester."

Anna's friend turned in her direction and flashed a small smile. She lumbered over to Anna. "What are you doing out here? You're going to catch cold."

"You sound like *Babička*."

"I'm going to miss you, dear friend." Ester dropped her suitcases on the damp ground and drew Anna into an embrace.

How much more of this could she survive? Her heart could only break so many times. "And I'm going to miss you. God go with you and watch over you."

"When this is all over, we'll find each other again. I promise."

"I hope so."

After one more squeeze, Ester picked up her bags and joined her family as they wound their way down the long, narrow street.

Anna struggled to bring some music to mind, but the songs refused to obey her.

Behind her, the heavy wooden door to her own building opened and clicked shut. "*Fraulein* Zadoková?"

She turned toward the sound of *Hauptmann* Engel's voice.

"What are you doing out here?"

"My friend and her family are being deported today. I said farewell to yet another person I love."

"Come inside. You're soaked through."

His concern for her well-being struck her as funny. Why should he care? She followed him into the building and up the stairs to her flat.

"May I come in? I have news for you."

"Sure. Make yourself comfortable." She opened the door. *Babička* sat in the chair by the window, her Bible on her lap.

"I saw your brother again."

Anna spun around. "You did?"

"I brought him some food." The crease beside his mouth deepened.

What was she supposed to say? "*Děkuji.* How was he?"

"Thin. But feisty. He wasn't too happy that I only brought food for him. He told me to stay away if I didn't have enough for everyone. He's packed into a room no bigger than my living room with maybe eight or ten other men."

"That sounds like my brother. It's good to know he hasn't changed."

"I also found out about your parents."

"You did what?" She fussed with her dress's collar.

"When I was at Theresienstadt, I took the chance to peek at your family's files."

Blood pounded in her ears, almost drowning out his words. "What did you find?"

He studied the worn rug covering the wood floor. "In early October, they were transported to a camp called Auschwitz."

"That's it?"

He scuffed the toe of his shoe. Cleared his throat. Cracked his knuckles. He swallowed hard. "They were," he drew in a deep breath, "gassed upon their arrival."

Anna grabbed her middle. "*Ne, ne, ne.*"

Chapter Six

*H*orst turned away from Anna and her grandmother and stared at the crack in the plaster of the hundred-year-old apartment building's wall. Their anguish and grief tore at him. All of it inflicted on them by people like him. And all of it so unnecessary.

The fissure was like a snake, slithering, ready to devour its prey. Like the Nazi machine. Like the man he was.

Anna sobbed, heart-wrenching cries for the family she'd lost. Her grandmother spoke to her in low tones, her voice cracking with sadness, her sorrow no less. She'd lost a child and grandchildren.

He, too, suffered great loss when his older brother, Otto, died. Horst had been young, but his mother never got over the death of her firstborn. To this day, more than fifteen years later, she cried for him every night.

He turned around and studied Anna, nestled in her grandmother's embrace. After a long while, her weeping slowed. She leaned away from her grandmother's shoulders and stared at him with watery eyes.

What could he say to her? None of this was right or fair. "I'm sorry."

Anna pursed her lips and wiped the moisture from her face.

"My brother died when I was ten."

Anna swallowed hard and stepped from her grandmother's hold, but continued to clasp her hand.

"I understand what you are going through."

"You don't." Anna's face reddened.

"I watched my parents mourn for him. They still do. I miss him to this day."

"How did he die?"

"Polio." The same polio he'd survived.

"Was he taken from his home at gunpoint?"

Horst shook his head.

"Was he treated more like an animal than a human?"

"*Nein*." His parents had procured the best treatment available in Munich for their son.

"Was he forced to live in the crowded, filthy conditions you described at Terezín?" Her voice rose in pitch.

"*Nein*."

She released her grip on her grandmother and marched two steps toward him. "You have no idea how this feels, this stabbing pain in my chest. You have no idea what my family endured before men like you transported them who knows where and subjected them to who knows what before they met their end at the hands of their enemies. You lost a brother. I lost a mother, a father, and two sisters. My grandmother lost a daughter and two granddaughters. You have no comprehension of our grief."

Anna didn't inhale during her entire rant. When she finished, she panted, her breath ragged and shallow.

He had no answer for her. She was right. His grief was small compared to hers. His brother had died a dignified death. Her family hadn't.

In a short space of time, the red eked from her face, leaving it as white as the Alpine snows. He motioned to the sofa behind her. "Sit down and let me get you a glass of water." He added a please so it sounded like less of an order.

Her grandmother tried to steer her to the couch. Anna shook her off and tottered another step in Horst's direction. "After what you did to them, you want to get me a drink? Do you think that will heal my heart? You may hold sway over me, *Hauptmann* Engel, but unless you are here to arrest me and *Babička*, you have no right to be in my home. For now, it belongs to me and is private property. Get out of here and leave us to mourn."

Her wrath broke over him like a storm. "You're right. I don't understand. But let me help you."

"Help me? You want to help me? Why should I accept help from someone who wants to kill all of us for no other reason than our ethnic background? I told you to get out, and I meant it." She launched toward him, her fists clenched, her jaw tight.

He ducked out of the door before she poured more fury on him.

As he clicked it shut, she wailed. "*Máma, Máma, Táta, Táta.* Oh God, why did you take them from me?"

He leaned against the stairway wall and bowed his head.

Patricie stood in the middle of Georg Klima's tiny flat, nothing more than a lumpy sofa and an uneven table occupying the living area. Nothing pretentious, nothing to attract attention. The heat from the small, black stove in the corner didn't do much to warm the space.

Georg tented his long fingers in front of his boyish face. "How many do you need this week?"

"The number in hiding has grown to fifteen. I must have enough to last me five days at least."

"Where do you have them all stashed?"

"With just about everyone I know and can trust. At one apartment, there are five. It's too many, but I don't have anywhere else to put them. Yet they keep coming."

"Or you go to them."

"I had several Jewish friends at the music conservatory. I can't allow anything happen to them."

"What will you do when the next ones arrive on your doorstep?"

She peered at the man across the table from her. He'd dyed his red hair brown so he wouldn't attract too much attention. A wise thing to do if you're stealing ration cards. "I will find a place for them."

"You can't turn anyone away, but it's dangerous to stuff them into every nook and cranny in the city."

"If that's what I have to do in order to save them, I'll do it."

"Patricie—"

She waved him off, waved off the words that were coming. She cut off his protestations of love and his warnings of danger. "Not now, Georg. This isn't the time for that."

She loved him, it was true. She had for a very long time. But this wasn't the moment for beginning a family. Though it broke her heart, she forced herself to keep him at arm's length. Especially with *Hauptsturmführer* Jaeger's attention on her.

He flashed a tipped smile, but the light left his green eyes. "Someday."

"When someday comes, we can talk. Until then, we have work to do. We don't know what the next minute may bring."

"All the more reason. Won't you consider it?"

Should she tell him about *Hauptsturmführer* Jaeger?

She shook her head, answering both Georg's question and her own. *Hauptsturmführer* Jaeger may never have anything to do with her again. At least, she prayed he wouldn't. And she prayed that, at the end of this, Georg still would want her.

He lifted a floorboard and drew out a bundle of cards, peeling off what Patricie needed to feed that number of people for that amount of time.

She accepted the stack of ration cards from him and stuffed them into the lining of her coat. "Thank you."

"You're my best customer." This time, he offered her a genuine grin. He walked her to the door and pecked her on the cheek. "Be careful."

"I always am."

She bounced down the stairs, in a hurry to get home, take out the cards, and hide them. Her pounding of her heart matched the pace of her feet as she scurried down the hall, so many cards in her possession. Not that anyone knew, but she wouldn't rest easy until she got home.

She stopped short when she reached the street.

Hauptsturmführer Jaeger stood on the walk. He nodded at her.

What was he doing here? How could he have known where she was unless he'd followed her? Her heart tripped over itself.

"*Guten aben, fräulein.*"

"Good afternoon, *Hauptsturmführer* Jaeger." She worked hard to keep the tremor from her voice. "What a surprise to see you here." Her coat weighed her down.

"I hoped to run into you."

How much did he know? "It looks like you did."

"Who were you visiting?"

"A childhood friend." That much was not a lie. "What brings you to this part of the city?"

"I was out exploring. I don't believe I've ever been to this neighborhood."

"*Ne*, I suppose not." It wasn't trendy. It didn't offer any entertainment. The only reasonable explanation was that he'd followed her.

"Allow me to drive you home."

She gazed at the shiny black car parked nearby. "It's a beautiful day. I think I'll walk and enjoy it. During winter, you have to take advantage of this nice weather when you get it."

With slight pressure on the small of her back, he guided her to the curb and opened the door. "I insist."

Of course he did. She tried a grateful smile on for size and slipped into the car. Once he closed the door, her stomach cartwheeled in her midsection. She shouldn't have done this. She should have declined. Even if she had to slip under his arm and sprint down the street, she should never have gotten in this vehicle with him.

What was she going to do?

She grasped the door handle.

Before she formulated a plan, he slid into the driver's seat and pulled into the street. In moments, they arrived in a part of the city she wasn't familiar with. "Where are you taking me?"

"I have a surprise for you." He turned to her and winked.

The ration cards in her coat bumped her calf as she crossed her legs. She clasped her hands to keep them from trembling.

Lord, help!

The sun teased at Anna's eyelids until she opened them. The little round alarm clock on the bedside table read two o'clock.

But this wasn't her room. She'd fallen asleep in her parent's bed. She brushed a lock of hair from her itchy eyes. Her nose was stuffed.

With the force of a cannonball, she remembered why.

They were gone.

All of them.

She ran to the bathroom and lost the small lunch *Babička* had insisted she eat. Once empty, she sat on the floor, shivering.

The mother who'd given her life. The father who'd held her hand when she crossed the street. The sisters who'd giggled with her. All dead.

Babička snored in the other room. That, at least, was good.

Anna forced her weak legs to support her. As she stumbled down the hall to the living room, she leaned on the wall. Her violin laid in the middle of the sofa.

She sat on the flowered cushion and opened the case's lid. She caressed the rich tiger-maple wood.

The music refused to come. Her head was empty.

Her heart was empty.

Her life was empty.

Out of instinct, she raised the instrument to her chin, fingers on the strings. A requiem. She needed to hear the music of the Bach *Violin Sonata No. 2 in A Minor*.

Tentative, she played the first few notes. The mournful sound flooded her soul. Her fingers picked out the next measure, then the third. Somehow, they remembered. They danced their way up and down the fingerboard. From a place deep inside, the music came. Not the music of joy, but the melody of mourning.

She poured out her heart and everything inside of her. Tears streaked down her cheeks, blurring her vision, but she didn't need to see. She breathed it. Became it. The music carried her to days spent in the kitchen with *Máma* and nights on *Táta*'s lap in front of the fire. To summer afternoons with Jana and Lada swimming in the Vltava River and fall evenings exploring the city with David.

Those days were gone forever.

The music cried. So did she.

Had she told them enough that she loved them? Why had she ever grumbled or complained or disobeyed? What had been her last words to them?

Her fingers halted.

She couldn't remember. Oh, she couldn't remember.

Chapter Seven

*A*nna sat across the small kitchen table from *Babička* and traced the rim of her bright blue, orange, and yellow cup, the edge smooth and cool. With her stomach churning, she couldn't force herself to drink the concoction that passed for coffee these days. A gray rain fell outside, the chilly dampness seeping into the old walls of the building.

Babička stroked the back of Anna's hand with her own wrinkled one. "I know it's hard."

Anna bit back the tears that choked her. "For you too."

"When you live as long as I do, you experience much loss throughout your life. So many loved ones have come and gone. Yet they all left an impression on me that made me the person I am today. I have loved and have let go. But I wouldn't wish my life any other way. I trust that God's plan is perfect."

Ever since she could remember, Anna had heard about God's all-wise plan. "What is so perfect about my life? About losing my parents and my sisters?"

"You may not see it now, but God knows the outcome."

"You are sad, angry, and maybe even scared, *ne?*"

Tears welled in *Babička*'s gray eyes. "There is an empty place in my heart. I should not outlive my children. Your mother was one of God's greatest gifts to me. All I want to do now is go home." She clutched her heart, her hand trembling.

Anna squeezed her grandmother's fingers. "*Ne,* not you too. I couldn't bear another grief right now."

"When it is my time, He will call me home. And I want you to remember the good and think about where I will be. That is what I am doing now with my darling Eva. I can hear her singing childish songs when she was little. I think of her walking down the aisle in our church to her groom. I see her holding you when you were born."

Babička sipped her coffee. "Look around us and the suffering of this world. *Hauptmann* Engel described Terezín as an awful place. I imagine the camp they went to must be much worse. But they suffer no more. They are in heaven, where God wipes away all pain and tears."

"Is that why you want to go there?"

Babička's mouth trembled. "Yes. What more do I have to live for? Whether the Lord calls me home today or years from now, I will be content."

"I wish I could be."

"That is a gift that comes with time. The world will dim, and heaven will grow brighter."

A knock came at the door, followed by a call from *Hauptmann* Engel. "Frau Doubeková, Fraulein Zadoková, I have your mail."

The grief in Anna's throat hardened at his voice. It shouldn't surprise her that he went through their post, but her midsection burned to think of yet another violation. She hustled to the door and flung it open. "I will take that and thank you not to touch our mail again." She wrenched the letters from his grasp.

He stood in the doorway, his mouth a gaping hole.

One envelope fluttered to the floor. She grabbed it before he could pick it up.

It bore an official mark.

She had seen it before.

The world spun around her.

He caught her as she sank to the floor. His warmth enveloped her. For the briefest of moments, she enjoyed it.

"Fraulein Zadoková, is something is wrong?" His words broke through her haze.

She shook her head. "I'm fine. Please let go of me." She stumbled back as he did her bidding.

"You aren't fine. What made you so woozy?"

Babička hobbled to Anna's side. "What is that letter?"

Anna clutched it. "You don't want to know."

"I do know."

Hauptmann Engel leaned over. "It's from the government. Open it."

The furrow of his brow must be part of his act. "Why should I, when we all know what it is?"

Babička pried it from Anna's hands and slid her finger under the envelope's flap. Anna closed her eyes while her grandmother scanned the document.

"We have two weeks until we have to report. Two weeks to put our things in order. They list what we can bring with us."

"I don't even need to see it. I remember *Máma* packing before they were deported."

Hauptmann Engel sucked in his breath. "It's your deportation notice?"

"Yes. Did you think our friend would protect us forever? We have two weeks left of life as we know it. Then, it will only be a matter of time before your friends, your countrymen, cart us off to our deaths, just as they did our family." Heat rose in Anna's neck. "And you are the one taking us there."

Patricie clung to the car's door handle, the bundle of ration coupons tucked inside her coat, as *Hauptsturmführer* Jaeger wove his way through Prague's narrow, ancient streets. What would the labor camp be like? How long would she be there? Would they torture her for information?

She now understood the fear of the people she hid and fed. Not knowing where you were going, only that it wasn't good and none returned, was sheer terror itself.

Hauptsturmführer Jaeger laughed, the sound of it like a frozen arctic tundra. Patricie shivered.

"Don't worry so much, my little bird."

She cringed at the term of endearment.

"This is a good surprise. You studied at the Prague Conservatory, did you not?"

"Is that what the surprise has to do with?" Many of her former classmates now resided at Terezín. Was she to join them there?

"You will see. Now, loosen your grasp on the door handle and enjoy the ride. Has it been such a long time since you've been in an auto?"

"Quite awhile." Her parents never had money for one. Georg took her for a ride in his car a couple of times, but that was it.

"Then sit back and have fun. I have quite the afternoon planned for us."

"But I truly have much to do at home. With my job at the shop taking so much time, it's rare I have a day off." She had to get rid of the ration cards before he discovered them.

"Then you should enjoy this."

She sat back but couldn't unwind. For the entire trip, her heart pulsed against her chest. At last, he pulled up to a restaurant overflowing with German officers like himself. Nazi flags festooned the outside and swastikas hung everywhere.

And here she came, contraband stuffed inside her coat's lining. *Hauptsturmführer* Jaeger led her into the dark interior. The owners set tables in front of a stage. "There is a fine orchestra playing today. Since you are a music connoisseur, I thought you would appreciate it."

Any other time, any other place, with any other person, perhaps she would. But not now. Not here. And not with him. She gave him another painted-on smile. "*Děkuji.* It was kind of you to think of me."

He stepped behind her. At his breath on her neck, the little hairs on her arms stood upright. "Let me take your coat."

She clung to its lapels and spun around so fast the cards bumped against her leg. "*Ne.* I'm rather chilly. If you don't mind, I'll keep it on." She sat so he wouldn't tug it from her shoulders.

"Suit yourself." He pulled the table's other chair beside her and sat.

After she consumed two glasses of water, the musicians took the stage and tuned their instruments. She recognized several of the players. They were Jewish. The yellow stars on their jackets confirmed that. Why would the Germans choose them as part of the group?

And then, they played. They were the finest the city had to offer.

They performed some Wagner and Beethoven. Her oboe sat silent in a corner of her flat. The war had stolen her desire for its song, yet this music flooded her soul. The cards in her coat and the Nazi officer sitting too close to her faded into the background. Beauty and serenity surrounded her.

Before she was ready for it, the performance ended. She turned to *Hauptsturmführer* Jaeger who leaned over, his nose mere centimeters from hers.

"Ah, your face is glowing. You enjoyed it, just as I knew you would."

"Yes, *děkuji*, I did. Do they often have music like this here?"

"Sometimes. Other times they have Czech jazz, but I don't care for that uneven rhythm as much. Do you?"

"Not at all. Give me Beethoven any day."

"We have much in common, then."

One shared taste did not mean they had similar views on everything. "Yes, we do."

"I would very much like to get to know you better, Patricie. You intrigue me."

"With your research, I thought you knew everything about me by now."

He laughed, another sinister sound. "Not quite. I don't understand why you were in that neighborhood. You pop up in unusual places in the city."

"And where you come from, don't you have friends all over town?"

"I was busy taking care of my mother and sister. I never had much time for friends."

"No friends?"

"*Nein.* Not anyone close to me. I was provider and protector for my family. I spent all my effort on fulfilling my duty to them."

"Your mother and sister must appreciate your care for them."

His features softened for the tiniest, littlest bit. "It's what you do. Protect them from those trying to take advantage of them. But I don't understand having friends so spread out."

"With my church, my job, and my schooling, I have acquaintances all over the place." Friends who counterfeited ration cards and hid Jews. "And I like to explore. You never know what you will find."

Hauptsturmführer Jaeger leaned ever closer. The malty odor of beer on his breath touched her. "How true that is."

Then he kissed her on the lips.

She chomped back the bile rising in her throat.

Dearest Mutti,

Horst bit the top of his pen and stared at the drawing he'd made of Anna that now sat on his desk. In her hands, she held her violin, enraptured by the music she played. He could stare at it all day.

But he had a dilemma. How should he word this letter to his mother? He had to be careful how he said things so she would catch his meaning but the censors wouldn't.

How do we know right from wrong? I have a beautiful woman for an upstairs neighbor in my new flat. She has had some devastating news and doesn't know what to do about it. I want to help her, but how? Doing so may anger some influential people and affect me in ways I'm not sure I'm ready for.

Would she understand?

I wish you were here so we could speak face to face about this matter. I need your advice. Vater would disapprove of my wanting to help this woman. He would tell me I'm not a good German officer. But I want to know what you would think.

I can guess at your words. You would tell me to seek the Lord and follow His will. But that is difficult in this situation. It could cost me my life.

Horst laughed a wry chuckle as he wrote the last sentence. It was as if his mother stood beside him, quoting scripture, her voice firm, unwavering. "'Then said Jesus unto his disciples, If any man will come after me, let him deny himself, and take up his cross, and follow me.

For whosoever will save his life shall lose it: and whosoever will lose his life for my sake shall find it.'"

From upstairs sprang the beautiful melody of Anna's violin. He reveled in the sound which erased his doubts and eased his fears. The tune brought him back to those wonderful evenings with his mother at the symphony. The way she would relax against the velvet upholstered seat as the music softened the lines radiating from her eyes. The way she'd laugh when she bought him a seltzer water during intermission.

Those days of innocence, before he'd learned why his mother only smiled at the symphony. How his brother's death had changed his father and torn their family apart.

Thank you, Mutti, for your wise words as I grew up. I may not have you by my side right now, but I will always have your insight and the wisdom you ingrained in me.

He tapped the ashes from the tip of his cigarette. On that awful day following that terrible night, she'd read him the passage about no Jews or Greeks. He'd never forget.

It will be difficult and perhaps impossible, but I will try to help the woman upstairs.

He didn't want Anna's music to end.

At a sharp knock at the door, his pen skidded across the page. Horst crumpled the paper and tossed it in the trash can before answering. "Ah, *Hauptsturmführer* Jaeger, what a surprise." He couldn't bring himself to add the word pleasant.

"I was sorry you didn't join us at the restaurant for the performance today. You told me you enjoy classical music so much."

Horst tried to keep his gaze from the waste can. He couldn't appear guilty. "I just wanted a quiet day at home to get caught up on some letter writing and such."

"I'm sure your father is pleased to hear how you have impressed your superiors."

"He is."

From upstairs drifted the most beautiful, most mournful music Horst ever heard. Stefan stopped for a moment. "Who is that?"

"My neighbor."

"A Jewess, I believe."

Of course Stefan would know. He made it his business to know everything about everyone. "*Ja.* Listen to her play, so beautiful and with such tone. That's why I bent the rule and allowed her to keep her instrument."

"Rules are not meant to be broken." Stefan started for the door.

A lump formed in Horst's chest. He grabbed Stefan. "She's soon to be deported, if I'm not mistaken. Let me enjoy her music for now. Such a shame she'll be gone when she plays so well. Perhaps you could get her name erased?"

"Why would you ask me that? Do you have a personal interest in her?" Stefan searched Horst's face.

"*Nein, nein, nein.*"

"Only the guilty protest so much."

Chapter Eight

There wasn't much to pack. Anna stuffed as much as she could in the two cases the order allowed them each to bring. Fifty kilos a piece. A bedroll. Blankets. Household utensils like pots and bowls and tea strainers. Warm clothes. As many socks and stockings as they had. *Babička*'s heart medication. Vitamin tablets. An extra pair of shoes. In the midst of it all, her violin.

But did it matter what they brought? They faced the same fate as the rest of their family. No one knew how long until their turn came, but it would come.

Would they see David at Terezín? Her day brightened. He held to some strange philosophies and teachings that *Táta* and *Máma* disapproved of, and ran with the secular intellectuals of the city, but he was her brother. Her flesh and blood. Other than *Babička*, all she had left. How good it would be to embrace him, to hold a part of *Táta* and *Máma* again.

Babička hobbled into the living room from the bedroom, dragging her two suitcases behind her. The load was too much for her to carry. Anna packed as many of *Babička*'s things into her own cases as she could. Her grandmother may have to leave hers behind at some point. They needed to walk. She couldn't lift the heavy bags.

How long would she survive? Days? Weeks? Tears, Anna's regular companion now, gathered in the corners of her eyes. She blinked them away and drew in a deep breath, letting it out little by little. "You are ready, *ne*?"

Babička's hand trembled as she stroked Anna's cheek in the way she had a thousand times before. "Yes, I am, for whatever the Lord has prepared. I'm ready to meet my Savior at the time He has appointed."

"Don't talk like that, please. I'll take good care of you. Stay strong. I need you."

"I trust Him, Anna."

"And I do too."

"Then all will be well. Underneath, deep down inside, you have more strength than you know because He has given it to you."

"At least it's not raining. We can be grateful for a beautiful winter day. I'm afraid the cold will return soon enough. Do you have all that you need? Are you sure you have plenty of warm clothes? You can't have too many. It may be very chilly."

Babička smoothed back a piece of gray hair which had escaped the knot on the top of her head. "Don't fuss so. I'm prepared."

Anna surveyed the flat again. Times had been difficult, but happiness and joy and celebrations had filled the space. Her parents made sure of that. Their voices echoed here.

Years ago, when they had the chance to flee, she hadn't wanted to move from Prague. Leaving her beautiful city ripped her apart.

But she was never destined to stay here.

Would she still be able to hear her family's voices when she left?

Anna helped *Babička* on with her boots, then slipped her own feet into her fur-lined ones. Today they may be too warm, but in the coming weeks, she would appreciate them. She grabbed both of her valises. *Babička* moved to follow suit.

"*Ne, ne.* Leave your bags. Once I have mine down, I'll bring yours. I'll take care of them."

"You can't. We have too much."

"Don't say that. We'll get it all to the train somehow." Those cases contained all that remained of her past.

They exited the apartment to the tiled hall, then down the curved staircase with its wrought-iron rails to the main floor. She left her bags at the bottom of the steps, then retrieved *Babička*'s.

No more turning back. The time had arrived to face the future.

Anna grasped the door knob.

"Wait. Stop."

She jumped. What did *Hauptmann* Engel want? "We have to leave, or we'll be late."

"Don't go."

She didn't want to. "We don't have a choice. You have commanded it."

"Not me. I want to offer you a different option."

Babička stepped beside her. "What are you saying?"

"Come inside, and let me explain how I plan to help you. To save you."

Anna shook her head. "You have no such thing in mind. We're dirty Jews to you. I don't know what you have planned. Perhaps you think I know where there are Jews in hiding, and you want me to give them up in exchange for keeping our names off the list for a few more weeks. But I know no such thing, nor would I ever divulge it to you."

He finger-combed his light, straight hair. "You have to trust me."

She clutched the handles of the suitcases ever tighter. "I could never trust you. I never will."

As she turned for the door, he grabbed her by the arm. "Fraulein Zadoková, please. Frau Doubeková, talk to her."

Babička set down her valises. "What do you have in mind?"

"I can't tell you in the hall. Come inside."

Her grandmother picked up her suitcases and followed *Hauptmann* Engel into his flat.

"*Babička*, wait. How can you trust him?"

"I can't. But I trust the Lord."

Horst breathed a sigh of relief when Frau Doubeková and Anna followed him into his flat. He'd prepared everything for them, knew just what he would say to them, what he would do. What he hadn't expected was Anna's resistance. How could she turn down his offer of help? Of salvation? Did she truly want to go to her death?

"Please, sit down." He motioned to the green sofa against the wall. "Let me get you a cup of tea."

Anna helped her grandmother to sit, then turned to him. "No tea.

Just tell us what you have planned for us. How you say you're going to help." Her dark eyes were wide, her skin pale. She bit her full lip.

Her fear was understandable. He nodded. "You're going to stay here. I'm going to hide you."

She tugged on her ear. "Here?"

The old woman grinned. "The Lord has provided, Anna. I prayed for salvation from this fate if it be His will, and He has made a way."

"You can't be sure of that. *Hauptmann* Engel might be plotting something else."

He sat beside Anna, her hands small and dainty. Like his mother's. "I know you don't trust me. I struggled with this, but I believe the Lord wants me to help you. I can't let you go to the camp."

"Why? So that I can continue to play for you whenever you demand it?"

"I can't deny that I love your playing, but that is not the reason. What my fellow countrymen are doing is wrong. I can't allow them to take you and do to you and your grandmother what they did to the rest of your family. David begged me to help, and so I am."

Anna's grandmother took over. "*Děkuji*. May the Lord bless you for what you're doing."

With that, Horst and Frau Doubeková made the decision. Anna slumped against the lumpy couch cushions and closed her eyes.

"I will take care of you. I promise."

"And where will you hide us when the Gestapo comes looking for us? You know they will when we don't show up at the exhibition hall."

Of course. He couldn't have Anna and her grandmother sitting on the sofa in the living room when his German friends knocked at his door and demanded entrance. He had put away his drawing of her. Why hadn't he devised a way to conceal them? "We'll think of a place to hide you."

"You need to think fast. It's only a matter of time before they get here. And you promised to take care of us."

He prayed it was a promise he could keep.

The soft, gray blanket of evening covered the city of Prague. The distinct chilliness of winter hung in the air. Anna stood in Horst's kitchen, cleaning up the few dishes from supper. He loved the clink of dishes, her soft humming. The place was homier with her here.

He stirred the fire in the living room's stove, then turned to Frau Doubeková. "Are you warm enough? Perhaps you need a blanket for your lap?"

She shook her head. "Your mother raised you well. Not many young men would bother with an old lady like me."

"You aren't a bother. I think my mother would like you." He sat on the sofa and pulled out his sketch pad. The way the dying light caught Anna tonight as she had played for him. The image seared itself into his brain, but he had to record that moment. He leaned against the back cushion, drew up his knees, and worked on imitating Anna's likeness on paper.

"What is that?"

The pencil slid from his hand when Anna spoke. He hadn't heard her come into the room and slip into the spot beside him. "You."

"I see that. You have some artistic talent."

"Most architects do."

"But why draw me?"

"Because you're beautiful." His heart gave one good, hard knock against his ribs.

"I'm nothing special. There are many other interesting things to draw in Prague. There is the Charles Bridge. With all thirty of its statues, it should take you some time. The Klementinum isn't far from there, with the elaborate Mirror Chapel, the Baroque Library Hall loaded with inlaid wood and a massive fresco, and the Astronomical Clock, which is one of my favorite places in the entire city."

A chuckle escaped his lips. "You are passionate about Prague."

"There's nowhere else on earth I'd rather live. I hope, as Minister of Architectural Preservation, you are as fervent about it as I am."

"I'll be sure to visit all of those sights. But I like to draw things other than buildings. Anything of beauty that captures my eye. Like you. Especially when you're playing. You radiate the loveliness of the music."

"Your time would be better spent on saving the charm that is Prague."

From the bowed living room window, a movement caught his eye. A green, canvas-covered truck screeched to a halt in front of his apartment building.

The moment they knew was coming arrived on their doorstep.

He dropped the pencil on the floor. "The Gestapo is here. Time to head to the cellar." He tore the page from his book, folded it, and stuffed it in his pants pocket.

With a bit of effort, Frau Doubeková pushed herself to her feet. "Can you help me, young man? These old legs don't work as well as they used to."

Horst seized Anna's grandmother by the hand and pulled her along as fast as she could manage. The three of them slipped into the hall. The truck's door slammed shut. Voices sounded on the front steps.

"Hurry, hurry." He opened the cellar door. Anna skipped down the stairs. The building's old entry door squeaked open. His hands dampened. They had no time to lose. He scooped up Anna's grandmother and hustled to the bottom of the steps. The clomp of jackboots sounded on the floorboards above them.

He shushed the women.

They scurried to the back corner of the stone cellar where a little nook, used for cold storage at some past time, hid behind a door. Earlier, he had torn out the shelves. "You'll have to squeeze together."

Anna bit the inside of her cheek. "Please don't turn us in."

"Never." Was she more afraid of the Gestapo or of him?

A deep voice above them shouted orders for the house to be searched.

This hiding place wasn't perfect. No doubt about that. He'd have to use his position as a German officer to convince his colleagues that there were no Jews here.

He shut the door to the little room. Wiped his damp hands on his khaki pants. Hurried upstairs. At the top, he met a Gestapo officer dressed in black garb who gave him a straight-arm salute.

Horst returned the greeting. "Why are you here?"

The soldier peered down his nose at Horst. "Who are you?"

"*Hauptmann* Engel. Minister of Architectural Preservation for Prague. I'm billeted here. Let me repeat my question. Why are you here?"

"Did you know Jews lived in this building?"

"*Ja.* They were deported today." He forced the corners of his mouth to turn upward, as if happy about this turn of events.

"They never showed up as ordered."

Horst touched his chest. "They didn't? But I saw them leave the building myself. They turned down the street in the direction of the exhibition hall."

"Where did they go?" The man stepped forward and glared at Horst.

"How should I know? I never kept track of them. They told me they received their notices and were leaving. That was it. Otherwise, they steered clear of me."

"My men are searching the building now." A thump from upstairs confirmed his statement. "Stand aside. Let me look in the cellar."

Horst didn't move, though his legs wouldn't hold him upright much longer. "No need. I was just down there. I heard a noise a bit ago and investigated it. A mouse. He disappeared into a little hole in the wall. No Jews down there. And like I said, I saw them leave this morning. They are gone."

"They could have returned and hidden somewhere here."

"That's possible, I suppose. But if they aren't upstairs, then they aren't here. I chased that mouse all around. If they hid in the cellar, I would have discovered them."

One of the underlings strode down the hall and opened the door to Horst's flat.

His stomach performed loop-di-loops. He'd shoved the women's suitcases under the bed, but they weren't well hidden. His plan had been for them to take their valises when the soldiers arrived, but they didn't have time to grab them and make it into the cellar. "*Halten sie.* There is no need to search my quarters. Why on earth would any Jews be in there? Get out, and leave my place alone."

The commander nodded. The man backed away from Horst's apartment.

"Have you found anything?"

"*Nein*. Not a trace of any Jews besides what they left behind in their flat. Nothing of value."

"Then we are finished." He turned to Horst, his shoulders raised, his chin upturned. Every inch in control. "I will watch you. If I find that you are hiding these women here, your punishment will be swift and lethal."

Chapter Nine

*T*he dark pressed in on Anna, little air in the miniscule shelter to provide relief. She leaned away from *Babička* to avoid crushing her frail grandmother. The floorboards above them creaked with the weight of German soldiers.

Hauptmann Engel had shoved them into this tiny space. It wasn't even safe. Anyone who came into the cellar would see the door, open it, and find them. Her breath came in gasps. "Why did we trust him? He has no intention of protecting us. He plans to lead the Gestapo right to us."

Babička's whisper was firm. "Thinking the worst is not good. Why would he stop us from going to the hall this morning if he didn't plan on caring for us? Why did he go to the trouble of making this hiding place for us if he meant to turn us in? It would have been easier for him to let us go with the transport."

What *Babička* said made sense, but it didn't stop Anna's cold sweat. "The soldiers will come down here and find us right away. This isn't a good spot."

"It's fine. He won't allow the Gestapo down the stairs."

"And what about our bags in his flat? How will he explain those away?"

"Don't create problems, Anna."

If she had room, Anna would stomp her foot. "I'm not creating them. They already exist. This is never going to work. And our fate will be worse. If the Germans don't shoot us on the spot when they find us, they will certainly skip Terezín and transport us directly to the eastern camp and gas us."

"Then that is God's will."

"How can this be His will?"

"We don't understand it, but it is."

"Believe something you don't understand? That's impossible."

"No, *beruško*, that is faith. Look at how He has provided thus far. We should be on the train right now."

If she had to choose between a transport train or hiding in this cellar, she supposed she would choose the cellar. It gave *Babička* an extra few days of life, at least.

Voices came from the top of the stairs, one angry and demanding, the other calm and sure. If the angry one opened the door . . .

Anna's hands ached from clenching them. Jackboots thudded above them. More German voices speaking words she couldn't decipher. The darkness strangled her.

After a long while, the footsteps moved in the direction of the front door. It clicked open, then shut. Silence descended. *Hauptmann* Engel didn't come for them. How much longer would they have to wait for release? Maybe the soldiers arrested him, and he'd never come.

Should they slip out on their own? She reached for the knob. *Babička* stopped her. "He is waiting to be sure they are gone and that they are not coming back."

Anna held her breath. *Keep them away, Lord.*

More time passed. How long had they had been stuffed into this closet? Her feet throbbed from standing so long. Her head buzzed. A round of dizziness swirled her brain inside her skull.

When she was sure she would faint, the basement stairs creaked. Moments later, the door opened. Anna fell out of the closet and into *Hauptmann* Engel's arms. She peered into his crystal blue eyes. "They are gone, *ne?*"

"*Ja.*" The crease around his mouth deepened.

Her vertigo faded. She pushed against his solid chest and righted herself. "What if they return?"

"I don't think they will."

Anna helped *Babička* from the hiding spot. She stared at her grand-mother, whose hands and mouth shook.

Their survival depended on him being right.

David made his way through the darkened streets of Terezín. The little village hummed, but not with the sounds of happy families around their dinner tables nor of children playing in their yards. Heart-wrenching weeping filled the air, the gut-twisting cries of suffering.

He coughed into his handkerchief, now stained brown.

Yet over this pitiful din drifted the lullaby of strings and the song of a piano. Its plaintive melody guided him to a ramshackle building, where a single bare bulb lit a large but dingy room.

Egon Ledeč nodded to him without missing a note of the song he played. He closed his eyes, his face peaceful, though its features were sunken. He drew his bow against the violin strings with studied ease, much the way Anna did.

Anna. How was she doing? And *Babička*. How was she holding up under the rigors of war? Jakub wouldn't be able to keep them off the deportation list forever. It was only a matter of time until they arrived.

Against David's wishes, that German soldier came now and then to see him, each time with a bit of food. Not enough to make a difference, but just enough to put all of them in increased danger. David didn't eat any of it but divided it among the men in his room. They'd lost two roommates but gained four.

The other two members of the ensemble arrived. Though David had worked hard in the rock yard today and would rather be sleeping on his pallet in his room, their captors demanded they practice for hours each evening.

And then the music enveloped him, carried him far from this place. He sailed above Terezín's confines, peering down on this miserable lot. He soared above green fields, majestic mountains of blue, shimmering turquoise oceans. Away, far away from the misery of his soul. The terrible ache in his heart over the loss of his parents, of his family faded.

Only beauty remained.

The last notes of the piece died away. Someone applauded. David opened his eyes and sucked in his breath when he discovered *Hauptmann* Engel in the audience.

"Your patron is here, David." Viktor clapped him on the back.

"I wish he would leave me alone. Haven't he and his like caused us enough grief?"

"I'm glad I'm not you." Egon gave a crooked grin, packed up his violin with a great deal of haste, and hurried into the night.

Only David and the officer remained in the building. He approached the Nazi, glancing over the man's shoulder a time or two as he made his way down the aisle. "What are you doing here?"

"I told you I would return. I have some supplies for you in my car. Tinned meat, bread, soap, and the like."

"Do you know what you're doing to me?" David bored his gaze into the middle of *Hauptmann* Engel's chest.

"I'm helping. Keeping you alive for your sister's sake."

"I don't need your kind of help." David turned to walk away.

The German grabbed him by the arm. David ripped himself from his grasp and shrunk back, his heart hammering in his chest.

"Why shouldn't I help you?"

"You aren't helping. Don't you see that? My roommates look at me with jealousy, like they might kill me for a bite of bread or a forkful of peaches. I've endured more fights in the past few weeks than in all my growing up years. I'm alienated. And here, to be alone is to die."

"I—"

"And what if you get caught? Have you thought about that? They would shoot you." He clapped his hands, and *Hauptmann* Engel jumped. "Exactly. But do you think they would stop there? Who would they turn their rifles on next? Think about that."

Hauptmann Engel didn't back down. "I have thought about it. What they are doing to you and the others is wrong. I'm not afraid to die on the side of right. I'm not fearful of the sacrifice." The man spoke with bravado, but did he feel it?

"Except it isn't only you who would be sacrificed." David stood with his legs spread apart. Couldn't this man see reason? Perhaps that flaw ran in Aryan blood.

"Your sister and grandmother got their deportation notices. They were to leave a few days ago."

David's stomach fell like a rock tossed off the top of the Eiffel Tower. "They are coming here?"

Hauptmann Engel shook his head.

David's legs lost all feeling. He sat down. "They are going directly to the extermination camp?"

Again, the Nazi shook his head.

"They aren't … ?" David held his breath.

Color flooded the man's cheeks. "I'm hiding them."

David released the air from his lungs. "Excuse me?"

"I brought them into my apartment. They are living with me, under my protection."

"You said you were hiding them."

"I am."

Was the man out of his mind? "Then they aren't under your protection. You all are in grave danger."

"You wanted me to stand by and watch them leave on the transport?"

"*Ne*. I mean, I don't know. I want my family to be restored to me." In more ways than one. He'd missed his parents and sisters in the years they had been estranged. And now … He swallowed the lump in his throat.

Hauptmann Engel sat across the aisle from David. "Believe me, I would like nothing more. That's not reality, though. Until then, I will do all I can to protect you. All of you. Tell me what is the best way to bring supplies into the camp, and I will do it."

"You can't. Putting yourself in harm's way is out of the question. If something happens to you, what will become of my sister and grandmother? I forbid it. Do whatever it takes to keep them safe. Forget about me. Don't return here. If you're followed, you'll lead them to Anna and *Babička*. Above all, you have to shield them." David mussed his already unruly hair. "You have to promise me."

"You should know there are no guarantees in this life."

"Lie to me, then, so I'll be able to sleep at night. I have nothing left here except for my music and my dreams."

Hauptmann Engel kicked the floor with the tip of his shoe. It took a moment for him to answer. "I promise to keep them safe."

For the time being, that would have to be enough.

Anna took her time washing the lunch dishes in the tiny kitchen tucked into the back of the flat. Here, no sun filtered through the curtains, no brightness to add to the days.

Life would be like this until the war ended. *Táta* said the Allies would come soon and free them. Almost a year had passed since he'd uttered those words, and still no British or American boots had set foot on continental European soil. For now, she and her grandmother could only hide in the shadows and pray that no German eye spotted them.

Babička shuffled into the dark little room with her plate and cup. "Why so sad, my *beruško*? I haven't seen you smile since we arrived here. And it's been a long time since you played."

Anna took the colorful dinnerware from her grandmother. *Ne*, she hadn't picked up her violin since the day *Hauptmann* Engel told her of her family's fate. Not even for him. "Why should I?" She plunged her hands in the water.

"I am disappointed in you."

She turned her attention from the dishes to stare at her gray-haired grandmother. "Why?"

"God has provided, yet you act like He hasn't."

"I know I should be thankful. I know. But are our lives more valuable than our freedom?"

"You are longing for home." It was a statement, not a question.

"Yes." But not the home *Babička* had in mind. "I yearn for the past. I would even take days from two years ago. We lived stuffed into the flat, but we were together. At the time, I didn't appreciate it enough."

"None of us did. Perhaps that is the lesson to be learned here. Cling to your memories, yes. They are good, a blessing from the Lord. But if you allow the past to weigh you down, you cannot move forward. You have to deal with the present and reach for the future."

"Maybe." Anna picked up another glass and dunked it into the water. Much as she hated to admit it, *Babička* was right. Maybe dwelling on the past only brought more heartache. Yet how could she bear to let it go? "You had a good nap, *ne?*"

"Not really. I couldn't sleep."

Anna took a good look at *Babička*. Had she shrunk another few centimeters in the weeks they'd been hiding here? She did tremble more than ever. The war took a toll on her. Anna couldn't stand losing her. *God, don't take her, too.*

Babička leaned against the counter. "Where did *Hauptmann* Engel go?"

Anna shrugged. "He left a few hours ago without saying. I guess there are things he cannot share with us. Don't forget, he is the enemy. There must be things he doesn't want us to know."

"You don't like him?"

"It's not that. Are you forgetting that I'm a Jew? This is an impossible situation. Dangerous, even."

"I see good in him."

"It doesn't bother you in the least that he is an officer in the Nazi army? That his countrymen sent your daughter and her family to their deaths? That he might send you to yours?"

"Don't judge him by the uniform he wears, but by the kind of person he is underneath."

Anna kissed her grandmother's wrinkled cheek and fought back the tears. "You always see the bright and not the dark. I wish I were like that. That is why I love you." And why she couldn't lose her.

Babička sat for a while, still and quiet. Anna couldn't follow her lead. What about *Hauptmann* Engel? Where was he, and what was he doing? When might he decide to turn them in?

"I think I might be sleepy enough to take that nap now." *Babička* pushed herself from the sofa. "Don't think ill of him just because of his blood. That is what the Nazis are doing to us."

Her grandmother made her way to the bedroom. The door closed with a soft click. The flat fell silent.

Anna picked up a book from the end table, one she'd brought with her from upstairs, one she'd read a dozen times at least. Her mind refused to focus on the words. She returned the book to the table, got up, and paced the living room. When would *Hauptmann* Engel arrive home? And with whom?

She daydreamed of the summer afternoons she'd spent at the café with Ester, of the winter evenings the string quartet had gathered at her home and practiced, of the brisk fall days she'd walked to the market and chatted with the grocer.

Hauptmann Engel was gone so much, and *Babička* often napped or read her Bible. If the war dragged on much longer, how would she stand the quiet? They didn't dare make noise during the day when he was away and the flat was supposed to be empty.

After she listened for sounds of *Babička* stirring or *Hauptmann* Engel arriving home, she wandered to the window overlooking the street and pulled aside the curtain. Here, on the edge of the Jewish quarter, life slowed. Too many of its residents had disappeared into the great unknown.

Before she dropped the drape, a Nazi officer popped into view. He turned in front of the building and climbed the steps.

Anna spun from the window and clutched her chest, as if she might keep her heart inside.

The officer banged and pounded on the door. "I know you're in there."

She couldn't breathe.

They'd been caught.

Chapter Ten

*H*orst stood in the midst of the grandeur that was Smetana Hall. Spectacular. Prague's monument to the Art Nouveau movement. Rows of electric lights accented the buttresses of the soaring ceilings. Sculpture groups known as the Degradation of the People and the Resurrection of the People flanked either side of the concert hall. Rather ironic.

The ceiling's glass dome drew his gaze upward. The frescoes were allegories of music, drama, dance, and poetry. The organ, surrounded by gilded bronze reliefs, occupied center stage.

All in all, it took Horst's breath away. He could stand here the entire day and admire it. A place of beauty, both in architecture and in music, as it housed the Prague Symphony Orchestra. Surely, Anna had been here. Perhaps even played here.

He would have loved to have heard her.

Because the Germans marched into Prague with little resistance, they'd spared the many beautiful buildings this city boasted. Not like London.

He shook his head. He hadn't come here to daydream but to work. He slid a pen from his uniform pocket and took notes on a pad of paper. The building was only thirty years old, but he marked several items that needed improvement.

Václav Smetáček, the conductor Horst met on a previous visit, entered and rifled through his music. Violinists, cellists, flutists, and others trickled in. Practice time was upon them. The musicians warmed up, a cacophony of sound.

Horst strolled around the edge of the great hall, jotting down the reliefs that required touching up and the spots that begged for gilding. In between his notes, he slipped out his sketchbook and drew the boxes above him, attempting to capture the heavy folds of the drapery. And failing. His pen refused to translate the awe of this place to paper.

The conductor gave a few instructions Horst couldn't decipher. Music then floated from the stage, a great blending of the voices into one. He stood transfixed, his pencil grasped in his hand. He'd heard this piece of music with *Mutti*.

The nightmares plagued him again. Unconscious memories of breaking glass. Cursing brown coats. Screaming Jews.

Mutti had always taken him to the music hall in Munich to soothe his frayed nerves. To help him forget, if only for a little while, what had happened on that horrible night.

Conductor Smetáček tapped his baton on his stand and the melody stopped. Horst screeched back to reality, to the olive-green uniform he wore, the Nazi swastika on his forearm.

He had to get out of here. Even the beauty of this place haunted him.

Still holding his pencil and notebooks, he was halfway up the red-carpeted aisle when *Oberleutnant* Meier, his superior, entered. Horst pocketed his sketchbook and met Meier halfway, giving a Heil Hitler.

Horst returned the salute. "What brings you by today?"

Meier craned his long neck and whistled. "Look at that. I had been told how amazing this place was to behold, but every account has been lacking. I will have to attend a concert here."

Horst nodded in the musicians' direction. "They are practicing Anton Bruckner's *Ninth Symphony in D Minor*. One of my favorites. You would enjoy it."

"I believe I would." Meier returned his attention to Horst. "I'm glad I tracked you down. You are a difficult man to find."

"The nature of the job." Horst grinned. "Just the way I like it."

"I imagine. You are good at what you do. I can see you are committed to the Fatherland and the Führer. But here you are, stuck inside of buildings all day long."

"I enjoy it. And many days, I spend as much time outside as I do inside."

"Your service has been noted."

"By whom?" Perspiration dampened his hands.

"You are being offered a promotion."

He didn't want one. "I'm flattered."

Meier stroked his long, pointed chin. "You have visited Theresienstadt with *Hauptsturmführer* Jaeger?"

"*Ja.* Twice." What did Theresienstadt have to do with this?

"You are being offered the position as director of deportations there."

To be transferred ... What would happen to Anna and her grandmother? And deportations? He couldn't do it. Wouldn't do it. "*Danke* for the recognition, sir, but I cannot accept. As I said before, I enjoy my work here. It is what I went to university for, what I studied many long years to achieve. And I'm just settling in to Prague and finding I like living here."

"You are turning down this opportunity?" Meier's green eyes darkened.

Horst studied his spit-and-polished black boots. "My father bought me this commission."

Meier crossed his arms in front of himself. "Do you not realize what total war means to the German people? There must be absolute unity in thought and moral conduct. You are no longer serving just yourself but all of Germany." His voice rang throughout the hall, reaching over the music. "Together, in step with each other, we forge a better place for our people. We make the world and Germany what it should be. Strong. Proud. Free from the impure. That cannot be done if we only look to our own selfish desires. No one is immune from sacrifice. Greatness will not be achieved without giving up self. Your circle of responsibility is growing. As it should. It is your duty."

Duty. *Vater* ever only spoke of duty. *Do your duty, Horst. Don't shirk your duty, Horst. Horst, it is your duty.*

But protecting Anna and her grandmother was his duty. He could not fulfill that responsibility at the same time as the one now thrust upon him.

And head of deportation? Would he be the man to send Anna and Frau Doubeková to their deaths?

Meier leaned in. "You would be wise to accept."

Anna hung onto the back of the old wing chair in the alcove the bay window formed. The German officer continued to pound on the door.

Thank goodness *Babička* had gone to take a nap. He wouldn't see her. At least, not right away. But he would search the apartment and find her. It would take too much time for Anna to hustle *Babička* to the cellar, to the hiding place *Hauptmann* Engel created for them. The man wouldn't wait that long. Besides, he already stood at the door. Blocked their path.

The knocking continued. Anna shuffled in the direction of the entrance. And what about *Hauptmann* Engel? He would be implicated. The punishment for being Jewish was severe. What about the punishment for a German officer caught hiding Jews?

She shivered as she turned the knob and cracked the door. "Can I help you?" She spoke in Czech.

The man furrowed his brows. Without an invitation, he pushed the door open and stepped over the threshold.

Anna dared not glance at the bodice of her navy-blue dress where a star once resided. *Hauptmann* Engel had insisted she rip it off, rip all her stars off, and burn them. His foresight proved invaluable.

"Who are you?" He spoke decent Czech. With his cold, blue eyes, he scanned her up and down and up once more.

She didn't appear Aryan. Her hair was dark and so were her eyes. There was no hiding her Jewishness. But it was worth a try. Her fate couldn't get any worse. "I am the maid."

"The maid?"

"Yes, sir."

"Who is your employer?"

"*Pan* Engel. He is good to me."

"He didn't tell me he hired a maid. I've been here before and never seen you." He narrowed his gaze.

"I am new here."

He stepped around her. "Do you have papers?"

She stopped breathing mid-gasp. Her papers labeled her as a Jew. And *Hauptmann* Engel had returned them to the upstairs flat soon after he'd taken her and her grandmother in, to make it appear as if they'd fled and changed their identities. She kept her back to the man. "I have lost them."

"No papers?"

"*Ne.*"

He twirled her around to face him, his grasp tight on her upper arm. She bit her lip to keep from crying out. His breath heated her cheek. "What shall I do with you, then?" His words carried a sneer.

"You can ask *Hauptmann* Engel when he returns. He saw my papers before I lost them."

The officer touched the length of her dark hair. "And I suppose he confirmed you were Aryan?"

"Yes, sir."

He stroked her cheek. She fought the urge to vomit.

"You are the darkest Aryan I have ever met."

"I am Eastern European."

"Slovak, then?"

She fisted her hands. Had she made a fatal mistake? The Germans hated the Slovaks almost as much as they despised the Jews. The Nazis didn't spare their wrath on their eastern neighbors. "*Ne.* Not Slovak at all. Just Bohemian."

He whispered in her ear. "A filthy Jew pig."

The bile in her throat threatened to bubble over. "*Ne.*"

"Not even a little bit?"

She shook her head, not trusting her voice.

He stepped back, and she allowed herself to breathe again. With his hands behind his back, he walked the perimeter of the small living room. What if he went to the bedroom and discovered *Babička* in the bed? Or Anna's clothes in her suitcase? Thankfully, they hadn't unpacked or put their clothes in the wardrobe. Too hard to explain away. And she'd finished the dishes and put them all in the cupboard, so he wouldn't question why so many were out.

He wandered to the alcove. At the same moment she did, he spied what lay on the chair there. He picked up her violin case. "And what would this be?"

"A violin."

He took two long strides in her direction, his jaw firm. "Do not toy with me. I know what it is. What is it doing here? *Hauptmann* Engel told me that, though he enjoys music, he does not play an instrument. Who does this belong to?"

"To me." Her voice squeaked.

"And why is it here? Has Engel gone and gotten himself a Jew whore?"

Not only did her blood drain from her face, but from her entire body. "I would thank you not to use such crude language in front of a lady."

His hard features didn't soften. "Are you his Jewish mistress?"

"*Ne.* Not at all." She trembled under his gaze. "I told you, I lost my papers." A weak argument, even to her ears.

The officer once again stood right in front of her. He pushed her against the wall, pinned her shoulders to the plaster, nose to nose with her. "You are lying to me."

"Would *Hauptmann* Engel be pleased to come home and find you harassing his Czech maid?" Where had that chutzpah come from?

But he stepped backward. "If that is indeed what you are."

"I am. And it would anger my employer to find out that you have accused me of such vile deeds. A good, Christian woman such as I am. You know that man. You know he would have nothing to do with the Jews."

"And where do you live?" He furrowed his brows.

"A few blocks from here."

"In the heart of the Jewish quarter?"

"*Ne*. Just the opposite. Farther from it."

He eyed her a bit more, then stepped closer yet again. She willed her soft knees to support her.

"You think you are so smart. What is your name?"

Zadoková couldn't be more Jewish. If she told him her real name, she would find herself on the very next transport to Terezín. "Anna."

"You try my patience. Full name."

"Anna Maria Kostachek." She stared at him.

Footsteps thumped in the hall. The Nazi pulled away.

The door to the flat swung open.

Hauptmann Engel stood on the threshold.

He paled.

She wilted.

Their stories wouldn't match.

Chapter Eleven

*A*nna stood rooted to the spot when *Hauptmann* Engel flung open the apartment's door. The Nazi officer who interrogated her faced him, his back to her.

"*Hauptsturmführer* Jaeger. How good to see you." *Hauptmann* Engel sounded more confident than his wide-eyed expression painted him.

"Heil Hitler."

A bit of red seeped into her protector's face. "Heil Hitler."

"Who is this woman?"

And now this *Hauptsturmführer* Jaeger would discover their secret, because *Hauptmann* Engel would give the wrong answer. She mouthed maid. He had to understand her. Had to.

"Who do you think she is?"

Behind *Hauptsturmführer* Jaeger's back, Anna wrote the letters in the air.

"Your little Jewish secret."

He roared with laughter. "You think she and I . . . *Danke*, Stefan. After the day I had today, I needed a good chuckle. As if I would ever have anything to do with the likes of them."

"This woman plays the violin."

"Very well, too, I might add."

"You listened to the concert at Terezín. Asked me to keep your neighbor's name from the transport list so you could continue to listen to her music."

He doubled over in peals of laughter. Quite the actor. "And that makes me a Jew lover? Stop it, Stefan, stop it. You're giving me a stitch in my side. You were at that concert, too."

Hauptsturmführer Jaeger's face darkened. "Is this your maid?"

Anna bobbed her head.

"Yes, she is."

"You didn't tell me you hired one."

"It slipped my mind. Now, come on, you look like you could use something to drink. And you," he peeked over *Hauptsturmführer* Jaeger's shoulder at her, "go and put my coat in my wardrobe." He tossed it to her, and she scampered away, grateful to no longer be in the room with the man.

And how had *Hauptmann* Engel known she wanted to check on *Babička*? Or did he intend to treat her like the maid? Whatever the reason, it didn't matter. It gave her the chance to leave and see to her grandmother.

She slipped inside the bedroom without opening the door too much.

"Anna, what is going on?" *Babička* sat in bed, her hairbrush in her hand, her thin gray hair around her shoulders.

"We were almost caught. It's too dangerous for us to stay here any longer. That friend of *Hauptmann* Engel discovered me. I told him I was the maid, but I don't think he believes me. He asked me all kinds of questions, and called me the worst of names." Tears clogged her throat, and she pinched the bridge of her nose to keep them from spilling over.

"As it is, we might not be out of the woods yet. *Hauptmann* Engel doesn't know the story I told. If he tells this man my name, my true name, he'll haul us out of here within minutes." She pounded down the fluttering rising in her chest.

Even *Babička*'s eyes grew wide. "You used a false name?"

"I couldn't very well tell him I was Anna Zadoková. Why did *Máma* and *Táta* have to use such a Jewish name for me?"

"Because you have been chosen by God. Twice. Chosen to be born of Jewish descent and chosen as a true daughter of Abraham."

Anna sat on the bed and rubbed her face. "When did you get to be so wise?"

"I only became wise when you started listening to me." She hid her laugh behind her hand.

"Hush, or you'll alert that Nazi you're here. I don't think he'll believe you're the cook."

Anna moved to the wardrobe to put away *Hauptmann* Engel's coat. She would return it to his room when *Hauptsturmführer* Jaeger left. As she pushed aside the various uniforms, pressed pants, and starched shirts he kept in this wardrobe, something flashed black.

She moved a jacket. What was this? A worn tin train. She pulled it out and examined it. Judging by the flaking paint, many children had loved it throughout the years.

What was it doing in here?

Wait a minute. Where had she seen this before? Yes, when she visited *Paní* Schniz.

This was her little boy's train. Anna had sat on the floor with him, making whistle sounds. He'd laughed his little baby laugh. Such a sweet child. Where was he? Was he even alive?

But a larger question loomed. Why did *Hauptmann* Engel keep it?

Hauptsturmführer Jaeger's voice sounded from the lounge. "Where is that maid? Tell her I need a stiff drink. We have business to discuss."

Anna rubbed her hands.

Babička looked to the ceiling. *Ne*, to the heavens. "Protect us, Lord." Then she nodded in the direction of the door. "You had better go."

Anna stumbled out of the room on shaky legs, wishing *Babička* would have prayed for steady hands for her. "Yes, sir?"

Hauptsturmführer Jaeger cocked his head. "A glass of water. I forgot that Engel here is a teetotaler."

Thankful that she didn't have to mix a cocktail she had no idea how to prepare, she moved to the kitchen and took a glass from the cabinet.

"What is it that's so important?" *Hauptmann* Engel's voice was as casual as if he sat on a beach by the sea. How could he remain so calm? Perhaps if *Hauptsturmführer* Jaeger discovered her Jewish roots, *Hauptmann* Engel would act shocked at the revelation and save his own skin.

"A little bit of interesting news."

"You have my curiosity piqued."

Anna turned on the faucet and let the water rise to the cup's brim.

"You know that Jew you spoke to after the Terezín concert?"

"*Ja*. I congratulated him on a job well done. I've always had an affinity for good music."

"Did you catch his name?"

A moment of silence. *Hauptmann* Engel must be shaking his head.

"It's David Zadok."

"You don't say."

"The brother of the Jew living above you. The Jew who, according to you, disappeared into thin air."

The glass of water slid from Anna's hand and crashed to the floor.

Patricie settled the picnic basket handle over the crook of her arm and lifted her face to the sun. If only she could enjoy the day. With the chilly temperatures, *Hauptsturmführer* Jaeger was crazy for this suggestion. Though her hamper boasted nuts, cheese, and *koláček* bought with his extra ration coupons, she couldn't summon any excitement for this outing.

He'd insisted on having the picnic in his office.

She spotted his headquarters in a rather modern building and took the paternoster lift to his floor. Nazis in dark uniforms filled the halls, moving with long strides, shoulders back, a proud set to their chins. Chills ran up and down her arms. The medals on the officers' chests glinted in the lights. German words swirled in the air.

Patricie's stomach roiled. She stood outside of his office door, her hands trembling. Why had he picked her, of all people, to be his special pet? Why had he singled her out? She wasn't pretty by any means, nothing to attract such an important and powerful man. He could have any woman in the Reich. Why her?

The problem was, she couldn't refuse him. Doing so would set off suspicion, perhaps an investigation of her and her activities.

Although he had already dug into her past, and probably continued to dig. And investigated her present, as well.

He suddenly appeared at her side. She gasped and clutched her chest.

He grinned, a strange look in his eyes. "Did I surprise you, my little bird?"

She took a deep breath, willing her heart to slow its rapid pace. "*Ja*. I didn't see you coming. I'm a bit early."

He ushered her into his office and shut the door with a soft click. "I like to keep you on your toes."

The words came off more threatening than playful. She needed to keep the atmosphere light. "No more than my brothers did when we were young."

"And where are your brothers now?" He pulled two chairs up to the desk, flipped open the basket's lid, and rummaged through its contents.

"One brother works for an engineering consulting firm in Dresden. The other I haven't heard from since the beginning of the war." But she had. He assisted in her illicit activities.

"You must be so afraid for him." He drew out a bottle of apple juice, his thunderous look telling her the beverage choice displeased him.

She stared at her best green dress, worrying the hem. Truth be told, she *was* afraid for her brother. Afraid *Hauptsturmführer* Jaeger would catch him counterfeiting papers and passports and printing underground fliers that would have him on the next train east if the Gestapo caught him. "I am."

He patted her hand. "I would be frantic if I didn't know where my sister was. If you want, I could help you find your brother. I have sources."

She held her breath to keep from sucking in the air. Why had she mentioned her brothers at all? "*Ne*." She exhaled bit by bit. "I mean, that is very kind of you, but not necessary. He will come home when he is ready."

"He has run away before?"

She bit the inside of her cheek before sitting back. "Let's not talk of him anymore. It makes me too sad." She swallowed like the thought of him brought her to tears. "Today is a day to enjoy."

"Perhaps, by the time we have another picnic, spring will have arrived." He winked.

Her arms broke out in goose flesh. "Let's hope it comes soon."

He poured two glasses of juice and handed one to her. "Cheers. Though you know I prefer a drink with a bit more punch."

"Cheers."

"Relax. I don't bite." He gazed at her hand.

She clutched the glass in a death grip. As she loosened her hold, she giggled.

"Do I make you nervous?"

More than he would ever know. "Not at all."

"Then look at me."

Steeling herself, she peered into his chilly blue eyes.

"You have nothing to fear from me. I'm just a boy from a small German village."

"Of course you are." One with the power to send countless people to their deaths. How many warrants had he already signed?

"Unless you have something to hide."

"Why would you think that?"

"We all do, don't we?"

"You have me there. I'm ready to confess."

If possible, his eyes turned harder.

"When I was seven, I ate all of the cookies from *Máma*'s cookie jar. I blamed my brothers, and she never found out it was me."

He roared with laughter. "And I have a confession. My sister didn't push me into the river. I went there all on my own to wade, though *Mutti* warned me not to do so right before church."

"The things we blame on our siblings. Will they ever forgive us?"

"My sister adores me. She said there was nothing to forgive. And I adore her right back."

What was this? A tender side to the man?

He polished off the remainder of the basket's contents. "I knew there was a less-serious side to you. I'm glad you showed me."

Hauptsturmführer Jaeger was handsome, intelligent, and charming. He had a quick wit and knew how to carry a conversation. Everything she wanted in a man.

Everything she already had in Georg.

She shook her head.

As the sun slipped behind Prague's colorful, time-worn buildings, the slight warmth of the day fled. The office darkened. Patricie shivered. "I need to get home. There are things I must attend to."

He slid off his military jacket and slipped it around her shoulders. "Let me walk you there. You have never showed me your apartment."

What did it matter? Most likely, he already knew. "That would be delightful. Thank you."

He picked up the hamper and helped Patricie to her feet. He held her hand the entire walk. It was warm and smooth yet strong. The stroll was only a couple of blocks, and they arrived in short order.

He nodded in approval. "Very nice. But I've seen the outside. It's the inside I want a peek at."

She shivered. "It's an older building. The flats are small, but it's just me, so I don't mind. Nothing to see in there. The area was too good to pass up, with the shops and parks and restaurants nearby. I love to be in the middle of people. *Máma* always said I could never stand to miss out on anything."

He pulled her closer and shushed her with a finger to her lips. "I do make you nervous."

She shook her head. Her scalp prickled.

He leaned over and brushed her lips with his own. She quaked, and he tugged her even closer, his mouth pressing harder on hers.

He pulled away without warning. Then he stepped into the street where a child walked, his head down. "You filthy, vile Jew-boy. What are you doing here?"

The youngster kept his gaze focused on the cobblestone street. *Hauptsturmführer* Jaeger took a step toward him. "I asked you a question."

"My apologies."

Hauptsturmführer Jaeger spit at him.

Patricie wiped her mouth, bile rising in her throat. She should do something.

"You are nothing but trash. I should have you hauled away right here and now."

The boy cowered.

Hauptsturmführer Jaeger slapped him on the cheek.

The screams piercing Patricie's ears arose from her memory. From the day they took Eliška away. Her best friend. Her confidant. They had played together as children, grown up together, dreamed of their futures together.

Eliška had shrieked that day. Had cried as the officers led her away from the only place she'd ever called home. And what did they do to her? Bashed her on the head until she bled.

But still she wept.

And Patricie had done nothing but stand by and watch.

She wiped a tear from her cheek.

Her pulse pounded. She vaulted forward. "Stop it. He's only a child."

Tears streaked the boy's gaunt face.

Hauptsturmführer Jaeger turned in her direction, his face hard and dark. "He's vermin. Not fit to walk the same street as you. Women and children need to be protected from such as him."

He struck the child again. The boy fell to the ground, screaming in pain. "Help me! Help me!"

The Nazi kicked him in the gut.

She should stop him. Should do something to protect the boy. He was innocent. Blood gushed from a cut above his eye. Sweat matted his hair to his forehead.

But her midsection tightened. Her feet refused to move. Her mouth refused to open. Her hands refused to help.

Hauptsturmführer Jaeger pulled the child to his feet, and while holding the boy by the collar, stepped to her side. He planted a sloppy kiss on her cheek. "I'm sorry to end the day on such a note, but I have to take out the trash."

He dragged the crying, pleading Jewish kid down the street and around the corner.

Patricie fell to her knees. What had she become?

Chapter Twelve

Horst sat in the easy chair, fading daylight slithering through the bow window and falling on the paper he read. Glowing reports of German advances. How much could be true? How much did he even believe anymore?

The great and glorious Fatherland. A pure and proud people. *Ja*, he'd bought into that ideology once a long time ago, when his father had always been right. Before Horst had removed his blinders and seen what the world was becoming.

What he was becoming.

And the offer that *Oberleutnant* Meier made him? Horst set the paper on the small table and took a long drag on his cigarette. What was he supposed to do about that? He couldn't accept the position of head of deportation. He couldn't send all those people to the work camps. *Nein*, the extermination camps.

He refused to put Anna or her grandmother on an eastbound train. Anna, his one spot of beauty in this crazy, upside down world. His one moment of sanity during the day.

She moved him. Stirred something undefinable deep inside him.

Like an apparition, she appeared at his side. "May I talk to you?"

She was small, fine boned, delicate. Yet he sensed a depth to her, a strength she herself had yet to discover. He nodded in the direction of the wing chair opposite him. "What is it?"

She sat and gazed at her hands, folded in her lap. Those fingers that flew over the violin strings. "I wanted to thank you for covering for me yesterday. You could have turned us in. Pretended you didn't know we were Jewish."

He gave a half chuckle. "I don't think *Hauptsturmführer* Jaeger would have believed me. My life is as much on the line as yours."

"We are putting you in great danger, as well as ourselves. It's not safe here anymore. *Babička* and I need to leave."

He leaned forward. More than anything, he didn't want them to go. "*Ne.*"

"And what if *Hauptsturmführer* Jaeger returns?"

"We now have our cover story straight. He believed it. And you can hide in the cellar while he is here. I will tell him I let you go home early. Just stay away from the window and don't answer the door."

She sat back and studied the rose-flecked wallpaper above him. "That man knows you spoke to my brother. It won't take him long to fit the puzzle together. My brother is in more danger."

"I'm doing what I can for him, although he doesn't want my help. Told me to stay away."

"Then do that, please. Don't go to him. Keep him safe."

"You haven't seen Theresienstadt." He leaned toward her and touched her cheek so she would look him in the face. He dared to use her first name. They'd become close enough. "Anna, conditions there are terrible. People are crowded together shoulder to shoulder. Disease is rampant. Food is scarce. I may be saving your brother's life, and the lives of several others."

"And you may be signing his death warrant."

"I would never do anything to put him at increased risk. Everyday living is dangerous in that place. It's not a matter of if, but when, he'll be taken away. If I can help him stay strong, perhaps he'll survive."

She sat back in the chair and pulled her legs underneath her. Like the children on that horrible night he would rather forget. "Why would you do that? Why are you risking your life for us? That is what I don't understand. What I can't begin to come up with a reason for. You took us in as strangers, but your job is to kill us."

"My mother raised me to do what is right. I didn't always follow her teachings, to my great regret."

"You are doing this to absolve yourself of guilt, *ne?*"

"Not to absolve myself, but to try to right what is wrong."

"How many Jews have you sent away?"

He sat back like she shot him in the chest. "None. My job has nothing to do with Jews. Do you think most of us work in our offices all day planning of ways to get rid of your people?"

"Don't you?" She stood and moved behind the chair, as if using it to protect herself.

"Don't be silly. Of course not." But *Oberleutnant* Meier's offer rattled around in Horst's brain. How many would he be forced to load onto cattle cars and send east? He would become just like Stefan. Just like his father. The man who hated the Jews, whom he blamed for his son's death.

"You don't understand what life is like for us." Her brown eyes shimmered.

"I'm beginning to."

"Why didn't your people stop this madman? You should have known, should have seen, what was coming. You could have been rid of him with a single uprising. By Kristallnacht, you should have seen his true colors. Didn't the shattered glass and the shattered lives give you a clue?"

Horst clenched his fists. "Enough!" he roared at her in German.

Anna scampered away like a frightened kitten and slammed the door to her room.

He mussed his hair, a wicked headache picking that moment to careen into him.

What was he going to do?

Hauptmann Engel left the flat very early the next morning without saying another word to Anna. And that was fine with her. Never in her life had she seen anyone angrier, except when her father had found out David was involved with the intellectual types like Franz Kafka. When his son turned his back on their faith, *Táta* was furious.

She could understand her father's rage. She couldn't understand *Hauptmann* Engel's. She'd said nothing to arouse his ire to that degree.

Perhaps she'd angered him by the way she spoke about Hitler. That had to be it. He loved the man and fancied him to be his country's savior. She'd spoken blasphemy against their dear Führer.

She made *Babička's* breakfast and washed the dishes when they finished eating. She read his newspaper, folding it just so when she was done, so it would appear unread. No need in upsetting him again.

She itched to touch her violin strings, to feel the weight of it in her hands, to draw the bow across it and produce the music that stirred her soul.

She pulled out the case, opened the squeaky hinges, and lifted out the beautiful tiger-maple instrument. She turned it over in her hands and tucked it under her cheek, loving the way it fit. Just perfect.

In her hands, she grasped an imaginary bow and played a tune only she could hear. Her fingers flew across the strings during long passages of sixteenth notes. Her body swayed when she came to the measures full of heartrending beauty and pain.

When she finished, she stood breathless.

"Anna." *Babička's* weak cry came from the bathroom. "Anna."

How long had her grandmother been calling for her? Anna dropped her violin on the sofa and flew across the apartment, her heart pounding as fast as her fingers had moved. *Babička* lay on the wood floor. Anna slid to her knees, propping *Babička's* head under a towel. "What's wrong? What happened?"

"The pain in my chest." *Babička's* breath came in spurts, her shaking hands clutching her blouse.

Anna's own hands trembled. "I'll get your medicine." She rose to retrieve it from the cabinet where *Hauptmann* Engel allowed her to store it. She rifled through the manly contents like razors and shaving cream, not finding what she needed.

"I took the last of it yesterday."

"So you haven't been feeling well for a while?"

"A few days. There are so many troubling things happening, I didn't want to burden you. But now you have to get more."

Anna knelt again. "Let me get you to bed. Perhaps you will feel better then."

Babička's face paled another shade. "You know these attacks. Only the medicine helps."

"But what if someone notices me? Someone who knows I'm not supposed to be here. What if a soldier asks to see my papers?"

Babička clutched her chest.

"Is the pain worse?"

She nodded.

Anna grabbed her own middle, her heart throbbing against her ribs. "Can we trust Dr. Skala? Are you sure he won't turn me in? He might have found out about our disappearance."

"How?"

"I don't know. But, but …"

"What about *Hauptmann* Engel? Or Sabina?"

"He is gone, and I don't know when he'll be back. And I would have to go out to get word to *Paní* Buraneková."

"What other choice is there?"

A cold sweat dotted Anna's forehead as she lifted her grandmother to a sitting position. "I'm not going to lose you. I will do whatever is necessary to keep you alive." She bit back the lump in her throat about to choke her. "You are all I have. You and David. So you aren't allowed to die. Can you stand?"

"If you help me, I think I can."

Anna managed to get *Babička* to her feet. Several times on the way down the short hall they had to stop so *Babička* could catch her breath. Ten minutes later, Anna tucked her grandmother into the large bed that occupied most of the space in the small bedroom.

"Anna?"

"Yes, *Babička*?"

"I love you, child."

"I love you too. Please hold on until I get back. Doctor Skala's home isn't far from here. Are you sure we can trust him?"

"*Ne*, but I trust God."

Anna fussed with her grandmother's blanket. "I won't be long."

With one last kiss for *Babička*, Anna sprinted from the bedroom, grabbed her coat, and slipped out of the flat. Her own breath came in gasps.

But she didn't have time for fear. *Babička* needed her. And soon. All she had to do was to keep her head down and pray no one noticed her.

And that they could trust Dr. Skala.

Chapter Thirteen

Oberleutnant Meier stood in front of his office window looking over Theresienstadt, his back to Horst. Rolls of gray clouds hung low over the chilly ghetto. The man took a long drag on his cigarette and blew out a puff of smoke.

He turned to Horst and stared at him across the mahogany desk. "The position I'm offering you is lucrative. To oversee scheduling the deportations is quite the responsibility. And a step up from your current position, which will win you no honor. No one cares about buildings. But helping to free the Reich from the impure? That will make you a man to be noticed. Reckoned with."

Horst wiped his sweaty palms on his pants. "But my job now is a pleasure."

"What greater pleasure is there than to rid Germany of all that makes it weak? These people have stolen what belongs to us. What all Aryans deserve. A homeland. Good jobs. Peace and prosperity."

Horst stepped backward. He didn't want any part of this. His hands would forever be stained with blood. Meier's gaze drilled through his middle. Horst turned his attention to the pictures on the wall, all painted by great masters. All stolen from the Jews.

If they only knew who lived in his flat.

"You participated in Kristallnacht, if I remember correctly."

Horst scanned the room for a chair as his legs went weak. "How did you find that out?"

"It's in your records."

Of course. They'd examined his records down to the last detail of his life.

"Your enthusiasm for the event was noted."

An enthusiasm which had turned to cold, hard regret when he'd opened his eyes the following morning.

He had stared at the Danish *Mutti* had placed in front of him for breakfast, afraid to look at her.

"Did you hear what happened last night?" She stood beside the table and wiped her hands on her apron.

He nodded, afraid to trust his voice.

"What a senseless waste. The Jews weren't hurting anyone. We need their businesses. For them to have windows broken and stores burned because of who they are is inhumane. And some of them were beaten and arrested, just because they are different. My heart aches today. What is becoming of us?" She touched the top of his head and turned to the stove to poach *Vater's* egg.

She knew where he'd been without ever asking the question.

Once *Vater* had come to the table, they'd eaten in silence, *Vater* smiling throughout the meal, *Mutti* frowning. Then she cleared their plates and brought out the family Bible. Resuming her seat, she flipped the pages until she came to the passage where Paul said there would be no free or slave, male or female, Jew or Greek, because we would all be one in Christ.

Her voice rang clear and true, steady as she spoke the words of God.

Vater's face, on the other hand, reddened as she continued. "Enough."

Mutti stared at him, her mouth wide open.

He reached over and slammed the book shut. Then he struck her across the cheek.

"*Nein, nein.*" Horst rushed to his mother's side.

"Last night I thought you were a man." *Vater's* eyes bulged. "Now I see that you are nothing more than a spoiled, wimpy excuse for a man."

Then his father's hand came across his own cheek. His insides burned almost as much as the spot on his face.

He would never forget.

That was the last time he could be called a good Nazi. That was when the awful dreams began.

Oberleutnant Meier cleared his throat, jerking Horst back to the present. Not any nicer of a reality. "What has become of you since that night?"

"I'm sure there is someone more suitable for the position. Honestly, I don't know why I was chosen. Does this have anything to do with my father?"

The man straightened to his full height, towering over Horst.

"I see." Horst paced across the small room and back again. "He got me this position in Prague to butter me up, just a prelude to the job he really wanted me to have." His pulse pounded in his wrist. "Tell him *danke*, but *nein*. I will not accept the position. Ever. Especially knowing it came from him."

The room's door banged opened. "You will accept this position."

Horst spun around. "*Vater*." The walls closed in on him.

His father strode into the room. Though they stood at the same height, *Vater* still towered over him. "How dare you turn it down."

Horst clenched and unclenched his fists and tried to keep his voice steady, even though his entire body shook. "I refuse to do your dirty work. If you want to send the Jews east, do it yourself."

Vater turned to Meier. "Leave us. I'll teach this boy some manners."

Horst fingered his sidearm. If he had to use it, could he?

The door clicked shut behind Meier.

"I will not have my son behaving in such a fashion." *Vater* took a step forward, his usually pale face burning red. "Do you understand me? You will not speak in such a manner to a superior officer. Or to me."

"I don't believe I'm under any obligation to take the offer. What are you doing here, anyway?"

"I traveled all the way from Berlin to congratulate you on your new position. To celebrate with my only remaining child as he finally becomes a man. And then, I hear this."

"You should have saved yourself the trouble. I won't do it."

"You're a coward." *Vater* spat on Horst's shoes.

"I'm nothing of the sort." He wasn't, was he?

"A disgrace to the Fatherland. And to me. How could you do this to me? Otto wouldn't have been so ungrateful. So stubborn. He would have done what I asked. Would have shared our vision for a strong Germany."

Horst sucked in a breath. He turned from his father and stared out the window at the work detail returning from a hard day's labor. "Well, I'm not Otto, am I? And that's what you can't stand the most. Go dig up his bones, attach strings to them, and make him dance for you. I refuse to do it."

"You're a Jew lover, aren't you?"

Horst held his breath.

"Well, aren't you?" *Vater* grabbed him by the upper arm, his grasp vise-like. "That's why you refuse such an important position."

"*Nein.*" *Ja. Ja*, he was. But that would be the death of him.

"Then I order you to take the job. I'll have the transfer papers drawn up immediately."

Horst shook himself free of *Vater*'s hold and spun to face him. He squared his shoulders, straightened, and puffed out his chest. "You will do no such thing. If I ever want such a job, I will earn it, like every other German soldier must. Until then, I will continue as Minister of Architectural Preservation in Prague. And don't you ever, ever pay me a surprise visit again. If you don't leave me alone, I'll render you unable to bother me." He clutched the revolver's grip. "Do I make myself clear?"

A vein bulged in *Vater*'s neck. "You are no son of mine. Do I make myself clear?"

The slamming of the door reverberated in Horst's ears.

How could he have ever tried to win *Vater*'s favor?

How could he have ever wanted to be like him?

The sun just touched the western horizon as German soldiers marched David and the rest of his work detail into the gate at Terezín, under the arch in the thick stone wall. A different gate, the one into the small fortress, read *Arbeit Macht Frei*. Work Makes You Free.

His body ached from splitting rocks all day long. What on earth could the Germans need with so many stones? They could have built ten pyramids with the ones he split just himself.

A violent cough racked his body. He struggled for breath.

Egon grabbed him by the hand. "Come on. You have to keep up."

A difficult directive, more so each passing day. His legs were as heavy as any of the rocks in the quarry. He dragged his mallet through the mud, lacking the strength to carry it.

And he had to go to practice yet tonight. If he could only curl up on his pallet and sleep away the war.

"*Schnell, schnell.*"

The German guard's attention landed on him. The consequences if he fell too far behind were unthinkable. With everything left inside of him, he lifted his legs.

They burned. The world spun. Blackness crouched at the corners of his vision. He breathed in. Coughed. The blackness seeped further into his consciousness.

Voices around him drifted like they were underwater.

A guard shouted at Egon. "Keep going."

"My friend." Egon turned his attention to David. "You have to get moving. Don't give up."

Over Egon's shoulder, the soldier lifted his weapon.

"*Nein. Halten sie.*"

A familiar voice. Who?

"What do you want?" The guard didn't lower his gun.

"Don't strike that man."

Hauptmann Engel. David's worst nightmare. Anna's savior.

The soldier stared at the officer with hard, hazel eyes. "Why shouldn't I?"

Hauptmann Engel peered at David as if he didn't know who he was. Then his eyes widened and his mouth dropped into an O. "He's done nothing wrong."

"He can't keep up with the others. He's useless."

"He's ill."

The guard took three steps forward until he stood mere centimeters from *Hauptmann* Engel. "Are you a Jew lover?"

"*Nein.*"

"But you care what happens to this man. That makes you a Jew lover in my book."

"I care that you have enough men to fill your work detail."

Hauptmann Engel's counterpart snickered. "Look around you. There are plenty of men to work. One more or less doesn't make a difference to me."

"Let me take care of him, then."

The guard glanced all around. Would he strike the officer? Kill them both? David should be frightened, but he didn't have the energy.

After a long moment, the guard backed down. "Have it your way." He returned to his duty. "Let's go. Nothing more to see here." He herded the men away.

As soon as the group marched out of hearing range, *Hauptmann* Engel knelt in the mucky road beside David. "What's wrong?"

David struggled to sit, backing away. "My life is nothing to me, but yours should mean something to you. If not yours, my sister's." Another coughing fit stole his breath. He wiped his dirty sleeve across his bloody mouth.

"You're the one who is sick."

David's head hurt. "Don't you realize what you're doing? You're getting yourself labeled as a Jew lover. Good enough to get you shipped east if you're lucky, shot if you're not. And I'm not going to get either chance because my many roommates will beat me to a pulp first. Can't you go away and mind your own business?"

"If I minded my own business, your sister would be here instead of safe inside my apartment. And your grandmother . . ." Without asking, he grabbed David under the shoulders and lifted him to his feet. "There is a hospital here?"

"Just take me to my room. There is nothing they can do for me at the hospital."

"How do you know? For Anna's sake, you have to get better. You and your grandmother are all she has left."

"Why do you care so much about my sister?"

"I care about all people."

If he had the strength, David would have spat. "A German who cares about all people? Impossible. They are mutually exclusive."

They made their way through the ghetto one small step at a time. "Not all Germans are evil. My *mutti* isn't. She is a good, Christian woman."

"In my estimation, being Christian doesn't make her good. I bet that more than ninety percent of these Nazis grew up in the church. And what a lot of good it did for me. Look at where being a Christian got me." He would have spat again.

They walked in silence for several minutes.

"You're surprised to hear that from me, aren't you?" David leaned more on *Hauptmann* Engel the farther they walked.

"*Ja*, I suppose I am. After listening to Anna and your grandmother, I assumed you all to be Christians. Though she did mention you were estranged from your parents."

"Because I didn't share their faith. Imagine that. Aren't Christians supposed to love everyone?" Yet, his heart twinged. His family. Gone. Everyone gone. He bit back the tears.

"Did you manage to talk to them while they were here?"

"Worried that I didn't make my peace with them when I had the chance?" They had to stop as David coughed again. The frequent fits now lasted longer, sending cold shivers down his spine.

He had seen his parents here at the camp. They'd spoken a few times. The last time ... Oh, if only he could go back and relive that moment. He'd stomped away after another argument with *Táta*. He'd give his last crumb of bread for a chance to see his parents one more time.

What would have been so hard about listening to them? Speaking kind words to them instead of shouting at them in a vain attempt to get them to listen to his philosophies?

"Won't you let me know what is wrong?"

"You'll run home and tell Anna and *Babička*, and I don't want them to worry." David had never met anyone so bent on giving assistance. Why had this officer singled him out?

"I won't share it with them if you don't want me to. But I'd like to know so I can help."

"You can help by leaving me alone." David sucked in his breath at the venom in his weak voice. "Go away and forget about me."

Hauptmann Engel tightened his grip. "If you think I'm doing this for you, you're wrong. Are you happy about that admission? I'm doing it for your sister. When I met you, I had to tell her about you. And now she wants me to keep in touch with you. She can't receive your post-cards anymore. Without me, she is cut off from the only family she has left, other than your grandmother. Think of her rather than yourself."

"I am thinking of her." Perhaps if the man knew the truth, he would leave him alone. "I'm dying."

Patricie sat at her small kitchen table, her cold hands clutching a cup of bitter ersatz coffee. The chill in the flat seeped deeper than into her flesh. It permeated her very soul.

She couldn't sleep. Hadn't slept in countless nights. The little Jewish boy's innocent face haunted her dreams. The memories of his screams blended with the memories of Eliška's cries.

No matter what she did, she couldn't shake the images of them being dragged away to their deaths.

She wiped a tear from her face. Why hadn't she done more to protect either of them? One, the sister of her soul. The other, a helpless child. She'd stood by, hands at her sides, mouth clamped shut, as those vile Nazis carted them away to an uncertain fate. She was no better than the Germans who committed these crimes.

Since the day those brutes beat her dearest friend and hauled her away, Patricie had worked to stop the Nazis from hurting anyone else.

Her acquaintances from the conservatory. Shopkeepers whose stores she frequented. Complete strangers.

Yet she hadn't helped her friend. Or the little boy.

Paul in the Bible held the cloaks of those who stoned Stephen, giving his approval to the dastardly deed.

That was her.

That was what she had become.

She swirled her coffee. If only she could drown in the depths of it.

A knock came at the door. She sloshed her drink, stumbled to the door, half-drunk on lack of sleep, and opened it.

Georg stood on her threshold. On most days, her heart thrilled to see him. Not today. Not after she became a disgrace to their cause. "Come in." She stood to the side, and he entered.

"You look worse than my cat after I give him a bath."

"Not today, Georg." She turned from him.

He grabbed her by the shoulder and spun her around. "What's wrong?"

If she spoke, she would burst into tears. Instead, she broke from his grasp, grabbed the coffee pot from the stove, and poured him a cup. He sat at the table and drank the offering.

Patricie took a swig of the bitter brew. "I think spring is on its way very soon. No more damp, chilly days."

"I hope you're right. The world is a better, happier place in the sunshine."

"Perhaps when the war is over, I'll move to Naples. Or Barcelona. Some place where the sun always shines." Away from her crimes.

He touched her hand. "Patricie, this isn't like you. We don't talk about the weather. We've known each other too long. We have important work to do."

She recoiled at his touch. "What is the matter with chatting with a friend? Does it have to always be about the work?"

He gazed at her, his green eyes as dark as a pine tree. "You know I can't stay long. I'm only here for a few minutes to check on you."

"I needed a little bit of lightness before we got down to why you are here. Life doesn't have to be about the war all of the time."

"You're wrong. The war dominates everything we do. Every part of our lives. It consumes every waking moment."

She slid her chair away from the table and stood, knocking over her cup, spilling the last few sips of the fake coffee. She ran for a rag and wiped up the mess.

And then her tears flowed. Fast and furious. Unabated.

Georg wrenched the dish cloth from her grasp and took her in his arms. He stroked her back and whispered in her ear. He did what she'd longed for him to do for many years.

But not now. Not like this.

She broke away, leaning back on her haunches, sobbing.

He touched her knee. "Please, darling, please. Tell me what is wrong."

She shook her head.

"Whatever it is, just say it."

She swallowed her tears and forced her voice to work. "I want out. I don't want to do this anymore."

The hardest, most heart-wrenching words she ever uttered.

Chapter Fourteen

Anna braced herself against the wind, a breeze that hadn't mussed her hair in a few weeks, a gust that burned her cheeks. Ah, how good. How free.

She hurried toward Doctor Skala's office, her head down, her eyes averted. *Lord, let him be trustworthy. Send a cover of protection.*

So as not to draw attention to herself, she measured her steps, yet her mind raced far ahead. The Nazis didn't allow Jews to go to Aryan doctors. According to the law, no Czech physician could treat a Jew. Even if he didn't know about their notices and didn't turn them in, grave danger hung over them both. If the Germans discovered them, they would take both Anna and the doctor away.

But *Babička*. Whatever the cost, Anna had to be brave. She had to do this so *Babička* would live.

Not far now. Just a few more blocks. Her racing heart calmed a little. Everything would turn out fine. No need to doubt that.

A tap at her shoulder sent her jumping almost as high as the moon. She covered her mouth to keep from screaming. She whirled around, shaking. Who would she see? An acquaintance from church? A German soldier?

"Jakub." She took a deep breath.

David's friend scrunched his thick eyebrows. "Your names appeared on the deportation list. I thought you left for Terezín."

She pulled him to the side and lowered her voice. "We're in hiding."

Now he raised his brows as his hazel eyes widened. "You don't look very well hidden to me."

"It's *Babička*'s heart. I need medicine for her."

119

He glanced over his shoulder. "Are you being followed?"

"*Ne*. I don't think so. I don't know why I would be. The Germans believe I'm gone."

Was it even safe for her to speak to Jakub? She inched away.

"Who is hiding you?"

"The German officer downstairs from our flat."

Jakub tousled his dark, curly hair. "You moved downstairs with a Nazi, and you think you're in hiding?"

"There is a place for us in the cellar when we need to disappear. Otherwise, we don't make noise during the day when *Hauptmann* Engel isn't home." Precious moments ticked away for *Babička* while she tried to make Jakub see what she did. "I have to go and get that medicine."

"Anna, you have lost your mind. You can't trust this man."

"But we can trust God."

"You sound like your grandmother. He'll turn you in the first chance he gets."

She leaned closer to Jakub. "What other choice did we have? Our time was up. We were on the way out the door when he took us in. So what difference does it make? If he turns us in, and why would he when he would be in trouble himself, we end up at the same place we would have if we went when our notices came. This way, I might have bought *Babička* some time. But only if I get her that medicine."

Without waiting for Jakub to answer, she hurried on her way. He was right, of course. She couldn't trust *Hauptmann* Engel. She couldn't trust anyone. Even Jakub.

And certainly not Dr. Skala. Before she was ready, she reached his house on a tree-lined street. She stared at the imposing, pink-painted, three-story residence, nestled in a row of similar homes. She shouldn't be here. Her presence spelled trouble for herself. And for him.

With feet that might as well have had weights tied to them, she climbed the stone steps to the front door. He had always been good to her family. He'd delivered her and her siblings, cared for her grandfather when he became ill, and set *Táta*'s broken arm when he fell on an icy street.

But that was all before the Germans had prohibited Aryan doctors from treating Jewish patients. She squared her shoulders and lifted the knocker. A young woman answered. "May I help you?"

"I need to see Dr. Skala, please."

The brown-haired, blue-eyed maid studied Anna's coat. She looked down. Much to her horror, there remained the darker outline of the star. Over the years, the material around it faded. Though she took it off, the shadow of it stayed.

"I'm sorry. He can't help you." The maid moved to close the door.

Anna stepped on the threshold and blocked the way. "I need to speak to him. That's all. I'm not here for treatment." Were treatment and medication the same thing?

"What are you doing? There is nothing I can help you with. Nothing he can do for you. If you know what's good for you, you'll leave."

She hadn't come this far to fail. "I'm not going until I see Dr. Skala."

"I can't do this anymore." The words burned Patricie's tongue. "I'm not going to work with you. Or with the resistance at all."

Georg stared at her as if she had grown two horns and a beard. "You aren't serious."

"I am." She pulled a handkerchief from her skirt pocket, wiped her nose, and then lifted the floorboard underneath her small kitchen table. She drew out stacks of ration cards and forged papers her brother had given her. "Here." She held them out to Georg.

He shook his head. "Patricie, please. Think about this more. We need you. All those Jews in hiding depend on you. Who will take over your work? You know the names of them all, where they are, who they are with, who will accommodate more."

"Someone will step up."

"You know how hard that is. Not since Heydrich decimated the resistance. Even since his assassination, it's almost impossible to recruit workers. Everyone is afraid of more reprisals, afraid of the streets running red with blood again, afraid of more towns like Lidice being wiped off the map."

She shivered, the horror of those days less than two years ago still fresh in her mind.

"Not to mention that your brother can come and go here without anyone giving a second thought. He's a vital link between you and the rest of the movement."

"That's not true anymore."

Georg rubbed his temples. "What's not true?"

"My brother can no longer visit me here."

He paled. "Has something happened to him?"

She picked a string from her sleeve. "*Ne*."

"Are you being watched? Do you need to move?"

"Moving me won't make a difference."

"Then the Germans have you under surveillance?"

"You could say that."

"Why aren't you being direct with me? Why am I fishing for information?" He touched her cheek.

The tears threatened to spill over once more. "Circumstances have changed."

"We've been friends for more years than I can count. You know how I feel."

And she had planned to reveal her love for him one day. But that was never going to happen now. "I'm dating a German officer."

Patricie couldn't look at Georg. He inhaled a sharp breath. "*Ne*." He whispered the word.

She carried the dirty rag she used to mop up the coffee to the sink and washed it out, keeping her back to him. "Don't worry. I won't tell him any of your secrets. Our secrets. But you see now why I have to cut all ties with the movement. It isn't prudent for me to continue the work. Not for anyone." Could he read between the lines? Tell that *Hauptsturmführer* Jaeger's presence in her life wasn't her choice? Cutting off Georg like this was like cutting off one of her own fingers.

"I can't believe you would do this to me. To us."

If only she could tell him this wasn't voluntary. But after what she had done, or hadn't done, she didn't deserve to be part of the resistance. Because she didn't stand up for that boy, didn't try to save his life no matter the cost to her own, she couldn't be trusted to do the right thing in any given situation. "I'm doing this to protect you."

"I don't need protecting. I'm a grown man. It's the little kids, the old people, the helpless who need protecting. Who is going to get the identity cards for us?"

"I will give you my brother's information. You can contact him and get the books from him. I'll even tell him to expect you. That won't be a problem."

Georg rubbed the smooth table top. "Who will shop?"

"The families hiding the Jews. It's no more dangerous for them to go out and do it than it is for me to bring the food to them. You see, I wasn't much help to you in the first place."

"That is where you are wrong. Very wrong. Please, you have to reconsider. How much does this man mean to you?"

"It's complicated." She twisted her apron string around her finger.

"Tell me. Make me understand."

"I'm not sure I can."

"Or you don't want to." Pain laced his words.

"Don't say it like that."

"What other way is there to say it? I thought you were dedicated to the cause. That the plight of these people moved you and compelled you to aid them. I thought you were a woman who cared about the helpless. Perhaps I was wrong, because no Christian woman would turn her back on the persecuted like this to cavort with the enemy." Georg scraped his chair back and marched from the flat, slamming the door.

A pain stabbed at her gut, so real that she clutched her middle.

She'd failed the movement. Failed Georg.

She'd failed God.

Horst was more than happy to walk up the steps in front of the stone building he began to think of as home, its graceful arches welcoming him, promising respite. The day had drained him. First *Oberleutnant* Meier, then his father.

His father. Horst clenched his jaw. He'd known the man had something to do with the job offer. Always pushing him to do things that went against everything *Mutti* had taught him.

But no more. Today was the final strike of the axe on the wedge that broke their relationship apart, an irreparable split.

No longer would he be the man's puppet.

No matter the cost.

And David. Dying of tuberculosis. How was he ever going to tell Anna she was about to lose yet another family member? This was getting to be too much. Where would it all end?

He couldn't let her know. Even if David didn't forbid it, he couldn't deal her another blow. She wouldn't be able to stand it.

A pair of slippers, a warm dinner, and Anna's music would help to right day. He let himself into the flat. All was quiet. Good. Perhaps the scare with Stefan had made Anna more cautious. He hadn't meant to get so angry with her, but she'd put herself in danger peering out windows and opening the door.

"Anna?"

She didn't answer.

"Anna?" He called a little louder.

Still no response.

Maybe she napped. He knocked on the bedroom door.

"*Ja?*"

He peeked in. "Frau Doubeková?"

"Horst. I'm glad you're home."

"Where is Anna?"

"Out."

He hadn't heard right. "What do you mean by out?"

"Not in. I had a spell with my heart earlier this afternoon. She went to get more medication."

"How are you? What do you need? She shouldn't be in public." He circled the room as he spoke.

"I'm better, but I need that medication."

He knelt beside Frau Doubeková. "I understand. You were in an impossible situation. I'm sorry. I got called away. If only I had been here."

She clasped her hands together. "Do you believe in God? Are you a Christian?"

The question startled him. "*Mutti* took me to church every Sunday. She read the Bible to me every night, so I guess I am."

"That isn't enough."

That much was true. It wasn't enough. His life wasn't the same since he'd become lazy with church and Bible reading. Right now, he didn't have time for God. And God didn't have time for him.

"Faith is precious. Cherish it. Hunger for it. Protect it."

"Anna has been gone for a while?"

She smoothed back a piece of gray hair. "I don't know. I fell asleep."

"Tell me where the doctor is. I'm going to find her. Before someone else does."

Anna's grandmother gave him the directions to the man's house. Anna wouldn't dare go to his office, because seeing him was illegal.

Horst patted the old woman's hand. "Thank you. For everything." He turned to leave.

"Young man?"

He redirected his attention. "*Ja?*"

"I know the Lord has great things in store for you. Just remember what your mother taught you when you were young. That will serve you well. God is testing you. Molding you. Shaping you. Allow Him to complete His work."

"I'll be back with your medicine as soon as possible." He didn't want to think about what she said. He would work hard and try to do the right thing no matter the cost. But trusting God to take care of him and to lead him? That was another matter.

People on their way home from their offices and jobs clogged the streets this late in the afternoon. Despite the war, life went on. He dodged a streetcar and several bicycles, their riders ringing their bells at him. Then he crossed the famous Charles Bridge with its graceful stone arches. All along the way, he scanned the area, searching for Anna's dark head.

Daylight faded as he arrived in the doctor's residential neighborhood. The street boasted yellow and pink and green homes crunched together, like a child had glued them side by side. Elaborate reliefs, some painted gold, framed the multi-paned windows. Dentil molding separated the windows from the roofline. Anna made it easy for him to find the right house.

She stood on the front step.

"I'm not leaving until I see Dr. Skala." She refused to permit the woman to shut the door.

"I cannot allow that." The young woman who, by her dark dress, Horst took as the maid, tried to push Anna out of the way.

"Please. I beg you."

The girl shook her head.

Horst rushed forward. "*Halten sie.*"

The maid let go of the doorknob and stepped backward. Anna, also, shrank back.

"You must admit this woman."

The maid nodded.

Horst grabbed Anna by the wrist and dragged her into the house. He shut the door behind them. No need making a scene for everyone on the street to witness. "Dr. Skala. I must see him."

Again, the girl nodded and turned to scamper away.

"Wait. I will come with you." He didn't want the doctor to slip out the back entrance when he heard a German officer with a Jewish woman in tow hunted for him. "And you will lead me to him. Do you understand? I will not accept that he is out for the evening."

"Yes, sir. I will take you to see him."

Anna's hand trembled in his. They followed the maid down the hall and to a room on the left. The girl tapped at the door.

"Come in."

The middle-aged, balding doctor sat behind his desk, files spread out before him. When he looked up, he stood and gave a Heil Hitler. Anna hid behind Horst.

He pulled her to stand beside him. "You treated this woman and her family in the past?"

The doctor sat once more and fumbled with the gold fountain pen he clutched. "*Ne*. I have never seen her before."

Anna gasped.

Horst leaned over the desk and narrowed his eyes. "That is a lie. Now, I would like the truth. And all of it. Am I making myself clear?"

The man paled and nodded.

"Have you ever treated this woman or any member of her family?"

"*Ja*. But not since the rules about treating Jews went into effect."

"Another lie. You must have helped them, or else why would she have come here?"

"Sir, I have made it my business not to have anything to do with them. This woman came here today without my knowledge."

The maid spoke up from behind Horst. "I told her to go away. That the doctor wouldn't treat her."

"But you will give her whatever she asks for."

The doctor put down the pen. "I refuse."

"Let me make myself very clear." Horst spoke in his most authoritative voice, one his father would have used. It rang in the small room. "Take care of this woman or face the consequences."

Chapter Fifteen

Anna stared at *Hauptmann* Engel, her mouth dry, her breath coming in short bursts. The way he spoke to Dr. Skala, the way he glared at the man, he was every inch the German officer.

One to be feared.

The physician stood, papers fluttering to the floor. "Whatever you need, I will get it for you."

Hauptmann Engel curved up one corner of his mouth, almost in a sneer. "That is better. Frau Doubeková needs her heart medication."

Anna shrank back. This wasn't the same man who listened to her evening concerts with rapt attention.

Dr. Skala nodded. "But I don't have it here. I need to go to my office to retrieve it."

"Do whatever you have to." *Hauptmann* Engel lifted his chin, tall and proud and condescending. "I expect it to be delivered to Frau Doubeková's residence within the hour. Do I make myself clear?"

The stout doctor swallowed. "*Ja.* It will be there."

"Good. I will come back for you if it doesn't arrive."

"No need of that, sir."

Hauptmann Engel clicked the heels of jackboots together, gave a Heil Hitler, and strode out the door. Anna followed in his wake. Did he even notice her behind him?

They trod a short distance down the block before he blew out a breath. His proud shoulders relaxed, and he laughed. "We did it."

Anna shuddered.

"What's the matter?"

She couldn't find her voice.

"What were you doing on the streets in the first place? You know how dangerous it is for you."

"Why do you ask me that? You know." She hurried to keep pace with his long strides.

"It's dangerous. If anyone recognized you—"

"My grandmother is more important to me than my own life."

"If they find you, they will find her. Did you think about that?" His voice raised in pitch.

She bit the inside of her cheek. Did he regret taking them in?

A muscle jumped in his jaw. "I'm just trying to protect you. All of us."

"I suppose I should thank you for getting *Babička*'s medicine." Though she hated how he went about it. Which man was the real one?

"You don't need to thank me. I don't want to see anything happen to you. Or her."

They crossed the bridge over the river. The wind here bit through Anna's coat, and she shivered.

"Are you cold?"

"We'll be home soon."

He unbuttoned his greatcoat and slipped it from his shoulders. "Here." He offered it to her.

She shook her head. "You can't be seen giving your jacket to a Jew. Look, the star left a shadow on my coat. What would the people, your colleagues, think of you?" What did she think of him? He was a man of contrasts. From now on, she would have to watch her step around him.

As they crested the bridge and started downhill, they encountered a group of German soldiers. They laughed and slapped each other on the back. Perhaps they had gotten off duty early and visited one of the area's establishments.

When they noticed *Hauptmann* Engel, they extended the one-arm salute. He returned the gesture she hated.

The biggest, most muscular of the gang ogled her. "What do we have here? A pretty little Jew by the looks of it."

"Leave her alone." Again, an authoritative chill colored his words. She scooted behind him.

"And why should we?" The soldier licked his lips.

"Because I told you to."

"And you are so high and mighty?"

"I outrank you."

The soldier stepped to Anna's side and touched her overheated cheek. "Very nice."

Hauptmann Engel pushed him away. He stumbled backward, then sprang forward. "Protecting the little Jew. How noble of you."

"You're nothing more than an overgrown schoolyard bully." He clenched his fists.

The man spit in Anna's face. Her throat closed so she couldn't breathe. She didn't dare wipe the moisture away.

"That is enough." The red in *Hauptmann* Engel's face must match that in hers.

The ringleader chortled. "Let me see her papers."

Now, Anna's stomach clenched. They were trapped.

One of the darker haired of the bunch fingered his weapon.

A scream burst from her. "Horst!"

Horst spun around at the piercing screech of Anna's scream. She turned pale and trembled from head to toe.

"Ah, she knows your name." The muscular soldier swung.

Horst ducked, the breeze of the man's fist passing over his head. He grabbed the young soldier by the front of his shirt. A gun cocked, but he ignored the sound. "Listen to me, and listen well. I can have all of you written up for harassing an officer. Would you like that?"

One of the other men broke away from the group, a revolver in his hand. "And we could turn you in for relations with a Jew. Would you like that?" He grabbed the hair at the back of Horst's head and yanked.

Horst kneed him in the groin. The man yelped in pain, dropping the pistol. Horst snatched Anna by the hand and raced away.

The crack of a gunshot reverberated in the air. He didn't stop running. Anna came along with him, so the bullet must not have found its mark. Residents heading home after a long day stared at them. They made a spectacle of themselves. Attracted attention. Something they couldn't afford to do.

Horst slowed. Anna gripped his sweaty hand, breathing hard. He dragged her around a corner onto a quieter side street before stopping. He turned to her, scanning her for blood. "Are you hurt?"

She shook her head.

"I'm sorry. It was foolish of us to take such a main road. We should have sneaked around a back way. What was I thinking? We were asking for trouble."

Anna pulled herself free from him. "I thought they were going to kill you, then take me away."

"I think they would have. I'm thankful you weren't hurt." He reached out to stroke her arm, to comfort her, but she pulled away. "What is the matter?"

"You are the problem."

He stepped backward at her harsh words. "What do you mean?"

Her brown eyes widened.

"You don't have to be afraid of me." Or did she? Blood whooshed in his ears. The brute from Kristallnacht reemerged with too much ease. That time, he'd been the follower. This time, he was the initiator. Was that all he was? A tyrant? An oppressor to be feared?

"Why shouldn't I be? You are the enemy. You and your people want to rid the world of me and my people. At any moment, *Babička* and I could be arrested, taken away, sent to die. My family has been. My dear friend has been. Soon it will be me."

"*Ne.* I'm going to make sure that doesn't happen."

"You're such a man of contrasts. You bullied the doctor into giving you the medicine, yet you keep a child's toy hidden in an armoire."

Ah, she'd found the little boy's train. "I couldn't dispose of it. It meant something to that family, so it means something to me."

She stared at him, hard, long, intense. "Who are you?"

She didn't trust him. The truth slammed into him harder than if he walked into a brick wall. And why should she? She was right. He was the enemy. In front of him lay an opportunity to send thousands upon thousands of people to their deaths. If he wanted the power and the prestige, he could have it in a moment.

But those things meant little to him. Her in his arms. That's what he wanted. For a moment, he couldn't draw a breath.

He stared at her. She didn't smile, didn't relax.

What was it going to take for her to trust him?

Horst bumped along the country road, headed toward Theresienstadt once again. For someone who despised the place, he came here often enough. He needed an excuse to see David, so he told *Oberleutnant* Meier that he wanted to meet with him once more about the position.

Not that he had any intention of accepting it. What his fellow countrymen did to other human beings sickened his stomach. Though he tried to block out the images of ill, suffering, dying people, they haunted him day and night. For weeks now, deep sleep had eluded him.

The appearance of distrust on Anna's face that day on the bridge haunted him even more than the people of Theresienstadt. Not that he blamed her. Look what had happened to her family. What was happening to her brother.

But hadn't he proved himself to her? Proved himself to be better than almost everyone else who wore this uniform and spoke this language? He took her in. Got her grandmother medicine. Protected her on the bridge.

Yet it wasn't enough. Unless . . .

Nein, it was too crazy. Out of the question. Then again. . .? He rubbed his temple. Where had this sudden idea come from? Was God trying to get his attention?

It was insanity, really. Pure, true insanity.

He gripped the steering wheel until he lost feeling in his fingers. *Nein*. He would do nothing crazy. Just see Meier and try to sneak David a little food. That was all.

He honked for a gaggle of geese crossing the road to hurry on. When the birds reached the other side, he stepped on the gas a bit harder. If he allowed this foolish idea to take hold, he couldn't race ahead and put any plan into motion before he fully developed it.

He arrived at the little village now bursting at the seams. More Jews had arrived since his last visit, and the place was more crowded than ever. Already tens of thousands inhabited the few square kilometers. How would they ever fit in even one more person? He could never allow Anna and her grandmother to end up here.

He parked the car alongside the main barracks and made his way up the steep stairs to *Oberleutnant* Meier's offices. The dark, dingy little room reeked of stale cigarette smoke. The Czech secretary, haggard and frumpy, showed him into the main office. "*Oberleutnant* Meier stepped out for just a moment. Wait here. He will be back soon." She shut the door behind him.

He lit a cigarette as he studied the faces staring back at him from the pictures on Meier's desk. Two little kids, almost cherubic, a boy and a girl. A beaming bride on Meier's arm. An older couple, hands clasped, in front of a mountain chalet.

How would Meier feel if someone hunted down his loved ones like they were animals?

A click interrupted his musings as Meier entered. "*Hauptmann* Engel, I'm surprised to see you here. You made your decision quite clear the last time we spoke."

"I want to apologize for that. I was out of line for speaking in such a manner. I am flattered by the offer. What I would like to know, before I give my final answer, is a little bit more about the position."

Meier stared at him for a long minute, his green eyes hard. "Why?"

Horst squirmed under the scrutiny, taking a long drag on his smoke. "My father would be disappointed if I didn't at least hear you out."

"You want to appease your father? That is why you are here? But I heard your argument with him. You sounded like your mind was pretty much made up."

Horst steadied his breath. Meier had cut through his façade fast enough. "You may yet be able to convince me this is the best move for me." He offered Meier a cigarette.

The man sat behind the metal desk and accepted, pressing his thin lips around the roll of tobacco. "Don't flatter me. Your little sniveling visit here isn't impressing me. You were foolish to turn down the offer, but brave enough to say so to my face. Now that you're afraid of your father, you come groveling. Go back to him. You aren't worthy to be an officer in the German army."

Chapter Sixteen

*H*orst's heart hammered in his throat as he made his way across Theresienstadt's ghetto in search of David. His meeting with Meier had not gone the way he'd hoped. The man was too perceptive, something Horst hadn't counted on. How foolish to think he could waltz into that office and not have Meier see right through him.

He thumped his head. From now on, he had to watch his every step. He couldn't afford to be so careless.

The sights and smells of the place no longer assaulted him the way they had on his first few visits. He had become desensitized to the eye-watering odor of decaying flesh, the stomach-churning smell of excrement. It must be the same for everyone. How could a man work here without hardening his soul? How could anyone survive here without shutting out the worst of the suffering?

That must be why the Nazis demanded the orchestra practice and perform. For a little while, they could all erase what they had become or what was happening to them. The way the music allowed his mother to forget. Him to forget. Anna to forget.

The early spring chill seeped through his heavy wool coat. How had Theresienstadt's residents born the awful cold with their thin clothes in their unheated living spaces? He shivered, not entirely because of the weather.

The full orchestra played tonight. If David were among the performers, it would make it easier to locate him and less conspicuous to talk to him. This time, Horst didn't sit in a seat up front but leaned against the wall in the back of the concrete former warehouse. The masses huddled together, most likely glad for the reprieve from the icy wind.

Oberleutnant Meier entered, and Horst slunk farther into the corner. Maybe the man wouldn't notice him. From the arrogant tilt of his chin to the way he strode toward the best chair in the front, he hadn't.

Horst picked David from the group of musicians. He had lost weight and coughed more than the last time Horst visited. For any plan to work, they needed to act as soon as possible, before David's condition worsened.

The conductor stepped to the front and the music began. Horst relaxed and lost himself in Beethoven's *Fourth Symphony*.

All too soon, the performance ended. The crowd cheered. All except for the Germans in attendance. They turned a cool shoulder to their prisoners and left in much the same haughty manner as they entered.

The room emptied little by little. Horst waited until almost everyone had left before approaching David. He tried to make his way up front in as casual a manner as possible. Even so, his stomach jumped in his midsection.

The ideas fell together like parts of an auto. What he was about to undertake was as risky as it got. He stopped and scribbled something on a scrap of paper.

But, if his plan succeeded, the payoff would be as big as they came.

"Engel, what are you still doing here?"

Horst jumped as if a gun went off next to his head. He spun around. Meier strode down the aisle. "The orchestra enticed me."

"For that, you are easily enticed. It makes me wonder about you. I come back for the handkerchief I left and find you moving to the front. Toward the Jews."

"I thought I saw a Guarneri violin. One of the most prized makers in the world. I meant to inquire where a Jew would get an instrument like that."

"And now you are a musical instrument expert?"

"I know enough."

"You would recognize one?"

"As you stated, I'm not an expert. But I might."

"Who has it?"

A dribble of sweat rolled down Horst's back. What now? Would pointing out a specific player send them to their death? He fingered the piece of paper in his pocket before nodding in David's direction.

Meier waved his hand. "You there, come here. And bring your instrument."

The wide-eyed young man's hands shook as he made his way forward. Horst prayed he didn't own a Guarneri violin.

Meier glared at Anna's brother. "Who is the maker of that instrument?"

Horst held his breath.

"I don't know, sir."

Meier smacked him across the face.

Horst flinched.

"Don't be impertinent. Tell me who made it."

David swallowed hard. "It isn't labeled. Possibly German, that's all I know."

"A professional with a violin of unknown origin. You want me to believe it?"

David nodded. "My better one was confiscated. This is the one I was given to play when I arrived here."

Horst stepped forward. "Permit me, *Oberleutnant* Meier, to have a look."

David passed him the violin. As they made the swap, Horst pressed the piece of paper into David's hand. Closing one eye, he peered through the F hole. He stood. "Have a look for yourself, *Oberleutnant* Meier. No label. If it had been a Guarneri, it would have had one. He was one of the most consistent label makers of all time."

Meier inspected the instrument himself. Satisfied at last, he returned the violin to David. "You may go." Once Anna's brother shuffled away, Meier turned to Horst. "I don't ever want to see you here again. You have no business in this place. If I discover you, I will have to assume you have some nefarious business and will have you arrested. Is that clear?"

"Perfectly."

Too perfectly clear.

Anna tucked the blanket around *Babička*'s shoulders and kissed her wrinkled cheek. "Have a good nap." Since the incident with her heart, *Babička* was more tired and spent most of the afternoon resting.

"Thank you, *beruško*. You are a good girl. But isn't it a bit chilly in here? I could use another blanket."

Even with winter departing and spring entering, *Babička* couldn't get warm. They hadn't been as cold this year because of *Hauptmann* Engel. The Germans made sure he had heat, unlike the Jews, who were forbidden from purchasing coal. She opened the wardrobe's door and dug out the heavy quilt from the bottom. As she did so, something clattered to the floor.

She picked up the little tin train with a string to pull it across the room. It was old, the paint chipped in several places. Well worn. Well loved.

Still shoved in here.

She closed her eyes, trying to shut out the child's cries and those of his parents. Where were they? What had happened to them? *Lord, don't let them have met the same fate as Máma and Táta.*

Hauptmann Engel told her he'd found it in the flat and hid it in the cabinet. Did he have a heart? Did he wonder about the boy who spent many happy hours playing with this toy? Perhaps he'd had a train like this that he loved as a child.

How could people be so cruel? She didn't understand what made them turn their backs on the good and do evil.

She picked up the train and fingered the small smokestack, spun one of the wheels.

"What do you have there?"

Anna turned. "The little boy who lived here left it behind. *Hauptmann* Engel discovered it and stored it in here."

Babička smiled. "Your uncle had one like that as I recall. He loved it. All day long he pulled it behind himself. The clatter almost drove me crazy. I would tell him to put it away and five minutes later, he would have it out again. What I would give to have him pulling that thing around the flat once more."

Babička's son, Anna's uncle, went to America eight years ago, and *Babička* hadn't seen him since. "Do you wish you would have emigrated with Uncle Ivan? He perceived what was coming, felt the undercurrents, the rumblings of persecution, and didn't want to take any chances. He ran when he could. Do you think you should have gone, too?"

"You can look back on your life and wish you had made different decisions, or you can look at the here and now and thank the Lord for what He has given you."

Anna set the toy on the bedside table and covered *Babička* with the red and blue quilt. "I don't want the philosophical answer. I want your heart answer."

Babička worried the edge of the coverlet. "That is a difficult question."

"I wish we would have."

"Don't you remember? At the time, you didn't want to. You cried to your parents and you cried to me about how much you would miss your friends and how you wouldn't be able to speak the language and not be able to go to the conservatory to study when you got old enough."

Yes. Anna had been a stubborn teenager who wanted her way, pouting for months until *Máma* and *Táta* dropped the idea. She sat down hard on the bed, almost on top of *Babička*'s legs. "It was my fault they didn't go. They would be alive if not for me."

"*Ne*, not at all. They weren't swayed by your theatrics."

"Then why didn't they leave?"

"It isn't the easiest thing to pick up your life and everything you've ever known and move to a different country. There is a new language to learn, a new culture to adapt to. Though your uncle insisted it wasn't the case, they were convinced that what was happening in Germany would never affect them.

"They enjoyed a comfortable life here. Czechoslovakia was prosperous, and they benefited from that good fortune. Your father had an excellent job as head of the accounting department with Škoda autos.

The city teemed with musicians, artists, philosophers, and they wanted to be a part of the vibrancy that was Prague. They weren't ready to leave it behind."

"I wish they would have gone. We could be together now. What a different life we would have had."

"But it wasn't the one God wanted for us. You're dwelling on things you can't change. Focus on what you can."

Anna fussed with the covers. "Have a good nap." She shut the bedroom door behind her. Yes, *Babička* spoke the truth. God had a different plan for them. But her heart railed against that. Why couldn't His plan have been for them to go to America?

Too many questions today that didn't have answers. Too much that left her frightened and confused.

She lifted the violin case's lid and stroked the silky tiger-maple wood. The instrument laughed with her and cried with her. In her hands, it came alive. She came alive.

Images flashed in front of her. America's big farms, grain waving in the breeze. Palm trees on sandy beaches, the scent of salt in the air. Its bustling cities and skyscrapers reaching to the heavens. A land flowing with milk and honey.

She slammed the lid shut. Perhaps she would go lay down with *Babička*. She couldn't look out of the window, couldn't even walk around much or turn on the lights.

"Why, *Máma*? Why, *Táta*? Why did you leave me? Why couldn't we be together? God, why was all of this in Your will?"

Yes, she was living in the past, trying to change things she couldn't. But how did you let go of all you loved?

Then someone knocked. She held her breath. *Go away. Please, go away.*

The sound came again, this time accompanied by an insistent whisper. "Anna. Anna, open up."

"Jakub?" She tiptoed to the door.

"Yes, it's Jakub. Let me in before someone sees me."

She undid the lock, and he slipped inside.

"What are you doing here?"

"That's a nice way to greet a friend." He dropped a peck on her cheek. He'd been sweet on her for a long time, but she didn't share his views the way David did. "It's dangerous for you to be here."

"Thank you for pointing that out." He rubbed his head, his black hair wilder than ever. "I came to see you one last time."

"One last time?"

He offered her a crooked smile, but his hazel eyes held no trace of laughter. "For now, anyway."

"But you're a member of the Jewish council. You have an important job. They can't send you away."

"It seems that I've worked myself out of a position."

"That's impossible, *ne*?"

"The Germans have managed to cleanse Prague of almost all its Jews. It is a racially pure city, just like they wanted."

She clutched the back of the sofa. "No more Jews? That can't be."

"I'm sure there are some in hiding. That is why you have to be more careful than ever. You cannot be seen on the streets, no matter what. You can't use the excuse of not getting your deportation notices anymore."

A lump developed in the back of Anna's throat, and she swallowed it away. Jakub's friendship with David had caused a rift in their family, but she couldn't deny he had been good to them, keeping her and *Babička* off the deportation lists for as long as he did.

"Is there a message you want me to bring to David?"

Her day brightened. "Oh yes, would you? Wait a moment." She scampered to *Hauptmann* Engel's little desk and drew out a sheet of paper and a pen.

Jakub followed her. "You can't write one. If the Nazis find it, they will know I had contact with you. They would—"

She interrupted him with a wave of her hand. "I'm sorry. I didn't think."

He spun her to face him, his eyes and cheeks hollow. "You have to promise me that from now on you will think. Think about every little move you make, every little word you say. Don't do anything without thinking. Taking a moment to ponder the consequences might save your life and your grandmother's."

"Oh, Jakub."

He opened his arms, and she stepped into his embrace, tears flowing down her face. At this moment, the family differences didn't matter. Besides her grandmother, he was her last link to the past. Her last link to a way a life that was lost forever. She spoke into his age-softened shirt. "Tell David that I love him. That I miss him so much it hurts. Be sure he knows that we're well and safe. Tell him that we pray for him without ceasing."

Jakub stroked her hair. "I'm sure that will be a comfort to him."

"And we'll pray for you, too, Jakub. We'll pray that you are able to stay off the transport lists there. And that you will know God's peace."

Before all of this, Jakub would have objected to such religious sentiments. Today, he didn't. Perhaps God was softening his heart. Perhaps God would soften David's heart as well.

She had to say good-bye to him. To all of them.

"Anna."

She hadn't heard the flat's door click open.

Hauptmann Engel stood just inside, thunder breaking across his face. He clenched his fists. Commanded her in German. "I demand to know who this man is and why he's in my apartment."

Blood whooshed through her ears. She couldn't formulate a sentence if her life depended on it.

Did it?

Chapter Seventeen

$\mathcal{P}$atricie opened the door to her little flat and a gust of spring wind ushered in *Hauptsturmführer* Jaeger. He wore his finest dress uniform, jet black with a red armband, a silver eagle on the right breast, and a white bow tie around his neck.

Now that she'd stopped working for the resistance, there was no reason why he shouldn't come here. She had tired of making up excuses to keep him away, even though she now broadcast her status as a Nazi girlfriend.

She steeled herself.

He kissed her cheek as he entered, his lips cold. "Hello, my little bird. You look lovely tonight."

She smoothed her red dress over her stomach. "Always good to see you." The lie tasted bitter on her tongue.

"Why do you never seem to mean that?"

She took out her best smile and put it on. "I don't know what you're talking about. I always anticipate your arrival, counting down the days until you come for me." That much was the truth.

"But you are so sad."

Sad because she missed her work and hated herself for what she had become. "If that is the case, there is one thing you can do to cheer me."

"Name it."

"Take me to the store and buy me a new coat." The words slipped unrehearsed from her lips, but as they did, she formulated a plan. She might as well get all she could from him, not for herself, but for the Jews in hiding. Perhaps at some point, all of it would come in handy. Maybe one of these days, she could be useful again.

He tipped his head and studied her as if seeing her with fresh eyes. "You have never asked for anything before."

"There is a first time, isn't there? But if I'm to be seen around the city with you, shouldn't I look the part? You can hardly bring me to parties and concerts when I'm frumpy. Please?"

He shrugged. "Whatever you wish. Tomorrow, we shall go. Tonight, it is time for a concert. Are you ready?"

She made great show of slipping on her truly threadbare red coat, her black peep-toes, and a pair of stained white gloves. He glanced at her hands.

"I'll keep them in my pockets."

"Perhaps we will need to add those to the shopping list." He escorted her from the building to the car waiting at the curb. While she didn't deserve to enjoy the good things that came her way because of her relationship with him, she couldn't help but be glad for the warm, comfortable automobile.

They arrived at Smetana Hall in plenty of time to get to their seats. The majestic, domed glass ceiling rose above them, taking her breath away. She stared at it for many long moments. "It's truly amazing."

"Have you never been here?"

She focused her gaze on her feet. "A few times. I even played here once. But the sight of it never ceases to fill me with wonder."

"I thought this would have been your second home."

"You know we didn't have the money for it."

"How did you afford the conservatory, then?"

"A scholarship. Without it, I would have been working in the same shop as my father long ago. It's a shame the school closed before I graduated. Perhaps I would be playing with the symphony tonight." She itched to hold her instrument, the wood smooth and the metal keys cool beneath her fingers. To have the music flow from her heart and over her once more. After all this, could she go back there?

"And you should be. If you would excuse me a moment." He rose and crossed the room to where another German officer sat. They had a brief discussion before *Hauptsturmführer* Jaeger returned to his seat.

"Who was that?"

"*Hauptmann* Horst Engel. I've gotten to know him since his father bought a comfortable position for him here as head of architectural preservation or some such ridiculous nonsense. Most of us joined the military to protect our families and our Fatherland. We had to work very hard to rise through the ranks. His father, for whom he doesn't care, handed his position to him on a silver platter."

"You sound like you don't like him."

"He didn't earn his title, nor does he deserve it."

"I will take that to mean that you don't."

"*Ne*, I don't. He was only here for a few weeks before a senior official at Theresienstadt offered him a lucrative post there with the power and prestige to match. That man told me *Hauptmann* Engel's father had a hand in that, too."

"A post which you would have loved to have been yours."

"And I wouldn't have turned it down the way Engel did. He is ungrateful, snobbish, and a disgrace to the German forces."

"He declined? Why?" Not that it mattered one way or another about the man, but it was curious. Most Nazis she had the misfortune to encounter jumped at any chance for advancement.

"That's the mystery. Then that same ranking official told me Horst came back a few weeks ago asking for more information about the position even though he had no intention of accepting it. Later, he found him ready to speak to members of the Jewish orchestra there."

Hauptsturmführer Jaeger had told her before that those musicians deported to Terezín were allowed, and more likely commanded, to play for the Germans. But she couldn't believe that an officer would take an interest in those who played.

"And it wasn't the first time he went there. Apparently, he keeps showing up on concert nights."

Patricie folded her hands and crossed her legs, trying to keep from glancing at this *Hauptmann* Engel. Why did he take such a keen interest in the Jews? Did he have some connection to them?

"I tried to take him under my wing and show him how to behave as a German officer in Prague. One day, I went to his flat, and discovered a woman there."

"That's unusual?"

A muscle in his jaw twitched. Had she spoken out loud?

"The young woman was jumpy and uneasy when I questioned her."

"You do have something of an intimidating presence." She well knew it.

"She claimed to be the maid, but she had dark looks. Not Aryan, that's for sure."

"What do you mean?"

"I mean that I think *Hauptmann* Engel is not all that meets the eye."

Patricie shivered and pulled her coat tighter.

Horst sat at his little desk, rubbing his temples for the longest time. The clock ticked away the minutes. If he could only come up with a way to rescue Anna's brother.

Thanks to *Oberleutnant* Meier, he could no longer show his face in Theresienstadt. His going there to see the man had been a terrible mistake. A grave miscalculation. He'd underestimated Meier. His error might cost Anna her brother.

He had planned every little detail of the plot. It was perfect. And now it lay in shambles. He had no ideas. David might be dead already.

He took a drag on his cigarette.

"Horst?"

Anna's voice at his shoulder surprised him. He hadn't heard her come up behind him.

"What?" He didn't mean to be gruff.

"I'm sorry. I interrupted you, *ne?*"

She didn't deserve his harsh treatment. He turned to face her. "*Ne.* It's I who should be sorry. I didn't mean to snap at you."

"You have been out of sorts for a while. Is something wrong?" She searched his eyes with such intensity. "Did *Babička* or I anger you? Are you still upset about Jakub?"

He tapped the ashes off the end of his cigarette. "I was never upset about that."

"You didn't talk to me for days afterward."

How could he explain to her that he was afraid she was in love with the young man in his living room? That it had stirred something new in him, something akin to jealousy? "It wasn't you. I had a difficult meeting. I told you that."

"But something is bothering you."

He hadn't given her details of her brother's illness nor of his plan to help him. It didn't matter anymore at this point. He had to tell her something, though, or she would continue to pester him. "That day, I got a job offer at Theresienstadt."

"You didn't tell me about it." Her tight, quiet words pierced him. "When do you leave? When do we leave?"

"We're not going there. None of us. I turned it down."

"Because of us?"

"Yes, and because the tens of thousands of others like you there. I was offered the head of deportation. I would have sent who knows how many Jews to the extermination camps."

She wiped her hands on her navy dress sprigged with yellow flowers, his favorite, the one that just skimmed her knees. "And you turned it down?"

He stood and held her at arm's length, her shoulder muscles taut under his fingers. "Of course I did. I didn't even have to think about it for a moment. I could never take such a position. If I had to send even one Jew, one person like you, to that miserable place, I would never be able to sleep at night again. It would kill me."

Her muscles relaxed, and her brown eyes swam with tears. She blinked them away and licked her lips. "I'm glad you didn't take the offer."

"It's good to know at least one person is happy about it. *Vater* was there to surprise me and congratulate me. Instead, we engaged in a screaming match. I'd be happy to never speak to him again."

"Your father?"

Her teary eyes broadcast her longing for her father. And here he was, not wishing to reconcile with his. "He's not the kind of man you want for a father. Or a role model. Or an acquaintance, either. I will leave it up to God to judge him, but that doesn't mean I have to speak to him."

"I'm sorry." She worried the edge of her red shawl. "Did you take us in to spite him?"

"What? *Ne.* Not even close. That's too dangerous of a game to play. I did it out of . . . well, out of compassion for my fellow human beings. I couldn't stand it if you became like the people I saw at Theresienstadt."

"It's that bad?"

Why did he have to bring that up? He should seal his lips and never utter another word. "I didn't mean to upset you."

She broke down in tears, in silent weeping for all she lost. He could do nothing to erase her hurt, so he swept her into his embrace and held her as she grieved. "Anna, if only I could ease your suffering. If I could just bring your family back to you. Stop this madness and restore the world to the way it should be."

He stroked her back and whispered into her hair. She nestled into the crook of his arm. Yes, if only . . .

A pounding at the door interrupted them. "Horst, it's Stefan."

Anna wriggled from his arms and raced, sobbing, to the bedroom where her grandmother napped.

He swallowed hard and ushered in Stefan. "What brings you to this neighborhood?"

"Rather fitting that they billet you on the edge of the Jewish quarter."

What did Stefan mean? Did he have a clue about the women in his flat? "A cup of coffee for you?"

Stefan shook his head. "I thought I saw you through the curtain embracing a woman."

He would have to get heavier drapes. Immediately. "You are mistaken."

"The little maid you have hired, perhaps?"

"Why on earth would I hug my help?"

"That is my question." Stefan tugged off his gloves and laid his hat on the table beside the sofa before taking a seat and crossing one leg over his knee. He didn't remove his shoes, an insult to the Czech people. "Never mind. It's none of my business what happens in your personal life. Actually, I've come with an offer. I'm going to Theresienstadt tomorrow and wondered if you would like to ride with me."

What a wonderful opportunity. Perhaps all was not lost when it came to David. Then Horst's excitement crashed to the floor. "I'm afraid I can't. The last time I was there to speak to *Oberleutnant* Meier, I angered him. He forbade me from returning."

"What in the name of goodness did you say to earn the man's ire?"

Horst paced back and forth in front of Stefan. How much should he share? How much did Stefan already know? "I didn't make a very good impression on him. He thinks I'm young and soft."

A glint flared in Stefan's cool blue eyes, and he rubbed his chin. "That is where I can help you. You don't even have to go to Theresienstadt. I have a way you can prove to him that there is much more to you than he realizes. That you truly are a man and worthy of a German officer's uniform."

A way to redeem himself? Horst clasped his hands together. Stefan knew too much. Perhaps suspected what Horst was up to. But he couldn't turn down his superior officer. He ignored the fluttering in his stomach. "Tell me what time I need to be ready."

Then, from the bedroom, came the crashing and shattering of a dish on the floor.

Horst clutched his head. Screams impaled his memory. Weeping, wailing, and splintering glass. Broken windows littering the sidewalks, sparkling in the streetlights. The brown coats dragging away Herr Feldman, the gentle, old Jewish clockmaker. Horst's neighbor.

He'd passed many hours in that shop, the owner telling him stories of magic watches and fairy timekeepers. Herr Feldman fed him sausages and kuchen. And those wretches had held Horst's friend by the coat collar, thrown him in the back of a truck, and sped off down the narrow street, the petrol fumes sickening Horst.

He shouldn't have been there.

He shouldn't have thrown the first rock.

Stefan jumped to his feet, flinging Horst back to the present. "Who is here?"

Chapter Eighteen

*A*nna slipped into the room she shared with *Babička* and shut the door behind her with as little noise as possible. Her grandmother sat in bed reading the same book she probably read ten times before. Anna leaned against the door and wiped the tears from her cheek.

"What on earth is wrong, *beruško*?"

She shushed her. "That same officer who saw me before is back." She didn't dare say more, even in a whisper. And that was fine. Right now, she wasn't sure she could explain her feelings. They tumbled and jumbled inside of her. Horst had been gentle with her, kind and caring. For a moment, they weren't enemies.

She couldn't allow her heart to rule her head, no matter what her heart said. If she lost favor with him again, as she did when he'd caught her in Jakub's arms, he might turn on them and send them to Terezín without a second thought.

But the way he'd caressed her back and spoken to her. For that one tiny moment, she was safe, protected, cared for in a way she hadn't been since *Máma* and *Táta* walked into that exhibition hall. Yes, she had *Babička* here with her, but she was responsible for her grandmother. In that moment, Horst had lifted that burden and cared for her.

It took a few minutes, but she managed to compose herself and still her trembling hands. The male voices floated under the door, but not loud enough so she could make out the words.

Babička went back to reading. Anna stood straight, then picked up her embroidery. The sampler she stitched helped to pass the time. She included different Czech patterns, brilliant primary colors against a black background. Flowers, scrolls, leaves. Today, she worked on adding her family member's names and the dates of their births and deaths. Here in the back of the flat, though, not much sun filtered in.

The drapes remained drawn to hide Anna and *Babička*'s presence, but a small bit of light filtered through the crack between the panels, providing a little more illumination. She grabbed the chair to move it from the bedside. When she did so, her hip bumped the small table where her grandmother kept a glass of water.

The glass tipped, then fell, rolled off the table and onto the floor, and shattered at Anna's feet.

"Who is here?"

Anna froze, holding her breath at *Hauptsturmführer* Jaeger's mighty roar. Did he hear the way her heart banged against her ribcage?

Had she just given them all away?

"Only my maid. She must have dropped something while dusting." Horst's voice didn't waver.

Anna released her breath, a tiny amount at a time.

"How can you allow such a clumsy woman to work for you? Tell her to come here."

Anna folded her hands, said a quick prayer for protection, then scurried to the living room. "*Hauptmann* Engel, I do apologize. I am sorry. As I dusted the night stand in your room, I tipped over your glass, and it broke. Please, you can take it out of my salary. It won't happen again." She stared at the floor.

"And you better believe that I will. Double the worth of the glass will be taken from your pay to teach you a lesson." The man who'd caressed her back and whispered such comforting words, so sweet a few minutes before, had changed into an angry bear, his eyes narrowed, the muscles in his jaw tight.

"What was your name again?" *Hauptsturmführer* Jaeger's booming voice filled the room.

She didn't look at the other officer, though he asked her the question. "Anna Kostachek."

"Fraulein Kostachek, where do you come from?"

"A small town to the east of here. I'm sure you never heard of it."

"Now you have me curious. I'd like to know."

Why was *Hauptsturmführer* Jaeger interrogating her? With her dark looks, did he have an inkling of her true identity?

Horst stood between her and *Hauptsturmführer* Jaeger. "Really, Stefan, she is nothing more than a maid. As I told you before, I checked her identity before I hired her. She is of no consequence. Now, I'm sure you have business you must get to if you are to be away all day tomorrow, as do I. Let me show you out."

He nodded to Anna, and she again scampered to the bedroom. As she left, *Hauptsturmführer* Jaeger's loud words reached her. "It's very odd to me, Horst. Your little maid intrigues me. Her looks. And the fact that she speaks perfect German. Like all of Prague's Jews. Are you sure you did a thorough investigation? Perhaps I should call in my sources."

How could she have been so stupid? German. Why didn't she speak to him in Czech? Why let on that she understood him? What had she done?

"No need for that, no need at all. She is clean, from top to bottom."

But Anna went cold all over when Horst's voice cracked.

He was nervous.

And she should be, too.

Stefan led Horst through the streets of Prague. The late spring sunshine filtered through the trees' leaves. Birds called and sang to each other over the hustle and bustle of the city. Horst never tired of this place. When he'd come here as a young man before the war, it had hummed with life. Intellectuals. Musicians. Artists of all kinds.

Though his fellow Germans worked hard to preserve the cultural heart of this city, without the Jews, it didn't possess the same vibrancy. It lost its soul. Gone were the thinkers, the painters, and the violinists. The coffee shops and restaurants no longer teemed with philosophers arguing with each other over the meaning of life. The streets were no longer home to artists who labored to capture the city's majesty on canvas. The performance halls no longer rang with music.

But the city trudged forward. The streetcar rang its bell as it glided down the road next to the people. Housewives grasped their coupon books in one hand and their children in the other and made their way to the market. Men in business suits hurried to their offices and shops.

Stefan rubbed his hands. "Nothing could be finer than a bright, warm day. I have a mind to take a long weekend and go to the mountains. Have you ever been?"

"*Ja*, I've been skiing there. I'm from Bayern, remember, the skiing capital of the Reich. *Mutti* didn't care for it much, but *Vater* and I did." The sport was the one thing he had in common with the man who had raised him.

"Then come with me. We can lift a pint and celebrate your victory."

"Victory? What do you have in mind for me? I wish you would share a detail or two at least." Horst fingered the pistol Stefan had insisted he bring along. His mouth went dry. What could it be for?

"All in good time. Don't rush ahead of me. I decided to walk today because the fresh air enlivens me. We get caught behind our desks and don't enjoy the outdoors as we should. Such a shame. The Führer recommends exercise. It's good for the body and the brain."

Horst tuned out Stefan's idle chatter as they left behind the commercial district and headed to a more residential area of the city. Through his work, Horst had become familiar with Prague's neighborhoods, but he didn't remember being here before. Paint peeled from the doors and shutters of the small, dingy windows overlooking the street.

Stefan made his way down the walk, a spring in his step. Gone was the hard, dark man of yesterday, replaced with an exuberant child. Horst trudged behind him.

"We're almost there now. Are you ready? It is time to prove yourself." They stopped in front of a nondescript home. Chunks of the faded, yellow paint were missing. Curtains covered the cracked window. A flowerpot sporting dead roses sat on the front stoop.

"Do you have your weapon?"

Horst nodded. He couldn't speak. Stefan's plan came into focus.

"We have reason to believe there are Jews hiding in this house. A truck is waiting for us around the corner. The driver will be here in a moment. We are going to break into the home and search it for Jews. Any we find, we must arrest. Do not be afraid to use force. In fact, it would impress *Oberleutnant* Meier even more if you did. Are my instructions clear?"

A chill raced through Horst. His stomach tightened. How could he rip people from their homes? He couldn't do this. He'd already done it to the family who'd occupied his flat before him. He closed his eyes. His mother's face the morning after Kristallnacht floated before him. Her pain. Her disappointment.

There is neither Jew nor Greek.

Stefan waited for acknowledgment.

What would Anna think if she found out?

What would God think?

Horst shoved those musings aside. He nodded.

Stefan led the way to the entry. He pounded and shouted. "Open up. Open up." Without giving the occupants time to respond, he kicked in the door.

Horst followed. "Papers. Let me see everyone's papers." A stall tactic. A chance for any Jews here to get into hiding.

What would he do if the Gestapo broke into his flat this way? Anna and her grandmother would never get into their tucked-away spot in time. They'd made it before with not a second to spare.

He came upon a middle-aged woman in the front room. Fine lines etched the areas around her eyes and mouth, her face calm and serene. She nodded at his command, opened a drawer in an old rolltop desk, and produced what he demanded.

Horst took his time examining the identification booklet, pretending to go over every detail. Her credentials were impeccable. He handed them back to her.

Stefan stood behind him. "Never mind about those. We're looking for the Jews." The hardness returned to his voice. "I can smell them. I know they are here. It's up to you, *Hauptmann* Engel, to find them."

He balled his fists to keep his fingers from trembling. "Everything appears to be in order."

"Search the house." Stefan's booming command gave Horst a jump start. He had to comply with the demand.

If anyone's here, keep them well hidden, Lord.

He rummaged through the kitchen cabinets and the wardrobes. He got down on his knees and peered under the beds. He tapped on walls and listened for any points that might be hollow.

"*Nein, nein*, that's not the way to investigate." Stefan pulled a bookcase from the wall in the living room. "They build secret rooms and hide the entrances behind furniture."

"*Ja*, I see." Horst didn't want Stefan to do any more searching. To keep him from looking, Horst climbed the stairs and moved the bureau in the bedroom. He gasped, then covered his mouth to keep his comrade from hearing.

In the wall, a door. He had stumbled upon just what Stefan hunted for.

"Get me a glass of water." Stefan ordered the woman about. Good. He was distracted downstairs.

Horst pushed the door opened. Five wide-eyed Jews huddled together in a corner of the tiny room. One of the women held a baby to her breast, rocking as much as she could in the crowded space. A gray-haired woman clasped her husband's hand.

Here was his chance to prove himself. To raise himself in *Oberleutnant* Meier's esteem. To earn the respect of his superiors. To demonstrate that he was a good officer.

There is neither Jew nor Greek.

The echoes of *Mutti*'s voice rang in his head. "You know what's right, Horst."

Oh, God, do I know? How do I choose?

"Engel, what are you doing up there? Find those Jews and bring them to me."

Before he could answer, the infant ceased nursing and let out a mighty wail.

Chapter Nineteen

N *ein, God, nein!*

"Hush it." Horst spat the words at the Jewish woman holding the baby.

She stared at him with stricken eyes as she covered her child's mouth. The group closed ranks, their faces pale.

A moment later, boots sounded on the stairs.

A noose-like tightness gripped Horst's throat. He shut the door and shoved the wardrobe into position.

"What do we have here?"

He turned as Stefan strode across the room. A half-grin brightened his face. "Good work, Engel. I think you found them."

Not good work at all. The worst work he could have done. He struggled to take a breath.

While Horst stood still, unable to do anything to stop him, Stefan pushed the piece of furniture away and exposed the door. Jaeger rubbed his hands together as if he were about to eat a plate of beef rouladen. "Open it." He barked the command, a wolf who had found his prey.

Heaven forgive him.

Horst pulled open the door and exposed its terrified residents. The infant screamed as his mother squeezed him.

Stefan slapped Horst on the back. "Well done. I didn't think you had it in you, but you proved yourself. Fine job." He brandished his weapon and pulled out the old couple, the woman with the child, and a young man, probably no more than eighteen. "Bring them downstairs."

Though he had no intention of using it, Horst pulled his revolver from its holster and herded the people out of the bedroom. His hand sweated so much, the weapon almost slipped from his grasp.

His actions just condemned five people to very uncertain fates. The only one the camps had use for was the teenager. The rest didn't stand a chance.

They filed down the stairs into the living room. The old man limped, his legs stiff, and he had a difficult time keeping up with the rest of the group. Stefan turned, his eyebrows crunched together. "Get him moving."

"*Schnell, schnell.*" Horst gave the man a small push to speed him on his way. Not a big thrust, nothing hard, simply a nudge.

But the aging man tottered, stumbled, and fell. Horst bent down and grasped the man by his hand.

Stefan shoved his way around the group and back to Horst. "What are you doing? You don't help people like him."

Jaeger raised his pistol and shot. The man crumpled. His wife screamed.

Horst went numb. His nightmare came to life.

Stefan snickered. "Get in the truck. Engel, do your job."

He nodded. Like a wooden soldier, he moved his charges along, out into the warm, bright light, into the truck spitting diesel fumes. The teen helped the two women aboard.

Stefan brought the woman of the house out at gunpoint and dumped her into the vehicle as well. "We'll send someone to arrest her husband at his office." He went around to speak to the driver.

Horst stared unblinking at the group of people huddled together on one bench, tears streaming down the women's faces, the baby inconsolable. "I'm sorry," he mouthed. And he was sorrier than he had ever been in his entire life.

He had turned into his father.

Patricie wasn't at all surprised to open the door and find *Hauptsturm-führer* Jaeger on the other side. He waltzed over the threshold, never waiting for her to invite him, never removing his shoes. She steeled herself as he placed a peck on her cheek.

He thrust out a package. "For you. I want you to get dolled up because we are going out on the town tonight. The woman at the shop said this was all the fashion and assured me it would fit. Go put it on. *Schnell*. I don't want to wait too long."

She didn't have a chance to say a word. Though she suffered a low-grade headache, she couldn't refuse him. Instead, she headed to her bedroom and opened the box.

Despite herself, she gasped when she pulled away the tissue paper. Inside lay a silky yellow dress, tucked and fitted in all the right places. She was almost afraid to touch it. When she did, it was like butter under her fingers, so smooth it was.

She undressed, then slipped the new creation over her head. It fit to perfection, the hem brushing her knees, the neckline gracing her collarbone. She gave herself a second look in the mirror and spun around. Could she be gorgeous, even?

Only an important man could get such a garment. Where had the silk come from? What had he done to procure it?

"Are you ready yet?"

"You have to give a woman a few minutes." She fixed her hair, applied a bit of make-up, her lipstick tube almost empty, and slid on her best, but still scuffed, black peep-toe shoes.

When she emerged, he raked his gaze over her. "The saleslady was right. It's like it was made for you. You look lovely."

Her headache disappeared. She flashed him a genuine smile before floating down the stairs and into the car. "Where are we going?"

"There is a reception for German diplomats this evening. When I first received the invitation, I didn't think I would attend. But I'm in the mood for celebrating tonight."

They merged onto the almost-deserted street. Between the black-outs and gas rationing, very few drove their cars anymore. "Why are you in such high spirits?"

"A good day at the office, you might say."

"And what constitutes a good day at the office?"

"The streets are safer for you now, my little bird, the city cleaner than this morning. Doing my job and doing it well makes me happy. And seeing other people prove their worth."

She forced herself to close her mind to what he did. Otherwise, she would go crazy. "I've never been to an elegant occasion like this."

"Then you are in for a treat."

Darkness bathed the residence as they pulled up to it. No lights shone from the windows, the black-out curtains drawn. But once she stepped inside, another world emerged. Chandeliers blazed and gilded mirror frames and wall sconces gleamed.

Waiters in tails and white gloves passed hors d'oeuvres while waitresses in white caps and black dresses presented silver trays loaded with champagne glasses. *Hauptsturmführer* Jaeger took two and offered her one.

"I don't drink, remember?

"But this is a special occasion. I insist. Have just a little bit."

She accepted the glass but didn't sip from it.

An orchestra struck up a waltz and couples twirled around the floor. "Do you dance?"

"I have no objection to it, but I don't do it very well." She shifted her weight.

He downed his bubbly, drank her glass too, then led her onto the ballroom floor. He gripped her around the waist a bit harder than she liked and held her closer than she was comfortable with.

He spun her around until the room swayed as if she had consumed the drink. "You never told me just what we are celebrating."

"My triumph."

"Triumph?"

"Well, perhaps triumph is a bit too strong of a word. How about my success?"

"What were you successful at?"

"Do you remember that night at the symphony, when I spoke to that young officer? I told you he was a disgrace to the Fatherland?"

She nodded. What had *Hauptsturmführer* Jaeger done?

"Well, I had a tip on the location of some Jews."

Patricie sucked in her breath. Which ones? *Dear God, let them not have found any.*

"I took *Hauptmann* Engel with me. I wanted to test his mettle. If he were working against us, he wouldn't have been able to do what I asked of him."

Her queasy stomach churned. She was glad she hadn't imbibed. "What was that?"

"I told him to find the Jews and arrest them. He located them and did just as I instructed. I will admit that I misjudged him. I had to shoot the old man, but all in all, Engel did a fine job."

Patricie's knees went weak, and she clung to him to keep from falling.

Just more evidence that she held a hand stained with innocent blood.

Chapter Twenty

avid paced the tiny Terezín flat, coughing up blood from time to time. He'd burned the paper the German officer had given him within minutes of returning to his room, but the words seared onto his brain. *Be prepared. Zacchaeus.*

That was months ago. *Hauptmann* Engel hadn't come again, hadn't brought him any more news. What did the strange message mean? Be prepared, he understood. Something was going to happen. But what? And when?

And Zacchaeus? That was the strangest part. What did the Bible story have to do with anything?

The aroma of boiled cabbage mingled with the smell of rotting flesh. All that faded into the background as the story of Zacchaeus flooded him.

He had sat at his grandmother's feet, his legs folded underneath him. He recalled her as a beautiful woman, even though gray hair crowned her head. Her green eyes shone. "What Bible lesson shall we have today?"

"Zacchaeus, please, *Babička*. That's my favorite." He loved the rhythm of her voice, like music, as she spun the tales.

She reached down and pulled him to her lap. "That's the story you want every day. Don't you want to hear about Joseph or Paul or Jonah?"

"Anna likes Jonah the best, but I like Zacchaeus."

Babička laughed, the pitch a pure E. "Then Zacchaeus it will be." And she told him about the little man who climbed a tree to see Jesus walk by. Who scrambled down to prepare a feast for the teacher. Who gave his dirty profits back to those from whom he'd stolen them.

"David, are you listening?" *Babička* spoke to get his attention.

"David, are you listening?"

He snapped to reality, the stench of unwashed bodies gagging him. Jan, one of his six roommates, stood in front of him.

"What is it you want?"

"You're mumbling to yourself, calling for your grandmother. Sit down and stop pacing."

"We're caged tigers, made to perform at the whim of our captors."

"Ah, the philosopher speaks." Jan brought him a dipper of dirty water. "I thought you were a musician."

"None of us are anything right now." David sipped the offering.

"True enough. But what were you dreaming about? Or were you hallucinating?"

"Zacchaeus."

"Who?" Jan slapped away the fleas that covered his scrawny body with red bites.

"A Bible story my grandmother told me when I was a child. My favorite."

"Why would she tell you that?"

"She was a Christian."

"Then why doesn't she get you out of this mess?"

"She was also a Jew."

"I'm sorry."

But David wasn't. The memory sparked a tiny flicker inside him. A hunger for all the days his parents and grandparents had spent teaching him about the Lord. His throat swelled, cutting off what little air he could draw into his lungs. If only he could sink to the floor and sob. But here, you couldn't show any sign of weakness. In a life and death struggle such as this, weakness could be your undoing.

"Don't let that mess you up. There is nothing beyond the here and now."

For years, that philosophy had infiltrated David's mind. Wove a web through him. That way of thinking appealed to a young man. Gratify the flesh now. Who knows what tomorrow will bring. There is nothing beyond this life, so enjoy what you have.

The lines etched in his parents' faces had deepened when he'd announced he wouldn't go to church with them anymore, and again when he'd told them he planned to live with Jakub and his friends. All young men who believed what he believed.

Coughs racked David's body, which grew frailer with each passing day. Each miserable, horrible, unbearable day. "What hope is there, then?"

"Only the hope we make ourselves."

"Not much hope at all."

"We'd take you with us if we could, but you'd impede our progress and give us away with your coughing."

David scrunched his eyebrows. "What are you talking about?"

"Gustav, Artur, and I are making plans to get out of here."

"The only way out of here is on a train or in a coffin."

Jan leaned in. "We'll make it. You'll see. I'm sorry to leave you behind."

"You'll never taste freedom. Even if you get out of these gates, what waits for you out there? Nothing better, that's for sure."

"You're a pessimist."

"*Ne*, a realist. What good does deluding ourselves do?"

Shots rang out on the street below. Not an unusual sound. If a prisoner got out of line or couldn't work, the Nazis drew their pistols and rid themselves of the problem. Tonight, though, the sound resonated hollower than ever. Such finality.

"We can't wait for salvation to come from Moses or Jesus or even the Americans. We have to make our own salvation. I'm trusting you with this information, even though you've spoken with that Nazi. I like you. If you betray us, I'll beat you to a pulp myself."

"Your secret is safe with me. That man wanted to help."

"Bah, what help do we want from him? Those pigs are all the same."

David held his tongue. He had no idea what the scrawled message *Hauptmann* Engel had given him meant. If only he could remember more about Zacchaeus's story. But maybe it meant nothing more than to be prepared to be deported. Like *Táta* and *Máma* and his little sisters. Was there a heaven where they were now? If only he could be sure. If only he could speak to them one more time.

As the weeks and months passed, the memory of their voices dimmed. But he heard *Táta* as clearly as if he stood beside him. *You know.* David shivered.

"When is this escape going to happen?" David held up his hand to stop Jan. "Never mind, I don't want to know. Don't tell me any details. If I know nothing, they can't force me to give up anything."

"You play for them. I think they'll keep you around as long as you're able to stand on two feet."

"And that won't be long." Yet another bloody cough punctuated his words.

"Let me get the doctor for you. Maybe he can help."

David waved him away. "He has no medicine, nothing to cure me. Nothing to even make me comfortable. Don't waste your time."

"At least let me see if I can find another blanket around here. Simon Bergmann died last night. Maybe no one claimed his yet." Jan left the stuffy attic room, slamming the door behind him, the entire building shaking.

He returned without one. Someone else had probably snatched it within minutes of Simon's passing.

Salvation. The word from Jan's lips echoed in David's mind. Salvation. Like a long-forgotten flavor on the tongue.

Salvation.

This day is salvation come to this house.

From the story of Zacchaeus.

Is that what *Hauptmann* Engel had meant? Was David's own salvation at hand?

Anna sat in the front room with her knitting. The bright summer light fingered its way into the room, filtering around the curtains they kept drawn. During the day, with Horst gone, she and *Babička* stayed as quiet as possible. *Babička* napped twice a day now. Her health declined. How much longer could she hold on? The hours stretched out long in front of the them.

Her fingers ached to play again. She could do without food and water. She couldn't live without her music.

The flat's walls closed in on her. Summer beckoned with its balmy temperatures and streaming sunshine. Warm rays on her skin. A soft breeze on her cheek. Clean air in her lungs.

Horst came home as she dumped the paprika into the pot for goulash, his boot falls heavy, no whistling as usual. He entered and closed the door as hard as possible. She went to the front hall to greet him. He scowled, his lips tight.

She sucked in her breath. What was wrong? "Hello."

He grunted.

"Dinner is almost ready." She couldn't make him thick bread dumplings. They didn't have much, because he didn't have ration cards for them. He couldn't get them without explaining who they were for. But a little warm goulash would keep their bellies from complaining.

"I'm not hungry. You and your grandmother can eat. Don't bother with me."

"What's wrong?" She trembled. Was he angry with her? Was he going to turn them out?

"I don't want to talk about it. Leave me alone. Just leave me be." His words bounced around the room.

Babička shuffled out. "What a commotion. I thought the Gestapo had come."

Horst softened. "*Ne*, I'm sorry. A bad day. My apologies."

"We all have days like that. Music calms the soul. David played for King Saul." *Babička* nodded. "Not that you're insane, but you are troubled."

"Fine. Let a man get in the door and get his house slippers on."

Anna went to the back bedroom to get her violin for the first time in many weeks. *Babička* followed.

"Why did you say I would play? He's angry with me."

"Not with you. With someone or something, but not with you. I watch him when you play. He enjoys it. His life is hard, Anna."

"And ours isn't? Look at us. Hiding in our enemy's home. Cowering in our room when people stop by. Not able to go outside. And what about David in the camp? His life is much worse than ours. Or think of the horror our family endured before their deaths. Don't tell me his life is hard."

"But it is. Not physically, but in many other ways. We don't know what he's forced to do each day."

"He works for architectural preservation. Not what I would call difficult."

"He's seen things, seen how his people treat ours. Believe it or not, he has a sensitive, gentle soul. The carnage hurts him. And now he has responsibility for us. That's an extra burden on him."

"I'll play for him so that we can have a peaceful evening at home, but I refuse to believe his problems are equal to ours."

Anna grabbed her instrument and marched to the front room. She pulled it from its case, set the case on the couch beside Horst, and plucked the strings to tune. Within a few minutes, strains of Mozart filled the flat.

He sat for a few moments, then rose and paced. He rubbed his chin and his back. He stared at her, his look hard and unreadable. After another circuit of the room, he returned to his seat and scrubbed his face.

She missed a note.

He slammed the case shut. Spoke in German. "Enough. That's enough for tonight. Put it away. I don't want to hear it."

"But—"

"I said enough." He strode across the room and down the hall.

Anna laid her violin on the sofa and turned to *Babička*. "Maybe he's more like King Saul than you thought."

"Go to him."

She turned on her heel. "*Ne.* I won't. Not when he's been short and cross with me, with us, tonight."

"He's scared."

"Scared of what?"

"I don't know. That's what you need to find out. He's here, alone, with no family, no friends. He needs to talk to you."

"He has that friend who came here and almost arrested us."

"That's no friend to him."

"Please, I don't want to."

"Trust me."

"I have trusted you enough, *ne?*" But she had already lost the battle.

"He needs you more than he realizes."

Anna went to his room and rapped on his door. Maybe he wouldn't answer. Maybe he had fallen asleep.

"Come in."

She entered. Feminine touches brightened the space. Doilies on the table. A lace-edged blanket on the bed. Items *Paní* Schniz had left behind. "I'm sorry I upset you."

He sat on the bed, his sketchbook open on his lap. "And I'm sorry I snapped. I didn't mean to. You didn't do anything. This has nothing to do with you."

She caught a glimpse of his drawing. Hard, dark lines. Ghosts of people, their faces drawn and gaunt. Piles of bodies along a road.

Terezín.

Did it bother him? Make him angry? *Babička's* words, the ones that sent her in here, nudged at her. "Do you want to talk about it?"

"Not really." Fine lines radiated from his blue eyes. The creases around his mouth deepened.

"You haven't been sleeping well, have you? I heard you call out the other night."

"*Ne*, I haven't."

"I want to be a friend to you."

"Do you really?"

Did she? He was her enemy. And savior. He could have turned them in more than once. He didn't. Every day, he risked his life for them. What a small thing she could offer to repay him. "Yes, I do."

"You may not like me very much afterward. I want you to trust me, but you may hate me."

"I trust you." And she meant it. "You saved me on the bridge."

"I sent five Jews to their deaths today."

Her knees buckled. She fell to the floor.

Chapter Twenty-One

Horst sprang from the bed and grabbed Anna before she hit her head on the wardrobe. He should never have told her. He wanted to block the entire incident from his mind. Why say the words? "Anna, I'm sorry."

"How could you? We trusted you."

"You can trust me."

"I'm not sure we can. Perhaps our trust was misplaced. Please, don't turn us in."

"I won't."

"Then why did you do it?"

"Sit down." He led her to the small arm chair by the window. "I didn't want to."

"Then why did you?"

"*Hauptsturmführer* Jaeger brought me to a house without telling me why. When we arrived, he ordered me to search the place. I found them. With everything in me, I didn't want to, but I did. Before I slid the door to their hiding spot closed, the baby inside cried. Jaeger heard him. He arrested them."

"You didn't arrest them, then?"

"*Nein.*" He couldn't tell her, wouldn't tell her the rest. The sound of that gunshot would haunt him the rest of his life.

"How can it be your fault?" Her face radiated such innocence. Even after all she'd seen, she exuded naiveté.

"I should have refused orders."

"At the cost of your own life."

"Is my life worth more than theirs? Can you put a price on a human and say one is more valuable than the next?"

"Hitler believes you can."

He paced in front of her. "Hitler is a madman. That's not the way my mother brought me up. My father would agree with Hitler. She would not."

"Why?"

"She is a devout Christian, never wavering in her faith. My father used to be like that. He went to church with us, led our family devotions, told others about the Lord."

"What happened to change him?"

He covered his ears, as if he could blot out the sound of his father's rage. "My brother was the spitting image of my father, not only in looks, but also in temperament, likes, dislikes. Everything. When polio struck, both of us were sick, but I got better. Otto did not."

"But how does that explain his hatred for a certain race of people?"

"Otto's doctor was Jewish. He tried to save my brother, but there was nothing he could do. When Otto died, my father flew into a rage about the man. Lashed out at each and every Jew around him. As if that would bring his son back."

"And that same grief and fury still drives him?"

"*Ja.* Like a car coasting downhill gathers speed, so each year, his hatred only increases. At some point, he will crash."

Anna leaned forward in the chair. "And what about you? What do you say?" She whispered, and he strained to hear her.

He stopped in his tracks. Sending those Jews to their certain deaths made him no better than his father. The question hung in the air. The all-important, all-defining question. Did God create him, a pure Aryan, to be better than the Jews? How about the disabled? The old? *For there is neither Jew nor Greek.* "If you believe the Bible to be true, you have to say no."

"I'm not asking about anyone other than you. Are you better than other people?" Anna fixed her gaze on him, her look boring through him, deep into his soul.

She laid him bare. Exposed him. "*Mutti* taught me better than that. But after Otto died, *Vater* tried to dissuade me from her teaching. From God's teaching."

He knelt in front of her. "You're showing me otherwise, Anna. I used to turn my head away from the horrific acts around me because I couldn't stand the sight of suffering. Now, I've seen it through your eyes. Realized that what repulses me is one human being degraded and defiled by another human. We are all made in God's image."

He'd been so blind, his heart calloused. And he'd been a coward. "I should have done more today, tried harder to save them. Even if it meant my own life."

Anna reached out and caressed his clenched fists until his muscles relaxed, and he opened his palms. "You were in an impossible situation. It's not your fault, what happened. If you hadn't found them today, *Hauptsturmführer* Jaeger may have found them tomorrow. Or located them himself. That baby would have cried and given them away."

"You don't know that." He stood again and rubbed his aching temple. "What could I have done? A thousand different things."

The color in her cheeks heightened. "*Babička* once reminded me we can't live in the past. Ever since my parents and siblings went away, I've wanted to do just that." A sob caught in her throat. She pinched the bridge of her nose, her eyes shining with tears. "But what would it accomplish? It can't bring them back. It can't undo anything I ever did. Wishing you acted in another manner doesn't make it so. That's a lesson I'm trying to learn."

Her words stirred more turmoil in his gut. "Don't torture me." He choked out the sentence.

She rose and touched his shoulder, then down his arm. He shivered. They stood, flesh to flesh. "You are not like your father. God is working in you, showing you right from wrong."

He gathered her to himself, her tiny body warm against his. He whispered into her soft hair. If only he believed her. "Am I? I want to be. I want to please Him."

She leaned back and tipped his head so he stared at her, into her shimmering brown eyes. "If He wasn't contending with you, you wouldn't be torn over what happened today. Do you think *Hauptsturm-führer* Jaeger is sitting at home, wondering if he did the right thing? If he can't sit still because of what he saw?"

"I'm sure he's out celebrating how he broke me and made me into a man. Some kind of man I am."

"Force doesn't make a boy a man. Honesty, compassion, faith. Those turn a child into a grown-up."

Her dark hair framed her thin face. She drew in a ragged breath. He'd never seen a more beautiful creature.

He bent and kissed her.

A knock at the front door. "Engel, I've come to celebrate with you." Stefan.

Horst let go of Anna so fast, she stumbled from his embrace. Her blood whooshed in her ears. "What is *Hauptsturmführer* Jaeger doing here?"

"You heard him. You were right. He thinks my actions today warrant a party. Stay here. I have to answer the door."

After he left, she hugged herself to ward off the chill that raced through her. He'd kissed her. She'd let him kiss her. He opened himself to her and let her see a side of him she doubted anyone else saw. He struggled, and that endeared him to her. She understood his outbursts better. He wasn't upset with her but with himself.

He had to be in a terrible position, knowing the right, and knowing doing the right demanded the ultimate cost. Going to work each day had to be torture.

Would she have done differently? Acted in any other way than he did? *Ne*, she might not have.

Hauptsturmführer Jaeger's jubilant voice carried throughout the flat. Horst answered him in more subdued tones. And then, a woman spoke.

A woman? Who had that man brought with him? Anna crept to the door and listened to as much of the conversation as she could.

"Patricie and I were at a reception for German diplomats. But why should we have all the fun? Come out with us, and let's toast your success today."

"I'm exhausted. Perhaps coming down with a cold. I should stay in and get a good night's sleep." Horst coughed. Rather convincing. "I hope you two enjoy yourselves."

"*Nein*, I insist. There is time for sleeping later. You don't have to go to the office tomorrow, so enjoy the evening. Don't spoil our fun."

"I don't think my staying in will ruin your plans."

"If you're holding back because you don't have a date, bring that little maid of yours along. I know you have a thing for her."

Horst coughed harder. "My maid?"

"Is she here? I want to see her again."

Anna's heart rate kicked up to the level of an Olympic sprinter's.

"What was her name again? Anna, wasn't that it? Anna, Anna, come out here." *Hauptsturmführer* Jaeger slurred his words.

She pressed against the wall. The man pounded down the hall, his jackboots marching out the time. She dared a breath only every ten seconds or so.

"Stefan, really. She's not here. She's gone for the night."

"I can smell her. The scent of a woman. Where is she?" He thundered into the room.

Every muscle in her body tensed. She sweated and shivered at the same time.

He flung back the blanket. "Ah, Engel, I'm disappointed in you. She's not in your bed. Too bad for you. If she's a Jew whore, she'd be great fun."

If she could have melted into the wall, she would have.

Horst entered the room. "You're making a fool of yourself, Jaeger."

"The only fool in the room is you." *Hauptsturmführer* Jaeger whipped around and struck Horst on the cheek.

Anna covered her mouth to keep from crying out.

Horst stepped backward.

In her direction.

Hauptsturmführer Jaeger's eyes widened. "Ah, there she is." He grabbed her and pulled her from her hiding spot. Had he done the same to the other Jews today? He squeezed her upper arm until she bit her lip. "Maybe you were about to have some fun of your own. That's why you didn't want to go out."

Horst laughed. This time, his performance fell flat. "Then why don't you leave us to have our own good time?"

"*Nein*, she can celebrate with us." He wrenched her arm as he pulled her down the hall to the living room.

"*Slečna* Zadoková? What on earth are you doing here?"

Anna froze. The woman used her real name. Her Jewish name.

Hauptsturmführer Jaeger yanked his date to his side. Patricie Kadlecová. An acquaintance from the music conservatory.

A line of sweat worked its way down Anna's back. "*Slečna* Kadlecová, how good to see you again."

Perhaps because of his state of inebriation, *Hauptsturmführer* Jaeger missed Patricie's use of her name. He released his grip on Anna and addressed her friend. "You know this woman?"

"We went to the conservatory together."

"Ah, another musician in our midst. What a delight."

Behind Jaeger's back, Anna mouthed to Patricie, "Please, don't tell. Please." She trembled like a small bird.

Horst came beside her. He didn't touch her, but a current passed between them. "We won't go out tonight, Jaeger. I'm not feeling well. You and Fraulein Kadlecová have a good time."

"Be a man."

Horst stiffened. "I'm not sure you know the definition of that word."

"Then show me. You show me what a man looks like."

Horst didn't break off staring at *Hauptsturmführer* Jaeger.

Patricie gave him a side hug. "Let's not bother these people. They don't want to come with us. Leave them to themselves. We'll have a good time without them."

Hauptsturmführer Jaeger turned his attention back to Anna. "If you're a musician, talented enough to study at the conservatory, why are you a maid?"

Anna swallowed hard, praying her words would come out more than a squeak. "The music schools are all closed. I didn't finish my education, so I'm forced to get whatever work I can."

"Interesting. Very interesting." He stroked his chin. "Get your jackets. The evening air is cool. You're coming with us." He stepped close enough for Anna to smell the liquor on his breath.

Horst wriggled between them. "You're drunk. Quit bullying us into going out. I'd much rather not. Please, it's getting late. Leave us in peace."

"Fine, you don't have to come." He reached around Horst. "But she's going with me."

Horst shoved Jaeger. "Don't touch her."

He slapped Horst's other cheek. "I outrank you by a kilometer. What I say goes. I'll get your jacket." He stormed into Anna's bedroom.

She and Horst followed him. *Babička* was in there. How would they explain if he saw her? They had to get him out. "Fine, I'll go with you. Leave me so I can change."

"You won't go anywhere with him." Horst moved to pull Jaeger from the wardrobe.

He flung Horst away like a rag doll. "Ah, here's your sweater. Put it on." He tossed it to her.

She caught it. But it wasn't hers. This one belonged to *Babička*, who huddled underneath the quilt.

Though she'd removed the yellow Star of David patch and pulled out all the threads, the outline of it remained where the sweater had faded around it after years of washing it. Just like her coat. Anna tingled all over. What should she do? "I'm not that cool. I'll leave it here."

"Put it on." Jaeger spoke through clenched teeth.

"I'll be too warm and catch cold myself."

"Listen to me." His hot breath scorched her face.

She shrank back, unable to still the wild thumping in her temple.

"That's enough, Jaeger. More than enough." Horst pulled *Hauptsturmführer* Jaeger away from her. "You will leave. Right now. You may outrank me, but in my home, I'm the general. If you don't get out this instant, I'll call the authorities. I'm sure they'll be interested to hear how you're harassing a fellow countryman who did his job with valor today." With each word, Horst's voice rose in pitch.

Hauptsturmführer Jaeger ripped the sweater from her grasp. "Fine. Stay here."

Anna exhaled. Horst stood up to Jaeger. Now, if he'd just leave . . .

He threw the sweater into the wardrobe.

Then he stopped.

Picked it up.

"What's this?" He held the garment to the light.

The star's shadow.

"Jew. Dirty, vile pig Jew."

With one swipe, he struck both Anna and Horst.

And drew his pistol.

Chapter Twenty-Two

*P*atricie sat on the green sofa in the comfortable room, but she couldn't settle into the seat. *Hauptsturmführer* Jaeger told her the authorities had issued *Hauptmann* Engel a flat that a Jewish family used to own. A family that was no doubt at Terezín now, if not beyond. She shivered and pulled her light sweater around her.

And then Anna Zadoková came from the bedroom. What on earth was she doing here? Did *Hauptmann* Engel know her true identity? That she was Jewish? With a last name like Zadoková, how could he not?

And how could *Hauptsturmführer* Jaeger not have made the connection when she'd blurted out Anna's last name? She had almost jeopardized their lives.

A thousand other questions raced through her head.

If he would just take her home so she could block out the world for a while. He'd drunk far too much tonight. A pain started behind her eye at his thundering. She hated this. Hated all of this. When would the nightmare end?

The one man's tenor voice rose in pitch until she understood the words. "You're harassing a fellow countryman who did his job with valor today."

"Fine. Stay here." *Hauptsturmführer* Jaeger's harsh voice dripped with anger.

Silence for a moment. He said something else she didn't catch.

But she understood the rest. "Jew. Dirty, vile pig Jew."

She turned cold all over. He must know, must have figured out Anna's secret. What should she do? Her heart told her what was right. Her head told her not to jeopardize herself.

But the wide eyes of the people she'd helped save haunted her. Could she sit back and allow him to arrest Anna?

Eliška. Her screams echoed in Patricie's head.

The Jewish boy. His cries tore at her chest.

"Whatsoever you do to the least of these ..."

She rose and followed the sounds of the commotion to the end of the hall.

Hauptsturmführer Jaeger stood in front of Anna and *Hauptmann* Engel. The color of Anna's face matched that of the first winter snow.

Hauptsturmführer Jaeger pointed his pistol at them.

At Anna's head.

Adrenaline pumped through Patricie's body. She rushed between him and Anna. "*Ne.* Don't shoot her. You don't want to do this."

"Get out of my way. Or do you want me to put a bullet in you, too?"

Even though her legs trembled, she stood her ground. "You're drunk. Not thinking clearly. Put your gun away. Send them to Terezín. Get some work out of them."

He blinked, his eyes bloodshot. "Maybe her. But not him. Hiding a Jew. Any Jew lover in our ranks must be eliminated." He turned the weapon on his comrade.

Patricie's heart hammered so hard she had a difficult time hearing her own words. "Give me the gun. Remember, you parked in front of the wrong building. Go get the car, and I'll watch them. They might try to escape if you parade them down the street."

"And you." His stare seared her to the soul. He flashed the gun around. "You knew her. Knew she was a Jew. Yet you didn't tell me."

She wiped her hands on the silky yellow dress. "How was I supposed to recall such a detail? It's been a long time since we were at the conservatory. And I didn't know her all that well. We were acquaintances, nothing more. Maybe I never knew."

He staggered to one side before regaining his balance.

"You can trust me." She kept her voice mirror smooth. "Give me the gun, and get the car. We'll turn them in, then celebrate another victory. That many fewer Jews in Prague. The cleansing one step closer to completion."

Stefan stared at her for a long moment.

"If you let them go, I'll send you to your grave along with them."

She didn't doubt he would. But he handed her the pistol, the metal warm from his grasp. She grabbed it and pointed it in Anna's direction. "Go now. Hurry."

He hustled out of the room.

"*Slečna* Kadlecová, please, don't do this." Anna's voice trembled.

Patricie held her breath until the door slammed. She allowed another minute to pass before she relaxed her muscles and dropped the weapon to the floor. She spoke just loud enough for them to hear. "We don't have much time. I'm banking on him being too drunk to find the car. Let's get out of here."

Hauptmann Engel spoke up. "You're going to help us?"

She turned to Anna. "Is he trustworthy?" Patricie nodded in the man's direction.

"He's hidden me and my grandmother for several months."

"He knew your background?"

"I did."

A stooped, older woman popped from underneath the bed covers. "Is he gone? I prayed the Lord would make him go away."

Anna embraced the woman. "He's going to arrest us. He'll be back."

"We're wasting time. Let's go." The elderly lady would slow them down. Precious seconds ticked away. Seconds that might mean the different between life and death.

Anna scanned the room. "We have to grab a few items. My grandmother's medication, at least."

"The medication. That's it. Hurry, hurry. Is there a back way out?"

"Down the building's main hall." Anna scampered to the bedside table and dropped what Patricie figured to be the grandmother's pill bottle into her pocket.

"Fast, fast, fast." She herded them out of the flat and to the back door.

The grandmother stumbled. She impeded their progress.

"*Hauptmann* Engel, can you carry the old woman?"

"I think I can."

"Then do it. And don't waste time." Were those his footsteps she heard? "Come on, come on."

He scooped up the woman. They hustled out the door. The soft evening air cooled her burning cheeks.

"I have the car. Let's get them out of here."

Patricie closed the door behind her, careful to not make a sound. The blackout covered them in darkness.

"Did you grab the gun?" The Nazi panted as he sprinted down the alley.

"Didn't you?"

"*Nein.* You hustled us out of there so fast, I didn't have a chance. And I thought you would."

"It would have helped, but there's nothing we can do about it now."

"Next time you have a weapon in your hand, don't let it go. Where are you taking us? Do you have a plan?" The German's question was a good one.

"I've been doing this for the entire war. Of course I have a plan." Which house should she take them to? A long while had passed since she told Georg she couldn't work for him anymore. She didn't know which, if any, locations had been compromised.

Georg would know. He could help.

If he forgave her for deserting him.

Anna, Horst, and Patricie ran down the narrow alley as fast as possible. Horst carried *Babička*, which slowed the group. Any moment, Anna expected the sear of a bullet to pierce her back.

Horst stumbled.

"Put me down." *Babička*'s voice carried in the still night air. "Leave me behind."

"Hush." Patricie scanned the area. Not that she would see anything in the near-perfect darkness. "Do you want him to find us?"

"You aren't staying behind. How could I bear to lose you, too?" Anna kept her voice low.

"This is no time for arguing. We're all going. Now. Fast." Patricie resumed the flight.

Down the alley, *Hauptsturmführer* Jaeger hollered for them. The blackness of the night should keep him from seeing them. As long as he didn't hear the crazy thrashing of her heart.

Anna's breath came in short gasps. The tightness of her chest kept her from drawing in enough air. And not from the pace of their run. They measured themselves so Horst could keep up.

Where was Patricie taking them? Anna couldn't fill her lungs enough to ask. How long would Horst be able to carry her grandmother?

They came to the end of the alley. This road led out of the Jewish quarter. "Put her down." As Horst set *Babička* on her feet, Patricie took hold of her. "*Hauptmann* Engel and Anna, hold hands. You're a couple out for a little night air. I'll follow with ... I'm sorry, what's your name?"

"That's my grandmother, Jana Doubeková."

"I'll follow with *Paní* Doubeková. We're your chaperones, should anyone ask. I doubt they will."

Horst leaned over and whispered in her ear. "Your grandmother's sweater. What if someone else sees the remnants of the star?"

"*Babička*, turn your sweater inside out. *Hauptsturmführer* Jaeger saw the imprint the star left on it. We can't take a chance. Even though it's dark, we don't want anyone else noticing it." Anna helped *Babička* slip it off, turn it around, and put it back over her shoulders.

"Where are we going?" Horst grasped Anna's hand and squeezed it. His warm presence eased her trembling.

"How well do you know the city?"

"I'm the architectural minister."

"Do you know how to get to Wenceslas Square?"

"I'm acquainted with the area."

"Then let's go."

The group didn't say another word as they stepped onto the street. A few of Prague's citizens moved about the city to enjoy the night. Curfew approached. They must hurry. Though they walked with as much nonchalance as they could muster, Anna feared they stuck out like a weed among roses. She crushed Horst's fingers.

He moved down the street. She forced herself to match his strides, to keep up with him. She might as well be wearing shoes weighted with lead.

A man brushed against her.

She recoiled. *Hauptsturmführer* Jaeger?

"Terribly sorry, miss."

Ne, just a stranger. He didn't suspect anything.

But what if the next person they ran into was German? What if they asked for their papers?

After about ten minutes, Horst led them down a quieter street. Less chance of meeting the wrong people. Or anyone, for that matter.

Still, no one conversed.

"I need to rest." *Babička's* weak voice cut through the silence.

Horst paused. "It's not far now. *Slečna* Kadlecová, you may have to lead from here. I don't know the exact place you're taking us."

"Is it safe?" Anna bent over, trying in vain to still her runaway heart.

"As safe as anywhere can be." Patricie remained calm. How could she be?

"Does *Hauptsturmführer* Jaeger know about it?" Anna fought for her breath.

The other woman gasped. "*Ne*, I don't think he does. This is the home of the leader of the resistance ring I used to belong to."

"Used to?"

"I quit a few months ago, afraid my relationship with *Hauptsturm-führer* Jaeger would compromise the group."

A song floated toward them from farther down the street.

"That's enough of a rest. We have to keep moving. We'll be at Georg's soon."

Questions flooded Anna's mind. Was this place safe enough? *Hauptsturmführer* Jaeger proved himself to be wily. Maybe he already knew about it. Waited to make his move on Patricie.

They went another block or so until they discovered the origin of the music. Off-key, raucous music.

German music. A group of drunken soldiers.

Did they all imbibe? Maybe they needed the liquor to dull the sting of their consciences.

"Let's turn down the next street." Patricie gave the order.

But the Nazis came toward them at a rapid pace. Their song, if you could call it that, grew louder. Anna caught a glimpse of them in the dull pool of light leaking from a shop's blackout shades.

Her stomach clenched. What would they do to them?

Horst pressed her hand. "Don't worry."

She had to trust him. Had to trust the Lord. Had no other choice.

Patricie motioned them to the side. "Stay close to the buildings. Give them plenty of room to pass."

The soldiers approached. A couple of them went by without incident. Anna sighed. Then one of them grabbed her by the upper arm.

"What do we have here?"

Horst yanked her behind him. "Don't touch my girl."

"Yours?"

"My wife. Don't dishonor me or the Fatherland."

Anna held back a cough.

"So sorry." The man hurried on his way.

"That was too close for comfort. *Hauptmann* Engel, you'll have to take *Paní* Doubeková again. We need to make better time." As soon as Horst swooped up *Babička*, Patricie set a rapid pace toward a poorer section of town.

Anna and *Máma* had come here once to bring meals to the less fortunate and share the gospel with them. How long ago that seemed.

At last, Patricie halted. "This is the building."

No traces of light emanated from any of the windows. "Are you sure this is the right place?"

"I know it as well as I know my own home."

Patricie led them up four flights of stairs to the top, and *Babička* and Horst followed.

Patricie knocked twice. A small man answered, his hairline receding, wire-rimmed spectacles sliding down his angular nose. In another time, another place, he might have been one of David's friends.

When he saw the group, he pulled them inside, shutting the door and sliding the bolt locked. "What are you doing here?"

They all worked to remove their shoes. Patricie tilted her head in their direction. "These people were about to be arrested."

"A German officer. Are you out of your mind, Patricie?"

"He hid these Jews, Georg."

"Well, he can't stay here. None of them can. It's not safe."

Chapter Twenty-Three

"It's not safe here? You're supposed to work hiding people, and this isn't a safe place?" Horst didn't dare raise his voice above a whisper. But his palms sweated, and his head pounded. Any moment, he expected Stefan to burst through the door.

The young man with round spectacles sat at his place at the uneven table. He directed his attention to the woman who'd rescued them. "What do you mean bringing them here? Him?" He pointed at Horst, still dressed in his olive-green uniform.

Patricie stepped into the weak circle of light cast by the small, dusty chandelier. "I know, I know. I'll explain it to you later. But he hid these two women, kept them safe. The Nazi pointed his gun at this man as well as at the young woman. Anna Zadoková. I know her from the conservatory. If she trusts him, so do I."

Anna, clinging to her grandmother, still trembled. "I do. He had ample opportunity to turn us in. He didn't. It was his idea to hide us. We were ready for Terezín."

"Well, the Germans raided one of our houses today. I don't know how they found out. Maybe a leak in our system? Or they were spotted by a window? Who knows. But they arrested an older woman, a teenage boy, and a young mother and her infant. And killed the old woman's husband."

The truth hit Horst in the gut, as if someone sucker-punched him. He'd arrested those people. This man must have a network of places where he hid Jews. And Stefan knew of one of them. How many more did he have on the list? "You're right. It's not safe here. How many homes do you have?"

Georg cracked his knuckles. "Do you think I would tell you anything? How do I know you won't run with the information to your superiors? Or arrest us all yourself?"

"He won't." Patricie sat beside the man she called Georg and touched his arm. "He needs to go into hiding, along with *Slečna* Zadoková and her grandmother. For now, please, help me find a safe place for them. And myself."

The young man's look softened when he gazed at Patricie. "You? Why?"

"I helped them escape. The soldier knows me, and knows where I live."

"This is the one you've been seeing."

"Yes."

"Listen, this is no time for conversation." Horst pulled out a chair for Frau Doubeková and motioned for her to sit. "We need a place to stay. Now. As fast as you can arrange it. I can't guarantee that we haven't been followed."

Patricie tugged on a stray strand of her brown hair. "I was careful. He didn't see where we went. No one followed us."

"You may be sure, but I'm not. Stefan is crafty and shrewd. He'll spring on you without a moment's notice."

"I know that." The young woman barely came to his shoulder, but a sharpness, a fierceness, edged her words. "I've been dating him for a few months now. Not by my own choice."

Horst turned back to Georg. "You must know of a safe place for us. One not far. The running is hard on Frau Doubeková."

"Don't worry about me." Anna's grandmother cut in on the conversation. "Take care of yourselves. You're young. I'm a hindrance."

Anna hugged her grandmother from behind. "You're no such thing."

Horst nodded. "If one goes, we all go. Now, that's settled. Where to, Georg?"

"There is a farm outside of the city, near Libochovice. I haven't used it before because it's so far out. Right now, it's the best option."

"How do we get there?"

"I have to think." Georg paced the tiny room. "A vehicle would be too suspicious. And you don't have the proper identification for the train. It has to be a farm wagon. Less likely to be noticed by the authorities and less likely to be searched. At least, I hope that's the case. But it will take me some time to contact the farmer and arrange for him to bring his wagon here."

"Time we don't have." Horst pounded the table. "What else?"

"That's all. If you don't like the proposal, go somewhere else."

Anna stood beside Horst. "What other options do we have? Where would we go? Do you have a hiding place?"

Horst fidgeted. He didn't have any other ideas. It was his fault Georg had no secure place in the city. The pain of his actions stabbed Horst's heart.

He was a victim of his own cowardice. Now he had Stefan hot on his trail. And very few outsmarted that man, even in his current state of inebriation. Could they find shelter in one of the buildings Horst inspected? He knew every nook and cranny of a few of them. But none of them provided what they needed. He shook his head.

"Then we have to take what *Slečna* Kadlecová and her friend offer us. While it may not be ideal, it's all we have at this point. We didn't notify him we were on our way."

Horst's stomach tightened, relaxed, then tightened again. Anna was right. At the moment, their choices were limited. Actually, there was only one choice. "Fine. There is no other way. We have to take what we can get."

Georg narrowed his eyes as he stared at Horst. "I want you out of here as fast as you want to be gone. Let's get you settled so I can make the arrangements." He showed the group a mattress for the women to share and the couch for Horst. "If the Germans raid us, it's imperative to put everything away. And do it fast. I live alone here. They can't discover any evidence to the contrary.

"After that's been stashed, you need to hide. There is a false door in the attic with a small room behind it. While I let the soldiers in, you scamper up there. You close the door from the inside. Is that all clear?"

"Will the plan work?" Horst cracked his knuckles. Would they be able to get Anna's grandmother into hiding fast enough?

Georg pushed up his glasses. "We can only pray it will."

Anna settled her grandmother onto the mattress and tucked the thin blanket around her. Patricie and Georg sat at the ancient table and spoke in tones so low that, despite the minute size of the flat, Horst couldn't hear their conversation. He reclined on the lumpy couch and rubbed his tense shoulders.

How long before Stefan arrived? If only Horst had stood up to him today. Maybe they would all be safe now. Perhaps not him, but Anna and Frau Doubeková.

How would he ever look *Mutti* in the eye again?

Anna kissed her grandmother's forehead and came and sat beside him. "What's wrong?"

He gave a short laugh. "We're running for our lives, and you ask what's wrong?"

"This, we were prepared for. We knew the day might come when the Nazis discovered us. But there is more. I see it in the set of your jaw."

Did she know him that well already? "It doesn't have anything to do with you."

"It pertains to what you told me earlier, *ne*? About the raid?"

She'd pierced to the heart of the matter in a few, simple words. Had he become transparent?

He swallowed as the words lodged in his throat. He cleared it. "*Ja*."

"What?"

"My actions put you and your grandmother into danger. *Slečna* Kadlecová, too."

"How? I don't understand."

"That was the raid I was involved in. Because of me, Georg's operation is compromised."

"With or without you, *Hauptsturmführer* Jaeger would have gone to that house today. Would have found the Jews there. It's not because of you that Georg is in danger, but because of him."

Horst listened to her. Even when she spoke, her words lilted like music. But she didn't know the entire story. "Didn't you hear Georg? Stefan killed the old man. And I did nothing."

"You can't save the entire world."

Nein, he couldn't. Too much madness permeated the earth. Too much for one man. "But I didn't make a difference when I should have."

"To *Babička* and me, you have made a difference. Because of you, we aren't at Terezín, facing the deplorable living conditions. I believe she would be dead by now if we had gone. And maybe I would be, too. You saved our lives. You made a difference."

But he wanted to do more. He hadn't helped her brother yet.

Even though forced to go underground, he would. Somehow, he'd find a way.

Anna and *Hauptmann* Engel sat together on the couch, he bent over, she rubbing his back. Patricie observed them for a moment. What was their relationship? Had it progressed beyond rescuer and rescued? Is that why he protected Anna and her grandmother?

Georg fiddled with his brown sweater's frayed hem. "Why are you back here?"

"Because I need a safe place for these people. And myself. Where else could I go?"

"So I was a last resort. The only resort."

"*Ne*, not like that at all. I didn't want to leave the organization." She paused and licked her lips. "Or you."

"Then why did you?"

"For your own good. Don't you see? *Hauptsturmführer* Jaeger demanded more and more of my time. He knew where I lived. Sometimes, he ran into me, and by no coincidence, to be sure. I didn't want to lead him here, or to anywhere the Jews hid. I couldn't take that chance. Leaving the work was my only option."

"You ripped my heart out." Georg took off his glasses and rubbed the bridge of his nose.

"I'm so sorry. I couldn't explain."

"He meant that much to you?"

"He means nothing. You have to believe me. He chose me. And when a high-ranking SS officer chooses you, you don't refuse him."

"We all have choices in life. There is always a way out."

"You don't understand. There wasn't." But had she been firmer in her refusal, would he have left her alone?

"An important, influential, handsome man notices you, and you're flattered. You liked the attention. I can't blame you. What do I offer? I'm poor, awkward, and caught up in the cause."

"That's not it at all." But was it? Did Georg speak the truth?

"Take a good look at yourself. Can you live with what you did?" He scraped his chair back and stood. "Get some rest. I have to work on moving you all to the country."

"Please, don't be upset with me."

"I'm not. Just disappointed in you."

No more disappointed than she was in herself.

And then a knock came at the door.

Chapter Twenty-Four

At the sound of a knock on the door, Anna's heart rate kicked up, racing along at a breakneck speed. *Hauptsturmführer* Jaeger already?

Georg motioned for them to be quiet. He crept to the door. "Who is there?"

"Open up."

Georg looked to Patricie, who shook her head no. It wasn't the man they escaped from. But neither Georg nor Patricie recognized the voice.

Horst caressed her hand. "Don't worry."

A moment before, she'd comforted him. With him by her side, her breaths remained even.

"To the attic, everyone. Take your shoes and head to the back entry that leads to the hallway to the stairs. As soon as you're by that door, I'll open this one. Slip out as fast as possible and make as little noise as you can. Hurry."

Horst helped *Babička* to her feet and led her in the direction of the back door. Anna had never seen a flat with two doors before. Who knew how handy they would prove?

The three of them tiptoed to the exit. Anna prayed her wobbling legs would hold her upright.

Georg leaned against the door. "You, too, Patricie. The Germans will be looking for you as well."

She joined them. The second Georg turned the knob, Horst poked out of the door to make sure the hall was empty. He nodded. The group slipped out the back way and up the stairs. An old riser creaked under Anna's foot.

Everyone froze. Holding her breath, she peered down the corridor. No one. Good. They hurried the rest of the way up the steps, *Babička* bringing up the rear. She was clutching her chest by the time they reached the attic.

"Is it your heart?" The coldness in the pit of Anna's stomach never went way these days.

"*Ne*. I'm just a worn out old woman. Why do you bother with me?"

"Because I love you. And I made a promise to *Máma* and *Táta*. One I intend to keep."

Horst groped the wall. "Georg said to press on the panel, and it will come loose. I just need to find it." A very long minute later, the wall opened to reveal a small space. "I'm not sure we will all fit."

"You have to squeeze in." Patricie slipped inside first. "They cannot be large or they will draw suspicion. The SS is smart." She eyed the eagle on Horst's chest.

Anna pushed *Babička* inside next and followed her. They stood shoulder to shoulder. A large person would never fit. Horst wormed his way beside her and slid the door shut.

Absolute darkness consumed them. No moonlight slithered under the door. Anna's hands trembled, despite her best efforts to still them. Whoever came to Georg's flat might hear the pounding of her heart. That sound alone might give them away.

"How are you doing?" Horst's soft words in her ear sent a tingle up her spine.

"The life is ebbing out of me."

"Ebbing out of you?"

"I'm scared. A few times, I thought we might be sent to Terezín. But even under cover, I'm vulnerable."

"This must be what the Jews I arrested this morning felt like." His words were subdued.

"There isn't music here. It's silent. That's what I hate the most." She leaned on his strong chest. His heart tapped out a rhythm similar to hers.

"You'll make beautiful music again soon. Don't let us rob you of that."

"Us? Don't group yourself with those people." Her throat tightened.

"You're not like them. Look at what you've done for my grandmother and me. Please, don't say that."

"I took your music from you."

The creaking of the stair jolted her to silence. Someone was coming? Who?

Whoever it was didn't shout or make a ruckus like a group of soldiers might. If only she could see Horst's face, to read the emotions there. She didn't dare speak. Maybe the Germans heard the two of them. She might have given them away.

Her small dinner churned inside her. She fought to keep the food down.

The footsteps stopped in front of them. *Babička* squeezed Anna's hand. She returned the gesture. Would her grandmother survive even the trip to Terezín?

The door slid open. "It's safe. You can come out."

Georg. Horst left the hiding spot. Anna stumbled after him. "I'm so glad it's you."

Patricie exited after *Babička*. "Who was it?"

"Václav Bosko."

"You told him about us?"

Horst supported Anna around her waist. "Someone else knows we're here?"

"He works with us. He has a cold. That's why we didn't recognize his voice. Don't worry. I trust him with my life."

"And you trust him with mine? And with the lives of these women?"

"Yes, I do. You have nothing to fear. He is going to contact the farmer to take you from the city. He expects the man will arrived a few hours after that. The plan to get you out of here is in motion."

They followed Georg downstairs. From a small wardrobe, Patricie brought out a set of sheets and several blankets. "I know it's difficult to put your lives in the hands of complete strangers, people who have no seeming motivation to help you. But we have a reason. No one should be hunted because of the blood that flows in their veins. We're all created in God's image. That is worth protecting."

Anna marveled at Patricie as the two of them worked to make up the mattress. "Have you been involved long?"

"Almost from the beginning. I knew too many Jews from the conservatory. They're good people. They don't deserve the treatment the Germans are doling out to them. But you. I knew you were Jewish, though I didn't think of you like that."

"With a last name like Zadok?"

"I guess because you spoke about going to church."

"My physical ancestry is Jewish. My spiritual ancestry is Christian." Anna tucked in the blanket.

They all settled down for the night. Horst's even snoring warmed her. With him a few meters away from her, the world wasn't as frightening of a place. Still, she couldn't sleep. Insomnia had plagued her since childhood. Often, she imagined playing a piece of music, and the waves of sound lulled her to slumber.

But no melody came to her tonight. Like she'd told Horst, this place sucked it all from her. She couldn't bring to mind even a simple tune.

She hugged *Babička*.

"What's troubling you, *beruško*?"

"Aren't you frightened? What's going to happen next? Will we be safe at the farm?"

"God gives me peace."

"How can you say that?"

"My heart pounded as fast and as hard as yours in that closet."

"You are afraid."

"At first, I was. But I prayed. I'm always praying. For strength. For peace. For deliverance."

"And it helps?"

"God is faithful."

Oh, how easy to say the words. How difficult to believe them.

Especially when the days, weeks, and months ahead promised nothing but blackness.

A shaft of sun poked into the tiny apartment. Horst worked to keep his voice down. "A pony and cart? This is your grand plan to get us from the city?" He stood across the minuscule kitchen table from Georg, convinced the man had lost his mind. "These are three women, one of them elderly and with a heart condition. It's out of the question."

Georg didn't flinch. "You are just what I expected. An arrogant, self-centered, spoiled German. My guess is that you grew up pampered and that your father bought you this commission so you wouldn't have to get your hands dirty."

"You know nothing about me." But the man's words hit too close to the mark.

"Then enlighten me. Tell me all about your hard upbringing. How your family slaved each day to eke out just enough of a living to put a cabbage and a couple potatoes on the table for nine children. How you watched your siblings die of hardship and disease. How you didn't have enough money to pay for coal in the winter. Tell me."

Horst sat hard on the kitchen chair.

"That's what I thought. Don't come in here with your manicured hands and pressed clothes and presume to know better than I do how to take care of women and old people. It's thanks to the likes of you that we have to do this at all." A vein bulged in Georg's neck.

Patricie touched his upper arm. "Shouting won't solve anything. I think *Hauptmann* Engel wanted to express his concern for *Paní* Doubeková. It will be a long and difficult trip for her."

Horst glanced over his shoulder at Anna and her grandmother as they sat on the couch. "And you will come with us."

Frau Doubeková laughed. "I didn't say anything. Please, don't worry about me. Remember, I was around before all these fancy inventions like cars and telephones and such. We lived different kinds of lives in those days. My family had money, but I knew some who wore gloves with the fingertips cut out during the winter so they could play the piano."

"Then it's settled." Georg pounded the table like a judge pounded his bench with a gavel.

"*Ne*, it's not. Figure out a different strategy. We don't have boots or hats or warm clothes. Nothing but what we wear on our backs."

"The farmer will bring what you need. And *Paní* Doubeková won't ride in the back, covered with straw. He has his mother's papers, which should do fine for her. Do you have any other questions?"

Anna left her grandmother's side to stand beside Horst. He stared down at her, so small, her brown eyes wide and large. "It's fine. As long as *Babička* is comfortable, I don't care."

He rubbed the chill from her hands. "Will the cold affect your playing? The lead violinist with the Munich symphony walked around with woolen mittens all winter to protect his fingers."

"What does it matter? My violin is …" Her voice broke.

"It's in the flat with everything else." He shouldn't have brought it up. "I'm sorry. That's why you told me yesterday the life drained out of you. I'll get it for you."

Georg snorted. "I went to all this work to try to save your life so you can risk it again for a musical instrument? Aren't lives more precious than possessions?"

Horst wrapped Anna in an embrace. "You don't understand. This possession is her life. She, the violin, and her music are intertwined. To her, it's like air."

She relaxed against him. The warmth of her body seeped through the thin shirt he'd borrowed from Georg after they burned his uniform. "How do you know this? How is it you understand?"

"You forget that I've watched you these past months. When you play, your face comes alive. Your entire body." She mesmerized him. Capture and enchanted him. But he couldn't tell her such things in public. He'd already said too much.

"*Pan* Karas will be at the grocer's around the corner in thirty minutes. You can take the alley over there. He will park his cart in back while he brings in the potatoes. Help *Paní* Doubeková onto the seat and slip under the straw. If you are not there when he is ready to leave, he will go without you. Is this all clear? Patricie?"

She kissed Georg's cheek. "I've taken care of situations like this many times before."

"But this time, you're on the other side of the operation. Be careful." Georg lifted his glasses and wiped his sleeve across his eyes. "You are precious to me, Patricie. You always have been. You always will be. God go with you."

"And with you."

They exited the building into the dark, dingy alley. Horst kept his guard up, alert to every sound, every movement, his muscles tense. Stefan could jump at them at any opening.

Anna tugged on his sleeve. "Stop. Please. I want to take one more look at Prague. Let me peek at the street."

"That's not a good idea. Someone might see you."

"I'll be careful to stay in the shadows. I beg you."

He couldn't deny her. He motioned for the others to wait for them. At the corner, he and Anna crept between the buildings to where the city opened before them. She pointed in one direction. "Over there is the Prague Castle with its many spires reaching to the sky. And beyond it is the Charles Bridge.

"In that direction is the Orloj, the astronomical clock in Old Town Square. *Táta* took me there as a child. I tried to figure out which of the carved figures were the apostles Peter and John. I stared at the gold and blue dial faces, trying to make sense of it all. He told me one day I would understand."

She quaked against him, the sunlight brightening strands of her dark hair. "Do you think someday we will understand all of this?"

He had no answer for her. Instead, he held her until her trembling eased.

"It's time to go."

"I fear I'll never see this city again."

He feared she was right.

Chapter Twenty-Five

January 1945

Anna stared out the dingy window. The rain wept from the trees in the farmyard at the edge of the hamlet where they had lived these past months. She couldn't weep. Not any longer. Enough tears had fallen from her eyes to fill a small lake.

Because inside, she was as empty as the milk can in the morning. For months, she'd heard no music. Harbored no melodies in her soul. Nothing but a yawning void.

Even if she had her instrument, she had no song to play.

Babička and Maria Karas, the middle-aged farmer's wife, sat at the scarred kitchen table, peeling potatoes to fry for dinner. Patricie curled up on the narrow divan, reading a book. Horst set aside his sketch pad, came to Anna's side, and lifted the lace curtain a little more. "All you do is gaze outside, all day long. What's wrong, *beruško*?"

The ache in her chest compressed at the sound of her father's nickname for her. "I can't feel it."

"What?"

"The music. Inside, I'm dry. And scared. Scared I'll never be able to make music again."

"You're mourning the loss of your violin."

"The loss of music." She dropped the curtain and turned to him. "I thought you understood. When you spoke to Georg at his flat that night, I thought you knew what music means to me."

"I do." His blue eyes, which she had first thought icy, now warmed to the color of the sea. "You leave this place and go to another of pure beauty. I know because, although I don't play, I can also find escape in music. And in drawing."

"And you haven't drawn much since we came here, so I believe you do understand." Still, it amazed her that he did. "But my violin is in Prague. If it exists anymore. I think your friend smashed it when he couldn't find us."

"I want to give you hope, but I wouldn't put it past him."

"Why do you think he hasn't found us yet?"

"Because *Pan* Klima and *Slečna* Kadlecová are good at what they do." Horst caressed the back of her neck. "He would never think to look for us here."

"He's given up?"

He sighed and turned his attention to the rainy scene in front of them.

"Tell me the truth." Anna touched his cheek, roughened with stubble, and he gazed back at her with incredible intensity. Maybe she should never have asked him.

"*Ne.* Stefan is a driven man. He doesn't quit until he gets what he wants."

A bolt of cold raced through her.

He pulled her into an embrace. She rested against his chest.

The rate of his heartbeat did nothing to soothe her nerves. "And what has you so troubled? I see it in your eyes, too. Are you also scared?"

"*Ne.* That's not what bothers me."

She tried to pull away, but he held her fast. "Then what? Why do you stare at the walls for hours on end, your pencil in your hand?"

He glanced at the ceiling, back at her, then at the ceiling again. "Are you sure to want to know? I'm not the man I appear to be."

Her stomach did a little bounce. "Yes, I do."

"Come with me, and I will tell you." He led the way to the top of the stairs and motioned for her to sit. "This will give us a bit of privacy while preserving your reputation." He winked.

Her cheeks warmed, even though the cold remained in the pit of her stomach. "Will you answer my question now?"

"My past haunts me."

She rubbed her knees. "What did you do?"

He stared at the ceiling, his jaw tight. "Growing up, we lived next door to a Jewish watchmaker. I spent many happy hours there."

She went cold all over.

"On Kristallnacht, I led a group of Hitler Youth who went to his shop, broke his windows, and looted his merchandise." He swallowed hard.

"Oh, Horst." Her words came out in a breathless whisper.

"I wanted my father to be proud of me, so I took part in beating him."

Her held-back sob strangled her.

"What I did was wrong. That night, I got caught up in the mob mentality of my Hitler Youth group. I regretted it right away, but the damage was done. Nightmares plague me. Your music soothes me. You are my salvation."

"*Ne.* I'm not." Anna hugged herself. She understood at last why he was so upset about finding the Jews in their hiding spot.

"Can you forgive me for what I did?"

"It's not my place to absolve you."

"But now you will be afraid of me?"

She studied her fingernails. "I don't know."

He scooted in her direction. "I couldn't bear it if you were."

"I can't answer that now." With that, she fled to the room she shared with *Babička* and covered her head with her pillow. If only the tears would flow.

When darkness fell, Horst took advantage of the cover of night to get a breath of fresh air. The walls of the tiny house closed in on him from time to time. The farmer, Karel Karas, and his wife couldn't be more gracious. But six people crowded into the cramped living quarters without relief. They didn't dare move about in the daylight. Even the small countryside hamlet had eyes.

His cigarette cravings gnawed at him, but smokes were impossible to get.

The rain had stopped about an hour before sunset, but had done its job in turning the farmyard into a muddy mess. Footsteps squished behind him.

"*Hauptmann* Engel, what are you doing out here?"

He stopped, and Patricie caught up to him.

"I needed to get outside for a while. To be free, if only for a moment."

"I'm sorry if I disturbed you."

"Not at all. You might be able to help."

"Me?"

"Tell me about your operation. How does it work? What does it do?"

In the dull light, she gave a wide gesture. "This is it."

"This?"

"We forge identity papers, print pamphlets, and counterfeit ration cards. That's what my brother does. This is a small part of the resistance movement. We, they, hide Jews and others the Nazis slate for arrest. Most of the Jews went to Terezín when their notices came. There aren't many like *Slečna* Zadoková and her grandmother who hid."

"And they would have gone if I hadn't stopped them. Is that all?"

"You've seen the people come each week with ration cards and supplies to feed us. That's what we do. What we'll continue to do until our land is rid of the Germans."

"Of men like me."

"*Ne*, not like you. You see *Slečna* Zadoková and *Paní* Doubeková as people, not an ethnicity. You care about them. About her."

"I do. And that's what concerns me."

"How so?"

They entered the barn. Horst took a risk and lit the lamp. Patricie smoothed back her brown hair.

"Haven't you noticed how she longs for her violin?"

"I have. The same longing plagues me. To be without music is like going without vegetables. You live, but your body isn't the same."

"Her clothes hang on her. The light left her eyes the moment we set foot outside of Prague. I'm no musician, but I understand how our present circumstances dull the senses. I've tried and failed to appreciate this house's architecture."

"It's simple and sweet. And our sanctuary. That alone should convince you it's beautiful."

"I never thought of it like that. Under that gabled roof, God protects us. Hides us. Yes, that is true loveliness." Patricie couldn't match him in height, but she outshone him in faith.

"Is that what you needed help with?"

"*Ne.*" He sat on a bale of hay and motioned for her to do the same. A horse whinnied in its stall. "I need your expertise."

"In music?"

"In underground work."

"What are you plotting?" She wrinkled her forehead.

"You have broken people out of prison?"

She gave a short, high-pitched laugh. "Out of prison? *Ne*, never. Who do you want released?"

"Anna's brother."

"You are touched in the head if you think you're going to rescue a single soul from Terezín. People who go there never come back. Never. The place is fortified, walled, and guarded." She jumped to her feet and paced in front of him. "No matter what you plan, it will never work."

Maybe not. But he had to try. Had to prove to himself that he was better than his father. "But I've been there. I know the lay of the land."

"Are you suggesting you'll go in there yourself?"

He nodded.

"Have you forgotten you're a wanted man?"

"That does make the situation more complicated."

"Complicated isn't the word for it."

"Hush. Keep your voice down. I don't want Anna, or anyone else, to know about this."

"I should imagine not. She'd try to talk you out of it."

"But if I can get her brother out and a violin, too, maybe she would eat again. I'm worried about her."

"Getting yourself killed won't help her feel better. And if they catch you, they'll torture you for our location. Going into that place will endanger all of us. Think about this more."

He stood in front of her to stop her back and forth. "I have to try. I can't stand seeing her so dejected and melancholy."

"Cheer her up some other way. Pick a few daffodils. Write her a poem. Draw her a picture."

"You studied at the conservatory."

"And what good does that do me now? You Germans stole my career from me. Before we had to flee, *Hauptsturmführer* Jaeger said he would arrange for me to play with the symphony. But here I am, forced once more to give that up. Here I sit, in the middle of the countryside, away from all I love." She stared straight into his eyes.

Horst backed down. "I'm sorry. Each of us has had to make sacrifices. It's not easy for anyone."

She relaxed her stance. "I'm sorry, too. I shouldn't take out my frustration on you."

"But that leaves us in the same place." He made a circuit around the hay bale. "I want to help. My *mutti* was right. After Kristallnacht, she aided our Jewish neighbors. God commands us to love all people, doesn't He? We're all created in His image."

"That's why I do what I do."

"But I can't. Before, my uniform, my position, prevented me from doing any good in any small way."

"You hid *Slečna* Zadoková and *Paní* Doubeková."

"But I didn't keep them safe. Or happy. I know it's a risk to try to rescue her brother. And yes, I'm doing it for her, to put a smile back on her face. To hear her music again. In the end, though, I want to do this for myself. It's selfish, that's true. I sent people to their sure deaths. I can't undo my crimes. Maybe I hope to absolve myself."

"Only God can rid you of your guilt."

"Can you help me? Will you?"

Lightning brightened the still-dark horizon as an early-season storm built. Through the flashes of light, Patricie worked to pack the cart with all the supplies Horst needed. "You are crazy to do this, you know that?"

LIZ TOLSMA

"Of course I am. But Anna's worth it. And I need to prove to her that I've changed. That I'm not the same person I was all those years ago."

Patricie had a man like that. One who would put his life on the line for her. Georg would make the ultimate sacrifice, if he had to. But this life didn't leave any time for love. She couldn't, wouldn't, commit to him until the insanity came to an end. If it ever did.

Because if she gave her heart to him and lost him, she'd break into a million little pieces. As it was, she had so little left. Not her music. The world inside of her was still. Silent. Too quiet.

She worked the kinks out of her shoulder muscles and stuffed several blankets under the straw. "Where's *Slečna* Zadoková?"

Horst added a few loaves of bread and a wheel of cheese. "She's helping *Paní* Doubeková get dressed for the day. We have to hurry. I don't want her to catch me leaving. She'll worry. And remember your promise not to tell her."

"It's a conditional promise. If I feel it's necessary for whatever reason, I'll share your secret."

"Fair enough."

"The beard is a nice touch. It helps to hide that crease by your mouth and your square chin."

"Anna questioned why I grew it. I wish it were fuller, but there is no time for that now." He pulled up the farmer's rough pants, much too large for him. "And no one will recognize me in these clothes. Nor will they want to get close to me."

"They do smell of cow."

"Perfect. I don't want the guards giving me too thorough an inspection."

"Just remember to give your German a Czech accent."

"That could be a little more difficult."

She laughed at his clumsy attempt. "Keep working at it." A curtain in the kitchen window fluttered. "Hurry. Someone in the house is watching."

Another peal of thunder rumbled in the distance. Horst stiffened, then shuddered. "Everything will be wet. I wanted to make David comfortable."

204

"I put most of the supplies in a knapsack. Especially the clothes he'll need. But if conditions at Terezín are like you say, he won't mind."

An unreadable expression passed over Horst's face.

"What is it? What aren't you telling me?"

"Nothing. Nothing at all."

He was lying, but she didn't press the matter. "If you want to be there and home by dark, you need to get going. This journey will be all this old horse can handle." She patted the animal's rump.

"I think I have everything. The clothes and food. The bribe money, should I need it. The forged papers. You and Georg are good at what you do."

Did he mean his comment as a compliment? She'd rather have there be no need for the job. The war meant she'd had to put her dreams for a career with the symphony on hold, too.

And she'd left Georg on his own. Perhaps, like Horst, she was trying to make up for her wrongs. "You're all set then. I'll pray for you and for the success of your mission."

"Thank you. That means a great deal to me, knowing I won't be alone out there."

"If I could, I would come with you."

"I know. But it's best if I do this on my own. Farmers come in with supplies, true enough. But they don't often bring their wives. It's a scene women would rather not see."

Out of impulse, Patricie leaned over and gave him a peck on the cheek. "God go with you."

The door behind them banged shut. Anna marched toward them. "What are you doing? Why are you kissing him?"

Words failed Patricie.

"And where are you going?"

Chapter Twenty-Six

*A*nna stood in the predawn light, waiting for Horst to answer. Or Patricie. Either one. She shivered and wrapped her hand-me-down housecoat around her. "Will someone answer? What's going on? Where are you off to?" Did she even want to know the answers to her questions?

Horst stepped forward. "I didn't want you to find out."

"I'm sure you didn't." Why did she care so much? She'd let him into her heart, allowed herself to believe that he understood her so well. Of course, he would want nothing to do with a Jew. He had participated in Kristallnacht, after all. Her throat burned.

"That's not what I meant."

Patricie leaned against the cart, the swayback horse hitched to it and chomping at the bit. "It was a peck on the cheek, nothing more. Just to wish him well."

"Wish him well? Why?" And why would he take off without saying good-bye to her? The early morning chill seeped into her bones.

"I'd rather not tell you."

"I don't understand all this secrecy. Why can't you share with me what you're doing?"

"I don't want to get your hopes up. I'm off to get a surprise for you. Or I hope to get a surprise for you. If all goes well."

Anna resisted the urge to stomp her foot. "Now you have me more confused than ever. Please, start from the beginning."

"I don't have much time. Just trust me. And trust that *Slečna* Kadlecová gave me nothing more than a friendly kiss on the cheek."

He came to her and touched her upper arms. "You're the woman who has enchanted me. You're the one sending me on this crazy errand."

He wore rough clothes, the pants held up with a rope. "At least I know why you grew the beard. Whatever you have planned, you've put a great deal of thought into it. But is it enough to fool anyone?"

"It will have to be."

"Just tell me. How will I stand the worry when I don't even know where you're going? I can't pray if I don't know."

"You'll worry more if I tell you."

"He's going to Terezín."

Anna gasped at Patricie's words.

Horst hissed at her. "Why did you say anything?"

"Since this is about her, she deserves to know."

Anna stepped from Horst's grasp. "Enough. You're going to Terezín? Tell me the reason you are doing such a foolish thing."

"I'm going to see your brother."

"What will that accomplish?"

"I have a plan to help him escape."

The gooseflesh spread to her entire body. Her brother? Oh, to see David again, to have one piece of her family restored to her. But at what cost? Horst's life? "*Ne.* I forbid it. You can't go there. That place stole my parents, my sisters, and my brother. I can't have it swallowing you too. No matter how good your disguise, someone is bound to recognize you."

"Patricie helped me put the plan together. It's a solid plot. She knows what she's doing."

"But no scheme is foolproof." How could she choose one person she loved over the other? Then another thought assaulted her. "You're doing this to get back into my good graces."

He shook his head. "*Ne.* I thought of this plan months ago. Before we ever came here."

"But you're putting it into motion now. Don't think bringing my brother to me will change anything." Her midsection heated. "Don't try something so foolish to undo what you did in the past."

Patricie hugged herself. "Barring any unforeseen circumstances, *Hauptmann* Engel should have no problem getting in and out."

"It's the unforeseen circumstances that frighten me. I wish you would have consulted me before you put this crazy idea into motion. Then I could have stopped it before it got this far." Before she had that moment of hope, that one second of believing she just might get her brother back.

"*Ne*, you couldn't have." Horst tried to pull her close, but she stepped away from him. "Our flight to the country put it on hold, but it's time now to implement it. I have to hurry to make it to Terezín and home in one day. Earlier this week, Karel sent an official-looking notice to the head of the work details requesting that David be excused today. If I don't make good time, I'll miss my window of opportunity to sneak him out of there."

Like a swimmer about to plunge under the water, Anna took a deep breath. "I'm going with you."

"*Nein*."

She flinched at that harsh word.

"Hush." Patricie shook her head. "Do you want everyone to hear you?"

Horst switched back to Czech. "*Ne*. That, I forbid. My going involves a degree of risk. But the risk is multiplied far too much for you to go. Stay here. Pray for me. But don't come."

"My mind is made up." She only needed to convince her quivering insides this was a good idea. "I'm riding with you. This is my brother we're talking about, and you're doing it for me. If it's too dangerous for me, it's too dangerous for you."

"I don't have papers for you." Patricie's voice was firm. "My group is working on forging some, but it hasn't happened yet. You can't go out."

"Does *Hauptmann* Engel have any identification?"

"Yes, he does."

"Anna, be reasonable. I've put more than one person in that horrible place. It's time for me to get one out. I couldn't stand it if anything happened to you. If I fail, it's only my life. If you're with me when I fail, it's both our lives. Losing you is too great a price to pay."

The fight slipped from her body. She melded into his embrace. "I don't want you to do this. Not for me."

"One life saved is better than none."

"And nothing I say can persuade you otherwise?"

He kissed her forehead and each of her cheeks. "My little *beruško*. I can't tell you what you mean to me. I would go to the moon for you if I had to. You miss your family more than you let on, but I see it in your eyes, in your face, every day."

"And if I lose you, too?"

"Pray nothing happens." Horst mounted the wagon's seat and picked up the reins. Without a backward glance, he clucked to the old nag and pulled from the farmyard, his slouchy hat drawn low over his eyes.

She stood beside Patricie as Horst disappeared out of sight. When the horizon swallowed the little cart, she fled to the outhouse so no one would see her tears.

With winter losing its bitter grip, a renewed vigor infused David. His cough lessened. His weakness decreased. Perhaps the old Jewish doctor in the camp was wrong. He had no equipment to diagnose tuberculosis, no X-ray machine. How could he know?

The order not to report to his work detail today bothered him. What did it mean? A transport that points east? They'd stopped awhile ago, with the advance of the Soviet Army. Were they resuming? He huddled under his thin blanket as a storm built in the west. As of yet, no summons arrived. No indication his name was on the list, if there even was one.

He paced the room, no bigger than the bedroom in the home where he grew up. That room had housed no one but him. This one, though at one time bursting at the seams, now contained only a handful. The numbers fluctuated over the years, depending on who the Nazis sent east. And who died. And who failed in their escape attempts, like his roommates.

For a while, he'd waited for that German soldier who'd come from time to time to arrive and whisk him away. Take him home. But months had passed since *Hauptmann* Engel pressed that piece of paper into his hand.

Nothing.

Nothing but an empty promise.

Well, no use dwelling on it. Fantasies were for children. Not for grown men living in a world gone crazy.

Ah, if only he could figure out what this strange order meant.

The bulging citadel of Theresienstadt loomed in front of Horst. A large arch led through the thick brick wall into the camp. A bitter taste stung his tongue. Though the sun peeked through the breaks in the heavy clouds, darkness reigned in the town's environs. Mud-splattered walls enclosed the gloom and filth.

He drove the cart to the gate where two uniformed Gestapo soldiers stopped him. "Papers, please."

He fumbled in the worn knapsack the farmer's wife had given him, in a way to play the part, in a way because his fingers quivered so much he couldn't grasp the identification booklet. After a long few seconds, he pulled it out and presented it to them.

The man squinted and studied them. "This is hard to make out."

"My apologies. They got wet in the rainstorm on the way here."

"Dry them or get yourself some new ones."

"Very good. I will."

The officer paused a moment. Horst's heart skipped a beat. After returning the identification, the man motioned for Horst to pass.

He released a shaky breath. One obstacle down, who knew how many more to go.

The town had changed very little since his last visit several months before. The occupants' clothes hung on them more. They moved at a slower pace. The rotten stench of death, like decaying leaves, hung ever more in the air.

How did they survive the long, cold months? And now the rains. If he could only fit all of them in his small cart and bring each of them to freedom and safety.

No use dwelling on what could not be. Horst steered the horse down the town's narrow streets to the men's quarters in the Magdeburg barracks. He reined the nag to a stop in front of David's living space, such as it was.

David may not even be alive. He had no confirmation of it one way or the other. Patricie hadn't been able to find out. But to bring a smile to Anna's face, it was all worth it. No matter what happened. He did this for her.

He slipped into the dark building and climbed the narrow, creaky stairs to the uppermost floor. He rubbed the back of his neck, trying to work out the crick that had developed in it from hunching in the wagon the past several hours.

Should he knock? Just go in? He turned the knob and entered the room. He covered his mouth to keep from gagging on the stench. A single bulb lit the cold, dingy space.

And there stood David, his back to Horst, peering out the window. His hair had grown, but he stood straighter, taller.

Horst warmed at seeing Anna's brother alive and in what appeared to be rather good health. "Excuse me."

David spun around, his mouth wide open. "Who are you? What is this all about?"

"I'm sorry I didn't knock. Don't you recognize me?"

"*Ne.*"

Well, that was the entire point of the disguise. "I'm *Hauptmann* Engel, the soldier who hid your sister and grandmother."

David turned his back and resumed gazing out the window. "I don't know anyone by that name."

"You don't have to pretend with me. I'm truly him. I don't have time to explain."

"I told you, I don't know the man you speak about."

"One of Anna's favorite movies is *Andula Vyhrála,* she almost drowned in the Vltava River when she was eight, and she wears perfume that smells like lilies of the valley. Do you believe me now?"

David relaxed his shoulders but didn't face Horst. "Why the getup?"

"You understood my note?"

"That was months ago."

"Our circumstances changed."

That got David's attention. "Are Anna and *Babička* well?"

"They're fine. And anxious to see you. Are you ready to go? Is your violin with you?"

"They aren't going to let me march right through the gate."

"I have a cart downstairs. There's a false bottom covered with hay. No time for other questions. We have to leave now."

"How do I know you're not taking me somewhere else?"

"You have to trust me. You have no other choice. And where would I take you? Get your instrument, and let's go."

David grabbed his violin from beside his thin mattress. He joined Horst near the door and gave a slow nod. Horst peered through the entry and made sure no one else hung about the corridor. Then he slunk down the stairs. Again, at the bottom of the steps, he paused and opened the front door. Blood pounded in his ears, drowning out every other sound.

No one milled about the streets. Good. He motioned David forward and to the cart. Horst held his breath as David crawled under the hay and into the small, hidden compartment. Even though he was as thin as a sheet of paper, he was tall. He curled up and just fit so Horst could close the top.

He fixed the straw and hopped on front.

Thank You, Lord. The operation was going smoother than he dared to hope it would. All he had to do was get out the gates, and he might be able to enjoy the ride.

He maneuvered around a corner and spotted a group of soldiers making their way down the main street. It would be better to turn back until the road cleared, but that would only draw more attention. He allowed the horse to plod on.

He approached the group, focusing on the reins in his hands.

"Hey, you, farmer boy."

Oh, no, it couldn't be. *Dear God, no.*

"I'm talking to you, farmer."

Stefan.

Chapter Twenty-Seven

"Anna, you're pacing again." *Babička* sat at the kitchen table helping Maria peel a few boiled eggs they planned to pickle. "Come, sit down and make yourself useful."

"I'm not sure I can be still."

"What makes you so restless? The last time you were like this, Horst moved in downstairs."

"I know. I know. But my feet refuse to be quiet."

"It's not your body that won't settle down. It's your spirit." *Babička* had a habit of always piercing to the heart of the matter. "What is it, child?" She pushed the ceramic bowl to the side and motioned for Anna to join her at the table.

The farmer's wife, her hands and face worn by many years of hard labor, scraped her chair back. "I'll leave you two alone."

"There's no need. It's nothing personal or private. But it may involve all of us sooner rather than later."

Maria pushed her chair in and resumed her egg peeling. "Why?"

"Horst has gone to Terezín to try to rescue David."

A bevy of emotions played across *Babička's* wrinkled face. First, her eyes widened. Then, all her features softened and sank. "My grandson. My heart aches for him. But this is not a good idea."

"That's what I tried to tell Horst, but he refused to listen. That man has a head harder than a rock. And if he's captured, we all might be in danger." Anna stared out the window. The storm had passed, and the sun worked to break through the clouds. "The roads are sure to be muddy. Will he even be able to drive that cart all the way home without getting stuck?"

Babička joined Anna at the window. "That's not what has you distracted."

A bubble burst in Anna's chest. "It's all too much." The words eked from her throat.

"I know, child, I know. When someone you love is separated from you, your heart aches."

"I don't understand any of this. Why did God take *Máma* and *Táta* and my sisters from me? Even if I live to be an old woman, that pain will never leave. I'll never see them again. Never hear their words of advice, feel their touch on my shoulder, or see the warmth in their faces. Never. That's a very long time."

"And now Horst went away."

"What if I lose him, too?" Tears fell, unbidden.

"This happens because you feel for him."

"Of course I do." Anna wiped her eyes and drew a deep breath. "But there's something you don't know." She turned to Maria. "That neither of you know."

"And this makes a difference in your feelings for him?" Maria tapped an egg on the table.

"Yes. *Ne.* I don't know. It's all mixed up inside me." She shifted her weight from one foot to the other, then drew in a giant breath. "He terrorized his Jewish neighbor on Kristallnacht."

"And?" *Babička* turned Anna so she gazed at her grandmother.

"That's enough, *ne*? Enough to break my trust and erase the minute chance we had at a relationship."

"You know, Anna, he's not an evil monster. He's a human being trying to survive. Like any of us. And caught in circumstances beyond his control."

"No one forced him to break his neighbor's window. Or beat the man."

"You don't know what kind of pressure he faced from his peers. And we all make mistakes in our youth."

"Mistakes, yes. Harming others, *ne*. Why doesn't this upset you?"

Maria wiped her hands on her apron. "It's a shocking revelation. But you have to look at the sum of his actions, not one small part. If he continued down that path, he wouldn't have rescued you. He would have carried your bags to the exhibition hall for you and would have put you on the train himself."

Anna nodded, but crossed her arms.

Babička patted her hand. "True, true. He's had ample opportunity to hurt us, but he has been nothing but kind. And now, he's risking his life to bring your brother to you. To break him out of the prison camp. What does that tell you?"

Anna stiffened. "If he truly were a good man, he never would have done what he did. He's trying to rectify a wrong he committed."

"Do you believe that?" *Babička* rubbed her arm, and Anna relaxed.

Did she? What did she believe about Horst anymore? "I'm ... I'm not sure. Nothing is as it should be these days."

Babička leaned over. "What is in your heart? Look there. Don't let your head do all the thinking."

"In my heart?" What did her heart say to her about Horst? She trembled to even venture into this territory. How could she, a Jew, feel these things for a Nazi?

But yet, he wasn't a Nazi in the truest sense of the word. He didn't hate her, didn't want to exterminate her race. He was kind, compassionate. Like that day in the flat in Prague, before *Hauptsturmführer* Jaeger came, when he'd spoken to her and calmed her.

In the midst of their flight, he'd made sure *Babička* was comfortable. He'd put himself in danger to bring food to David. And now, he'd gone to rescue her brother.

He was a haven in a hurricane.

When he wasn't near, a chill pervaded her. Like she was without an arm or a leg.

Could it be?

A shaft of sunlight pierced the clouds. "I love him." She leaned against the wall, her knees weak.

"Yes, that's what has been in your heart these past weeks. What makes you not eat or sleep." Maria grinned. "I've watched you. I knew. Your grandmother did, too. We all did."

"I thought love made you happy."

Babička pulled back a stray strand of gray hair. "This love frightens you."

Anna rubbed the plastered wall. "Loving him is forbidden. It's dangerous. Impossible. What kind of future do we have? And I question if I can trust him."

"At some point, the war will end. You'll be free once more, free to love him."

"If we survive that long."

"God has protected us this far."

"And how much longer will He watch over us? How long can we hold out? What if the war ends in victory for the Germans?"

"You are borrowing trouble."

"Trouble has found me."

Babička moved back to the table. For a moment, she sat and caught her breath. "I remember your mother as a child. So beautiful she was. Like you. She sat beside me on the piano bench, hour after hour, as I played. As she watched me, she laughed. She plunked out the melody, her tiny fingers stretched to reach the next key. And do you know what I thought about at those times?"

Anna shook her head.

"I wished for her to hurry and grow up, so I could listen to her play some of those same songs. And I got my wish. Before I knew it, she developed better tone and technique than me. Then she met your father, got married, and left the house. It was empty and silent. And I longed to have her next to me on the stool."

"And now she's gone. My pain is your pain."

Babička drew out the handkerchief she tucked underneath her watchband and dabbed at the moisture gathered in the corners of her eyes. "Don't worry about tomorrow. Each day has enough worry of its own."

Anna recognized the passage from the book of Matthew.

"Cherish today before it flits away. Horst is a changed man. Love him, and don't let this chance at happiness slip through your fingers. Your parents wanted this for you."

But how could she give herself to a man who had done the things Horst did?

Horst sat still on the cart's seat, clutching the horse's reins until his hands went numb. Could Stefan tell this wagon had a false bottom? Did he somehow know David lay inside? The straw. Had he covered up the opening well enough?

Stefan called to him again. "Farmer, *halten sie*. I want to inspect your load."

Horst pulled his slouchy hat farther down, over his face more, and stroked his beard. If he spoke, Stefan would recognize him. Instead, he nodded and tugged on the reins. The horse came to a stop.

"Climb down."

Horst obeyed the order. Why was Stefan even here? He liked to come, true enough, and enjoyed the power he had over the residents here. Now, he carried a rifle with a bayonet. Why? Perhaps the higher-ups had transferred him. Perhaps he'd taken the job first offered to Horst.

Stefan approached him. "Papers." His cold tone froze Horst to the core.

He produced the identification booklet, holding his breath. It had passed muster before. Would it now? Stefan was nothing if not meticulous.

"What is your business here?"

Great. Now he had to answer. "Delivery." He mumbled as much as possible.

"Speak up."

"Delivery." A nice, halting German accent. Believable, he hoped.

Stefan stepped right in front of Horst, nose to nose. "My patience with you is wearing thin. I want answers to my questions. What kind of delivery?"

Horst's mouth went dry. Under his beard, his upper lip sweat. Was this the fear Anna experienced when he first moved in? "Potatoes."

"That's all?"

"*Ja.*"

"Then let me see."

"Already delivered."

"Empty sacks."

"In the kitchen." Too much talking. Stefan would see through the disguise and the fake accent soon enough.

"Then let's see what's under that straw."

Trying to stop Stefan from searching the back of the cart would only serve to raise his suspicions. Horst gritted his teeth and put on as nonchalant a front as he could muster. He stroked the horse's nose to calm himself as much as the animal.

Stefan climbed in the back. With his bayonet, he stabbed at the straw. Would it penetrate the cart's wooden bottom? Injure David huddled underneath?

God, blind his eyes.

Stefan kicked at the straw. Horst's pulse raced. Stefan could uncover the trap door. When he did, he would lift it and find David.

Would he bother to arrest them or shoot them on the spot?

Mutti, sweeping glass from the watchmaker's shop's floor. *Vater*, demanding he be a man and serve his country. Anna, trembling in his arms, her brown eyes wide. All of this flashed through his mind in a split second.

Stefan grunted. "Nothing here. I thought for sure." He hopped down and pointed at Horst. "I'm going to be watching you from now on. See this eagle on my hat?" He pointed to it. "Like an eagle, stalking you until I catch you in the act. I know I've seen you before. And we will meet again."

With that, Stefan marched off, his hands clenched at his sides.

Horst couldn't scramble into the cart fast enough. They had to get out of here. He picked up the leather reins and slapped the horse's back. The ancient mare plodded down the street. Couldn't she increase her pace? The farmer should have given him a faster nag.

Each step, though maddening in its slowness, brought him closer to the gate. After a few minutes, though to Horst it could have been an hour, they arrived at Theresienstadt's entrance. The only way in. The only way out.

The same guards that permitted him to pass earlier stopped him now. They performed the same gut-checking inspection as Stefan.

One of the soldiers stopped after one stab in the straw. "Quiet. I think I heard something."

All three of them stood stock still. Had one of them injured David? Did he cry out in pain? *Nein, Lord, protect him under there. Keep him safe. And hidden.*

The stockier of the soldiers broke the silence. "You're hearing things. No contraband here. Let him go."

"I know I heard a sound. Like a groan."

Or a cough. If David could just have remained silent a few minutes more.

"You have a vivid imagination." The one guard nodded to Horst. "Proceed."

He hopped back up and drove that nag as fast as she would go. Unlike Lot's wife, he didn't dare turn back. He hoped never to see that miserable cesspool again.

Not until at least half an hour went by did he stop. By then, he figured them to be far enough away that if David's absence was noted, they had a good head start. But with his excuse from work, no one should notice until tomorrow. And with the rate of death in the camp, he doubted anyone would care.

He pulled off to the side of the road and slowed the horse. Unsure of what he might find, he climbed in the back, brushed away the straw, and slid the trap door open.

David uncoiled and climbed out of the small hole. A grin stretched across his thin face. "That was quite the adventure." He swiveled and surveyed the Czech countryside. He whistled. "Look at all of this. Open fields. Evergreen trees. Birds singing. There is beauty left in this world."

"Not much of it."

"Much better than that hole where you Germans condemned me and tens of thousands of others."

"I wish I could have taken more men."

"Is it safe for me to ride up front with you?"

It must be horrible, crammed in that tiny space kilometer after kilometer. "Maybe for a little while." No one used the road much.

David climbed beside him. "Why did you rescue me?"

"Because what my countrymen are doing to you is wrong. Atrocious. Unforgivable. I myself sent more than one person there."

"You want to absolve yourself, then?"

"Maybe. I don't know."

"Are you sweet on my sister?"

Horst didn't answer, either out loud to David or in his own heart.

"Where are we going? This isn't the way to Prague."

"We moved. I'll tell you about it as we go along."

By the time they neared the farmhouse on the outskirts of the tiny country hamlet, he'd related the entire story. Every sordid detail, including his own involvement in it. The young man beside him didn't interject a single comment. Not that Horst expected him to.

The farmhouse came into view, a sloping roof crowning the top of the white stucco home. He pulled into the yard. Before he'd even stopped, Anna raced from the house, her blue skirt flapping.

David climbed down, his steps slow and measured. His sister reached him and flung herself into his arms. Hopefully none of the neighbors witnessed the reunion.

Anna and her brother hugged each other, their sobs reaching Horst's ears. For a long, long time they stood there, clinging to each other.

David stepped back, pulled a handkerchief from his pocket, and coughed into it. He drew it away, but Anna caught him by the wrist. A red stain marked the white fabric.

She blanched. "What is this?"

Chapter Twenty-Eight

*A*nna stepped away from her brother, unable to believe her eyes. Here he stood, in front of her. In the flesh. Could it really be him? She reached out and touched him.

Ne, she didn't dream. He was here.

Horst did it. Snuck her brother out of that miserable place. She itched to pick up a violin and play. The music, so long gone, flooded her.

Then David coughed and pulled away the handkerchief red with blood.

Oh God, ne.

The melody inside her dimmed. "What's wrong, David? Please, tell me." Her stomach clenched.

"Let's enjoy our reunion. There will be plenty of time for other talk later. Nothing but happiness now."

She swallowed hard but nodded. "This is a time for joy. Wait until *Babička* sees you. She'll never get over it."

"How is she?" David walked to the house, his steps slow and careful.

"She's an old woman, and all of this has been hard on her. No one of her age should be forced to live like this. The move has taken its toll."

David pulled her into a side hug as they strolled. "I never thought I'd see any of my family again. *Táta* waved to me as I watched the guards close the train doors. The last glimpse I had of any of them." He glanced at the sky as two fat tears rolled down his sunken cheeks.

"How were they?"

"You know them." David gave a wry laugh and wiped his eyes. "I didn't see *Máma* and the girls much, but *Táta*, I did. He spoke to me about God, about God's protection. God didn't protect them. They're dead." Another tear dribbled down his face.

Anna pulled her brother to a stop and stood in front of him. She stroked his hollow cheek. "*Táta* would say God did protect them."

David scrunched his heavy eyebrows. "I don't understand. How is that?"

"The Lord brought them to heaven. They are safe with Him now. No more harm will ever come to them. No more tears. No more hardship. Nothing but peace and joy."

"I want to believe. But look around you. Is this what God wants for us?"

Behind her, a door banged open. "David? Is that you? Come here, my child, and let me see you." Anna turned. *Babička* stood in the entryway and motioned to her grandson.

David moved forward into his grandmother's embrace. Anna clutched her chest. How good this was for *Babička*. Perhaps it would revive her. Give her a reason to live once more.

Horst joined her. "I think she's happy to see him."

"How did you do it? How did you get him out?"

"Our plan worked with only one hitch or two."

"Something went wrong?" Patricie caught up to them.

"I met Stefan."

Anna sucked in her breath. "You what?"

"He stopped me on the street. I had already tucked David under the straw."

"He didn't recognize you?" Patricie widened her eyes.

"*Ne*. Your disguise was perfect. The beard, the hat, and the clothes. No flicker of recognition crossed his face. Let me tell you, I held my breath the entire time. The Lord watched over me, that's for sure. I thought he would remember my voice, but he didn't." Horst's face lit up like a child's on Christmas morning.

They came to the house, and Patricie entered. Anna tugged on Horst's rough wool shirt and halted him. She wanted to hold him, but resisted the urge. Instead, she smiled. "*Děkuji, děkuji.* I cannot thank you enough for what you did for David."

"I did it for you." He bit his lower lip. "To put that grin back on your face. To make the music sing in your heart again. Wait here. I have a surprise for you." He ran back to the wagon and opened the trap door.

Did her eyes deceive her? Was that . . . ?

He sprinted toward her and held out a violin case. David's?

"I know it's not yours, but perhaps he'll let you play it."

She took it, loving the weight of it in her hands. But no song danced in her head. The music, long absent, refused to come. "Perhaps he'll play for us."

"I would love for you to." Horst's voice was husky.

"And *Paní* Karas might set out a welcome home feast if we ask her."

"Ah, Anna." He brushed a lock of hair from her cheek.

A shiver raced down her spine.

He leaned over, ready to kiss her.

She licked her lips, a buzz about her. Then she turned from him. Not yet. She couldn't let him that close yet.

Babička opened the farmhouse door. "Anna, Horst, come in, come in. David wants his violin so he can play us a piece Egon Ledeč composed in the camp. Good, you have it." She motioned them inside.

Horst whispered to her as they entered. "I'll talk to you later."

She presented David's violin to him and settled next to Horst on the sofa to hear her brother play. The warmth of Horst's body seeped inside her.

David, very, very thin and frail, nonetheless coaxed a tune from his instrument, a lusty, boot-tapping, skirt-swinging Czech folk song. The group clapped along in time to the music. He played two more smooth, upbeat tunes before slumping onto an empty chair. They applauded.

"That is enough for now. I cannot play more than that."

The cold dread which had gripped her outside returned. "You're not well."

"Is anyone in that place?" He coughed, and again his handkerchief came away spotted with blood.

"We'll get you a doctor." *Babička* nodded, as if that settled the issue.

"What good will a doctor do me?"

Anna gripped the couch's rounded armrest. "Have you seen one already?"

"In the camp."

"They didn't have the medicine you need there. *Slečna* Kadlecová, is there one we can trust to see him?"

"I'll find out the next time someone from the resistance comes."

David plucked a few strings. "For you, to make you happy, I'll see a doctor if you find one. But I know what he'll say."

Anna braced herself for the news.

Babička fingered her sweater's sleeve. "You have tuberculosis."

David nodded. "The disease is progressing. I don't think I have long left."

Anna dove from her chair and knelt in front of her brother. "Maybe the fresh air here will do you good. You will grow stronger, you'll see. *Paní* Karas will feed you well. We'll get extra rations for you. You will get better. You have to."

"Anna, don't." David rubbed her shoulder. "Don't make this harder than it already is."

Ne, God, You can't take him. He just came back.
You can't.

"We'll do everything we can for you, David." Horst would go to whatever lengths it took to keep David alive. For Anna's sake.

David helped Anna to her feet. "I appreciate it. You aren't half bad, for a Nazi."

Horst took that as the highest compliment. Maybe David would go through with the plan to consult with a doctor. At the very least, to give Anna a sliver of hope. A bit of time to deal with the news.

Patricie leaned against the doorway into the kitchen, her arms crossed. "It bothers me that you met *Hauptsturmführer* Jaeger."

"Why? I told you, he didn't recognize me. He had no clue who he stopped. He thought I was some farmer bringing in supplies. Don't worry." He didn't want to alarm the women, but the concern did cross his mind.

Stefan wouldn't rest until he hunted down Horst. Anger, hatred, and evil drove that man to the brink of insanity. Maybe even over it. He would sniff out Horst and not stop until he found him and exterminated him. And everyone around him.

He shivered.

"You don't know that you weren't followed."

Horst tightened his jaw, then relaxed it. "I'm a trained German officer. Give me a little credit."

"Then maybe you're infiltrating us now. How can we be sure?" Patricie narrowed her eyes and stared at him until he squirmed.

"In that case, why would I risk my life to bring David here? He was already in the camp. You're not making any sense."

Anna dried her tears. "Stop it. Both of you. Patricie, I know it's easy to be paranoid. Don't you think I jump at every little sound, every car that passes, every knock on the door? But Horst has done much to prove himself. He won't turn us in."

Was that a crack in the wall between them? Dare he hope that his rescuing David had helped her believe he was a changed man? He wanted to swing her around the room in a dance. Instead, he held the feeling close. Savored it.

The urge to kiss her almost overtook him, even more than it had a few minutes ago outside. *Nein*, he didn't want to admit it to David or to himself.

It was too dangerous to say the words. Too dangerous to even think about. If Stefan ever knew ...

But he loved her.

Heaven help him, he loved her.

Crickets chirped underneath Horst's window. Winter had melted into early spring. The farmer planted his crops. Chicks hatched from their eggs. The cow gave birth to a calf. Horst almost dared to breathe a sigh of relief.

David snored in the bed beside him. Though the doctor confirmed the tuberculosis diagnosis, the fresh country air did improve David's condition. He remained weak, but he played his violin almost every day.

From downstairs came a creaking of the floorboards, then Anna's soft voice as she whispered to the cat and let him out for the night. Even when she spoke, and though she told him the music left her, her voice lilted.

Unable to resist the siren song, he flung the sheet away and pulled on a pair of pants. He slunk from the room and down the hall, careful to keep quiet. On childhood Christmas mornings, he'd always peek at the tree from the top of the stairs, not able to wait until his parents woke.

Watching Anna was much the same.

How much more time would it take for her to forgive him? To trust him again? He sat on the middle step and observed her through the railing. She turned off all the lights, opened the blackout curtains, and stood in a pool of moonlight with her back to him, her dark hair cascading down her back.

When he went to bed later, he would sketch her, capture her just this way and hold onto the moment forever.

For the longest time, she didn't move. Then she picked up David's violin and stroked it. She didn't lift it to her chin or grasp the bow. She simply caressed it.

He held his breath.

Then she set it on the couch.

"Anna?"

She turned and stared right at him. "You are spying on me, *ne*?"

He chuckled at the teasing tone in her voice. "You caught me."

"What are you doing out of bed?"

"I couldn't sleep." He descended the rest of the steps.

She came to him. "Have you been having nightmares?"

"Yes."

"Bad ones?"

"Worse than ever, since you stopped playing for me."

"David doesn't help?"

"Not like you did."

"I'm sorry. It . . . it just won't come." He'd never heard such wistfulness in his life.

"When this is all over, it will."

"It really helped you?" She hugged herself.

"*Mutti* and I went to the symphony every weekend. I listened to masters from all over Europe. Never did I hear one of them play as well as you. I'm sorry the laws forced you to stop your education. When this is over, you'll have a brilliant career. I have no doubt of it."

She stepped close, not quite touching him. "Life will never be the same. For any of us."

"This is temporary. God will not allow evil to win."

"The Americans joined the fight over three years ago. *Táta* told me to hold on because they would soon be here. Yes, they are now on European soil. Paris has been liberated. But how much longer do we have to hold out? How long until they slog their way here?"

"I don't know. I can't tell you. But I do know that it will end. It has to." Good would triumph, wouldn't it?

He leaned over and brushed a kiss against her soft cheek. He whispered into her hair. "I love you."

Light from a car's headlamps swept across the wall behind them. Gravel crunched under tires.

Anna stiffened. "Who's here?"

The moon illuminated the vehicle.

A German transport truck.

Chapter Twenty-Nine

$\mathscr{F}$ear slashed across Anna's middle as the headlights shone through the farmhouse's big window. She drew her housecoat around herself.

Horst peered outside. "A transport truck. They found us. Or, should I say, Stefan did."

How much longer would her legs support her? "What do we do now?"

"Get everyone up. Fast. The farmer's wife will have to stall."

Anna raced up the stairs to her grandmother's bedroom. *Babička* slept on her side, her mouth open as she snored. Anna shook her awake. "*Hauptsturmführer* Jaeger is here. Grab your coat and suitcase. I'll straighten your bed. We don't have time to waste."

The floors creaked as the rest of the household stirred. *Pan* Karas had devised a plan for just this scenario soon after they arrived. They'd practiced it several times, shaving off precious seconds, knowing just what to do. Putting the scheme into motion was another thing, however.

Anna pulled up the sheet and blanket on the bed and fluffed the pillows before picking up *Babička*'s suitcase. They could leave no trace of their presence. Even a hairpin on the floor might give them away.

In the other room, David coughed. Anna's hands trembled as she led *Babička* to the hall. The SS patrol rang the bell and butted their rifles against the door.

"I'm coming, I'm coming. Give a woman a chance to get decent." No fear marked *Paní* Karas's words.

Horst met Anna, *Babička*, David, and Patricie at the bottom of the stairs, his sketchbook in his hands. "Ready? Move as fast as possible. Make no noise."

The farmer stood in the middle of the kitchen, ready for action. He took charge. "Let's get *Paní* Doubeková and *Pan* Zadok into position first." He slid open the hinged china cabinet, revealing a hidden door. The tiny space allowed only *Babička* to hide in there.

Anna kissed her grandmother's cool, wrinkled cheek. "I love you. No matter what happens, always remember I love you."

Babička patted her face. "And I love you, my *beruško*. God be with you."

"And with you." Anna fought back the tears that threatened to fall. She forced herself to remain calm. If she got upset, she might make a mistake and give them all away.

While she bade her grandmother farewell, Karel moved the table to the side and lifted the worn rag rug, exposing a trap door. Conditions in the little hole under the floor were not ideal for David, but what could they do? He had to hide.

David coughed once more. "I promise not to do that down there. Whatever it takes, I will remain silent."

"God go with you."

David didn't echo her prayer. That cut her to the quick, maybe even more than the news that tuberculosis ravaged his body. When he did leave them, where would he go?

The farmer dropped the trapdoor into place. At the front, the Gestapo continued to demand entrance.

"Hurry, hurry. My wife can't hold them off much longer."

Horst, Anna, and Patricie slipped out the back door and tiptoed across the dew-moistened grass like stealth undercover agents.

The barn door creaked as Horst opened it. Anna held her breath, expecting the Nazis to sprint around the side of the house at any moment. Instead, they shouted from the front. "Open up now, or we will break down the door."

Her pulse throbbed in her neck. She couldn't swallow. Couldn't breathe. Couldn't even think.

They rushed by the cows who chewed their cud as if the world had not gone mad. Horst held the ladder as first Patricie, then Anna, ascended to the hayloft. He came behind them.

Once at the top, he kicked the ladder over. "Under the hay. Let's go. They might come in at any second."

"Horst, I'm frightened. *Hauptsturmführer* Jaeger won't send us to Terezín. He'll shoot us. You know he will."

"We have to trust the Lord to blind his eyes." He brushed her cheek. "I meant what I said before. I love you, Anna."

Could a moment be so beautiful and so horrible all at the same time? Yet, she held back.

"Now, go."

Anna scrambled under the haystack. The straw scratched her arms. Sweat rolled down her cheek. She pulled her little suitcase with her.

Wait. She hadn't grabbed everything. "David's violin. I left it laying on the couch. It's out there in the open. They'll see it. They'll know someone else was here."

Horst crawled in beside her. "It's fine. Don't worry about it."

Patricie moved beside her. "We train those who host *ponorky,* the submarines, what to do in such situations. *Paní* Karas is a savvy woman. She has a quick mind. She'll come up with some explanation."

But the assurances did nothing to calm Anna. How could she have been so careless? It wasn't only her life on the line. Six others depended on her to get it right. She'd let them down. "I'm so, so very sorry."

Horst squeezed her hand. "You have nothing to be sorry for. Like Patricie said, *Paní* Karas will think of a reason for it to be there."

Dear Lord, don't let them spot it. Avert their eyes.

Below them, the big barn door squeaked open. The guttural reverberation of German voices filled the air. Their words grated. Anna shivered. Her stomach heaved.

"Search everywhere. I know they're in here. They aren't that crafty."

Was that *Hauptsturmführer* Jaeger's voice? Anna couldn't be sure. It should be seared into her brain, but she couldn't bring it to mind.

No matter. Anyone could take them away.

Thunk. The ladder going into place? Yes. Boots creaked up it. Anna curled into a ball. As if that would do any good.

Though I pass through the valley of the shadow of death, I will fear no evil.

The clomp of boots drew nearer.

How long, O Lord, how long? When would she see His face?

"I can smell them."

She had no doubt.

Hauptsturmführer Jaeger.

Feet shuffled.

"Under the hay."

Ne, ne, ne.

Hauptsturmführer Jaeger's words rang in Patricie's head. "I know they're here."

He would never rest, never give up his search. Even if he left today, he would be back tomorrow. And the day after. And the day after. Until he nabbed them.

Not them. Patricie doubted he would put this much energy into finding a couple of Jews. *Ne.* She and Horst were the prizes. Anna and her grandmother were the bonuses.

The straw prickled Patricie's skin. The stiff grasses cut her cheek. *Hauptsturmführer* Jaeger's boots shuffled on the wood floor.

"Stab at the straw until you hit something."

They would be killed. All of them. And if he found Horst or Anna, he would assume the rest hid here, too.

She couldn't do that to them. Couldn't let him take them all away.

"It is better that one man die than for the nation to perish."

Was this what the Lord was asking of her? Was this what He wanted her to do?

"Sirs, you are upsetting my cows." Karel. God bless him for trying to distract the Gestapo. "The milk will sour."

"Shut up." Venom tainted *Hauptsturmführer* Jaeger's words. "Get this man out of here before I arrest him. Or worse."

She had never heard him angrier. How could he be so cruel? So heartless? Did he even have a soul?

Her stomach quivered. Blood whooshed in her ears. She labored for each breath.

If he caught them, he would show them no mercy. None at all.

God, what is the right thing to do? Please. Reveal Your will.

"Better that one man die …"

There had to be a different route.

"This cause might require your life." Georg had spoken those words as she'd sat at his petite kitchen table at the beginning of the war. She had watched, helpless, as Eliška fell into the Gestapo's grasp. Vanished into thin air. One day they'd laughed, sang, and played music together. The next, Eliška was gone, her breakfast cold on her plate. Her blood staining the ancient, cobblestone street.

"If my life is required of me, so be it." The words had flowed from Patricie's lips. "I'll be careful, Georg. You know me. You can trust me. I want to work with you. I don't know why you didn't tell me about this before. We've been best friends since we were children with the same music teacher."

Georg had leaned forward, the lines around his eyes and mouth changing him from a twenty-three-year-old man into a wise, old soul in an instant. "This isn't a game. I understand you want to help, but even knowing my secret puts you in danger. I never wanted to do that to you."

"I'm stronger than you give me credit for. And I will never, never give you away. No matter what they do to me."

"Don't you understand? People's lives depend on us. One wrong move, one slip-up, and it doesn't cost just us. Two, three, four, or more might lose everything. Can you do it? Take a long, hard look at yourself, Patricie, and tell me if you can do it."

"Do what?" She'd whispered, afraid to say the words aloud.

"Give your life for someone else."

"Find them. Find them now." *Hauptsturmführer* Jaeger's harsh words snapped Patricie out of her memories. "I smell Jew blood. I smell traitor blood."

She moved. Anna grabbed her. Held her in place.

Patricie shook free. Before she lost her nerve, she wriggled from under the hay.

"*Hauptsturmführer* Jaeger."

"Patricie." He focused his steely gaze on her. "I knew you were here. You stupid, insolent, filthy Jew lover." He slapped her across her cheek.

She stumbled backward. "You caught me."

"And where are the rest? I know you aren't alone."

"Would I be so foolish as to stay with them all this time? To put myself in more danger? *Ne*, I sent them across the border months ago. They're in Palestine now. Far, far out of your reach. And for that, I am glad." If he was about to shoot her, she might as well tell him her mind.

He withdrew his pistol. "I could kill you on the spot. I should." He raised the weapon.

"Do with me what you will. Soon I'll be with Jesus. Away from the pain and suffering of this world. But what about you? Do you have that assurance?"

"I'm warning you, woman. Do you think God will save you now? Do you think your talk will save me? Try again. I don't need you. I don't need anyone."

Hauptsturmführer Jaeger cocked his gun.

"God have mercy on your soul." Peace, joy, longing filled Patricie. Music flooded her.

She was ready.

Chapter Thirty

Ice ran through Anna's veins. What was Patricie doing? Thinking?

Oh God, protect her life.

Beside her, Horst stiffened. Coiled, as if about to pounce. She grabbed him. *Ne, ne,* she refused to let him give himself up. This had to stop.

He quieted.

Thank You, Lord.

"You can call off your dogs." Patricie's voice was strong. "No one else is here. And don't harm the family who lives here. They knew nothing of my presence on their property. I've been on the run and stopped here to sleep tonight. I never approached them."

"We'll see about that." Stefan clipped each word. "Arrest the farmer."

Patricie cried out. Had *Hauptsturmführer* Jaeger struck her? Anna clung to Horst and waited, not even daring to breathe.

"I knew," *Hauptsturmführer* Jaeger growled. "From the moment I met you, I knew. Carrying that heavy bag. Popping up in strange places around the city. Holding tight to the car door's handle. All of it gave you away. You are careless. Not a trait I admire. And now, I'll teach you a lesson. One you soon won't forget."

"Let go of me. I'll come with you willingly."

"Never. I don't trust you. I never did. I could have made you something. But you're nothing more than a vile, Jew-loving pig yourself."

The clomp of boots and the softer footfalls of oxfords sounded on the ladder. Voices faded. Time ticked away. Anna sweated, then shivered. Her back ached. Her legs ached. Still she didn't move.

The truck engine roared to life. Gravel crunched under the wheels. The world fell silent. Eerie. Strange. Frightening.

Did an eternity pass?

Horst stirred. He grasped Anna by the hand and helped her from under the haystack. He brushed her off and kissed the top of her head.

They descended the ladder and, after checking to be sure *Hauptsturmführer* Jaeger had left, returned to the house. *Paní* Karas stirred the fire in the stove, dried tears streaking her face. David and *Babička* sat at the table, each with a mug of fragrant rose hip tea.

"*Paní* Karas." Anna approached her.

The farmer's wife stilled, a single tear shimmering on her weathered cheek. "They took Karel."

"And *Slečna* Kadlecová." Horst's voice cracked.

Then she spied it on the counter. The smashed violin. *Hauptsturmführer* Jaeger had destroyed it.

Anna collapsed into a chair and rested on the table. Tears refused to come, unable to provide her release. She couldn't think about what had transpired in that barn.

Horst rubbed her back. *Babička* set a mug beside her, but she couldn't lift her head to sip it. The cuckoo announced the hour. One call.

Oh, that she might sleep and find this was a bad dream. To have *Máma* and *Táta* back, to not fear for her life, to not be hunted like an animal.

What had Patricie done? Why? If she could just understand.

But she couldn't.

More time slipped away. David cleared his throat. "What happened in the barn?"

Horst stopped his gentle rubbing. "Just as Stefan was about to stab at the straw, Patricie crawled out."

Anna sat up. "She gave herself up and told him to call off the search. Risky. Daring. But it worked. He came back in here, *ne?*"

The farmer's wife shook her head. "*Ne*. We watched through the window. They brought *Slečna* Kadlecová out, and my husband."

"*Paní* Karas told us what was going on." David stopped and

swallowed. "I thought for sure the next words from her would bring news of your arrest. And that it would be our turn after that."

"I waited for them to come for me." Maria rubbed her arms. "How did they not take me away for hiding her, only my husband? That I don't know. I can't answer. But she must have persuaded them."

Anna sipped her tea. "She did. She told them she didn't have any contact with you. That she'd only stopped here for the night and you didn't know. *Hauptsturmführer* Jaeger arrested your husband out of spite."

"He is an evil man." David coughed.

The question burning in Anna's chest flew from her lips. "Why? I don't understand. Do you? Any of you? How could she give her life for people who are almost strangers to her?"

Babička pushed her mug away from her. "Better love has no man than this, that he lay his life down for his friends."

"That's from the Bible." Anna remembered the passage.

"Yes, from John 15."

David finger-combed his wild brown hair. "I don't see it. What is the motivation? No one does anything without some driving force behind him. Many times, that force is self-preservation. That's what moves us all. It's what kept me alive in Terezín. What keeps me alive today. Simply moving forward, waking up with each sunrise. Life is nothing more than that. And when that will to live wanes, we die."

Anna longed to cover her ears, to drown out David's philosophical babble.

Babička patted her grandson's hand. "My boy, it's so much more than that. Remember what your mother and father taught you as a small child."

Another knock at the door. This one almost as wild as the last, but singular.

Had *Hauptsturmführer* Jaeger returned?

Pani Karas peered around the blackout shades. "No truck. No shouting. It's not him. This fellow is small. Stay where you are. I'll get rid of him." She slipped through the door.

A moment later, she returned with a short, bespectacled man.

Georg. The man from the flat the night they'd fled Prague. The one who loved Patricie.

"Come in, come in." *Pani* Karas bustled about, pulling another chair to the table, pouring another cup of tea. Calm, even in the face of her husband's arrest.

Georg joined them. Lines radiated from his youthful eyes. "I've come to warn you."

"*Hauptsturmführer* Jaeger was already here." Horst eyed him.

"Then I am too late. They raided my apartment when I was away. I had lists of homes where we hid Jews. This one wasn't on it, because I never used it before you, but I thought maybe the others gave away this location."

"That's how he knew where to find us." Anna warmed her hands on the teacup.

"I'm afraid so. I never went back inside, but informed our contacts they were in danger. They raided several homes and found some *ponorky*. You are my last stop. The farthest away. I thought I might make it here in time. Where is Patricie? I want to see her."

Silence enveloped the room. Anna took in a breath around the lump in her throat. How would she ever find the words?

"Patricie ... we were, I mean, all there. *Hauptmann* Engel and her and me. And she ..." Anna couldn't do it. Couldn't bring the words to her lips.

Horst rubbed his face. "Stefan was about to pierce the haystack with bayonets. We were dead no matter what. *Slečna* Kadlecová surrendered and managed to get him to leave without any further searching. We owe our lives to her. All of us."

"Is she ...?" Georg fisted his hands until his knuckles turned white.

"*Ne*. They took her. Somewhere. I don't know." Horst sighed.

Anna wiped away a tear. "How can we ever repay her?"

David clutched his chest, his lungs burning, as Georg absorbed the news about Patricie. First, his eyes widened, then they shimmered with tears. Then, the most curious emotion of all. Georg smiled.

Smiled.

Was the man deranged? Did he derive some sadistic pleasure from another's pain?

Georg removed his glasses. "I once asked her if she would be willing to give up her life for the cause. For a moment, she questioned me. But her faith shone through. In as clear of a voice as I ever heard, she answered she would. I'm proud of her."

David shook his head. "How can you say such a thing? Don't you want her to live? To be free?"

"Of course I do. I didn't wish this for her. I told her to stay out of it, but she refused. She wanted to help, needed to help. The Lord called her, and she answered. He called her again today, to make the sacrifice of which we spoke.

"I pray they aren't torturing her. That's the hardest part of all, what makes me tremble for her. I don't want her to suffer. Anything but that. If she dies, if they kill her, I have the assurance that she will be at peace with the Lord. And that's the most wonderful thing that could happen to a person."

Anna clutched her teacup's handle until she almost snapped it in two. "That's what she told *Hauptsturmführer* Jaeger. That she felt sorry for him because he doesn't have a right standing with God. I wouldn't be surprised if she continued witnessing to him in the truck. If she still is talking to him."

"That's my Patricie. That's why I love her so."

"And yet, you're not upset about her loss. I don't believe you." David coughed harder than he had in weeks. The damp air of his cellar hideout had done him no good.

Paní Karas handed him a glass of water. He downed every last drop.

"Yes, I long for her. Ache without her. I'm worried to death about her. What they might be doing to my beautiful love. If I could take her place, I would."

Anna and Horst nodded. *Babička* sipped her tea and cleared her throat. "That's what she did for us. Took our place. Just what Jesus did for us."

"I don't need a lecture." Why had he spoken with such harshness to his grandmother? "I'm sorry for snapping at you. But you know I don't believe what the rest of you do. It's a bunch of nonsense. We have the here and now, and that's all. Nothing beyond it. Only ourselves to rely on."

Babička's pale gray eyes took on a dreamy quality. "You are in a much worse place than *Slečna* Kadlecová. I worry more about you than her. One day you will find out you are wrong, and then what? It will be too late. At that point, there will be no going back, no chance to do life over. What a sad and sorry state. How do you live and move in this evil world without the assurance of more? Of salvation that leads to ultimate joy and happiness and freedom from pain? I know it will end soon, and I can't wait."

David scraped back his chair and paced the room. He didn't want to think about *Babička's* words. A god, the God, frightened him. But he didn't believe in God, right? So why should it? He couldn't explain. He rubbed his forehead.

"Think about what I said." *Babička* stood and shuffled to his side, embracing him as if he were still a little boy. "Dear Lord, please open David's eyes and let him see."

Her prayer pricked him. Wounded his soul. Excited him. He gave her a gentle squeeze.

She released him, yawning. "It's time for this old woman to get some sleep." She and *Paní* Karas drifted away to bed.

But the four young people remained at the table, the gas lamp hissing overhead. Georg turned his mug round and round. "Despite what Patricie did, this place is no longer a haven. If they torture her, they might get information from her. Or from *Pan* Karas. We have to prepare for that eventuality."

"They could return?" David struggled for breath.

"I would be surprised if they didn't."

"We have to move, then?" Horst kneaded the back of his neck.

"Yes, I'm afraid so."

"But where do we go? Is there anywhere safe in this insane world?"

"Out here, you haven't had much news. The Allies are advancing ever closer, as are the Soviets."

"Not good news for me." Horst flashed a wry smile.

"I agree. We can't allow you to fall into Russian hands. They won't see a man who saved lives. They'll see nothing more than a useless German."

David tensed. Horst might lash out. Might come down on Georg for the slur. But he didn't. He nodded.

"I want to move you all west. As close to the British and Americans as possible. Getting you over the border isn't going to happen, not with the battle raging. It's best to hide there and wait it out."

Anna bit her lip. "But *Babička* isn't strong enough to survive another trip. The one here was almost too much for her."

David's chest ached. Every day, his body lost strength. "I'm too frail. Moving isn't an option for me, either."

"And without *Babička* or David, I won't go."

"Then you will remain in danger." Georg shifted in his seat. "I can't protect you further. My operation is compromised. I won't stay here, and I can't come back. There will be no more rations, no more help. You'll be on your own."

What if something happened to his sister? David didn't want that. One member of their family deserved to survive this catastrophe. "Go, Anna. Go on without me. I'll take care of *Babička*. Live. For all of us, live."

Chapter Thirty-One

"Good morning, Paní Karas." Horst entered the kitchen where Maria stood at the stove.

"Or afternoon."

"Sleep came hard. How are you holding up?"

"I'm just praying *Slečna* Kadlecová will be able to convince that man to release Karel. We've been married for forty-five years. I don't remember life without him."

His parents' marriage wasn't one to be imitated. Until he met Karel and Maria, he never believed that a love like that could exist between two people after such a long time. "We're praying for him."

"I see that same look in your eyes for *Slečna* Zadoková as Karel has for me."

He sat at the table and accepted the cup of tea she brought him. "What kind of look is that?"

"You love her."

"Is there any use in denying it?"

"She told her grandmother and me what you shared with her."

He spluttered as the tea went down the wrong pipe. "She did?"

Maria nodded.

"Why haven't you kicked me out?"

"She's hurt. I've watched her, and trust doesn't come easy for her. But she loves you."

"Haven't I done enough to prove to her I'm not like that anymore?"

"It's not about what you do. She needs time. And you by her side, not giving up on her."

"Are you giving up on Karel?"

"Never."

He rose and squeezed Maria's shoulder. "*Děkuji*. You are a wise woman. Do you know where Anna is?"

"I saw her head to the barn earlier."

Horst hurried to the warm stable, the place that had sheltered and saved them last night. Anna stood staring at the hayloft.

"Anna?"

She spun around, grasping the front of her faded, flowered dress. "You frightened me."

She'd had to leave all her dresses, all of them blue, behind in Prague. She looked different, frailer, in this one. "I'm sorry."

"I didn't hear you come in."

"Did you sleep at all?"

"A little. How about you?"

"I did manage to doze for a while."

"Good."

"You're not going to leave, are you?"

She shook her head, her eyes dark and tired. "*Ne*. Not while David is alive. I can't go without him. Other than *Babička*, he's all I have left. You brought him to me. It would be wrong to leave him now."

"I understand."

"Do you think *Hauptsturmführer* Jaeger will be back?"

"That's hard to say."

"That means he will."

"Maybe not."

"We have to leave it in God's hands. I'm weary of it all."

"If I could only help you."

"There you are."

Horst jumped at Georg's voice. "What is it?"

"*Slečna* Zadoková needs to come to the house. It's her brother."

Anna shrunk in an instant, as frail as her grandmother and lone surviving sibling. A strong wind might blow her away. She brushed passed him.

"He will sustain you." But did he really know? *God, why now? Why at all?*

Only the lowing of the cow answered him.

He followed Anna and Georg back the cozy house. "I don't understand. When he went to bed a few hours ago, he was fine. How did he get ill so fast?"

Georg shrugged. "I don't know."

Anna rubbed her temple. "He shouldn't have been in that cellar. We might have squeezed him in the little nook with *Babička*. Breathing that damp air brought this on." She ran up the stairs.

Horst caught Georg at the bottom of the steps. "Is it that bad?"

"I'm no doctor. He's pale and sweating. Why did you ever bring him back to her? He's dying."

"I knew that when I rescued him. But she needed a few more moments with her brother. To say her goodbyes to him. And he has been feeling better."

"Who knows the ways of the Lord? But she needs you right now. I don't know why, but she does."

"*Děkuji.*"

"Against good reason, she trusts you."

"That means the world to me."

"Don't let it go to your head. I'm going to keep watching you."

"I thought you were leaving."

"And so I am. But while I'm here, I'll keep you under surveillance. How does that strike you?" Georg narrowed his eyes and stared at Horst.

"You do what you have to. And so will I." He marched up the flight of stairs to the first door to the right of the landing. A chill permeated the tiny bedroom.

Anna stood on one side of the narrow mattress, her grandmother on the other. David lay propped in between them, his face the same pale shade as the sheets, his lips as blue as the cloudless sky. "I woke up cold. Then hot. Couldn't stop coughing."

Anna leaned over her brother and smoothed away a lock of dark brown hair from his forehead. "Hush, you don't have to speak now. Save your strength."

"I don't have much to save."

The older woman stroked her grandson's hand. "Then you listen well to me."

Even Horst came to attention at her words.

"You know what's right and wrong. I don't need to spend time telling you again. When you were little, you loved God and let everyone know. You evangelized the entire neighborhood. Then you grew up and allowed the world to influence you."

"I did. I know I did."

She clucked her tongue. "You remember those lessons you learned from me, and your grandfather, and your parents."

"There has to be more."

"There is." Anna nodded. "*Máma* and *Táta* knew it. So did Jana and Lada. I'm glad you do, too."

David coughed, blood spilling from his lips. His grandmother, with trembling hands, dabbed it away. For a long moment, he struggled to catch his breath.

"That's enough talk for now." Anna pulled the blanket to his chin. "You rest."

"I'll think. I'll remember."

So would Horst.

The old woman kissed David's forehead. "I'm glad. Only Jesus."

Silence descended on the room as David drifted off to sleep, but no one moved. Only the ticking of the round alarm clock on the bedside table filled the air.

"There has to be more." David's words echoed in Horst's mind.

And there was. Like David's family had taught him the way of the Lord, so had Horst's mother taught him.

The darkness of Kristallnacht blotted out much of that. Pushed it into the deepest recesses of his soul.

But David's words had unleashed a flood inside Horst. There had to be more than just this life. This horrible, miserable, rotten life. If the world could be so evil and awful, how much worse could hell be? He'd had enough of misery and suffering already.

And there had to be more than guilt and penance. Like a distant echo, a memory flitted at the edge of his consciousness. Someone telling him, maybe preaching to him, that you could never earn your way to heaven.

He leaned against the wall and sucked in a breath. He wasn't good enough. He could never be good enough. No matter how many brave and heroic gestures he made, it would never be enough.

He alone couldn't make up for all he'd done. How he'd become like his father.

Only Jesus.

Oh Lord, what a fool I've been. I can't earn Your forgiveness. But I plead for it. Grant it to me. Cleanse me of my guilt. Wash me whiter than snow. Help me to rest in You and in You only.

A sunbeam slanted through the window, landing at Horst's feet.

For the first time since that awful night, a lightness and a peace settled in his soul. He'd come home.

Like Frau Doubeková, *Mutti* would be glad. Glad that Horst remembered where salvation and freedom came from.

David's lungs rattled as he breathed.

Paní Karas entered the room. "A bit of broth for him?"

Anna slipped out.

Horst followed her downstairs. "Anna, wait."

"What?"

"I know this is hard on you."

"Do you? Your family is alive and thriving."

"Have you so soon forgotten that I lost a brother?"

"And I've lost everyone. Everyone who mattered to me."

"You have your grandmother. And me. I hope I mean something to you."

"I don't know, I just don't know. I can't make sense of the world anymore. It's like looking through a kaleidoscope. Nothing more than broken pieces of glass that don't fit together."

"But if you turn the scope, a beautiful picture appears."

"If only they hadn't smashed his violin. If only."

He touched her upper arms. She flinched, so he backed off. "I know."

"Please, not now. I can't ..." She fled to her room.

Horst balled his fists. She was right, in a way. How would life ever be beautiful again? Maybe he shouldn't have rescued David. His being here only brought her more pain. It forced her to watch her brother die. She would never forget.

He paced the small living room. *Paní* Karas entered from the kitchen. "Come with me." She motioned for Horst to follow. "I have a job that will help you clear your head."

She led him to the back of the house, to an area protected by a stand of evergreen trees, away from prying eyes. A stack of wood waited to be split.

"Is this your way of getting your chores done?"

"Not at all. Work out your frustrations."

"What about you? Who knows what is happening with your husband?"

She closed her eyes, took a deep breath, and opened them again. "I'm worried about him. What they might be doing to him. It's hard. Now, I'm alone here. What will become of me? I have to lean on the Lord. Without Him, I won't be able to get through this."

"About that, you are right. *Děkuji*. What more can we do?"

Paní Karas returned to the house, her shoulders slumped. All of this wore on her. In rescuing them, she might have lost her husband. What a great price to pay.

Horst grasped the ax handle. He set the smaller log on top of a larger stump and swung. *Thwack.* The blade sunk into the wood. *Thwack. Thwack.* The log split in two.

For at least thirty minutes, he chopped wood for the fire. He stopped once to take off his jacket. He labored until sweat rolled down his face, his chest, and his back. With one last swing of the axe, he cut the final log into pieces. *Paní* Karas had enough firewood to last her a good, long while.

Horst's muscles ached, but in a refreshing, reviving way. He wiped his forehead with his sleeve.

Paní Karas came out with a glass of water. "Do you feel better?"

"I still need answers. How do I help her? When will all this end?"

She stroked the hem of her apron for a moment, her forehead furrowed. "Only He knows."

Horst threw the ax as far into the field as possible.

Hauptsturmführer Jaeger held Patricie in the Small Fortress at Terezín. She'd lost track of what day it was, what time of day. She sat alone in a rank, damp cell, a bare bulb her only light. The pungent odors of urine and excrement overwhelmed her senses. The food, what little there was of it, consisted of a thin, watery soup. On a good day, she got a potato. A mealy, rotten one.

Other prisoners moaned and groaned. All the time.

She shut her ears and her soul to it.

In her mind, she played symphonies, loud and swelling, to dim the misery, the melody rising in her chest once more. She rehearsed every note of Beethoven's *Ninth Symphony*. Over and over, until she fell asleep.

But when her dreams came, they consisted of nothing more than *Hauptsturmführer* Jaeger's face the moment she'd crawled from underneath the haystack. His lead-colored eyes wide, his jaw gaping, his nostrils flaring. Always, a forked tongue shot from his mouth and wrapped itself around·her neck.

He hissed. "I have you now. You're mine. You'll never get free. I'll eat you and spit out your bones."

She jerked awake, bathed in a sweat as cold as the Vltava River.

A key scraped in the cell's lock. She hadn't seen another person since they'd sealed her in here. A guard slid her meals through a slat under the door. She didn't know whether a man or a woman brought her gruel.

With a slow creak, the door opened. A large-boned woman, her dirty-blonde hair tucked under her creased cap, motioned to her. "You, come with me."

Patricie slid from the bed. Her muscles, weak from disuse, protested the movement. She limped to the doorway. "Where are you taking me?"

"That is not your concern."

Patricie wanted to differ, but didn't dare. Then again, how much more trouble could she be in? With stiff joints, she followed the woman into the courtyard, blinking in the bright light. Heavy metal doors lined the perimeter. Weeping, whimpering, and lamenting followed her.

She bit back the thousand questions rolling on her tongue. Simple ones, like the date. Harder ones, like who she was to see and the length of her confinement. Impossible ones, like why God abandoned His people.

But the guard would never answer.

Her limbs had loosened by the time the woman brought her to a tiny, square room. Two gray metal chairs occupied the space. Nothing else. She shook from head to toe, much like she did right before the surgeon had removed her appendix.

"You sit. He'll be in soon." The guard shoved her into one of the chairs, then left, the key grating in the lock.

"Who? Who?" Her cries went unanswered.

To keep herself from going insane, she examined her broken fingernails. Prior to her incarceration, she'd always kept them neat and trimmed. You couldn't play the oboe with long nails, not to mention ragged ones. When she was a teenager, some of the other girls in her music classes bemoaned the fact they had to keep their nails short. They wanted long, red-painted ones like movie actresses.

Not her. She wore her short nails as a badge of honor. She would do whatever it took to excel. Including cutting her nails short.

Pan Svoboda would look at her hands today and scold her.

She sat on them.

The door opened. "Ah, my little bird."

She stiffened and held her breath.

Hauptsturmführer Jaeger walked around to face her. "So, we meet again."

To avoid answering him, she pursed her lips.

"What, so quiet? And nervous as always around me. Now I know why."
She resisted the urge to spit in his face.

He sat down and leaned forward. "Tell me, how are you liking your accommodations?"

She refused to give him the satisfaction of an answer.

"No matter. You won't be here long."

"Where are you taking me?"

"Ah, you speak at last. Good to see you haven't lost your voice. Now that I know you aren't mute, you can tell me where you stashed the others in your group. That traitorous, Jew-loving German, his filthy, little whore, and your boyfriend."

An involuntary sucking in of her breath.

"*Ja*, I know about Georg Klima. How do you think I found you? He's an excellent record keeper. The rest of the resistance may have fallen apart after Reinhard Heydrich's assassination, but his little cell flourished. I traced his list of houses. Someone at the last one thought you might have gone to that farm."

"I have no idea where Georg is. I haven't spoken to him in months." The truth, much as it pained her.

He stood, knocking over his chair in the process. "You lie. Nothing but black lies from your lips." He slapped her hard across the mouth. The metallic flavor of blood coated her tongue.

"You have to believe me. I'm telling you the truth." She left her seat and stood toe-to-toe with him.

He choked her, shook her. "More lies. So false. So impure."

He released his grip, and she toppled backward. "I told you, I sent the others over the border. They're in Palestine now." A place he would never dare to set foot.

"Lies. Lies. Lies." With each word came a new, forceful strike to her cheek.

The room spun. She stumbled. Tripped over the chair. Fell to the cold, hard, concrete floor. "The truth. Don't you recognize it anymore?" She covered her mouth at her bold words.

He kicked her in the stomach, his jackboot connecting with the softest, most vulnerable part of her body. "You are incapable of telling it. I'm warning you, Patricie. You'd do well to listen to me. This isn't the end. *Nein*, it's only the beginning. Every day, you will come here. Piece by piece, I will break you until you spew out the truth."

"I've told you, more than once. I can't give you anything more." She scooted to the corner as he came for her once again.

Another kick to the gut. She vomited her small lunch, along with a good deal of blood.

"You're as vile as the rest of them. Get up. I'm done with you today."

She crawled up the wall until she stood, bent over from the pain.

"Tell me one thing, Patricie. Was it all worth it?"

Chapter Thirty-Two

For David, the days melded into each other. Time blurred. People came and went from his room. Memories bombarded him. He couldn't distinguish the past from the present. Anna and *Babička* were there, but so were *Máma* and *Táta*.

Máma smoothed his fevered forehead, her hand cool, soft, gentle. "My boy, so sick. I'm praying for you. And I'll be here for you. Everything will be all right. You'll see. Don't worry. Just sleep."

And he did. He dreamed of playing with his friends in Prague's narrow, ancient streets. They ran after each other, free, unfettered. Their lungs drew in air. They never tired. They ran over the bridges, up the castle steps, into the countryside. He never stopped.

And then he woke, coughing, gasping for oxygen. The pain, the blood, the horrible strangulation came. "Water."

Anna was at his bedside, smiling, her heart-shaped face so beautiful. With *Táta* gone, he would have to make sure no man took advantage of her. If only he could stay.

"Let me help you sit and take a drink." She lifted him from the pillows and placed the glass to his lips, tipping it so the water dribbled into his mouth.

He lapped a little, then pushed the cup away. "Enough."

"How about some broth? I slaughtered one of the chickens and made a little stock. You need to keep up your strength."

"*Ne.* I'm not hungry."

"For me. Please?" She pouted like when she was five.

He couldn't resist her then. He couldn't resist her now. "Fine. A little."

She moved from the room. Such a weight she carried on her shoulders. He was glad she had *Babička*, but for how long? Anna would soon be alone in the world. The Germans had taken so much from them. So very, very much.

She returned with a bowl and set it on the small, unsteady bedside table. The fragrance of chicken and onions wafted his way. It was probably tasty, but it didn't entice him. She lifted the spoon for him. Most of it dribbled down his chin. After three or four mouthfuls, he turned his head away. "That's all."

"You didn't eat much."

"Are you ever afraid?"

"All the time. I'm trying, really trying, to trust God. But it's hard. How can losing my family be best for me? Is He really taking care of me, or am I on my own?"

"Do you believe in heaven?"

"You know I do."

"When you are young and invincible, you don't think about things like dying. But then comes a point in your life when this world fades and you have to face it. For years, I've thought there is nothing but the present. Nothing but what I can see and touch and taste."

"Then dying is the end. Where do you go? To utter blackness? We came from somewhere. We must go somewhere."

"God moved my heart."

She rubbed the top of his hand. "I'm glad to hear that."

"I don't want death to be final. I want more. Eternity. Everlasting life. I'm not ready to be done. My life has been brief."

"Like *Babička* said, you know the truth. I don't have to preach to you. Do you believe in Jesus?"

"I did once."

"That's not good enough. Do you believe now?"

Did he? *God, are You there? Do You hear? Do You even exist?*

"Call to Him, David. He hears you. He knows you by name." Anna's soft voice cut through his fog

David had to see Him, to feel Him.

He had sat in his uncle's kitchen. His feet didn't even reach the floor when he perched on the chair. "Jesus loves you, Uncle Petr. I wish you loved him, too, so we could live in heaven together."

His big, burly uncle's laugh had filled the room. "If I go to church with you, will you stop pestering me?"

"Sure."

Uncle Petr was as good as his word. He went to church. David sat on the pew beside him. He didn't understand much of what the preacher spoke about, but he studied the beautiful stained-glass windows. One depicted Jesus gathering the little children on his lap. Oh, to be one of those children, safe and secure in the Lord's embrace.

Anna stroked his cheek. The memory dissipated. He clutched at her. "Is this why this is happening to me? Do you think God is trying to get my attention?"

"He very well might be. Listen to Him. He loves you, David. He is our rock, our shelter in the time of storm, our only hope of salvation."

"And you believe that?"

Her brown eyes shimmered with unshed tears. "I forget it too often, but yes, deep down, I believe that."

"I rejected Him."

"That doesn't matter. He forgives. Over and over again, if need be."

Forgiveness. Washing. Cleansing. The missing part of the equation. He couldn't come to the Lord without repentance, seeking God's mercy to cover his many sins.

Lord, I come in Jesus' name, and ask You to forgive me for His sake. It's His sacrifice I plead.

Like Patricie's sacrifice for them. She took their place. She didn't deserve the punishment the Nazis must be meting out to her. But because she gave herself up, they were safe and alive.

And that's what Jesus had done for him on the cross.

I don't deserve Your loving kindness, but I beg You for it.

At long last, he came home.

The melody of a simple hymn he'd learned as a child washed over him. He hummed, then sang, breathless, his voice cracking.

Once He came in blessing,
All our ills redressing;
Came in likeness lowly,
Son of God most holy;
Bore the cross to save us,
Hope and freedom gave us.

Thus, if thou hast known Him,
Not ashamed to own Him,
But wilt trust Him boldly
Nor dost love Him coldly,
He will then receive thee,
Heal thee, and forgive thee.

"I believe, Anna. I believe."

A week later, they buried David on a hill overlooking the Czech countryside. Afraid of being seen by the people of the hamlet, they held the funeral at night. No marker indicated his burial spot. No one in generations to come would know his body lay in that place.

Anna would never be able to visit any of her family's graves. She doubted the Nazis had marked her parents' and sisters' final resting places with headstones.

She had no family other than *Babička*.

Somehow, she gathered the strength to get out of bed the morning after David's funeral and fry potatoes for breakfast so *Paní* Karas could sleep. She stared at the always-drawn blackout shades and dreamed of the world beyond. What did America look like? Wide and open like the Czech countryside? Crowded, dirty cities, much different from Prague?

And would she ever play again? Would the music return? How could it? Everything else was gone.

Horst wandered downstairs first. She poured him a cup of dandelion tea that *Pani* Karas had made, and a cup for herself. He sat across the table from her. For a long moment, they sipped in silence.

Finally, Horst spoke. "How are you? I'm worried about you."

"Sad. Lonely."

"You are in mourning."

She bit back tears. "And in rejoicing, in a way. *Babička* told me that. We don't understand the Lord's ways. I don't know why He took my family from me. But David went home to be with Him. I will miss him very much. He would have been a great uncle. Someone to share stories from the past. But he's at peace. God saved him. That's enough right now. It's hard."

Horst kissed the back of her hand. "I love you more than you know."

She slid to the edge of her chair. "Our love is a problem."

He stroked his square chin. "I know. I have to face reality. The Allies are ever advancing. The Soviets are in Slovakia. The Americans are in Austria. They have forced the Germans into this little pocket in Bohemia. There is no more room for me to run and hide."

"What will you do?"

"We can't stay here. We have no idea where the Soviets and the Americans will meet. I want to surrender to the American forces. I believe they will be kind to me. The Soviets won't be so forgiving."

She didn't want to say the words, but the reality hung over their heads. "What about us, Horst? Our relationship?"

"More than anything, I want to promise you a future. But I'm afraid I can't."

"I know." It was the reason she'd held back from telling him she loved him.

"After the war, I will do everything in my power to find you again. I don't want to lose you, Anna. You're everything to me. If you'll have a German officer, that is."

She came around the table and sat on his knee, wrapping him in a hug. "When I look at you, I don't see German or Nazi or enemy. Do you know what I see?" Her heart flip-flopped in her chest. She could forgive him for what he'd done on Kristallnacht.

"*Ne.* What do you see?"

"A kind, gentle man, one who is loving, sensitive, caring. A man any woman would be proud to be with. When you put aside the façade of German officer, I got to know the man behind it. That's who you truly are. Please, find me again."

He nestled against her shoulder. "I will do whatever I have to in order to make that happen. But I can't ask you to wait for me. If you find someone—"

"Ahem. Am I interrupting something?" Georg stood in the kitchen doorway in *Pan* Karas's baggy work clothes.

Anna shot to her feet. "*Ne.* Sit down. I forgot about the potatoes." The smell of burning food registered. She grabbed the pan from the fire. "I am sorry."

"Never mind. A cup of tea will do me."

"Let me cut off the black part. The rest should still be good." She grabbed a knife and, holding the hot potato between her fingers, worked on making it edible.

"We have important business to discuss." Georg pulled out a chair and sat.

Horst scratched his cheek. "I know what it is. We have to leave."

"I'm surprised *Hauptsturmführer* Jaeger has left us in peace this long. He will be back. The noose is tightening. Nothing is more dangerous than a wounded animal. That is what he is. He has nothing to lose."

"But where will we go?"

Anna plated what little potato she managed to save, setting aside a few slices for *Babička* and *Pani* Karas when they awoke. "Surely not back to Prague." Nothing would give her more joy than to see the city of her birth, but it was too dangerous.

Georg leaned back. "Of course not. As we said before, we cannot allow Horst to fall into Russian hands. The Soviets will liberate Prague, but we won't be there. I refuse to sign anyone's death warrant."

"Very generous of you." Horst bit into a potato, grimacing as the smell of soot overtook the flavor.

"So, it's to be west, then. Where?"

"Plzeň."

"Is it far enough west?" Horst fiddled with the handle of his cup.

"I offer no guarantees. These days, all we can do is hope and pray."

Anna sat at the table and forked a piece of potato. "My reservation remains my grandmother."

"Plzeň isn't that far."

"I know, but her health isn't the best. She has heart problems. A bumpy ride in a farm wagon might be too much for her. And I won't leave her alone."

"Understandable." Georg peered at her through his spectacles. "But I have a way to get us there."

Horst wrinkled his forehead. "How?"

"By train."

Anna release her hold on her fork, which clattered to her plate. "Train? We're going to just march right on board?"

Georg reached into the pocket of his pants. He laid four identity cards on the table, like a poker master with a winning hand. "We'll use these."

Anna picked up one of the booklets. Her picture stared back at her, but the name typed on it wasn't hers. "Where did you get these?" There was no large J for Jew stamped on it.

"Patricie has a brother also in the underground. He makes false identity cards, among other things."

Horst turned his over and over. "He's good at what he does. This looks better than the one that the rain ruined when I went to Theresienstadt. We'll leave soon?"

"Two days."

"But we have no money." Anna's racing heart slowed almost to a stop. "How will we buy tickets?"

"I have enough for all of us sewn into the lining of my coat."

"You've been planning this for a while."

"I have. I'm sorry we were too late for Patricie." Georg's eyes misted over.

Anna touched his rough hand. "We all are. Why are you doing this? Why haven't you left like you threatened?"

"For Patricie. She would want me to help you to safety. To finish what she started. And I waited to tell you about the cards until after David's passing. I knew you wouldn't leave with him so ill."

"*Děkuji*. We cannot thank you enough."

"Don't thank me yet. This trip is fraught with danger."

Chapter Thirty-Three

Anna rubbed her eyes as she made her way to the chicken coop. She, Georg, and Horst had stayed up far into the early morning, discussing their plans for the future. Even now, *Hauptsturmführer* Jaeger might be watching the house. She'd dressed in *Paní* Karas's clothes, an embroidered black shawl over her head. Her breath puffed into clouds in front of her face.

Anna's stomach rumbled. Georg warned they would get no more help in terms of ration cards, and so they hadn't in the weeks since the raid. They'd had just enough to sustain them.

She entered the warm, smelly coop, pushed one chicken to the side, and gathered the egg into the basket she carried. Not all the hens were kind enough to offer up a prize. She moved to another. This little one refused to give up the egg. She pecked at Anna until she dropped the basket. Two of the four eggs she'd collected broke.

"Stupid, stupid chicken. See what you made me do? Now there won't be enough for breakfast." She kicked at the coop's wall. "Ouch." Her toe throbbed.

She sank to the floor, pulled the scarf over her face, and wept. Cried for the family she'd lost. For the home that was no more. For her virtual imprisonment.

Most of all, for the loss of music. For the emptiness of her soul.

The coop's little door creaked open. She didn't bother to lift her scarf to see who entered. She breathed in his masculine, woodsy scent. How did he smell that way without his cologne? His own clothes?

"Anna, what's the matter?"

She pinched the bridge of her nose to stem the tide. A few moments passed before she regained her composure. "The chicken pecked me."

Horst examined her hand, then kissed the top of it. "A few red marks, nothing more."

"And I dropped the eggs for breakfast. How will we eat?"

He righted the mess. "God provides."

That prompted her to remove her shawl and stare at Horst. "Does it look like He provides? Our lives are in as much danger as ever. Maybe more. We're hunted. Pursued. Tracked like animals."

"But here we are." His confident words almost disguised the clouded gaze of his pale blue eyes.

"You doubt, too."

"Trust isn't easy. I'm responsible for all of you. What's going to happen next? How can I keep you safe? And alive? I want to do it all. Yet, I can't. Only God can do those things for us. My head knows it. My heart needs more convincing."

"*Babička* would say to trust in the Lord with all thine heart, and He shall direct thy paths. That's from Proverbs. She would add that salvation comes only from Him."

"And you? What do you say?"

She turned her focus to the slanted roof. "It's so dark. Like the blackest of all moonless nights. Even the stars don't shine anymore. How will we find our way? Maybe none of us will even come out of this alive. Perhaps it's futile to try. Patricie saw that. She wanted relief. Escape."

Horst sat on the ground beside her, knee to knee. "*Ne*, that's not it. She wanted to save us, to keep us from being discovered. But I'm not ready to give up. I'm willing to fight. To live, like David told you."

"That's just him."

"Maybe, in part. But we have to hold on."

"For what? The music is gone. It won't return. Without it, I'm nothing." The blackness threatened to spill from her heart and mind to her soul.

He caressed her cheek and let his fingers skim her neck. Fire and ice raced through her. "You are more than just your music. Yes, it is part of you. A very important part of you. But not all of you. You are kindness and compassion, gentleness and faithfulness, loyalty and trustworthiness. They make you who you are. And that is all wrapped up in your music. But it's not gone."

"I have no instrument. No one to play for. *Hauptsturmführer* Jaeger, the Nazis, stole everything from me."

"You are the music."

"Those other things that make me who I am?"

"Yes."

"All my life, music has been there. My parents filled our home with it. When we were old enough to hold a violin, all of my siblings and I added to the symphony that was our household."

"But there was more to it than that."

"My mother had such a musical lilt to her voice. It was more like she sang than she spoke."

"Ah, that's where you get it from."

"But you're right." Her soul stirred a little bit. "They also taught us to be kind, compassionate, helpful, and so on. They tried to instill in us a love for the Lord."

"Even without an instrument in your hand, you are beautiful to watch, to listen to, to be around."

He saw those things in her? "But I feel empty without it. I can't even hear a note in my head. It's vanished."

"Often, when people lose a sense, another one is sharpened. Some who are blind are very sensitive to smell. Or noises. Maybe the Lord is training you to use your other senses. Your other gifts and talents."

"He's teaching me to be more compassionate, kinder."

"Possibly."

But why did the Lord have to take away her music to teach her those lessons? Did she need to trust in Him more? Yes, she did. She didn't rely on Him enough. When trouble came, she leaned on her violin more than on her Bible. Without her instrument, she had nowhere else to turn but to God.

"You said my music isn't gone."

"'O sing unto the Lord a new song.'"

"He's my audience?"

"Always." Horst clasped her hands, warming them through. "Close your eyes."

She obeyed.

"Reach deep down inside. Dig to the pit of your being. What is there, deep in your heart?"

A tiny sliver of light. "I don't know."

"You're not there yet. Delve inside. You'll find it. Trust me."

"We're alive."

"*Ja*, alive. I feel it, too. Breathe in. Breathe out."

She allowed the warm farm air to rush into and out of her lungs. He did the same. They took this journey together.

"We're safe." No thinking of the future or the past. Only this moment.

He squeezed her hand. "No prison. We have freedom, no matter how little."

Another fissure in the darkness of her heart. "My family is here." She brought *Babička* to mind.

"Family, *ja*. My *mutti* is alive and well."

"We have clothes, food, and provision." She licked her lips.

"Yes."

"We have each other." How could she have forgotten the love she harbored for this man?

"Each other. Anna, you have made this time in my life bearable for me. Even more than that."

The light broke the horizon of her mind. "We have salvation."

"In many forms." He rubbed her thumb.

"Yes, from all our sins. From Satan. From *Hauptsturmführer* Jaeger."

"God has been good to us. And He always will be."

"No matter what?" As they traveled west?

"Even when we walk the valley of the shadow of death, He'll be with us. Even if He takes our earthly lives from us, we'll have heavenly ones."

A note sounded in her mind, clear and true. Her fingers ached to hold a violin, to clutch a bow. Instead, she hummed the tune.

Horst echoed.

Warriors who for God are fighting,
And for His divine law,
Pray that His help be vouchsafed you;
With trust unto Him draw;
With Him you conquer,
In your foes inspire awe;
With Him you conquer,
In your foes inspire awe.

The rich notes of the old Czech warrior hymn filled the small space. Even the chickens paused their cackling. Anna turned to Horst. "You know Czech music?"

"When *Mutti* and I visited during the summers, we worshiped in local churches. *Vater* didn't approve, but we didn't tell him."

She brushed a kiss across his cheek. "*Děkuji.* You gave me back the music."

"I did no such thing. God gave it to you." He returned her kiss. For a moment, he sat back. Then he drew her close and kissed her on the lips. Runs, trills, vibrato coursed through her. A passion only music brought before now stirred in her.

They parted, breathless.

"I love you, Anna."

Could she ever say the words?

The wind whipped around Anna's bare legs as she stood on the knoll overlooking the Czech countryside. David's knoll, where his body rested. Daylight faded in the west. The west, where she was bound. Tomorrow, she would not be here. Where would the next weeks and months take her? Would she ever return?

She pulled *PPaní* Karas's black shawl around her shoulders, hoping

Hauptsturmführer Jaeger would stay far away. That they would manage to outrun the Nazis and the Soviets. Horst's only hope lay in getting to the Americans.

Kneeling, she picked up a clump of the fresh, soft dirt and sifted it through her fingers. "Oh David, I wish you were coming with us. But it's useless to think about the past, isn't it? No amount of longing is going to bring you back. Nor *Máma*, nor *Táta*, nor our sisters."

But how she ached for them. She would give her life for even one more minute as a family. In the past, she didn't treasure them the way she should have. And now . . .

"You're happy, David, and at peace. I want that for myself. Until that time comes, I pray for a measure of it on this earth. Maybe soon. If we survive."

Though she tried not to dwell on what lay behind, memories flooded her. Happy Easters, the family all decorating *kraslice*, the intricate hand-painted eggs girls gave to boys on Easter Monday. Excursions to the countryside, and *Táta* trying to paddle a boat. Chilly winter evenings spent on *Máma*'s lap as she read to her.

The tears came, fast and furious. Great sobs shook her entire body. She keened, rocking back and forth, back and forth, hugging herself. Cried for the nieces and nephews she would never know. For the wisdom she'd never receive from *Máma*. For the family reunions they would never enjoy.

How could she do this? How could she leave him? All of them? She trembled and rubbed her upper arms.

> *Thus, if thou hast known Him,*
> *Not ashamed to own Him,*
> *But wilt trust Him boldly*
> *Nor dost love Him coldly,*
> *He will then receive thee,*
> *Heal thee, and forgive thee.*

Trust Him boldly. So hard to do. Like throwing yourself from the Charles Bridge, hoping your father would catch you. This leaving was a free fall.

Lord, catch me. Oh please, catch me, or else I will drown.

The wind lashed at her face, cooling the tears that coursed down her cheeks.

"Good-bye, David." She turned to the northeast, to the place where the Germans had taken her family. "Good-bye *Máma, Táta*, Jana, Lada. Until we meet again."

Horst tucked his coat around himself to ward off the cold. Anna stood on the hill, the wind tossing her wavy, dark brown hair to and fro. She knelt. Her shoulders shook. She wept.

So small against the vastness of the sky. So helpless in the face of the storm. So vulnerable in light of the danger.

He climbed the small rise and stood behind her as she bade farewell to each member of her family. Then he knelt beside her and gathered her into his embrace. She cried into his coat until she hiccupped and finally stilled.

Silence settled over them.

How hard for her to leave all she knew. When, if, they met the Americans, none of them had any idea what might happen. His only hope lay in the Allies showing him mercy. He had no guarantee. They might throw him in prison. He didn't dare think of the other possibility.

He kissed the top of her head. "I will never leave you nor forsake you. That's God's promise to you."

"And to you." She drew back, her face stained by tears. "You are afraid, *ne?*"

"Apprehensive. The Americans can't be worse than the Soviets. Perhaps they'll treat me with kindness."

"I don't like not knowing what's in front of me. *Táta* bought me a flashlight to leave by my bed, so I could find my way to the restroom or to their bedroom in the middle of the night."

"That's what trust is about."

"It's not easy."

"*Ne*, it's not. If it was, it wouldn't be trust." *God, provide that trust in You, no matter what happens. My life is in Your hands.* The way his stomach tightened, he might as well have jumped out of an airplane. Would the parachute deploy in time? Or would he hit the ground at an incredible rate of speed?

She kissed his cheek over and over.

He kissed her salty, sweet lips. "I love you. Are you ready?"

"Are you?"

He squeezed her hand. "It's time to step out in faith."

Chapter Thirty-Four

A powerful pressure weighed on Horst's chest as he, Anna, her grandmother, and Georg stood on the platform at the small train station, just two valises between them. A few people milled about, going on with their business despite the end of the war looming on the horizon. The ticket agent sat behind the window, a shadowy beard covering his sunken face.

Georg stepped up. "Four tickets to Plzeň, please."

Even now, Horst held his breath. Would the man question why they went west?

He didn't. He simply took the money Georg slid across the counter and produced the tickets in exchange.

Horst released the air from his lungs. One hurdle cleared. Many, many more to go.

He and Georg returned to the women, huddled at one end of the platform. Both wore shawls over their heads. Anna blinked several times and bit her lip. He squeezed her hand. "Are you nervous?"

One corner of her mouth tipped up. "I'm trying not to let it show."

"You'll be fine."

"Once we reach Plzeň."

"And how are you, *Paní* Doubeková?"

The old woman leaned on a cane *Pan* Karas had carved from a gnarled tree limb. "I'm fine." But in the time he'd known her, she'd shrunk, smaller than her already short stature. More lines graced her face.

"Good."

"How long?" Anna still clung to him.

"It's not far."

"*Ne*, not that. How long until this miserable war ends? Until we are truly safe?"

"Only God knows." His pulse throbbed in his wrist.

"How long do you think?"

"Anna, don't pester the man. He doesn't know." The old woman's soft voice carried the authority of her years.

"That's fine. We all want to know. To have a date to shoot for. I understand. But I don't know the mind of the Allies. From what *Pan* Karas told me before his arrest, the Americans are going around Czechoslovakia into the heart of Germany. That makes sense. If they strike at the command center, the rest of the operation will fall."

Anna toed the wood deck. "It's been a long six years. It's like waiting for *Ježíšek*, the baby Jesus, to come on Christmas Eve, for *Máma* to ring the bell to let us know He'd brought us gifts. In January, you don't get too anxious or excited about it, because it is so far off. But as December draws on, it's harder and harder to wait."

Georg nodded. "We all feel that way right now. First things first. We have to get to Plzeň."

Off in the distance, a train whistle blew. A shiver ran down Horst's spine. The times he'd visited Theresienstadt, he heard that sound plenty. Trains bringing thousands of Jews to the camp. Trains packed with men, women, even little children, headed to Auschwitz.

The hulking, black behemoth chugged into the station, belching steam and soot.

Horst supported *Paní* Doubeková and helped her up the metal stairs. Georg and Anna followed them into the passenger compartment.

They passed a few private berths. "Stop there."

Horst turned around to make sure he'd heard Georg right. "This is ours?"

"It is."

He didn't say any more until the four of them tucked their small amount of luggage into the rack above them and sank into their worn velvet seats. "Why this?"

Georg shrugged. "I have a feeling my Reichsmarks will soon be useless. Might as well spend them. Besides, this is much more private. Less chance to be singled out."

Horst nodded. He sat beside Anna, very aware of her presence. Even though they didn't touch, the heat radiating from her body warmed his. She sat with her back rigid. He caressed her shoulder, trying to get her to relax. "It will be fine."

"I don't know. Such a bad feeling has settled in my stomach."

"Don't you trust me?" Georg crossed his arms.

"I trust God." *Paní* Doubeková grinned.

Anna remained tense. "I'm clinging to Him. That's all I can say."

Horst leaned just a little closer to her. "When I was a boy, *Mutti* took me to the market with her every Saturday. We rode the tram. While the workings of it fascinated me, getting on and off terrified me. I was afraid I might slip and the wheels would run over me. But I trusted *Mutti* and clung to her hand. She never let me down."

"Are you clinging, too?" She gazed at him with such intensity that it stabbed at his core. Like she wanted him to struggle along with her. She needed to know she wasn't alone.

"Yes, I am. To face this final journey is hard, not knowing what's ahead. I'm afraid of this, like I was of the tram's sharp, metal wheels."

Paní Doubeková tapped her cane on the train's floor. "Each of us clings, my *beruško*. That's all our frail human nature can do."

Anna snuggled into him. "If your heart is pounding like mine, *Babička*, you'll need your medicine."

The old woman touched her chest. "My heart is fine."

Georg shushed them. "Enough talk like that. We must appear as normal travelers. Any nervousness might give us away. Or at least, bring additional scrutiny we don't want."

Once again, the whistle blew its lonesome cry, and the wheels creaked and squeaked as they pulled from the station. Each slow turn brought them that much closer to the Americans. To possible freedom.

No guarantees. Life offered none of them.

But God does.

The small whisper in his heart brought Horst a measure of comfort.

God didn't guarantee ease in this life. He didn't guarantee anything other than peace in Him and eternal life for those who believe.

The checkered Czech countryside flew by the window, hypnotizing him. He dozed, Anna tucked in beside him.

A rap at the compartment's door roused him. Anna sat up. He, too, straightened as the visitor slid open the door.

A Wehrmacht soldier stood there. "Identification." The man stared at each of them for several seconds. Did his gaze rest on Horst longer? Did he look familiar? Maybe.

Nein, he had to be imagining things. He should have never shaved his beard. *God, don't let him look too hard.*

The soldier examined Anna, Georg, and *Paní* Doubeková's cards and handed them back to each person. He held onto Horst's. "I've seen you before."

He didn't want to speak too much. One thing Georg told them to do was to say as little as possible. "*Ne.*"

"Where are you from?"

"Prague."

"How long did you live there?"

The German pressed him for answers, forcing Horst to say more. "All my life."

"What is your occupation?"

"Architect."

"Do you speak German?"

"*Ja.*"

The soldier narrowed his green eyes and stared long and hard at Horst. "How do I know you aren't lying?" He spoke in German. "Who are these people with you?"

"My new wife, her grandmother, and a friend of ours."

"Your German is perfect."

"My parents lived in Austria. I learned from them."

"They failed to teach you good Czech."

Horst furrowed his brows, as if he didn't understand what the man meant. But his throat went dry.

The soldier didn't believe him.

He tapped the little identification book on his hand. "I know you. I have no doubt."

"Perhaps we met at a pub along the way."

"*Nein*, that's not it." He leaned in for a closer look.

Horst forced himself not to flinch.

"Your mouth. Your eyes. I know you. Let me think."

Horst would rather he didn't. "Perhaps we met long ago on a ski holiday."

"I don't forget people once I meet them."

"I don't recognize you. You must have me confused with someone else." That, at least, was the truth. He didn't know the man. Was pretty sure he had never seen him.

The soldier straightened. His face brightened.

Horst's midsection cramped.

"You aren't Czech."

He went cold all over.

"We were in the same class in military training."

Horst squinted, trying to remember.

The soldier took off his cap and tilted his head, revealing a shock of bright red hair.

The memory flooded back. Marcus Kuhn. They had been together in basic training.

Marcus also recalled it. "Horst. Horst Engel."

"*Nein*. You are mistaken."

"That is who you are." Marcus sneered. "The man missing for the past year. The man who hid Jews."

"*Ne*." Anna stood, dropping her own card on the floor. "I know him. He's my husband. We grew up together in Prague. We went through school together. There is no way he is the man you say he is."

Something about the way she phrased that hit him between the eyes. *He is not the man you say he is.*

No, he wasn't. He wasn't the Horst Engel who'd smashed windows, vandalized Jewish property, and beat a man on Kristallnacht just to please his father. He wasn't the Horst Engel who'd received a commission from the Reich's high command. And he wasn't the Horst Engel who'd arrived in Prague, proud of his position, unaware of what was expected of him.

"Does that mean you, too, are lying?" Marcus thundered, his words echoing throughout the cabin.

Anna shook her head. "It means you are wrong. Perhaps he looks like him, but this is not the man you seek."

"I should shoot you both."

Horst stepped in front of Anna. Marcus would not take the life of the woman he loved. Never. "I am Václav Filipek, like it says on card. Take me if you have to, but leave my wife alone. She is innocent."

"All of you are under arrest." The man tore Horst's identity booklet in two.

He slammed the compartment's door shut with a clang.

The clinking of the shutting door reverberated in Anna's ears. The soldier stood guard outside the compartment. Across from her, Georg sat with his mouth wide open. *Babička* clutched her cane, her knuckles white.

Anna gazed at Horst. He closed his eyes and bowed his head. His shoulders slumped. She rubbed small circles on his back. "It's not your fault."

"But it is. If not for me, he would have accepted your identification and let you go. I'm the one who put you in this predicament. It is my fault."

Georg returned his card to his pocket. "If I learned nothing else during the course of this war, I learned this. Nothing ever goes according to plan. Bumps and hiccups happen along the way. It's what you do about them that determines your fate."

"The Lord will save us." *Babička*'s mantra.

"She's right." Anna nodded.

Horst opened his spring-blue eyes and stared at her. "I'm not going to give up. Whatever I have to do, I will get you to safety. All of you. So far, none of us has accepted any Nazi directive."

Anna stopped rubbing. "My parents did. *Babička* and I would have if not for you. You delivered us."

"And put you in danger. But no more." His voice was more resolute than she'd heard it since the day he'd brought them into his flat. "We need a plan. A way to escape."

Anna pulled away. "Escape? You've gone mad, *ne*?"

"Young man, I think you forget that I'm a very old lady. I cannot outrun a trained military man in his prime. Never in my life, even in my younger days, could I get away from him."

"I am the only one who will have to outrun him."

Anna squeezed her hands together. "I know where you're going with this, and I don't like the sound of it. You can't be serious. You would give yourself up for us?"

"I don't intend for him to catch me. But if he does, it's what I have to do."

She went numb. "*Ne. Ne. Ne.* I can't . . . I won't . . . lose you. Not you. *Ne.*" She fidgeted in the seat.

Horst pulled her close. "Calm down. This is trust in action. You are going to have to remain composed and keep a level head. Can you do that?"

Could she when every part of her tensed in panic? Could she when his life depended on it? "I don't know."

He whispered into her hair, so only she heard his voice. His soothing words. "Yes, you can. I trust you."

She sucked in air and drew deep into herself. "Tell me what to do."

Chapter Thirty-Five

*O*nce, just once, did *Hauptsturmführer* Jaeger come for Patricie. She survived. Her injuries healed. Where was he? What was he plotting?

Fear left her. She had no strength for it. She didn't think about the future. Or the past. She concentrated on the moment, on getting through this particular slice of time.

The war's end had to be near. Had to be. The news *Pan* Karas had given her before her capture promised Allied victory in Europe soon. If she could hang on a few more minutes, hours, days, perhaps she would live. Would once again taste freedom.

And be able to tell Georg all he meant to her.

How foolish she had been. A man, a wonderful, tenderhearted man, loved her with great passion. And she loved him too. A physical ache pierced her chest whenever she thought of him.

But she'd put him off, thinking there would be a tomorrow. After the war. They could be together after the war. They could get married after the war. They could start a family after the war.

Now she knew better. Tomorrow might never come. Why had she ever put it off? She should have seized the moment. In his flat, after she'd failed to help the boy, she should have told him everything. Should have gone to him and allowed him to love her.

That time would never come again. She couldn't do it over.

But if she held on, just for a little while longer, perhaps God would grant them another chance. They could yet be happy. Marry. Have children. Grow old together.

How long, O Lord? How long?

The suffocating solitary confinement didn't end. Time had fused together into a single lump. Endless. Like the big, blue ocean she'd only heard about. Or the Czech countryside covered in snow.

Every part of her body ached. Each joint protested at the slightest movement. The pounding in her head didn't cease.

With a long, loud groan, the metal door holding Patricie inside the small fortress creaked open.

"Come with me." The guard, a different one than before, motioned for her to follow. He held a weapon in his hands.

She stood, the world spinning in circles. She leaned against the wall until the ground righted itself. "Where are we going?"

"You'll find out soon enough." The man cuffed her hands behind her back. With his rifled trained on her, he led her in a brisk walk through the courtyard.

She had a difficult time keeping up. Her lack of food and exercise over the past few weeks hindered her. "Please, stop. Let me rest." She glanced at him.

The tall, fair-haired guard grinned. But not a birthday-party sort of grin. More like a you'll-get-what's-coming-to-you one. "You'll have plenty of time to rest later." But he paused until she caught her breath.

"I haven't been out in, I don't know how long." Overhead, birds chirped. The grass shone emerald in the brilliant yellow sunshine. She basked in the warmth of it. "It's spring."

"May second, to be exact. You won't forget the date."

Her shrunken stomach clenched. Why wouldn't she? Was she to be released? Or tortured again?

As they progressed through the courtyard, they proceeded through a long, arched tunnel into another yard. A red brick wall rose on one side. Grass opened like a carpet in front of her.

A few other women and their guards occupied the space.

She searched their faces for a clue. Any clue. And *Hauptsturmführer* Jaeger. Where was he? She expected him to be here.

Women's faces, which should be round and soft, were hard, angled, withered. One lady whimpered. The rest hunched over.

Resigned.

"Line up against the wall." The guard grabbed her, his grip tight, and shoved her against the rough brick. A slight breeze stirred the air. The wind carried the odor of filth, illness, and decay.

But she inhaled the scent of roses and lilacs.

The guards lay prone on the grass, their weapons focused on the women.

The reality of what was about to happen dawned on her. Time ceased. Blood pounded in her ears, in her neck. Her breaths came in rapid succession.

Was it worth it? Hauptsturmführer Jaeger's last words to her played over in her mind. Visions of Eliška's and Anna's faces flashed before her. One she'd failed. The other she hadn't.

The crescendo of an orchestra washed over her. Tears streamed down her face.

Would she change anything? *Ne,* not a thing. Except maybe for Georg. But she followed God's leading in her life and accepted whatever fate that brought.

She was willing to give her life. She could make the ultimate sacrifice. *Was it worth it?*

She lifted her hands to heaven.

Yes, oh yes, it was.

"My life is nothing now. I'm surprised Marcus didn't shoot me right away. Deserters and traitors are not tolerated in the German army."

Horst's words froze Anna's heart. "Not to me, it isn't. Your life is very important. You have me to live for. Our future to fight for."

He stroked her cheek as the train wheels clacked westward on the track, the rhythm a drumbeat that matched the throbbing in her head. "And I will. I'll fight to the bitter end, if I have to. Believe me, I won't give in. He's just one man."

Should she be relieved or terrified? "One with a gun."

"Ah, but you forget that I knew him in military training. His looks have changed enough that I didn't recognize him at first, but I remember what he was like. His strengths. And weaknesses. That, I can use to my advantage."

"He has the same advantage."

"Oh, my Anna, please don't worry. Whatever the outcome, remember that I love you. And I'll find you. We'll be together some day."

"It won't be soon enough for me."

He kissed her then, right in front of Georg and *Babička*. But she didn't mind. Instead of words, she allowed the melody in her kiss to speak to him. To tell him of her love for him. To tell him she would wait for him. To tell him good-bye.

"I love you, Horst."

"Oh, my Anna." He caressed her cheek, kissed her forehead, her eyes, her mouth. "I love you more than you'll ever know. Leaving you is ripping my heart out." He kissed her again, hard, possessive. Then, he broke away and rubbed her arms.

He straightened, his tone turning serious and business-like. "Be ready to go at the next stop."

She clung to him.

Babička bowed her head in prayer. The words wouldn't come for Anna. *Please, please, please.* That was the only petition her broken heart cried.

Georg sat with his back straight. No emotion played across his thin face. She guessed he must be thinking about Patricie, wondering where she was, what was happening to her.

And in a matter of hours, she would be in the same position. Wondering about Horst. Where he was. If he was safe. Alive.

She inhaled, long and slow, even though her arms and legs, hands and feet all trembled. Like water over a dam, she would never be able to control the panic if it broke through. She had to remain calm. For all of them, she had to stay clearheaded.

Much too soon, the little hamlets strung out across the farm fields drew together, closer and closer as they approached the station at Žatec.

The train slowed.

So did time.

With one last screech of the brakes, the train jerked to a halt.

Anna glanced at the soldier. He remained at his post, legs akimbo, clenching his rifle.

Horst squeezed her hand and gave her one final peck on the cheek. Then he left her side. She shivered, but nodded to *Babička* and Georg. "Are you ready?"

Babička whispered, "Amen," and nodded. Georg did too.

Anna slid to the edge of her seat, ready to jump into action.

Horst moved to the door. Anna helped *Babička* to stand. Georg leaned forward, ready to spring.

She bit her lip as Horst slid the door open. "I need to have a word with you, Kuhn."

"I have nothing to say to you." *Hauptmann* Kuhn blocked the doorway. How would they ever get out?

Horst didn't wait for his rival to make a move. With one fluid motion, he punched Kuhn in the face. Kuhn staggered. Fell to the floor. Horst stood over him.

The doorway was clear. Anna grabbed *Babička* and headed for the exit. Her grandmother's cane tapped on the floor as they rushed out. They approached the steps and the line of people waiting to disembark.

They had to hurry. Had to get away from here. Couldn't these people move any faster?

Georg swept up *Babička* in his scrawny arms. How did he have the strength to carry her? "Excuse me." He wriggled to the side of a man in an old-fashioned business suit. "Pardon me." He pushed by a young woman loaded down with bags. "This old woman is ill. Please, let me through. We have to get medical care as soon as possible." His voice held a hint of panic. Genuine, to be sure.

He wormed his way down the steps. Anna followed in his wake.

They set foot on the wooden platform. She caught up to him. He spoke to her in a low tone. "Hurry, but don't run."

The flash of a gray-green German uniform in the crowd caught her eye. Her throat closed, allowing nothing but the smallest amount of air through.

"Go, go. To your left."

She wound her way through the crowd. "Let us through. My grand-mother is ill. Please, let us by." *Babička* even gave a convincing groan. The crowd parted for the three of them.

Lord, watch over Horst. Keep him safe, whatever is happening.

A tug on her shawl stopped her. "Do you need help?" A man in a bowler hat motioned in Georg's direction. "I can take you to the doctor."

Anna wormed her way to Georg's side. "*Ne.* Thank you. The motion of the train made her sick. As soon as we get her home and tucked in bed, she'll be fine. But her stomach is sour, and I don't want her to ..."

The man backed away. "Fine, then. Take her home."

Georg gave her a thin-lipped smile. For someone taught never to lie, that one had rolled off her tongue.

They cleared the group assembled on the platform to welcome arrivals and to see loved ones off. Warm sun greeted them.

"Which way now?"

Georg scanned the street in both directions.

A commotion broke out behind them. "Stop that man. Stop him."

"Don't look back." Georg shifted *Babička*'s weight.

Anna clamped her mouth to keep from crying out for Horst. But she had to know.

A gunshot. Two. Three.

"Horst!"

Screams rippled through the crowd.

"Run!" Georg sprinted off with *Babička*.

Anna turned around. Some people fell to the ground. Some scattered. Some froze to the spot.

"Anna, now!"

She spun back. Georg dashed away. She hurried to catch up.

They raced down a few blocks, passed little shops, their windows sparkling in the light. Passed quaint village cottages, white fences marking the property boundaries. Georg turned several times.

They came to a row of businesses. He hustled into the alley behind them and stopped. He set *Babička* down and bent over.

Anna raised her arms in order to catch her breath. A minute or two went by before she could speak. "Horst."

"You can't think about him."

"But they might have shot him. He might be—"

"Get that thought out of your mind. Right now, we have to find a way out of here. If he made it, we might be able to rejoin him in Plzeň. But Kuhn will be on the lookout for us. This town isn't safe."

"We can't leave him behind."

"We have to. You know that. Our plan never was to stay together. As soon as the situation there quiets down, we'll think about our next move. Right now, rest."

But how could she rest when Horst wasn't by her side? When he might be injured. Or worse.

"I'm going back."

Georg grabbed her so hard he must have left a bruise on her upper arm. "You are going nowhere. How are you going to help him? You'll only put him in more danger. And yourself. And your grandmother. Think."

She didn't want to think. Didn't want to face what her reality might be.

She hugged herself. Cold. Alone.

God, spare him.

Chapter Thirty-Six

Panting, Horst reached the train car's exit. A crowd gathered at the edge of the tracks. Czech? They might let him pass. German? Not a chance.

He raised the gun he'd wrestled from Kuhn in the air. "Out of my way, or I shoot."

Whatever nationality, they moved aside. He made for the steps.

From the top one, he caught a glimpse of Anna and the others hurrying away from the train into the large, many-windowed Beaux Arts station.

"*Halten sie.*" German. A Nazi soldier. In front of him. "You there, drop your weapon."

Horst hesitated no more than a second before lowering the gun. That's all the time his fellow countryman needed. One, two, three bullets ricocheted off the metal steps below him and the metal railing to his side. His stomach rattled around his midsection in much the same way.

He jumped from the top step and landed in the gravel with a thud.

The soldier marched in his direction.

Then, an unforgettable sight. The group of bystanders and passengers formed a barrier around him. They held the Nazi back. Refused to let him through.

Horst sucked in his breath.

"Move, or I'll shoot all of you."

The crowd didn't budge.

A young man grabbed Horst by the wrist. "Come with me."

Should he? Did he trust this person?

I trust God.

Horst followed him along the length of the train and into the open. Small stones crunched under their feet. Sweat soaked Horst's shirt.

They ran into a grove of trees some distance from the station. When Horst, winded from the fight and the sprint, didn't think he could manage another step, the man stopped. "You are a crazy person."

"Why did you help me?" Horst gulped air.

"You're German. Why was he after you?"

"I'm a deserter."

"A coward?"

"Not like you think. I protected a woman and had to go into hiding with her when the Nazis discovered us." Anna. This man led him away from where they disappeared. "I have to find her. She was with me."

"You truly are crazy if you go back into the town. I'm sure those Nazis have their German shepherds sniffing out your scent as we speak. *Ne*, you can't return there."

Anna had slipped through his fingers.

He had to trust the Lord. Trust Him to bring them together again someday. Soon.

"Can you help me get to Plzeň?"

"That's near the front, you know."

"I know. That's where they're headed."

"Come with me. I don't have transportation to get you there, but I'll give you what provisions I have and point you in the right direction."

"How far is it?"

"A few days' walk."

Days. He might not have days. The Nazis might pick him up along the way as they fled the advancing American troops.

But right now, he had no other choice.

"Now what?" Anna moved farther into the alley's shadow as a group of young girls passed by, their hair rolled, lines drawn down the backs of their legs to imitate stockings. "How are we going to get to Plzeň?"

Georg pushed his glasses up his nose. "We might have to walk."

"Walk? Plzeň is about eighty kilometers from Žatec. *Babička* can't make it that far. *Ne*, you need another plan. A better one."

Georg paced in the small space. "The train is out of the question. They'll have guards posted all over, waiting for us. Probably combing the town for us as we speak."

"Then we have to leave. Fast." Freedom lay less than one hundred kilometers to the southwest. So close. So far away.

"Bicycle. Could she ride?"

"Why ask the question when you know the answer?"

A burst of air escaped Georg's lips. "The only other options are a car or a wagon."

"And how do you propose getting either one of those?"

Babička rubbed Anna's arm. "Let the man think. Stop pestering him."

"I'm sorry. But please, hurry with a plan."

"I remember waiting for your grandfather."

"Where did he go?"

"He went to school in Vienna, to study banking. The years passed with a maddening slowness. I wanted them to hurry, so he would return. So we could be together forever."

"Exactly."

"But the Lord used our time apart. We grew as people. As Christians, we relied on our faith more than we ever did before. He did come home. What a time of rejoicing and celebration. I appreciated him more because of his absence and never took for granted a single day we had together. Our separation taught me to savor each moment with him. And I did."

"Now, he waits for you. But I don't even know if Horst is alive."

"You'll find out. Everything happens in the Lord's time."

Anna hugged *Babička*. "It's hard, because I want it to happen in my time."

"You'll look back on this, and it will be a small pebble in a rock quarry."

"What would I do without you? I wouldn't have made it this far."

"You would have. The Lord is faithful."

"I know your next words."

Babička nodded, a strand of gray hair sticking out from under her embroidered shawl. "Then follow my advice."

So easy to say. So much harder to do. *Lord, I'm trusting You with my life. With Horst's. Be with him wherever he is, whatever is happening to him. Have You taken him home? Please, Lord, don't let that be the case. Watch over him. Bring us together again. In Your time.*

She struggled with those last words. With meaning them and trusting them.

But her void wasn't as deep as it had been. God filled the empty place in her heart. Returned a soft background of music.

Georg sucked in a breath. "I know how we can get out of here."

Anna straightened. "Don't leave us in suspense."

"The Czechs have no petrol for their automobiles. The Germans are driving eastward."

"That doesn't sound like a plan."

"Let him explain, Anna."

"I have a contact. Well, a man I went to secondary school with. The last I heard, he lived around here. He was a mechanic."

"A mechanic?"

"*Beruško*, stop interrupting."

"Don't you see? He has access to cars."

"Can he get petrol?"

"It's our only chance. We'll have to find him first. I'm going on nothing more than a hunch. There is no other way."

If she wanted to be reunited with Horst, she had to get to Plzeň. "It's an idea, if nothing else. How do we locate him?"

"I'll go on my own and ask around. The authorities will be on alert for a man and two women, but not a man on his own."

Her legs shook. "*Ne*, you can't go. The people at the train station got a good look at you. But with my shawl over my head, they didn't catch a glimpse of me. I'll search. Tell me his name and what he looks like."

"Edvard Hornick. Tall, skinny fellow, at least in those days. Brown hair, brown eyes. He had a scar over his left eye. One winter, I hit him with an icy snowball, and it cut him."

With trembling hands, Anna lifted the dark shawl over her head. She stepped from the sunless alley into the waning daylight. Men hustled home from work. Women rushed back from the market with their meager supplies to start supper.

She approached one man. He nodded to a couple of people in passing. He must know the town well. "Pardon me, but do you know Edvard Hornick? He's an old friend of mine from school. He is a mechanic. Or was. I suspect the war put him out of business."

The man, his hair parted on the side and slicked back, shook his head. "Never heard of him. But I only came last year."

She stopped a woman coming from the bakery, no bulge in her shopping bag. "Do you know Edvard Hornick?"

She pursed her lips. "The name is familiar, but I can't place him. Sorry I can't help."

After a few more people indicated they didn't know Edvard, she entered a dressmaker's shop. The window sat barren, no dress forms draped in the latest fashions. For years now, Anna, as a Jew, hadn't been able to buy clothing or material. The same fate now befell the general population as the war's end approached.

The young woman behind the counter stood. She smoothed her slim-fitting flowered dress and tucked a blonde curl behind her ear. "May I help you, miss?"

Anna's energy rushed out of her body. She leaned on the counter. *Lord, let this be the place.* "I'm looking for Edvard Hornick."

The woman's blue eyes brightened. "I know him. He's my brother's friend."

Anna relaxed her shoulders. Could it be? God answered her so fast? "Where can I find him?"

"His shop is on the other side of town. I feel sorry for him. His only business in almost six years has been the Nazis. People around here don't like that he worked with them, but he had to earn a living. With no petrol, his usual customers didn't come."

"Can you write down directions for me to find him?"

"What is it you want with him?"

"I'm passing through town. He told me if I ever came to the area to find him. All these years later, here I am. With the war on, I know it's not the best time, but I always liked him." Heat rose in Anna's face from the lie. Hopefully, the woman would think it was from embarrassment over her admission.

"He's married now, with a little one on the way."

"I would love to meet his wife, then. And say hello."

The woman led the way to the door. "I'll take you to his house. You'll like his wife. She's very sweet. My name is Iva, by the way."

"Anna."

Iva led the way through the narrow streets of Žatec. Anna would never have found the house without her help. They came to a humble cottage on the edge of town. Iva knocked, and a woman, her belly rounded, answered the door. "How nice to see you, Iva. We were about to sit down to supper."

"I'm sorry to disturb you. I brought a friend of Edvard's with me. They went to school together in Prague. This is Anna."

"Nice to meet you, Anna. Won't you come in?"

A young man rose from the small table. He rubbed his head, his hair thinning. "I'm sorry, but I don't remember you. What did you say your name was again?"

I trust God.

"My name isn't important. I come on behalf of Georg Klima."

Edvard pointed at her. "Him, I remember."

"He and I and one other person are on our way to Plzeň. And we need your assistance."

"I don't have money for train fare."

"That's not what we need." She swallowed around the lump in her throat, her hands sweating. "We need a car to get us there. Can you help?"

Chapter Thirty-Seven

*E*dvard Hornick stood beside his table, the light dim in this little cottage at the edge of Žatec. Anna held her breath, afraid to hope.

"I don't know. It's risky. The only cars I have access to are Nazi vehicles."

"Do any of them have petrol?"

"Yes, a couple."

"Enough to get us to Plzeň?"

"I believe so." But he gave an almost imperceptible shake of his head.

He was going to turn them down. And then what? This was their one and only shot. "I know it's asking a great deal of you. I've come to you on blind faith that you might help us. My husband is waiting for me there, as is Georg's wife. We don't want to be trapped in Soviet territory when they're in American hands." She glanced at Edvard's wife. "You know how terrible that would be. To be separated from the one you love."

He gazed at his bride, his face glowing. She'd hit the mark.

"I can't imagine being parted with someone I love so dearly. I'll help you. But why didn't Georg come himself?"

"Help me find my way back to him, and you can speak to him."

Edvard's wife cried as she kissed her husband good-bye. Was Anna wrong for taking him from her while trying to reach Horst? Who knew any more in this topsy-turvy world.

Edvard and Anna hurried through the darkening streets. She led him to the alley where Georg and *Babička* waited.

Even in the low light, Anna caught how, like little boys, both men grinned when they recognized each other. They slapped each other on the back.

"How good to see you, Edvard."

"And you, Georg. Can you tell me why you sent this woman to help you find your wife?"

When Georg glanced at her, Anna shrugged.

"It's a bit more complicated than that. Someday, I'll explain it to you. For now, we need to get to Plzeň. *Paní* Doubeková can't walk, and there are reasons I can't explain to you why we can't take the train."

Edvard stared at Georg for a moment. "I can surmise. In school, you always were the first to help a classmate who fell on the playground or who didn't understand their math equations. Yes, the picture is clearer to me now."

"Will you help?"

"We'll have to go under the cover of darkness. A car heading to Plzeň during the day would draw too much attention."

"All the better." Georg clapped once. "When can we be on our way?"

"Right now."

"The last stage of our journey, *Babička*." Anna embraced her grandmother.

"I pray you're right."

Edvard retraced his steps through the town toward his shop. "The war will end within days. Mark my words. Hitler is dead. How much longer can the Germans go on?"

"Dead?" Georg stopped in his tracks.

"You didn't hear?"

"*Ne*. We haven't had access to any news for several days."

"General Doenitz is now in charge. Berlin is about to fall."

Goose bumps broke out on Anna's arms. Could it be that after six years of war, they were in the final hours of the battle? Czechoslovakia had been the first country to come under Nazi control. And, it looked like it would be the last country to taste liberation.

"It appears they'll make their final stand around Plzeň. Are you sure that's where you want to go?"

"Yes, we have to get there."

They came to the dingy shop. Edvard retrieved the keys to one of the automobiles and started it. Anna slid in beside her grandmother. "You can rest now, *Babička*. It's almost over."

Please, God, let Horst be alive. To come so close and to have him not survive would be too much. She couldn't stand another loss.

Edvard pulled out of the garage and into the inky night, his headlights off. "We have to be careful. The Americans have bombed Prague and a few other targets." The news would sadden Horst. All his preservation work for nothing.

The car motored down the road. Twice, they pulled to the side to let a convoy of German trucks by. Trucks heading east. Away from the battle. Perhaps they would give up without a fight.

Suddenly, the car veered to the right and bumped along the road. Edvard brought it to a halt. "Sorry. It seems we have a flat tire."

Would they never get to Plzeň?

Georg and Edvard went to work changing the tire. As they jacked the car down, the low hum of approaching trucks reached Anna's ears.

"Hurry, hurry." Georg urged on Edvard.

"I'm going as fast as I can."

The convoy came closer. Her heart threatened to jump out of her chest. One, two, three trucks passed them.

Her pulse slowed. Perhaps the Nazis, in their haste to get out of the Americans' way, wouldn't bother with them.

But the fourth truck screeched to a halt on the side of the road behind them. The vehicle's door slammed.

Anna held *Babička*'s trembling hand. "We've come so close."

"We'll get there. We'll get home."

But Anna didn't see how.

Horst sat back in the woods at the edge of the town. The German truck pulled up beside the stranded car. He shivered, and not because of the chilly night air. The soldier stepped from his vehicle and approached the two men working to change a flat tire.

"What are you doing? Identification." The soldier peered into the back window. "All of you. Out of the car. Let me see."

Two women stepped out. The soft moonlight illuminated them. One was small and thin, the other hunched over.

Could it be? Had he found them?

With a flashlight, the soldier examined their papers and handed them back to him. "Where are you going?"

"We're on our way to Plzeň." Horst recognized Georg's voice.

"What is your business there?"

"He's taking me to my father." Anna. With the lilt in her words, no mistake it was her. He itched to jump from his spot in the brush and run to her.

But he had no papers, no identification. He couldn't risk it.

"And just who is your father?"

A man Horst didn't know entered the conversation. "Herr Obermeister."

"Obermeister you say? Boris?"

"That's the fellow." The Czech man stood a head taller than Georg.

"I didn't realize he had a daughter."

This Czech took over, and probably for the best. "You know how private he is."

"*Ja*, that's true. Let me take you to him."

Georg cleared his throat. "Um, *nein*—I mean, we have this car. But—um, thank you."

"I insist."

Did Horst detect a hint of disbelief in the German's voice?

"Really, it's fine. I have permission to use this car."

"Come with me." The German left no option for them to object. He marched the four of them to his truck.

A transport truck.

Was he taking them to Plzeň? And then what? Anna was not Herr Obermeister's daughter. That truth would be uncovered as soon as they arrived.

He rubbed his arms as he sucked in his breath.

Dear God, protect them.

Anna and *Babička* clasped hands as they made their way from Edvard's car to the German truck. When would this nightmare end? Freedom proved to be elusive. Impossible, almost.

"Ladies, you can squeeze into the cab with me. Men, into the back." The German soldier was kind enough. "Though I don't see why you want to go to Plzeň. You'd be wise to get to Prague. Though I hear there is unrest there. Maybe staying put is the best decision."

Anna's throat clogged as she helped *Babička* into the vehicle. "We heard terrible rumors about the Russian soldiers and German women. We hope to reach the Americans."

The soldier bought her story and went around the back to make sure Edvard and Georg were in place. For six years, they'd managed to avoid being carted away by the =Germans. With liberty no more than a few days away, their nightmare transformed into reality.

"All will be well." *Babička* relaxed into the seat.

"I'm trying to trust God for salvation, but it's difficult."

"Yes, to put your life in someone else's hands is a hard thing to do. We want to be in control. But He will never fail us."

Lord, let Babička be right. Please, don't fail us now. I'm clinging to You. Be with us. Give us a way out of this situation.

The man jumped into the cab and started the engine. He turned around and drove toward Plzeň. At least he kept that part of their deal.

"Tell me about your father."

Anna paused a moment, almost ready to share her memories of *Táta*. But no, he asked about Herr Obermeister. A man she'd never met. Her dry tongue stuck to the top of her mouth. "I thought you knew him so well." Thank goodness for *Táta*'s time at the university in Austria and his insistence that his children learn perfect German.

"I thought I did, too. He never told me about a daughter. Or a grandmother. You look nothing like him."

"I favor my mother's side of the family."

"How long has it been since you've seen your father?"

"Not long. I'm anxious to be with him again, though. My husband and I have exciting news to share with him." She ended with a soft giggle. The perfect touch.

"What is that?"

"I can't tell you until I give it to him. But you can probably guess."

"So Boris is to be a grandfather. Congratulations. And will this be your first great-grandchild?"

"*Ja.*" *Babička*'s German wasn't as polished as Anna's, despite her spending time in Vienna. A good thing she kept her answers to single syllables.

"Boris never struck me as the family type."

"There is much people keep hidden from others." If he only knew her secret.

The soldier fell silent as they bumped along the road. *Babička*, squished between the man and Anna, dozed.

Anna gazed out the window into the blackness. Hopefully, Georg and Edvard were back there cooking up a plan to get them out of this trouble.

So many emotions churned inside her, she couldn't untangle them all. Would the longing for her family ever go away? Could she control the fear that her end, too, was near? Yet, a bright spot glowed. Her love for Horst. But where was he? The unknown gnawed at her.

Lord, You've brought me this far. You've kept me and Babička from danger. You have been watching us and caring for us each step of the way. Thank You. Please, continue to keep Your hand upon us. And be with Horst. Let him be alive. Bring us together again.

Peace washed over her. She would worry about their next step when the time came.

She dozed. And dreamed of an empty concert hall. She played Vivaldi's *Four Seasons.* But only one man sat in the seats.

Horst.

She awoke with a start when the German pulled the truck to a grinding stop in front of a large home in the center of a town.

This must be Plzeň.

She straightened and shook *Babička* awake. "We're here."

Babička squeezed her hand. "God is in control."

Yes, but how would they get out of this mess?

Maybe they wouldn't.

She slid from the seat, stood on stiff, shaky knees, and helped *Babička* down. Georg and Edvard came from the back. The German soldier held tight to his rifle.

And then . . .

Only God could have planted this idea. Her own muddled mind would never have produced such a scheme.

She clutched her middle and doubled over. "Ah! Oh, I'm having such pain. Georg, sweetheart, where are you?"

Georg came to her side and clasped her hand. "What is it, darling?"

"The baby. I'm afraid it's the baby."

"*Nein, nein.*"

Edvard jumped in, saving Georg from having to say more in his terrible German. He gestured at the soldier. "Get a doctor. Hurry. There isn't time to lose."

"Let me get your father."

"*Ne*, there isn't time. The baby. I'm losing the baby. The pain is horrible."

If she could but see the German's face. Would he go? And give them a chance to escape?

Chapter Thirty-Eight

$\mathcal{A}$nna hunched over in the middle of the street, feigning pain, praying for a chance to get out of the German's clutches. "My baby, my baby." She wailed and moaned.

Georg rubbed her back. Edvard turned to the soldier. "Get that doctor. You don't want to be responsible for Herr Obermeister's daughter's life, do you?"

"Help her in the truck. I'll take her to the hospital."

"*Nein. Nein.*" She couldn't allow him to do that. "I can't move. The pain is too bad. Bring him here. He'll know what to do. Oh, it's getting worse." She tried to imitate *Máma's* anguish as she'd brought Lada into the world.

"Don't stand there." Edvard's words carried a great deal of force. "You're wasting precious time."

The soldier ran to the front door and pounded on it. "Herr Obermeister. It's your daughter. I'm going to get the doctor."

"What is it?" A Czech woman answered the door.

"I brought Herr Obermeister's daughter and family. I have to get her help. Tell him."

What was her reaction? Anna couldn't interrupt her act to peek.

"What are you talking about?" She slammed the door.

Another door shut. The truck's, from the clanging, metallic sound of it. Good, the maid's words didn't register with the German.

The engine roared, then grew silent as the soldier sped away.

"Now, fast, before he returns."

Edvard hoisted *Babička* into his arms. He, Georg, and Anna raced down the street. What would happen if the maid came back? They had to hurry.

Not many people stirred this early in the morning. Dawn streaked the sky pink above them. A baker unlocked his door, the line for bread already around the corner.

Edvard, in the lead, slowed his pace and set down *Babička*. "Act as if nothing is out of the ordinary. We don't want to draw attention to ourselves."

Anna and *Babička* pulled their scarves over their heads. Edvard and Georg tugged their slouchy caps over their ears.

They melded into the line. The woman in front of them carried a large basket. A clean, white apron covered her pleated, gray skirt. She turned and gave a dimpled smile. "Good morning."

"Good morning to you."

"They say the Americans are only a few kilometers away. It's a good idea to stock up while you can. We don't know what's coming."

Anna nodded. "We have to be prepared."

"I haven't seen you before." The woman nodded in the direction of the others in line. "We've spent so many hours here in the past years, we know almost everyone."

Maybe blending in with the crowd wasn't the best idea.

Georg joined the conversation. "We just arrived from Prague."

"Trying to get away from those mad Soviets?"

"Something like that." Anna's nervous laugh grated on her own ears.

"I don't blame you. I am glad it looks like the Americans will be the ones to liberate us. It is a shame the Soviets are going to be in control of the rest of Czechoslovakia. I'm afraid it will mean hard times ahead for our country."

More heartache for herself and her countrymen? *Ne.* They must concentrate on the present.

Georg scrubbed his face, his eyes clouded. He glanced at Edvard, who nodded. "We're searching for accommodations. Do you know of a place to stay? Just until liberation."

The woman surveyed their crew. Anna drew *Babička* into a

protective embrace. "My grandmother is exhausted. We need some-where to rest."

"I have two spare rooms. We'll be tight, but the Americans will arrive any day, mark my words."

The specter of the German soldier hung over them. At this moment, he might be discovering they'd tricked him. He would launch an all-out search. They had to get tucked away as soon as possible. "I hate to take you away from the line, but my grandmother can't stand any longer. We will pay you extra if you bring us to your house now."

Georg flinched. But he was the one who'd said he had to spend his soon-to-be worthless Reichsmarks.

"Of course. I can come back later. It's only a few blocks."

She led them around a couple of corners to a small row house, with ornamentation surrounding the windows much like Anna's home in Prague. Once inside, she put the kettle on for tea and made up a bed for *Babička*. Anna secured the blanket around her grandmother and kissed her weathered cheek.

"This is it, *beruško*. The end of our journey."

"I pray you're right."

"God provided, didn't He? You trusted, and look where He brought you."

They may be safe, at least for the time being, but what about Horst? She wouldn't rest until she knew.

May 6, 1945

Horst woke to a windy, chilly, damp morning. Little light filtered into the barn where he'd spent the night. The farmer had no idea Horst took advantage of the warm building. He had to move on before the man came to do the morning chores.

He stretched his stiff muscles and shook the hay from his hair. His empty stomach cried out to be fed. Though he'd rationed the supplies the man from Žatec had given him, they'd dwindled to nothing. He needed a meal, a bath, and a shave.

But Plzeň lay on the horizon.

Freedom.

At least from the fear of being caught by his fellow Germans.

And Anna. Was she in the city? Safe somewhere? Even alive? He tried to push the questions aside, but with little luck. She haunted him every moment of every day. The only picture of her he managed to bring to mind included a German soldier herding her into a truck. Later, he would sketch her, fill another page in his book with her face.

Today's objective? Get to the city.

A round of sporadic shooting punctuated the early morning still-ness. Not far away. The Americans must be on the edge of town.

This would be the day he surrendered. The day the war ended for him.

He stood up and down on his tiptoes. He needed to get there as soon as possible and put this horrible chapter in his life to an end.

Maybe not the most horrible. Because of the war, he'd met Anna. He would never love another as much as her. And the Lord had worked in his heart. *Mutti* would be proud of the man God had changed him into.

With a deep breath, he climbed down the ladder from the hayloft. He'd just reached the main part of the barn when the door slid open. He stopped dead, allowing himself only small breaths.

A middle-aged farmer entered and took a few steps inside. Like Horst, he halted, stock still, when he spotted the intruder. "You there. What are you doing in my barn?" The farmer grabbed a nearby pitch-fork and pointed it in Horst's direction.

He raised his hands. Instead of surrendering to the Americans, he surrendered to a Czech farmer. "I mean no harm."

"German?"

"*Ja.*"

"I should run you through."

"I'm a deserter, a traitor to my country. I've been working with the Czech resistance." Partially true. He didn't want to mention he hid Jews, too, not knowing the man's sympathies.

"You people almost destroyed my farm. Confiscated my cows, stole my crops. Why shouldn't I exact my revenge on you?"

Horst's raised hands shook. "Because you would harm a man who tried to do right in the face of terrible wrong. Alone, I didn't do much, but I did my part. You have to believe me. I'm on my way to Plzeň to surrender to the Americans."

"No need to do that now, is there?" The man stood as tall and as broad as Horst.

"A compromise, then. Take me to the city yourself and turn me over to the American command. I'm unarmed." Horst opened his coat and turned his pockets inside out.

"Fine, fine. You Germans are barbarians. Czechoslovakia is a land of culture. I'll show you that. Move toward me. Slow. One step at a time. Keep your hands up."

Horst inched his way in the farmer's direction, watching the man the entire time. The farmer did the same.

"Good. Stop there. Turn around."

Horst hated to turn his back to the man. He might yet decide to pierce him with the pitchfork.

"Fine. Let's go. I have a couple chickens left to care for. Don't make any sudden moves, or I promise you, I will not show you mercy."

"Understood." Horst relaxed his shoulders. Maybe this was the better way to turn himself in. If he came alone, the Americans might shoot. Now, he was already in custody.

The farmer prodded him along, the sharp tines of the pitchfork against his back. They marched at a brisk pace to the city, only a couple of kilometers away.

A light mist fell, and the wind sneaked under his coat, the bottom of it flapping in the breeze. Yet Horst warmed as they ambled along. Part of him wanted to get there as fast as possible. Part of him didn't want to face what the Americans might have in mind for him. He'd heard they were kind to their prisoners, but was it true?

Then, the melody of church bells rang out, filling the air. Was Anna listening to this?

They arrived in the town packed with beautiful old buildings. His architect's eye caught the ovular curves in some of the buildings, suggesting Baroque Revival. Someday, perhaps, he would return here and draw them.

Shouts and cheers joined the bells' cacophony.

The Americans must have arrived.

No sounds of a battle. No gun blasts. No earth-shattering bombing. No screaming.

Just joy. The purest sort of joy.

The farmer marched him along until they came to the main road.

They couldn't see far, because the citizens of Plzeň clogged the streets. Like at a parade, they stood ten, twenty deep. Horst caught a glance at a tank's gun, raised high.

He sank to his knees and wept.

The stab of pitchfork tines in his back prodded him to his feet.

"This way." With the farming implement, the man directed Horst to the left, down a street paralleling the main one. "Fast. We want to catch the beginning of the line."

Horst, hands still raised, obeyed the command. After a few blocks, the farmer found a sliver a daylight between the people. "There. March there."

They made their way to the happy throng.

"Coming through. Let us by. German prisoner here."

The people around them ceased their cheering. Horst stared at the ground and moved forward. A wet wad of spit hit him in the cheek. He flinched. Another one. And another.

"You monster. Look what you did to us." More spit.

"I hope you get what you deserve."

"Good riddance. May you rot away."

The jeers bounced off him.

He glanced up. Crowds swarmed the American tanks. Women kissed the soldiers. Everyone waved American flags. Where had they gotten them?

The farmer prodded him forward. They approached the tank. Horst's heart pounded at the same rate as the motors ran. He stood tall.

And uttered the few English words he knew. "My name is *Hauptmann* Horst Engel. I surrender."

Chapter Thirty-Nine

"*Babička, Babička*, wake up." Anna shook her grandmother as hard as she could without rattling her bones. "Don't you hear that noise? Listen. Singing. Music. The Americans are here."

Babička roused and sat up. "Is it true? Go to the window and see. Tell me what is happening out there."

Like she had almost two years ago, Anna parted the curtains to observe the scene outside. This time was different. This time, she didn't peek out of them, afraid of what she would see. There were no Nazi officers. No one being pulled from their homes.

This time, she threw open the blackout shades and unlatched the window. A cool, damp gust of air invaded the room. She tingled. "You should see it. Come here. The American tanks are rolling down the street. Look at all of those flags. Czech and American. But, *Babička*, the best part is the music."

The bells pealed their triumphant song. The reverberations traveled through the floor and into Anna's soul. Her long-still fingers moved as they would if she held her violin. Like most of the city's residents, she wept.

Wept for joy.

Wept for loss.

Wept for uncertainty.

Babička came and wrapped her in an embrace. Tears, too, flowed down her lined cheeks. "I know, *beruško*, I know. They should be here. They should share in our joy."

"I'm glad I have you. What would I do if you weren't here?"

"You know." *Babička* paused, fighting for control. "Your parents accomplished what they wanted by leaving us behind. We survived. They would be happy to know that. To see one of their children make it to the end.

"Now, we need to celebrate. Dry your tears. They would want you on that street, searching for *Hauptmann* Engel, cheering and singing with the rest of the people. Enjoy the moment."

Anna took a deep breath and blew it out. "Come with me."

"I'll only hold you back. And I might get crushed in the mad rush."

"I won't let that happen. You should rejoice, too."

"It would be fun."

"Good." Anna squeezed *Babička*, then dressed for the day. She slipped on a red polka-dotted dress that the lady of the house had given her. She combed her dark hair, no longer a danger to her, and held it back with the barrettes she'd worn the day they escaped from the train.

If only she had a better fitting and prettier dress, one in blue, and had the tools to roll her hair the way many of the young women did. She should look her best for Horst. If she found him.

Georg joined them as they clomped down the stairs and into the flood of humanity, all pushing and shoving for a glimpse of the Americans. "What a day of rejoicing." His voice, though, held a hint of sadness.

Was Patricie rejoicing as well?

Anna held tight to *Babička*. The people waved flags and threw flowers. A few brazen women climbed on the tanks and kissed the soldiers. Heat flooded Anna's face as the memory of Horst's kisses filled her mind. *Ne*, she wouldn't greet the Yankees that way. Her kisses belonged only to him.

Dragging *Babička* behind her, she pushed through the crowd and toward the front. "Look, look." She pointed down the street. "They're marching prisoners of war this way." She couldn't voice the words. Maybe, just maybe, Horst was among them. She could know where he was. Know he was alive.

The long line of German soldiers, Czech collaborators, and Nazi commanders snaked passed. Anna stood on her tiptoes to get a better look. They all raised their hands. Their jackboots sounded on the wet pavement.

"Do you see him?" *Babička* clapped her hands like a little girl waiting for her father to return from a long trip.

"*Ne*, I don't. But there are so many. Where are they going? Let's follow them, if you're up to it. Maybe those in charge will help me."

"Not too fast. My poor heart can't take all of this excitement."

"Shall I bring you back to the house first?"

"Maybe that would be best."

"I can take her." Georg nodded to Anna. "Go, find *Hauptmann* Engel."

She wound her way through the sea of humanity to the town square. There, American tanks and Jeeps parked around the perimeter, containing hundreds and hundreds of prisoners. How would she ever find him?

"Horst Engel. I'm looking for Horst Engel." She repeated her words in German and Czech. She didn't know the English for what she wanted to say.

An American soldier came to her, his skin as dark as night. He couldn't be any older than eighteen or nineteen. He spoke to her.

She didn't understand him. "Horst Engel. *Hauptmann* Horst Engel. Please."

He answered in his strange language.

"Czech?"

He shook his head.

"German?"

Again, he shook his head. This time, he motioned to another just-as-young soldier, his coloring from European ancestors. They chatted, and the fair one smiled at her. "I speak some German."

"Good." She told her heart to stop its furious beating. "I'm looking for *Hauptmann* Horst Engel."

"He's a prisoner?"

"I don't know. I think so."

"Ma'am, we have over three thousand captives to process. Right now, I can't help you locate him. Come back later, or tomorrow. Then, we might be able to assist you."

A shot rang out.

"Snipers. Take cover."

She went cold all over. The war had ended, hadn't it? She ran and flattened herself against one of the buildings lining the square. She went cold all over.

Would she ever find Horst?

One, two shots echoed in the air. All fell still. The American's did away with the lone gunman in short order. On shaky knees, Anna traced her way to the woman's house, her steps slow. They'd come this far. So close.

Once home, she climbed the stairs to the room she shared with *Babička*. Her grandmother sat on the bed, combing out long strands of her silver-gray hair.

"I didn't locate him. They said to come back later or tomorrow."

Babička set down the brush and motioned for Anna to sit. She patted her on the knee, like she so often did when she was a child. "All in God's time, *beruško*. Trust that it will happen according to His perfect plan."

"What if Horst is dead?" .

"This, too, you'll discover when God is ready to reveal it to you."

But would that time ever come?

Chapter Forty

December 1946

*A*nna stood backstage at the concert hall in Munich, clutching her bow in her sweaty hands. Why this attack of nerves? Since moving to England with *Babička*, she had performed several times with the London symphony. Tonight, she guested with the Munich orchestra.

Really, the answer to her question was simple. She was in Horst's home town.

She tapped her foot and bit back the tears. More than a year and a half passed since she'd last seen him. Since he'd held her in his arms and promised to live for her.

The soldier at the train station in Žatec must have done his job. That was her only conclusion. All of her letters to the United States and German governments in search of information as to his whereabouts went unanswered.

That dream, the one of being his wife, had evaporated like the last notes of a requiem.

Again, she had no grave to visit, no memorial where she might lay a bouquet of flowers.

But she had her music. The melody God and Horst had restored to her. The song that remembered a most precious time in her life.

A prelude to whatever lay ahead.

"Are you ready?" The concertmaster tapped her on the shoulder and spoke to her in English.

Now, after much hard work, she understood his words. "I am."

He twitched his white mustache and strode onto the stage. Once the audience stopped applauding, he introduced her.

"This is for you, my love. It is your song." Anna stepped into the bright spotlights which obscured her view of the crowd.

The clapping died away, and an expectant hush fell over the auditorium. She closed her eyes and soared back to the little flat on Salvátorská Street in Prague, playing for Horst.

And only for him.

The smell of his cologne and his cigarettes tickled her nose.

One lone tear eked from her eye as she lifted the violin to her chin. She raised the bow. The orchestra played behind her. She stroked the first note of Vittorio Monti's *Csárdás*, one of the first pieces she had performed at Horst's request.

As the tune washed over her, it was as if he came to life once more. She witnessed the emotions playing on his face. Joy. Peace. Love.

Most of all love.

A love that drove him to shelter her. One that held on her in her darkest days. One that gave everything for her.

The softness of his lips caressed her cheeks. The warmth of his body radiated to her. The rough wool of his smoky jacket rubbed against her bare skin.

She played for him. And for *Táta*, *Máma*, her sisters, David. So many who were lost in those long, terrible years.

The music spoke of darkness and violence, but also of hope and trust.

The piece came to an end, the final note still reverberating in the massive hall, when the audience broke out into cheers, bravos, and calls for an encore. She curtsied. Imagine this outpouring of support from a people who, two years ago, had wanted her dead.

Was Horst's mother part of the crowd? Did she know anything about Anna?

She left the stage and collapsed into a chair. The concertmaster hurried to her. "You must go out there again. They're demanding an encore. They want to hear more."

"I cannot give it. In English, I do not know how to explain, but I cannot. I have no more in me. Already, I give them my song." Even if she mastered the language, there wouldn't be words to express how she played for Horst.

And for a brief moment, made him come alive again.

Horst sat in the concert hall, the ceiling soaring above him. He and *Mutti* had made it just as the house lights went down.

In the silence, the entire audience must have heard his heart pounding against his ribs. He tingled. He would see her once more. In the past year and a half, he'd drawn hundreds of pictures of her. Playing for him in the flat on Salvátorská Street. The night on the farm, standing in the puddle of moonlight. In the chicken coop, straw tangled in her hair.

But now, he would see her in person. His Anna, here. He held his breath.

The concertmaster entered the stage, bowed, and motioned for the evening's star to join him.

He leaned toward his mother. "There she is, *Mutti*. That's her." His Anna. Very much alive, still so tiny, still so beautiful. Just like the first time he'd seen her and his world changed forever. Though the war had stolen so much from her, it didn't rob her of her music.

Mutti patted his hand, her fingers long, like a pianist's. "She's beautiful. Everything you told me she was. I can't wait to hear her play."

For a long moment, she stood still, silent. Was she breathing? Her face, her entire body, relaxed. A smile crossed her lips. She touched the bow to the strings, and the melody poured forth.

The same one she first played for him.

Oh, his Anna. She hadn't forgotten him.

Without shame, he wept through the entire piece. As if she were in his arms, so small, so vulnerable, shaking in fear. He breathed in the rosy scent of her freshly washed hair. The notes spoke to him, declaring her love for him. During the selection, he relived every moment of the two years they had together. Remembered what she, and God, did for him.

Thunderous applause broke out when she played the final note. The crowd demanded an encore. There wouldn't be one. She'd given her all. The tilt of her head as she proceeded off stage told him she was exhausted.

While the audience cheered, he leapt from his seat. "We have to see her. Come, *Mutti*, and I'll introduce you." Together, they hustled back stage.

A stage hand blocked their way. "I'm sorry, this area is restricted."

"We need to see Anna Zadoková. Right now. My mother and me."

"That's impossible. She's in the middle of a concert."

"Trust me, she'll want to see me. I saved her life in Prague."

"You know her?"

"Better than anyone in the world. I love her, but I haven't seen her in more than eighteen months. Please, let us through." What if the man barred his way, and he couldn't get to her while she was here?

But, at least she was alive. She'd survived.

"You don't know what it would mean to me. To her."

"Very well. But I will keep my eye on you. If you harm her in any way, I'll be after you."

Horst rushed passed the man, *Mutti* following close behind. They made their way toward the stage.

And there she was, right in front of him. She sat in a straight-back chair, hunched over, covering her eyes.

He went to her and knelt in front of her. "My *beruško*."

She looked up and gasped.

"I promised I would find you."

"Horst? Is that really you? I am dreaming, *ne*?"

"You aren't dreaming, my *beruško*. I'm here."

"I—I thought you were dead. For so long, I searched for you, but you disappeared. No one knew of you." She threw herself into his embrace.

He clung to her, afraid to let her go in case she might walk out of his life again. "I'm sorry you thought that. I wrote letter after letter to your address in Prague. They returned to me unopened."

"Where have you been?"

"The Americans detained me for a while. They had to determine if

I'd committed any war crimes. They're prosecuting people like Stefan. Patricie is dead. Executed at Theresienstadt. He fled before her killing, but he ordered it. He's been sentenced to death for her murder, and the murder of thousands of others."

"But they released you?"

"They found no basis for any charges. But it took awhile for them to clear me. I did everything I could to locate you."

"I've been in London with *Babička*."

He gestured in *Mutti*'s direction. "This is my mother. Imagine my incredible joy when she told me about the concert given by a Jewish Czech violinist."

Mutti nodded. "I'm very pleased to meet you, Anna. Horst has told me so much about you. And the way you play. I've never heard finer."

Still half in his hold, Anna shook his mother's hand. "Thank you so much, Frau Engel. The pleasure is all mine." She turned to him and stroked his face. "Horst, you found me. I can't believe you found me."

He touched her tear-stained cheek, brushed away a strand of her dark hair. "Yes, I have. And I'm never going to let you go." He pulled away and reached into his pocket. He drew a box from it, knelt in front of her, and presented it to her.

"Anna Zadoková, you are the love of my life. These past months have been torture without you. You bring a melody to my soul that I never want to end. I want to fill our house with music, with love, with laughter. Erase all of the bad memories and build new, good ones."

His voice broke. How could he communicate to her all that she meant to him? "You are the song I sing in the morning, the tune I whistle at night, the music that swells deep within me. Anna, will you marry me?"

She sank to the floor beside him and nestled against his shoulder. "And you, Horst Engel, gave me my music back when I thought it had fled forever. You saved my life. You fill the empty spaces in my soul. Without you, I am nothing. Yes, oh my love, yes, yes, yes, I will marry you."

He slipped his grandmother's sapphire ring onto her finger. As they kissed, the orchestra's music reverberated, lifting him, filling him. The melody of the soul.

Notes

At Terezín, Egon Ledeč formed the Ledeč Quartet, with himself as first violinist, an amateur named Schneider as second violinist, Viktor Kohn as violist, and his brother Paul Kohn as the cellist. The Ledeč Quartet performed at the Magdeburg barrack. With the establishment of the *Freizeitgestaltung* (Leisure Time Committee) during the autumn of 1942 and the sanctioning of musical activities by the Nazis, the quartet began to perform for different audiences. Egon was transported to Auschwitz on October 16, 1944, and was gassed upon arrival.

While Anna and her grandmother go into hiding, most of Prague's Jews chose to follow the Nazi directive and report for transport to Terezín. Of the tens of thousands of Jews in the city at the war's beginning, only a little over 200 ever went into hiding. The Czech Resistance worked mostly publishing pamphlets and printing false passports and identity papers. With the assassination of Reinhard Heydrich in 1942 and the subsequent reprisals, the resistance movement was crushed. What little of it remained was splintered and mostly ineffective.

While Prague's Jewish residents were ordered to turn in their instruments, I found many instances of Jews awaiting transport at the exhibition hall, playing violins, and many reports of them playing their own instruments once at Terezín.

For a while, those brought to the ghetto were allowed to write cheerful and encouraging postcards home, extolling the virtues of the place. The Germans stopped that practice as the war went on.

Czech is a very formal language. The Czech people are quite reserved with strangers. They use titles instead of first names for a long time after meeting someone, until they are very close. Also, they add the feminine *-ová* to the end of a woman's surname. That is why Anna's last name is Zadoková and David's is Zadok. It is, really, the same family name.

I strove to be as accurate as possible when it came to historical events. Because communism quickly replaced German occupation in Czechoslovakia, certain documents and files have been lost forever. The exhibition hall really existed. Salvátorská Street is a real street on the edge of the Old Jewish Quarter in Prague. My description of the train stations at the end of the book is as close as I can come, based on photographs. The war did end in Plzeň on May 6, 1945, the last day of the conflict in Europe. The scene was much as I have described. By December 1946, symphony concerts had resumed in Munich.

Anna is based on Alice Herz-Sommer, a Jewish concert pianist in Prague at the time of the war. She hid her piccolo piano from the Germans and continued to play, despite the risk. Alice expressed how music was her joy, her happiness. She also called it her savior. That sparked the story idea. Music, however much we love it, however much it is ingrained in us, is not our savior. Only Christ is.

Horst is based, in part, on the German soldier who lived in the same building as Alice and loved to listen to her play. He is also based on Wilm Hosenfeld, a German officer in Poland who helped to hide and save several Poles, including Jews. He was captured by the Soviets at the end of the war and died in Russia.

Alice ended up at Terezín, along with her son. Her husband died of typhus in Dachau, but she survived. She died in 2014 at the age of 110, the oldest Holocaust survivor.

For further information on music and the Holocaust, visit http://holocaustmusic.ort.org/.

Acknowledgments

*N*o book is possible without the assistance of many people, and this one is no different. A huge thank you to David Muhlena, head librarian at the National Czech and Slovak Museum in Cedar Rapids, Iowa. The wonderful material you provided me with and your patience in answering my questions is very much appreciated. You helped with the historical details and the authenticity of the story. And thank you for your recommendation on a restaurant to try a true Czech goulash. It was an exceptional meal.

Thank you also to Jerry Farnik, missionary to the Czech Republic. I truly appreciate your help with the Czech vocabulary and with the nuances of the language, including the female versions of last names.

My sincerest appreciation to the wonderful team at Gilead Publishing. I'm so proud to be part of your family. Dan Balow, Becky Philpott, Kristen Gearhart, and Jordan Smith, you are all a pleasure to work with. Thank you for giving me the opportunity to tell this story. And special thanks to Julee Swartzburg, my terrific editor. Without you, this book wouldn't be what it is. My deepest gratitude for all you've taught me over the years.

Tamela Hancock Murray, thank you for being the greatest agent a writer could want. I shed a bucket-load of tears in the process of getting this story into print, and you held my hand the entire way. There aren't words to express my appreciation for your patience, your willingness to take my phone calls and emails, and your ability to talk me off the ledge.

My dear family, I often wonder how you put up with me when I'm in the middle of a book. You don't get home cooked dinners, you don't have much clean laundry, and you don't always have my fullest attention. But you willingly pitch in and cook, clean, and hold down the fort. I owe you everything. Doug, I'm so blessed to have you in my life. Only a woman married to such a wonderful husband and father could manage this kind of career. Thank you for being my rock. Brian, thank you for the sacrifices you make for your country. We live in the land of the free because of brave young men such as yourself. Alyssa, I'm so proud of the young woman you've become. God has great things in store for you. May he richly bless you as you fly the nest and embark on life's next adventure. And Jonalyn, thank you for reminding me that, at the end of the day, it doesn't matter how many contracts I have or how many books I sell, but how much I've loved and been loved.

And all praise to my Lord and Savior, Jesus Christ, who has blessed me in Christ with every spiritual blessing in the heavenly realms. Without Him, I'm nothing.

Soli Deo Gloria

About the Author

Liz Tolsma's specialty is historical fiction—from WWII to prairie romance. Her debut novel was a finalist for the 2014 Selah and Carol Award. She prides herself in excellent storytelling, presenting accurate historical details, and creating persevering characters.

Liz is also a popular speaker on topics such as writing, marriage, living with courage, and adoption. She and her husband have adopted all their children internationally. Liz resides in semi-rural Wisconsin with her husband and two daughters; her son currently serves as a U.S. Marine. Liz is a breast cancer survivor and lives her life to the fullest. In her free time, she enjoys reading, working in her large perennial garden, kayaking, and camping with her family.

Connect with Liz!
Visit her blog, The Story behind the Story, at www.liztolsma.com.
Facebook: www.facebook.com/liztolsma
Twitter: www.twitter.com/LizTolsma
Instagram: www.instagram.com/authorliztolsma

Coming Soon

The next stanza in the Music of Hope series.

Visit us online for the latest updates:

www.liztolsma.com

www.gileadpublishing.com

GILEAD
PUBLISHING

The melody continues in Fall 2018.